INVITATION
AND
INSTRUCTIONS

OPEN THE COVER OF THIS BOOK. LOOK INSIDE.

WELCOME TO THE LAND WHERE TALES ARE TOLD.

THERE IS A PATH UNFOLDING IN FRONT OF YOU, PAVED WITH WORDS, LEADING INTO SECRET PLACES –
THE DANGEROUS, THE REMEMBERED, THE FAMILIAR, THE UNKNOWN.

YOU WILL NEED MIND, HEART, AND SPIRIT TO MAKE THIS JOURNEY.

YOU MAY PICK FLOWERS AS YOU GO – AND THEY WILL HAVE NAMES –
COURAGE, EMPATHY, WISDOM, FAITH, IMAGINATION.
YOU CAN PRESS THEM LATER, FOR SOUVENIRS, BETWEEN PAGES OF OTHER BOOKS.

THEY WILL HELP TO GAIN YOU ENTRY INTO THIS TEMPLE, THE TEMPLE OF THE FAIRY TALE.
WHEN YOU REACH THE DEEPEST SECRET SANCTUARY IN THIS PLACE AND OFFER THEM UP... AND THEY
WILL BE RESTORED TO YOU, IF YOU DO... YOU MAY RECEIVE A VERY PRECIOUS THING IN RETURN.

WRAPPED IN MAGIC AND MYTH AND MYSTERY, FOLDED INTO THE SILVER TISSUE OF FICTION,
YOU WILL FIND THE SEED OF TRUTH.

PLANT IT IN A SAFE PLACE. TEND IT WELL.

MAY IT GRANT YOU SHELTER AND SHADE ALL THE DAYS OF YOUR LIFE.

fractured fairy tales

ALMA ALEXANDER

Book View Café

KOS BOOKS

Fractured Fairy Tales © 2021

All copyright © Alma Alexander

Published by Book View Café Publishing Cooperative/Kos Books

www.BookViewCafe.com

ISBN: 987-1-61138-960-9 (paperback)

ISBN: 978-1-61138-961-6 (ebook)

Cover illustration and design by James A. Owen

❀ Created with Vellum

DEDICATION

Deck

Because this is a book of fairy tales, the things that happen between Once Upon A Time and a Happily Ever After, there could be only one person to whom it could be dedicated. To the one who embodied those things for me, for twenty years. Twenty years which were too short, but apparently forever doesn't last as long as it used to. And you're gone – and you will never see this book – but you know it, because you read every single story in it, even the final two, which I wrote while you were in the hospital, which I brought to you as offerings, handing them to you to read while you sat there in your recliner, or your hospital bed.

One of those stories brought, for the last time, that thing I treasured from you – that gentle "I hate you", when I told you how long it had taken me to write it, and you held that you would never in a million years be able to write THAT story, a story like THAT, in the time frame specified. You told me once that you thought that you were a writer, but that was before you met me. But you WERE a storyteller. You chose our story, and you fought for that with every ounce of your strength, all the way, to your final hours. Always, always, you were 'coming home'. Coming home to me.

Except you never made it. Somewhere in the dark woods your light went out, and I lost you.

But you are still with me, will always be, here in my heart. We had a Happily, if not an Ever After. And I would not trade a year, a day, an hour, a minute, a moment of it.

Thank you, for all of it.

This book is for you. I put all of my fairy tales into your hands.

And I take my leave with the words which were the last we would say to each other at the close of every shared day of our lives.

Good night. I love you.

CONTENTS

ARIS

ALMOST FAIRY TALES

the first book:
the three fairy tales

The Perfect Rose

There lived once in a land far away to the east, so far that it sat right under the sun when it rose every morning, a great King.

He was a good King, a wise and powerful one; he was yet young and strong, and he loved his people, and they him.

There came a time for the King to choose a bride, and Ambassadors from many lands flocked to his City, each extolling the Princess of his own country. But when the Princesses arrived for him to choose, he looked at them all and immediately pointed to a very dark and very lovely Princess from a land close to his own borders.

"She and no other will be my Queen!" he vowed.

So the wedding was celebrated; and the people rejoiced, and threw rose petals and flowers of jasmine before her whenever she passed by. And she smiled at them with her little rosebud mouth and out of her slanting dark eyes, and waved with a dainty little hand, and her wrists were heavy with the gold and jewelled bracelets the King had given her to prove his love for her.

Now, the King had a Rose Garden in the grounds of his palace, hidden from all eyes by a high wall; and he loved this garden, and was proud of it. He often walked in it, along paths bordered by red, white and yellow roses, enjoying the fragrance that perfumed the air. Nobody else ever went there, not even the Queen. Never were the roses cut from the trees while still in bloom, but only when they were dry and ugly; then the King himself would cut them and take them away. No-one ever saw the roses except the King; it was his only selfishness in life, the only thing he did not share even with his dearly beloved Queen.

She, a spoiled Princess who had become a pampered Queen, grew more and more jealous of the Rose Garden. She even began to think that it must be that the King went there to meet another woman, whose eyes then saw what her own were denied; and her hate grew and festered because she never spoke of it to anybody. She became determined to see what she was forbidden to look upon. She made plans.

All of a sudden one day the Queen took to her bed with an inexplicable malady. It left her cheeks pale and her eyes dull, and she neither spoke nor smiled. The King, afraid for her life, sent all over his land for the best physicians he knew; and they all went away from the Queen's bedside saying that they knew not what ailed her, and that none of their remedies had worked a cure.

So the King sent them away, and tended her himself. For seven days and nights he sat by her, and she neither moved nor spoke; but he did not sleep because he wanted to be there if she needed him.

Finally, on the eighth evening, she turned to him and whispered,

"My Lord, why sittest thou there by the foot of my bed?"

"Because thou hast been ill, and I have tended thee. The physicians could not cure thee, and nobody knows what ails thee. Tell me, for if there is something that will make thee well, I shall do it myself."

"There is something, Lord," she said, and in her eyes there was a gleam of triumph and of malice. But he saw them not, saw only her.

"Speak!" he cried.

And she said, "I want the most perfect rose from thy Rose Garden."

And he frowned and drew back, and said, "If that is the only thing that will heal thee, then I shall find it. But my heart is troubled."

"It is the only thing," she said.

So he rose, and went out into the garden. And the moon was full, and the garden full of light, and all the roses seemed perfect to him. And he wandered for a long time, and finally cut the topmost bud from the youngest and loveliest rose tree. The night dew was still upon the bud, and sparkled like diamonds; and the white petals looked like wrought silver beneath them. And the King took up the rose and went into the Queen's bedchamber; and he said,

"Look! I have brought it. Here is the loveliest rose from my garden. Now, Beloved, let the roses return to thine own cheeks, and thy sickness lift."

But she looked on the rose and laughed, and said,

"Is that the best thou canst do? Thy garden is no marvel, then; but I have heard told of a magic Garden of roses, to be found further east still than thy Kingdom. There grows the most perfect rose in all the world. There must thou go; and that rose must thou bring before me. Otherwise I shall surely die."

So the King took the white rose away, for the Queen would have none of it, and placed it into his own bosom; and he ordered his horse saddled, and rode off from his Kingdom with a heavy heart to search for the perfect rose for his Queen.

He rode a long way; he passed the borders of his own country and entered a burning desert. It seemed to have no end, but stretched out all around him. He travelled in it for many days, and soon the day came when he had no water left to drink. He had seen no trace of it in the land he travelled. He sat down in the meagre shadow of a squat cactus, to at least partly shield himself from the merciless sun. His horse stood beside him on trembling legs; the King could not meet the animal's patient, pain-filled eyes. He buried his head in his hands in despair. And it was then that he heard a soft voice like the chiming of a thousand little bells. The voice spoke to him, and said,

"Be not afraid, O King, but take thy rose from thy bosom and take what it gives thee."

So the King reached for the white rose and lo! on its petals still shimmered the night dew that had fallen on them many nights ago in his garden. Wonderingly the King shook the drops of water onto his palm, and a little water collected there. It was not much, just a thin film of moisture, but the King offered it first to his horse. The animal licked off the water, but now looked at its master even more mournfully than before. The King said,

"Look! It was only the dew from the rose - and I have no more to give."

But as he looked on the rose he saw that there were still dewdrops on it, and he thought that now there were more than before. So he shook them off again; and the more they shook, the more there was, until both horse and man were satisfied. The King put the rose carefully back into his bosom and went on his way.

There came a time when the King and his horse shared out the last morsel of the food they had brought, and once more the King despaired, but again the voice like the chiming of a thousand bells spoke to him.

"Be not afraid, O King, but take thy rose from thy bosom and take what it gives thee."

So the King took out the rose again, and marvelled how fresh and lovely the flower still was even after many days in searing desert heat. he plucked off a velvet-soft white petal because it seemed the right thing to do, but he did not do it gladly, for it marred the rose. But even as he looked the rose was as before, and still he held the petal in his hand. He put the rose back into the folds of his garments and laid the petal down on the hot sand. And there the petal began to grow and grow; and it grew until it lay at the King's feet as a cloth of the finest white silk. And then the cloth brought forth food - a feast fit for an Emperor. And when both horse and man were satisfied, the sumptuous dishes vanished and the cloth became once more a rose petal. And the King gathered it up with care and placed it next to the rose from which it had been plucked.

And so the King journeyed on. When he needed water, he drank the dew from the rose; when he hungered, he ate from the cloth that the rose had spread before him. And the rose never faded, but was ever as fresh as on the day it had been plucked, and always as white as snow.

The King journeyed ever east, always searching for the fabulous Garden of his Queen's vision. He passed through many cities, and asked many people, but they all knew nothing. Some said they knew of it, but that it lay further east still, the next city, the next realm. And so he travelled on.

He came to a great sea, and knew not how to cross it. The shores were deserted, and they stretched out to his left and his right so that he could see no end to them. There was not even a fisherman's hut where he could find a boat to take him across. He gazed at the foam of salt water which swirled around his feet, and thought sadly that this must be where his journey ended. But again he heard the small voice like the chiming of a thousand bells, and it said,

"Be not afraid, O King, but take thy rose from thy bosom and take what it gives thee."

So the King took out the white rose again. He plucked another petal and let it float on the foam of the water. And it grew, and grew, and became a boat of the finest, lightest polished white wood, the like of which he had never seen before. He stepped on board, leading his horse, for there was easily room for both. And the boat, which sailed by itself with no sailor to tend it, reared up delicate white sails of silk and turned into the wind.

For many days the King sailed in the petal boat, for the sea was a wide one to cross; but at length he glimpsed the shadow of land on the horizon. And he shouted for joy as he looked on it. It had been a lonely voyage across the waters, and rejoiced that he would soon see people again.

The boat came ashore quietly on an empty beach of white sand; it came ashore, and then became once again a single white rose petal floating on the even whiter foam of the sea. And the King scooped it up lovingly and placed it with the rose again.

And then he was riding once again. And presently he began to look at the land around him first with puzzlement and then with a growing joy, for it was his own country that he was riding through. But then he looked closer, and his eyes clouded with pain and anger. For his fertile land was a tangle of wild bushes and weeds; the neat little houses of his people were dirty and ruinous, and thin and mangy dogs scavenged there and quarrelled over what meager food they found. The farther he rode the worse it became; even the great wide road he had been travelling on fell into disrepair. Grass grew on it and around it, and thorn bushes crowded around it and scratched at his legs and the flanks of his horse if he went too near. The King rode on with a sorely troubled heart and lamented the day he had left on his Quest, for it seemed that the land had been ruled most evilly in his absence and the glory of his Kingdom was forgotten.

He wept when he saw the city walls. The City that had once been the most beautiful in all the Kingdoms was now mean and sly; little, rat-like people scurried from one corner to the next and stared at the golden clasp on the King's cloak with avarice shining palely from their eyes.

"Where are all the people?" the King asked one, and

"Where is your Queen?" he asked another, and

"Where is your King, and what City is this now?" he asked of a third.

"We are the people, there are no other," said the first;

"We have no Queen," said the second;

"We have no King," said the third, "although it is said we once had one. And this is no city, these are but walls we live in, for safety's sake."

And the King pointed at the ruined wall that he knew had once been his palace, and asked a fourth man,

"What is that up there?"

And the man said, "It is nothing now. I have heard it said that it was once a great palace. Nobody goes there now, but I have heard it said that somewhere within there is a magic Rose Garden in which there grows the most perfect rose of all the world."

"So," said the King, "I have come to the end of my journey, and it is at the place of its beginning."

And he urged his horse towards the Garden, his Garden, the Garden of the Perfect Rose.

When he got to the palace, he saw that it really was no more. Rooms lay open to the sky; mildew had eaten the gold-embroidered tapestries, and cobwebs had taken their places. Where once carpets from Persia spread their luxurious tread there now grew grass and small field flowers, no less lovely for their humbler beginnings; and where spirited horses had lived in gold-embossed stables now mice and rats scurried and rustled in the rotting straw.

The palace was the King's no more. It had a different ruler now, for Nature had taken what she could and left what she could not touch to Decay, with whom she shared her Throne.

The King walked through the familiar corridors, and they echoed around him, hollow, empty. At length he reached the little door under the archway, the door that led to the garden. He took the key from where it hung around his neck on a silken cord and put it into the keyhole. At first it wouldn't turn; the years that had gone by had taken their toll even on the locked and untouched gate. But then, slowly and creakily, it gave; and the door swung inward on complaining hinges. And lo! out of the whole palace the Garden alone was as it had been, fresh and pure and lovely, and the same haunting scent of roses hung lightly in the air. Nobody had been inside that garden - not through that stiff and time-frozen door - yet there were no dead blooms on the rose trees, no dead twigs; they had been watered, and the weeds had been pulled, and the pathways tended. The King stood in the doorway and looked on in wonder, for he could not understand how these things could have been done.

Then he shut the door behind him, and walked over to the high eastern wall of the Garden and opened a little hidden window in the wall. he opened the window, and once more he wept, for out of that window he could see all too clearly the sordid alleys of his City that once had been so beautiful and the shabbiness of the countryside all around. He wept at the way the shine of glory had gone from his Kingdom, and the people had to live under this gloom - and he, their King, could do nothing because his people would no longer believe that he existed.

And then he heard the soft voice like the chiming of a thousand bells, and it said to him,

"Be not afraid, O King, but take thy rose from thy bosom and take what it gives thee."

The King did this, but he looked at the rose sorrowfully and said, "Alas, my faithful companion, I believe the remedy of this situation will tax even thy powers. For what canst thou do against fear and greed and disbelief? What canst thou do to restore the people to what they once were?"

And the voice spoke again, "It is the last thing I can do for thee, O King; I will cure thy Kingdom."

"I did not know thou couldst talk!" exclaimed the King in surprise.

"Thou didst not ask."

"Then the stories are true," said the King, "for I do indeed hold in my hand the most perfect rose that ever was."

"Nay," said the Rose, "that One was beyond thy powers to find. But here, within thy world, perhaps thou dost speak truly."

"Then why didst thou not tell me? For had I known, I would never have gone on this Quest, and my Kingdom would still be whole."

"Thou didst know. Why else wouldst thou have picked from the rose tree thou chose. It was thy wife who made thee believe otherwise; she knew not perfection when she saw it and she laughed at it. So she drove it away, and Kingdom wilted under her cruel hand."

"If I had known..."

"Thou didst know. Only thy love was too strong. And thou hast held the Perfection of thy Kingdom all this time safe next to thy heart. Thy love was worthy, King; thy Beloved was not. Therefore thou hadst to leave, before she destroyed thee."

The King bowed his head, and was silent for a long time.

The White Rose presently rustled again, and the voice like the chiming of a thousand little bells spoke once more.

"If thou dost want thy Kingdom back, then hearken. Pluck four petals, each with a drop of dew, and release each into a wind from a different corner of the world."

So the King did as he was bid; he plucked the four petals with dew on them from the White Rose. And the Winds swirled around his head. First came the North Wind, sullen and cold; he snatched the petal offered him and disappeared into the distance amid a great howling and moaning. The West Wind followed his brother, salty from the sea from which he hied. He murmured an apology for his brother from the North, for the West Wind was the peacemaker; and, with a word of welcome, also took up his petal and flew away. The East Wind arrived next, with sand from her deserts swirling around her skirts; her breath was hot and dry, and she curled the petal protectively around its dew so as not to harm it. She, too, offered a welcome before departing.

Lastly it was the turn of the South Wind, her breath sweet with the scent of frangipani and jasmine from the isles of the South. She took up her petal as gently as a mother would her babe, promised she would deliver it well, and planted a light, feathery kiss on the King's brow - then she, too was gone, and the voice of a thousand chiming bells spoke softly and it seemed to the King to be faint and very far away.

"Turn thy eyes outward, O King, and behold."

And the King did. And, as he watched, he understood how the rose garden had kept itself tended so well. For where the dew of the White Rose fell, the same dew that had quenched his thirst in the wilderness, all that was evil or foul melted away and there arose, like the phoenix from the ashes, the cleanliness and love and faith that had succoured his Kingdom before the evil times had come. And whichever side he looked it was the same picture - the land was coming back to life, and his people with it. And the King wept once again, but this time it was for joy.

But when he looked down at the rose in his hands, he saw that it had taken on the colour of cold ashes, and the smooth petals had shrivelled into wrinkles and lines. And he exclaimed,

"Thou art dying! What can I do to aid thee?"

"The new Glory of thy Kingdom will never fade, for it is the Glory of the Heart of the Rose. From this moment, thy Kingdom will be thy Garden; but this Garden will not bloom again - it will die, for it has given its heart away in four drops of its dew. I, too, must die with it. Farewell, O King. Thy Garden has repaid thy love."

And when the King looked again, he held naught but a handful of fine ash dust; and when he turned to look at the lovely Rose garden he had entered only a short time ago, all he saw was a waste, a graveyard of dry and dead rose trees. Around each, on the earth by its roots, lay a pale wreath of dust which had been its leaves and flowers.

The King came out of the dead Garden with a heart heavy with sorrow. The people, his people, such as he remembered them, came and thronged around him and shouted welcome from a thousand throats. And the King said to them,

"Peace! Be still, there is tale I have to tell you."

And so they fell quiet and listened as he related the history of the rose, and they were silent for a long time when he had finished speaking. And then the King asked after the finest gold- and silversmiths in the city, and the finest makers of gems, and they came forward. And to the first he said,

"You will coat all the rose trees in the Garden with the finest gold you can find, and fashion blossoms of red and yellow gold to adorn their branches forever."

To the second, he said, "You will make a White Rose out of the most fragile and precious silver."

"And you," he said to the third, "will form crystal dew drops out of the most perfect diamond gems, and adorn the rose of silver with them."

"This Rose," he then said, "will be placed upon the topmost tip of the rose bush which I shall show you. The Perfect Rose will bloom forever in the Garden it has made its own."

As he said, so it was done. The voice like the chiming of a thousand little bells may be silent, but the beauty of the White Rose, the most Perfect Rose that ever was, will never pass away.

My Music Was My Life, My Life My Music

✿❀✿

The old forest knew Niklas. He would come wandering along the shadowed paths playing his nut-brown fiddle, and the leaves on the trees would dance for the joy of his music. The stags would come to the edge of the paths to watch him go by, and the rabbits played leapfrog to his rhythms in the long grass of the clearings. Birds knew his tunes, and would sing along. Music always followed in Niklas's wake. He lived for the music, and the music came tremblingly alive for him, pouring from under his bow, wrapping the frets of his violin, making the forest laugh and lilt.

The fiddle had been a gift from his grandmother for Niklas's thirteenth birthday. The two of them lived alone in a cottage deep in the woods, and Niklas had never seen either his father or his mother. Grandmother would say nothing about the gift except that it had always belonged to the family, and was very old - and that it had been left for him to have when the time came. And it seemed to be a magic fiddle, because it seemed to teach Niklas how to play it, guided his fingers to play the right notes. The first time he held it in his hands he could play any tune he wanted. It was as though playing the fiddle was something he had always know how to do, and had merely remembered something that he had forgotten. And so taken was he by his gift

13

that he did not see his grandmother weep when she saw what had happened, and did not ask her why she was crying.

Niklas had been admonished not to leave the forest where he lived. Once he had asked his grandmother, when he was still very young, if the forest covered the whole world. She could have told him then that it did. But she had sighed, and sat him down, and explained that there was a whole wide world outside of the forest. That had been only the first time that she had told him that he must never enter it. There had never come another day when she did not repeat those words to Niklas. And, because he was happy, he did not wish to disobey her. The world held no call for him. He was happy to roam his forest home with his fiddle. The beasts all knew him and came to him if he called to them, and he could make the tiny wild flowers in the clearings sway to his music like graceful little dancers. He could make the nightingales sing for him. He was king of his kingdom. He was happy.

One day he was sitting on the low bough of a favourite oak tree and playing his fiddle when he heard an unfamiliar sound. He stopped playing to listen and soon the noise grew closer. Along the path that meandered beneath his swinging feet a procession of riders came slowly, weaving their way through the woods. There was an expression of fear on the lead rider's face, and he kept making strange signals with his hand, as though warding away evil spells. Behind him, on a milk-white palfrey, rode the most beautiful girl Niklas had ever seen. She had long golden hair that streamed like sunshine down her shoulders, and she had the eyes of a fawn. She didn't seem as afraid as her escort, because she was smiling as she looked around her, and she was humming a tune, very softly, under her breath. Niklas listened intently for a moment, and then, carried away with the girl's beauty, his fiddle seemed to leap into his hands and he played an echo of the tune she was humming. Instantly the cavalcade came to a milling halt beneath him, and scared voices were raised in raucous query. She alone, the girl, looked immediately up to where he was sitting, and smiled.

"Why, hello," she said. "That was well played. What are you doing here all alone?"

"Playing the fiddle," said Niklas.

"Come down! Come down here at once! Are you alone? Where are your parents?" chattered the lead rider, quite pale, but recovering. "Where did you come from, anyway? What is a youngster like you doing in the Enchanted Forest on his own? Who sent you here?"

"I live here," said Niklas, "with my grandmother."

"But nobody lives here," said the girl reasonably. "This is the Enchanted Forest."

"I do, I live here. Where are you from? Where are you going? I have never seen anyone pass this way before."

"I am..." she began, but the lead rider leaned over to clutch at her arm.

"Princess!" he remonstrated urgently.

"He is only a child, Ilon!" she said, shaking him off. "I am Princess Briagha. I come from my father's house, to marry Prince Balach. I go to my wedding, forest boy."

Niklas laughed, and played a snatch of a happy tune on his fiddle. "Luck to you, then!" he said, and laughed again. He played faster and faster, and soon the fear on everyone's faces began to melt as the smiles came. The princess clapped her hands in time to his music and laughed joyously, and even dour Ilon was surprised into a smile. When Niklas stopped, breathless, Princess Briagha held out her hands to him.

"Oh please come and play at my wedding, forest boy! You make such happy music, and I know that my betrothed will welcome you, as I do!"

Niklas laughed out loud and leapt down from his perch on the tree. Such was his joy at having been asked by this beautiful girl to play his music at her wedding feast that he quite forgot his grandmother's constant words of warning.

"You can ride behind Ban," said Princess Briagha, and a handsome young man swept off his plumed hat and laughed down at Niklas. The knight leaned down from his mount and helped Niklas clamber up behind him, his fiddle tucked between them. Then Ilon gave the signal and they moved off. The Princess rode beside Ban and Niklas, and talked happily about her wedding; Niklas listened avidly and it was only when he felt the sunshine hot on his bare head that he turned and saw the edge of the Enchanted Forest being relentlessly left behind him. For an instant his grandmother's voice came to him, and her words about the forest returned to touch his mind. He shivered where he sat with a sense of doom, knowing, for just an instant, that he had done something irrevocable. But then Briagha's lilting laugh drew him back, and he turned his back on the forest. Somewhere far ahead he thought he could see a castle of many turrets, each flying a white pennant to welcome the new bride. And soon he would be playing at a Royal wedding.

In the joyous chaos of their arrival at Prince Balach's castle, Niklas somehow seemed to be left behind in the throng. The cooks fed him, because he came in with the Princess and they assumed that he belonged to her. But he could not ever get close to her again, for she was always surrounded by throngs of other, more important people. Once he saw her walking with Prince Balach and came to bow to her, but she was laughing up into her Prince's eyes and did not see him, and Prince Balach merely swept past him with haughty eyes. Niklas retreated, and watched from a distance. It was not his lot to be numbered into the friends of the princely pair. The day of the nuptials was drawing near; and then, surely, Briagha would remember her strange troubadour.

In his innocence, Niklas had thought that he was to have been the only player at their feast. He stood in the decked hall with his violin, and surveyed the throngs of musicians and singers that milled about waiting their turn. If it had been within his power, Niklas would have turned and run all the way back to the Enchanted Forest, where he was loved and where his music was eagerly awaited. But once again he was stayed by the sight of the Princess, more beautiful than ever in her wedding gown. Surely she would remember him when the time came? Niklas found himself an unobtrusive place in the musicians' gallery, and settled down to wait.

Course after course of the wedding feast was served, and the music poured from the musicians' gallery like silver waterfalls. When one lot stopped, another began, and they in their turn were succeeded by others. Niklas waited, silent. He waited for a moment of silence when he would be called to play. But the moment never came, and the feast was already drawing to a close. Niklas's eyes filled with tears, because he finally knew that he had been a whim, chosen and then forgotten.

Uncalled, his violin leapt into his hands and he began playing, very softly, a quiet melody. At first nobody heard him over all the din, but soon the other musicians began to, and one by one the other instruments stopped. In the spreading silence from the musicians' gallery, the laughter and chatter in the hall began to still as the notes of Niklas's violin came sweeping down to them, suddenly filled with power. They carried a different message to all who heard him play, and Briagha was not the only one who wept behind her hands. But Niklas, seeing her weep, was moved once again by her beauty and the violin changed its tune. Soon he had the entire hall clapping their hands and stamping their feet, and the Royal couple were laughing with joy at one another and dancing in the midst of the hall.

Eventually Niklas's violin died slowly away and his hands dropped from the magical instrument, exhausted. There was a moment of silence while the guests realised that the music was over, and then the rafters shook with their cheers and their clapping. They brought Niklas down from the gallery on their hands, and set the finest of wines before him. Briagha herself sat beside him and fed him from her own plate.

"How handsome the lad is," the people murmured to themselves, seeing him sitting there. "And such golden hands. Surely there can be no better fiddler in the world!"

But when he was finally escorted, transported beyond happiness by the acclamation he had gathered at Briagha's wedding, to his new chambers, high up in the towers and close to Briagha's own, Niklas saw his reflection in a polished shield that hung on his wall, and he was no longer the boy who had left the Enchanted Forest only days ago. He was taller by a head, more; he had the rangy body of an adolescent and no longer the small round smiling face of the boy from the Enchanted Forest. His fingers were longer and stronger, and on his upper lip was the first faint shadow of down. Thus Niklas at last understood the price he had paid for trespassing beyond the borders of his forest. He would know adulation, and fame; but he would never again have immortality.

He stayed at Balach and Briagha's court for some time, their treasure and their pride; but he did not play often, and it was soon obvious that he aged a little every time he did. After a while Niklas slipped out one day and walked away. He did not look back. He did not know that he was missed, and looked for; but that all too soon he was put aside and replaced by newer entertainments. The name of Niklas the Fiddler became a tale.

Niklas traveled the world, playing the fiddle when he needed money to survive, and every time he played he aged a little more. In the space of a few years he had gone through adolescence into middle age; in a few more he was an old man. Soon the fiddle was put away, for Niklas feared that he would carry himself beyond the last boundary, and there was one thing he wanted to do before he laid down his charmed life. He wanted to go home. If the price of his final melody was to be his life, he wanted to play it beneath the eaves of the Enchanted Forest.

His travels took him, now a stooped and white-haired old man, past the castle where once he had played at a wedding feast. He knew he ought to have walked straight past and turned his back on the castle walls where he had known such bitter sorrow before he had known joy. But it was stronger than him. He walked inside and asked to see the Prince.

"The Prince, forsooth," said one of the knights in the entrance hall. "Do you think we allow every vagabond off the street to see the Prince? The Prince has better things to do."

"But he will want to see me," Niklas said, "he or Princess Briagha. Yes, she will remember me. It was she who brought me from the forest, a little Gypsy boy, to play at their wedding feast. I would like to play for her once again."

"Liar," said another knight, "I was at their wedding feast. The Gypsy who played for them was young, merely a boy. It has only been a few years since they were wed; the Gypsy boy could not have become a grandfather in that time."

"Please," said Niklas, "my music is my life, my life my music. Both are drawing to a close. Let me play for my beautiful Princess once more."

"Listen," said another voice, and Niklas turned, recognising it for that of Ban, who once carried him to this castle on his own horse. But

Ban showed no recognition, and he had not been speaking to him but to the other knights. "The old man wants to entertain us. Well, would you like to see an entertainment? I will throw him out myself. Come!"

Niklas started to speak, but Ban picked him up and carried him through the oaken gates into the courtyard, pitching him outside into the horse-churned mud beside the main paved roadway. He stood on the top step of the castle entrance, his hands on his hips. Behind him crowded the other knights. They were all laughing.

"Play, old man!" Ban called. "Play for Princess Briagha now!"

Niklas picked himself up painfully and dragged himself out of the outer gates, the knights' laughter following behind him. He glanced up once as he walked away, and ghostly white pennants seemed to fly from the battlements, as a different, kinder laughter flooded the courtyard in his memory. But then the pennants were gone, and he knew he would never hear Briagha laugh again. He hunched his shoulders against the cold and began shuffling slowly in the direction of the forest.

He had nothing to eat or drink, but something gave him strength to continue even when everything seemed lost. It was almost beyond his belief when he looked up and realised that the first branches of the Enchanted Forest were spreading over his head, and he wept when he saw them, recalling the days of his innocence in their shadow. He moved in deeper, deeper, until he could move no longer and simply sat down beneath an ancient oak. He drew out his violin and looked at it for a long time, his tears flowing freely; then he slowly lifted it up on his shoulder and laid his chin on the place it had worn smooth so many years ago. His hand was shaking as he laid the bow upon the strings, and he should have played false, his notes trembling out of true and discords marring the forest's peace. But the violin burst forth into a bubbling melody that flowed into the trees, seemingly unguided by Niklas's hands, finally asking the question as to who, here, was the player and who the played.

The stags heard the air and lifted their heads in wonder. The rabbits and the foxes pricked their ears. The flowers in the clearing, beginning to fade as the autumn set in, allowed the last of their summer colour to blaze out as they began swaying in a dance they had almost forgotten. Somewhere deep in the forest, an echo reached the cottage where Niklas's grandmother still dwelled in the forest peace and she stood quite still for a moment before reaching for her shawl and hurrying, led by an unerring instinct, towards the clearing where Niklas was playing his violin. The song had a name, and the name was woven of the words he himself had spoken in the castle courtyard to a jeering crowd: my music is my life, my life my music. And both were ebbing away, the melody dying on a high, sobbing note that only a violin can draw out from within the depths of a soul before flowing into a reverent silence made poignant by the absence of sound.

Niklas was dead by the time his grandmother reached him, his violin broken in two by his side. In the silence he was surrounded by the beasts who had loved him, and who were the only ones to grieve over his passing. And his Grandmother wept over the frail old man, for she knew of his journeys and his seeking, and the love that had destroyed him in the end. She raised a cairn over him where he had sat down to play his last air, over him and over the broken violin. And a new spell was woven about the Enchanted Forest. For the infrequent travellers who chanced its perilous paths now came out telling of a cairn in a clearing, the occasionally-glimpsed wraith of a small, dark-skinned boy, and a strange melody which now hung in the shadows between the trees, its sad refrain repeating the same few sorrowful words: *my music was my life, my life my music.*

The Dolphin's Daughter

There was once, long ago, a land by the sea. In a castle which stood on a high rock overhanging the sea, there lived a king and a queen with an only son, a prince that would one day inherit the kingdom. As the young prince grew into manhood, the time came for him to choose a bride, but none within in the borders of his kingdom suited him. So his father arranged a match with a young princess from a kingdom across the sea. Soon the matter was concluded and the bride set sail in a gilded ship from her land to come to her husband's kingdom and be wed.

The voyage was long, and often stray winds blew them off their course into strange waters, from which they then had to find their way back to their path. They saw strange golden fish that flew from the water and shone in the sunshine; once a shadow of something huge and dark passed underneath their ship, and the vessel rocked from the wake of its passing.

All was well until, almost within sight of the end of their journey, the skies darkened as though night had fallen in the middle of the day. The sun was hidden in darkness; the wind grew stronger and stronger. It whipped and tore at the sails. A bitter rain began to fall, and the black waves broke into white foam across the ship's bows. They had brought the princess, whose name was Lilla, into her cabin for safety when the storm broke, but there was no safety to be had from that storm. Soon the wind was too strong to fight. With a sigh of surrender, the main mast of the ship gave way and split with a crack of thunder, falling like a felled tree straight down through the ship's deck and into the ocean. Water poured into the hole it had made. Still attached to the ship by the ropes and the rigging and the heavy wet remains of ragged sails, the mast, bound with bands of black iron, began to sink slowly into the ocean depths and to drag the ship under with it.

In the confusion, many tried to save their own lives, forgetting about the precious passenger who had been entrusted to their care. Sailors leaped overboard and drowned in the foaming sea. The captain and the princess's personal attendants tried to get to her to save her, but all were swept away to their own dooms by the crashing waves and the roaring wind. Princess Lilla was flung into the angry ocean clinging to a piece of battered driftwood and for a while fought to stay afloat; but soon the weight of her soaked skirts and wet hair began to pull at her with invisible fingers. Her grip on her raft began to slip. She raised her beautiful eyes to the black and purple skies, and her tears mixed with the rain on her face.

"Ah, Prince Brion!" she sighed. "I was not fated to be your bride! I go rather to the halls of the King of the Sea, to see all the drowned sailors that the sea has taken to grace his court!"

As she let go of the raft, and watched it swirl away into the oblivion of close, wet darkness, she heard a voice at her side. "Land is not far, lovely lady, and I can take you there."

"Who speaks?"

"I am Atlan," said the voice, and a huge grey dolphin swam up beside her, buoying Lilla up and refusing to let her sink. "I will save you... but I ask a price, lovely lady."

"If I can pay it, it is yours," said Lilla.

"You will bear children," said Atlan. "Your eldest child shall be mine, the dolphin's daughter. You must bring your eldest daughter to the sea, to me, and let me take her. That is the price I ask."

Because children were far away and her own life was precious and so nearly gone, Lilla whispered, "I promise." Then she fainted away.

When she awoke, she was in a bed hung with pale blue velvet and a woman wearing a crown of gold was bending over her. "Lilla," the woman greeted her. "We were afraid we had lost you. But by a great miracle, while your ship was lost with all aboard, you were found, fainting but alive, on our beach two days ago. Luckily you were recognised from your portrait, and brought here. Now everything will be all right."

And so it was. When she recovered her strength, Lilla was wed to Brion. Within a year she reigned as Queen at King Brion's side when the old king passed away. In due time, the young Queen was brought to childbed and delivered of twin girls.

"Twins!" she thought. "That means there is no eldest daughter. The bargain is void." So she never told her husband of her miraculous survival from the shipwreck, or of its toll.

It soon became apparent that the dolphin's daughter was different from her sister. The younger twin, named Atalia, was bright and happy, with blue eyes and curly fair hair. The elder, called Delphine, was dark with huge eyes and heavy, straight black hair, and she never uttered a human sound. The King remarked on this difference before long. Lilla, who knew there was a reason behind it, was finally brought to confess her adventure in the sea. But Brion was a proud man, and unwilling to give of what was his.

"No child of mine belongs to another, whatever his claims!" Brion declared. "Whatever her faults, this is a princess of the royal line, and no daughter of a fish from the depths! Here she was born, and here she stays."

But Delphine was hard to be with, because she was always surrounded in an uncanny silence which made anyone near her uneasy and watchful. She was beautiful, in an eerie way, and her eyes were big and dark and dreamy, full of unfathomable secrets. All too soon everyone drifted away to the bright and captivating Atalia, and left the silent princess to herself. Before long, Delphine was lodged into a separate tower, which had long stood empty, right out over the emptiness of the water beneath its overhanging rock, crumbling away in places and with its own entrance through a small postern gate and a steep stair that led directly down to the sea.

The King and Queen soon forgot their oldest daughter, who lived alone but for a handful of attendants out in her tower. They had pretty Atalia to be proud of, and within three years of the birth of the twins, Queen Lilla gave birth to a son and heir to the kingdom. They called him Tarion, and the whole land celebrated his birth for a month. Tarion grew into boyhood, and by the time he was old enough to remember, his oldest sister was quite forgotten. So he grew up believing the while-and-golden Atalia to be his only sibling.

Delphine grew too, in her oblivion. She had always been striking, but she grew into a sleek and strange beauty that was quite as arresting as Atalia's much vaunted glory, although her own made no songs as her sister's did. The dolphin's daughter often came down from her tower in the early mornings, before anyone was awake, and sat watching the dawn break over the wide sea. It was as though she was waiting for something; but whatever it was, it never came.

The years passed, and the two royal sisters turned eighteen years old. Atalia had a court ball to celebrate her birthday; her sister celebrated hers alone, in the company of nobody but the few old servants assigned to her. They felt pity for the poor girl and baked her a special cake themselves, to mark the occasion as best they could. But Delphine only smiled at them with her eyes, and stroked their thin, veined old hangs. In all her eighteen years she had never been heard to utter a word, although one of her servants swore that she had once heard her singing by the ocean in the early morning light – a strange, plaintive tune with no words to speak of but with a melody that broke the heart.

The ball was still going on in the early hours of the morning. The night had been still, and only gentle waves were lapping on the shingle beach below Delphine's tower when she came down to the sea in the dark hour just before dawn. The moon was full and golden, and there was a silver-sparkling path laid at Delphine's feet from the shingle beach to the distant horizon. The Princess watched it for a long time, alone, and then she stepped into the water at its beginnings. The sparkling water swirled around her feet; the moonlight dressed her hair with gold and touched her raiment with silver. She took another step, and her gown lifted and swirled around her legs. Her hair flew like a silken flag in the soft breeze. The water was around her waist, her gown a lighter billow in the darkness around her, when suddenly the silence was broken by a cry from the other end of the beach, where one of Atalia's guests must have come out to clear his head in the morning air.

"Help! There is a woman drowning! Wait, wait, I will help you!"

Delphine turned her head at the sound, and saw a tall boy of perhaps fifteen years of age, dressed in a stiff court gold and brocade. He was flinging away his short cloak and racing across the shingle towards her. She had never seen her brother and did not know him; neither did he know of his hidden sister, or of the mystery of her life. All he saw was a woman in danger, and his actions were born of instinct and purity. All she saw was a bright youth rushing into danger. She raised her hands in a gesture of warding off, still silent but it was dark and he leaped into the sea without seeing. Their common blood spoke, and she loved him for coming without question, and he would sooner have died than had been thwarted in his rescue.

But there was another cry, a scream of anguish from the castle which began spilling its light and its people on to the beach. Even as it echoed out across the water, a huge wave rose above the two figures in the water and then crashed down on to the figure of the young prince, shrouding everything in a spray of foam. When the waters settled again, the Queen saw standing in the ocean a giant around whose knees the deep water swirled. In his hand was the limp body of her only son. There was nothing there to connect the giant with the dolphin who had brought her to safety many years ago to claim her crown – nothing except the darkness of his eyes, eyes which she only now really recognised as belonging to her eldest daughter: the dolphin's daughter.

"I am Atlan," said the giant. His voice shook the castle on its rock, and pieces of rubble broke off Delphine's tower and fell into the sea with white splashes. "I made a bargain with you long years ago, and even marked that which you bargained away as my own. You chose to keep what was mine. Today I exact a different price. I asked for a life; it is your choice that you paid with a death."

His fingers closed over the limp body of the prince that lay in his palm. For a while he stood there, impassive to Lilla's cries and Brion's raillery and Atalia's tears. He watched them all for a long, silent moment, and then stirred to return to his depths. The ocean whispered around his massive legs.

Then a different voice spoke. It cut through all the moans and cries and stifled everything into silence. Everyone who heard it heart it differently – some said they heard the deep and sombre darkness of the ocean's depths; other swore it was like the play of sunlight on the surface of the sea on a summer's day; still others spoke of distant and eerie melodies playing within it, like the songs of whales. But with one short word it stopped everything, and all eyes turned to the girl who had spoken – a slight, dark girl with the eyes of the sea who had never spoken before in all her eighteen years.

"Wait," she said, and they all did. The giant Atlan turned to look at her, standing at his feet, looking at him with his own eyes. "I was your price," Delphine said. "And every day for years I have come to the sea's edge and waited for you to call me. Why did you not come to me then? And even now, when I had started walking to you without your call, you come in wrath to take an innocent who tried naught but to save your child from what he thought was a certain death, as it would have been for any of his race? You now claim a death instead of the life that was owed you, and which has always been yours, unclaimed. So be it. But claim the death of that life, not of another's. Lay no revenge at the door of the innocents. Let my brother life; take your daughter in his place."

"It is too late," rumbled Atlan. "I took the death that was given."

"Mine is the death that is given – the one you hold you stole!" said Delphine. Father, take me – let him live."

"It was your life I wanted, beside me in the deeps," Atlan said. "Your death at my hand was never in the bargain."

"Rather at yours, who has claim, than at those of others who have no right," said Delphine.

Atlan stood in silence for a long time. Then, slowly, he stooped to lay the motionless body of Prince Tarion in the shallow water at his mother's feet. Delphine stooped over him and kissed him gently on his cool and marble-white brow, smoothing his wet hair away from his face. "Live, then, and remember me," she whispered very softly, and then turned at went willingly into Atlan's open hand. When his fingers touched her, she shivered and then lay limp at lifeless in his huge palm. At the same time, Tarion shuddered where he lay, and drew a shallow breath. They all bent to succour him, and so none but Tarion himself, whose eyes opened and looked past the crowds of those who would aid him on to the sea, saw the first touch of dawn on the waters. In silence so total it was deafening to Tarion's ear, the young prince saw the giant Atlan raise his eyes to the sky and open his mouth in a silent scream of anguish, and then fall, a wall of sparkling, disembodied foam, into the waters of his birth.

"Look," somebody called out, "the Princess! The Princess!"

Tarion sat up and looked where they had pointed. He saw lying in the shallows of the beach the body of the dark and lovely young woman whom he had tried to save from drowning only moments before. Her eyes were closed and she was smiling.

"Who was she?" the young Prince cried.

"The dolphin's daughter," said someone.

And so she remained. Royal she might have been, but over his priests in matters ecclesiastical her father had no rule, and because of her end none would bury her in sacred ground. She was laid in a distant grave, close to the sea; and often from it the people who passed near swore they heard plaintive song. Above her grave a tree grew, a tree the like of which grew nowhere else in the land. It had fruit that grew the colour of the eyes of Atlan, and it tasted of the ocean, or of tears.

eyer after

Princess of Ashes

I remember fire.

Fire rose all around me. There was no other color in the world except the grim and purifying red, and orange, and gold. It licked the walls, and brought them down, and then there was dust in the ashes, and the air was roiling smoke, a visible thing, thick and difficult to breathe. There were people who tried to wrap rags around my nose and mouth, to help me suck in what oxygen remained without inhaling the fine choking debris of what had once been home. There were people who helped me stagger out of the inferno, there were people who carried me for a while, after, because I was too weak to stand. I remember the strange stasis my mind was in, stuck in that fire. Part of me drifted without conscious thought in the shadows of that thick smoke – but when I was aware that I was thinking it was the flames that stayed with me.

It was a very long time before I began to think of other things, of the things *before* the flames, of the things the flames had devoured. And it was only then, really, that the pain began. When the flames were dead, and the air had cleared and got to the wounds the flames left behind.

· · ·

"*What is that one about, Grandfather?*"

"*That one is poetry. All of those are poetry. I read you some poems from that green book, remember? The one about the flowers?*"

"*But that one...?*"

He chuckled, a sound that was his alone, something that I would always carry with me as an identifying memory – that distinctive small laugh that was the expression of his delight, often aimed at the young me when I said something he found interesting or endearing.

"*There is time enough for that one, little one, when you understand a little more of what passes between a man and a woman. Some day. But that is still to come. We can read some more from the green book, for now.*"

He might as well have forbidden me to think about elephants (because we all know that once that is done we can think of nothing but elephants ever after). I listened dutifully as he read me more poems from the green book and they were lovely poems, to be sure, but now I knew that there were others that should have been mine, but were Not For Me, not just yet, there were things I was – well – not precisely forbidden, but told I would not understand.

And I rebelled against that. I would understand! There was a part of me that was wise! How dare anyone forbid me any words that existed out there, because they thought those words were beyond me?

The book I had asked about was not removed or sequestered. My grandfather's word was assumed to be enough – it was his library, after all, and I was his granddaughter, and we all lived under his rules. And, mostly, I obeyed them. Mostly.

I took down the book stealthily, later, and avidly turned the pages.

I was annoyed to discover that Grandfather had been right. I did not really understand what some of the poems meant, although the words themselves were not that hard – I understood the words perfectly, it was the truth behind them that eluded me. I was precocious in many ways but that in itself preserved other kinds of innocence. I was very learned with words and concepts – I understood much at a young age – but I sought my experiences within books and not really with people. Not then. Not yet. And words that spoke of passion for people were strange to me. That, I did not understand completely. The idea that communication could be through touch and scent and sound, as well as through the eyes and the mind. All that was still just a nebulous idea. After all, when I wasn't in this library, I was still playing with dolls.

Stories, even there. Making up stories about these blank-faced creatures with their staring eyes and painted half-smiles on rosebud mouths which hinted at secrets they would not tell me. So I made up my own stories about them, and made it their truth. Because they were silent, otherwise, and could not tell me different. After I had sneaked my look into the books with those other poems, the ones my grandfather told me were not for my eyes and soul yet, I tried those stories on the dolls, the stories that the poems were telling me. There was something strange and exciting and enticing about creating stories that I didn't fully understand but knew they were built on pure human passion, for these passionless frozen creatures who would never know any except what I chose to visit upon them. But still, those strange painted smiles. Maybe they knew more than ever they realized.

The smell of Grandmother's bread that sometimes greeted me when I woke into the warm light of the mornings of my life, rubbing my eyes free of sleep and the dreams that had come in the night. I would come downstairs to the kitchen and Grandmother would be there, and bread would be cooling on the rack on top of the range, and Grandfather might give me a quick smile over the top of his teacup. Mother might be fussing with breakfast. I don't remember my father in these scenes, much. I don't know why he seldom shared mornings. My mother used to say that he was grumpy when he woke up and that he was better left alone. I had visions of my father as a great bear waking from slumber, a creature not to be disturbed until he deigned to turn back into a mere man.

The smell. Of bread.
Just baked in a hot oven.
There was always fire, it seems.

There was the knitting. There were several bundled projects on individual sets of needles in various rooms, for the various women in my family to work on. At the same time, my grandmother might be working a pair of socks in the kitchen in the intervals between fussing with food and on a sweater for one of my cousins in the parlor. My mother might be purling up something that would end up on my back come winter, or else working the crochet hook diligently while she

33

created a baby blanket for someone in the family who was expecting (it was a rambling family and someone was always expecting).

I was taught, and there were times there were my projects in the works, too. I knitted things for the dolls, mostly, because the grown-ups had the real people covered. But I did a scarf, once. All by myself. And wore it proudly enough, despite the fact that I had made a mistake about halfway in and it had been too much effort to unravel and fix so I just ignored it and carried on as though it had never happened. It was a scarf that was made from ten different yarn remnants anyway, its textures wildly varying from lacy with long fragile hairy fibers to chunky solid knit that was close to three dimensional. I loved that scarf, actually. Mostly because... it was a story. It was a lot of stories, unfinished stories, knitted into one bigger story.

It was like my family, in a way. Like my days, raveled into a life. Like my country. Like my world. The scarf, itself, defined, described, identified, but with an identity that only existed because so many other smaller identities had been subsumed into it. Whispered memories of yarn remnants – 'I was made into a sweater' – 'I was made into a blanket' – 'I was socks, or mittens' – now all wrapped up into one – 'I am a scarf'. I am something different, new, whole. No matter how many remnants went into the making of me. No matter how many stories.

I was not a stupid or unobservant child and the things that went on in the wider world around me did not entirely fail to touch me. I knew there was trouble in the world. There was always trouble. I knew that sometimes my grandfather's worried frown would be smoothed over deliberately for my benefit when I walked into a room unexpectedly. There was at once a sense that he was reading those poetry books of his with a renewed passion, as though seeking salvation in them from something bigger and darker that he could see coming for him, and that he was not reading them at all anymore, because that bigger and darker thing had already eaten that part of him that knew how to care.

But words were his memories. They were what he carried with him.

"It will pass," he would say, cryptically, to me and not to me, staring out of the window into a street which was curiously empty – or maybe curiously full of hurrying and furtive people who were doing their best not to be seen by other hurrying and furtive people. You didn't want to know anyone else's business, in

*these days. It was dangerous. A little knowledge – even knowledge you didn't
realize you had – could destroy you.*

*I understood that. The poems, the stories, had taught me that a long
time ago.*

It will pass.

It will pass.

It was a hope, a prayer. But it was not answered.

Things do not pass. Things end. In fire.

They carried me, and many came beside us – some in cars and trucks,
but those were increasingly left behind by the wayside, abandoned, as
they ran out of gas and no more was to be found, or the seeking of it
would mean more danger than it was worth. After a while we all
walked. Even I, when they stopped carrying me and set me down on
my own feet. I walked.

It was cold, at night, when we would all stop and wait for day to
come again. I shivered. They found a blanket. I wondered what had
become of my scarf, whether it was part of the ashes and dust I
remembered.

What had become of the books, the poems, the stories, the dolls?
The unfinished knitting? The unbaked bread?

All, all fed into the fire...?

I bore its scars. My hand was burned, because I had been reaching
for something that was already out of reach. Perhaps the scarf. Who
could remember?

They picked ashes out of my clothes, from my hair. Someone had a
hairbrush and my mother drew it through my tangled locks, almost
tenderly.

"Look," she said, that first night, brushing my hair, "you still have
cinders in your hair. Poor baby. My poor poor baby. My little
Cinderella."

. . .

35

We walked. And I remembered fire. And I remembered ashes. And I thought about the cinders in my hair.

Someday, I will go back. I want to read those books that my grandfather had thought I had been too young for – someday, when I am old enough to understand. That was something that was taken from me, by fire, by ashes. But I will not let that fire consume my mind or my heart or the memories I carried away from the inferno.

Because one day, I will go back. And I will rebuild.

I will use the memory of fire. Ashes are fragile and without strength or substance... but they carry within them that memory. And if I have to, I will build from cinders.

Princess of Pain

There will be stories told, after. There always are.

They will be wrong. They often are.

Because this is the truth of it. Yes, I fell in love. Yes, I left the sea. But I never *wanted* to.

You don't need to know my name, or his. I was not a sea princess (as the tales will tell). He was not a prince. We were ordinary, he and I, of our kinds. And we met by accident – when I was singing on the rocks, as we all do, as we are supposed to do, singing the song of the sea, and he came by, on the shore, at an hour when none should have been abroad, and stopped to listen and was enthralled.

He never saw me. He only heard. I saw him, though. I saw him there on the shore in the moonlight, his fair hair shining in the bone white light, his arms bare and muscled coming out of a sleeveless jerkin which left them and his broad chest exposed, the tight dark trousers which hugged his slim legs, the broad bare feet planted into the sand.

His legs. His bare feet.

I faltered in my song, just a little. He never knew it. But the sea did, and the sea responded. There was a storm off the shore that day, a storm that raised waves higher than they remembered seeing before, a storm which shattered fishing boats against the pier where they had been tied. One of them, his. The man from the beach. The man the sight of whom had caused me to falter and fail and bring the storm upon the ocean, and upon those who walked the land that swept down to it.

They made me go, the powers of the sea. They took me, and they broke me. They took my voice so that I could never speak to him and make him understand; that I could never sing again. And they split apart my tail to give me the legs that I had so admired in the moonlight. They gave me the gift of grace, at that, and I never walked as though I had never walked before or didn't know how. I suppose I should thank them for *that*. But the gift was a sharp and bitter one and it came at such a price that it might not have been reckoned to have been a gift at all.

The pain.

The pain of the splitting of my tail to form these two legs, these two bare feet – rendered afresh with every step I took on dry land. I was driven from the water and made to walk on knives, out there on the ground. And I was never to show any of it. I could not. I was made not to. All the agony screamed on the inside. My face did not reflect it. My voice never could again.

There was some talk that if I atoned sufficiently – doing what, I was never quite clear – it might all be given back. But I already knew that I could not return. I was no longer the creature I had been, and would never be that creature again – a refugee from my own past, my own being, my own identity, driven away forever. I had to find a home, make a home, where I could – or drift forever, alone and unmoored, silent, in a world of pain.

He had a woman living in his cottage with him. Not his wife. Not a bad woman, simple, a little coarse, a woman of no sophistication or elegance or beauty. She was ordinary enough. But she clearly filled his need – she put food before him every day, she washed his clothing free of the smell of fish, she warmed his bed at night. There was a child, even – but the way he behaved towards the boy it might have been his son or it might have been someone else's, part of the bargain with the woman, that he would take them both in and give them a roof and their daily bread.

It was not with pleasure that I set out to destroy that, particularly since I heard them talk and laugh together and I knew that he would never talk or laugh like that with me. How could he? When I could not return any of it in kind? But even though it would matter at all whether or not I got him to swear he loved me – I would *never* get my tail back, or my song, or my life in the sea, no matter what I did – he was what had got me thrown out, driven away into exile. If I couldn't have my home and my identity, both taken from me, at least I would take him. Because he was the reason of my exile, he would be my reward, the only thing of value that was worth the price I had paid for all of this.

So I showed myself, a little, every day. I smiled at him. I know how to steal a man's soul. It's what we do, the sea creatures, we, and the sea, together, since time began. But it wasn't his soul I was taking, it was his heart, and his mind, and his body. And those were harder to get, and to keep.

She knew, his woman. She knew me for what I was – or she suspected something, anyway. She tried to warn him. But mine were eyes that were deep, the deep blue of the deepest ocean, and hers... were ordinary, brown, close-set, suspicious. Mine was the pale amber hair which spilled luxuriantly over my shoulders, falling down my back, forward over my breasts demurely tucked into their chemise, and hers... was straight and pale and lank, the color of dirty dishwater, and smelling of fish. Mine were lips the color of coral, and hers were sea-rough, chapped, split, broken. When he first kissed me, I knew that he tasted that difference – and it was already over, by then. Because by the time of the second kiss I was the one living in the cottage by the sea, not her, and not the child (I had been right about that. Not his. He would not have given up his so readily.)

I knew that after a while he regretted the bargain. That he missed her. And the boy.

But by then he was mine, and I was his, and that was the way things were.

That is the love story that they would write fairy tales about.

Only... they would paint it in a different palette. They would paint it with passion, and not with raw need. They would paint it with choice and not a desperate seeking of sanctuary and survival. They would paint it sweetly and prettily, and it was not. The coupling at night was sometimes hard, and harsh, and there was pain, on both sides. We loved one another, I think, yes. But not in the fairy tale way.

When the child came, it all broke open.

Because his daughter – I could never bear male progeny, he would have no sons of me – was born with the tail, and her voice, even then, at birth, when she first cried out, had the song of the sea in it. He might not have heard that song, perhaps, if all else had been equal – but the evidence of *otherness* was already there and once you saw the tail on the tiny creature you could not help hearing the difference in her voice.

I watched him fall to his knees beside the birthing chair where the midwife had abandoned me and my baby in horror and fled to spread the tale to the rest of the fisherfolk. I watched him kneel, and I watched him weep.

And because this was given to me – that once, just once, I might speak again aloud, here on the shore – I chose to do it now.

"I am sorry," I said to him, and my voice was harsh, rusty from disuse, bitter from its long silence. "I could not tell you. I was not permitted."

"Why?" he asked, he begged, turning his head away from the child. "Why? Why me?"

"You heard me sing," I said. "Once, on the shore. And I saw you there. And the sight of you broke my heart, and my song. And the sea does not forgive."

The other words were left unspoken but they were there. *Will you...? Can you? Can you forgive? Forgive this – the depth of this deception, as deep as the deep blue sea? How can you?*

"I needed you. I am sorry," I said again, only that, and then it was over, and I was locked into my silence again. This time, forever. Exiled, lost, perhaps soon to be driven away further, deeper, more alone.

But he had struggled to his feet, and he had steeled himself to take a look at the child. A long, long, long look. I feared he would never speak to me again, either, but at length he lifted his eyes from her and turned back to me again. They were wounded, bitter, even angry... but also there was something in there that gave me hope. And his words confirmed it.

"Is there something that is necessary...?" he asked. "For... for the child?"

I could not answer him in words, not ever again, but he read it from my face, from my blue, blue eyes.

And nodded. "I will see it done," he said.

And he took the child into his arms, and strode out into what was still night, in the cold still hours before dawn.

Down to the pier, where the boats were tied, there to gently put his newborn child into the embrace of the sea for which she had been born. He would give her that grace; he might be the only one who would understand because if he was seen − even if he wasn't seen, when the fisherfolk came crowding around to see what the story was when the midwife was done talking − if they couldn't find the child he, both of us, would be accused of murdering it. Not that anyone would blame us, after the midwife had described the monster that had come out of my womb. But we would be branded. And we would be watched. If a second pregnancy occurred... things would be difficult.

He knew that as well as I did. Because, when he came back, after he had spent only a few precious minutes giving his daughter the gift of his tears, as salt as the sea, he wasted no time in gathering together what little possessions he and I both had. And before anyone had a chance to come, to push closer, to see better, to gossip, to gloat... we were gone into the night. Both of us. Turning our back onto the sea, the sea which held my past, and the future which we had created together. We both knew we could not bear to hear her singing to us from the sea on some moonlit night to come.

. . .

We left the story behind. The story that would be told, and embroidered on, after, as always.

This time the story will be wrong. They often are.

Princess Of Dreams

I sleep.

My life is made of moments, and I know each as it comes, greet them as old friends. Other people might call them by their proper names – the moments of dawn, or noon, or dusk, or nightfall, or midnight. But I think of them as slices of being awake, or being asleep. Or falling asleep. Or swimming back towards wakefulness.

Because that is what I do in this camp of lost and dispossessed people, travelling from hellfire into uncertainty, perhaps going nowhere at all, doomed to live out their days trudging along until night should fall and an encampment needed to be raised.

I sleep. Because when I sleep, they sleep. And if I do not sleep, nobody does. And if they do not sleep, they do not dream. And without a dream, sometimes dipping into memory, life would soon become too unbearable. If I do not sleep, they die.

But the price... ah the price I pay.

I give them all dreams. At the price of my own.

You might ask, how did this happen? I would have to tell you right from the start that it wasn't an accident, and it wasn't coercion, and it wasn't something that anyone else had a hand in. I was not bullied into this place, or elected to it, or volunteered into it by others. When it became clear what was happening, I took this on – myself – my choice – no other voice asked for, or required.

In fact there voices raised against it. My parents had been aghast, and my mother had wept for days, and had gone around red-eyed and haggard and drawn, thinner and thinner, as though she was eating herself out with guilt over it all even though she had not been asked for permission, or a blessing, or a parental curse. She died, not long after. My father never told me that it had been I, and what I had taken on, that killed her – but he didn't have to. And anyway, by then, he barely spoke to me at all. I was alone by then, isolated, the sleeper, the dreamer, the solitary witch who made their existence possible.

There was only one other who played a part in this. He had a name, once; it was quickly forgotten as he stepped into his role. He became Prince Charming. That would be what he would be remembered as when he died. And if I survived him... then another would have to step into his place.

It all really began when the armies came. *Their* armies clashed with *our* armies, and where the armies passed only scorched earth and poisoned water remained. So the people who had dwelled in those places (theirs... or ours... in the end they mingled, in this exodus that we were all on, a journey to nowhere, it didn't matter in the end whose soldiers had passed last...) had little choice – stay and die, or pack up a few belongings light enough to carry, and leave, and maybe you would still die, eventually, far from your home, but at least you would have died trying to live.

In those first days, when we were still a small clutch of desperate people but accreting others fast as the fires of war burned past us, it really was that simple. We were a handful of families, then, and we knew one another, and we shared what we had even when we didn't have it. We ran, then – ran for our lives – and if nobody got a good night's sleep, back then, well, that wasn't surprising. We all slept with one eye open, watching out for armies. Theirs, or ours. By that stage it didn't matter. A gun was a gun and we were in everyone's way. But then they started trickling in, in ones, in couples, in families. Dragging children, carrying old people or pulling them in wagons for as long as they could make their frail old bodies endure. We still shared, what we could. But there was one thing that we could not share, because everyone clung to their own desperate shred of it, and it wasn't to be shared, or diluted.

Hope.

Nuggets of hope, hard as sharp stones, rolled around people's minds, roiled their spirits. And the longer the journey without end wore on, the smaller the nuggets, the harder to find, to cling to.

That's when people stopped dreaming.

Oh, they would sleep – everyone has to, sometime. So they closed their eyes as they lay down to rest, and perhaps they even slipped into what might be called sleep – but it was just an absence of consciousness, that was all. No dreams came.

You might think that is a minor thing, in the greater picture. For people who had lost everything they had – an absence of *dreams* would matter? But it did. It *did*. You could hear it in the whimpers of too-quiet children, in the moans of the aged ones who were praying for death to take them away as soon as it might be arranged, in the silence of everyone in between, those responsible for the young and the old, the ones who carried the survival of everybody on their shoulders. The women who tried to feed us all, on whatever they could. The men who worked silently and without joy at any task they were set to – making camp, breaking camp, building fires, sometimes hunting when they could, keeping guard at night so that we wouldn't be surprised by the armies. Theirs, or ours.

Sleep still came – but sleep was no longer an honored guest. It was a fleeting visitor, barely stopping to pass the time of day, no longer pleasant and familiar and known like a good neighbor, lingering only long enough to make people feel even more tired after they woke up than they had been before they had laid themselves down to rest.

I dreamed. *I* dreamed. I knew I did. I knew nobody else could. I did not know why. But in my mind the images unspooled, the memory of beloved trees which I never knew but which I somehow pulled from someone else's undreamed dream, faces I didn't recognize but knew that somebody out there had loved and lost, abandoned homes and hearths and fields and streams and animals who had been loved once. It was as though it was all being poured into my own head, through a funnel, until I was full of it all, brimming with it, overflowing with it, bursting with it.

I didn't know what to do with any of that. It seemed churlish to even ask those who were starved of dreams what to do with a surfeit of dreams that threatened to choke me. It smacked of hubris and of gluttony. So I held onto the secret, for a while. And I got fuller and fuller and fuller of dream and hope and memory.

Until the night I sat before the fire and I heard a voice beside my ear say, quite clearly,

"*Let it out.*"

I turned sharply but nobody was there. Only the firelight, only the shadows.

"*Sleep. Let it out. A little at a time, just enough.*"

"Enough for what?" I said, out loud. But there had been nobody near me at that time to ask me why I spoke to thin air beside me.

"*Enough for them to share. Enough so you don't have to carry so much. Enough.*"

I hesitated. "How...?"

"*Sleep.*"

"I do that every night. And nothing has ever..."

"*Sleep. Sleep deeply. And remember.*"

"Remember what?"

"*Remember everything. All of it, all of theirs, all of yours. And one more thing.*"

I waited, and the voice that wasn't there began to fade – but not before one last thing was whispered to me.

"*Do not forget to wake up.*"

I sat there by the fire for a long time – and after a while it became clear to me that I was waiting. I did not know for what, but I knew that it would become clear to me when the thing I waited for finally occurred – and it did, at last, when Philip, the younger (and only surviving) son of the family who had once been our first neighbors before we all left on this odyssey, came walking by, softly, with his head bowed in a posture that spoke of utter weariness.

"Philip," I said.

His head came up a fraction, but his eyes didn't meet mine. "Yes?"

"I need you to do something for me."

"What?" he asked, after a hesitation. It wasn't a hesitation of reluctance. Only of tiredness.

I felt my heart go out to him. To them all. And I bowed my head and took it on.

"I need to sleep," I said. "And what I need you to do... is wake me, when the sun comes up. Can you do that?"

This time he looked at me directly, his brows knitting a little quizzically. "Wake you?"

"I will be deeply asleep. Very deeply. And it is important that you wake me. Will you?"

He hesitated again, but nodded. He didn't understand.

He would, before the night was over. They all would.

That was the first night I slept the sleep of sharing. I closed my eyes and opened my mind and let the dreams find those from whom they had fled. I didn't know which dreams were whose. It wasn't my place to know. It was my place to carry them, and release them, and gather them, and keep them safe, and then do it again. And again. And again. But that first night – I knew nothing of what was still to come. I just did what the voice from the night had asked. I chose to do it. Freely. And I slept.

And in the morning, with the sky paling with dawn in the east, he was there, Philip, who would become known as Prince Charming, kneeling beside me, his fair hair falling into his eyes, lifting his head away from mine, his lips from my own. I could still feel the lingering kiss on my mouth as my own eyes fluttered open and met his. Met his, which were filled with tears.

"I think I know," he whispered. "I understand. Last night... we... for the first time in too long... I'm so sorry. But thank you. Thank you."

My limbs were still leaden, still heavy with the weight of dreams returning to me, to be carried, to be held and treasured until the next sharing.

"It is necessary, for the thing to be done," I said. And then, hesitating, "Will you stay by me?"

"For this?" he asked. "To wake you back into our grim world after you shared the sweetness and treasure of all that is lost with us all?"

"It needs to be done," I said, almost repeating myself, but not quite – now I was talking of him, not myself.

"Then it will be," he said. "I will never leave you. I will always protect you. If I have to do without sleep to watch over you as you sleep safely in the night, then I will do that too. I will stand between you and harm all my days. I will guard the sleeping beauty who guards our dreams."

I smiled a little, at that, and pushed back a hank of lanky unwashed hair. "Hardly beauty," I said.

"I will... we will all be the judge of that," Philip said firmly. "Are you ready to rise? I will go see about breakfast."

My life is made of moments, and I know each as it comes, greet them as old friends. Other people might call them dawn, or dusk, or nightfall, or midnight. But I think of them as slices of being awake, or being asleep. Of dreaming, so they all can.

That is what I am for. That is what I do in this camp. I sleep. Because when I sleep, they sleep. And if I do not sleep, nobody does, not any longer. There is no longer any sleep in this camp if I do not sleep. Because if I am not asleep, they do not truly sleep even if they appear to be doing so. And when they do not sleep, they do not dream. And without a dream, sometimes dipping into memory, life would soon become too unbearable. If I do not sleep, they die.

I understand that I have surrendered something, here. I will endure. There is a kind of immortality in it for me. I am the repository of dreams; I no longer eat, because there is no need for me to do so. I exist on the sustenance of dreams. Theirs, undreamed, somehow channeled into me and through me and then back into them, and I dole them out every night, and they smile in their sleep. And those people – the others – even my Prince Charming who kisses me awake every morning when I come back into the real world to ravel the dreams together once again – they are all human, they remain human, they live, they suffer, they die at the end of their allotted span. But I... I might outlive them all. And one day, when the armies – ours, and theirs – are done, and vanished – there may be nobody walking here at all, nobody except me, full to bursting with other people's dreams and hopes and memories. And one day I will sleep, and there will be nobody to wake me, and nowhere for the dreams to go. And I know that will be the last night. When sleeping beauty at last fails to wake, and the ravening dreams she carries finally devour her.

Princess of Lies

The mirrors reflected me as I walked by, always – and I would never look at them, not directly, not obviously. Because *she* said I was ugly. My features were imperfect. My eyes were different sizes (and she implied different colors as well). My nose was too big. My jaw was too round. My eyebrows were too strong (one of the ladies of the palace offered to pluck them for me, once, and I still don't know if it was malice or just a too-heavy hand but she didn't so much shape them as obliterate them – and then there was a laughter of another sort that followed me around, the titters behind concealing hands, at the eyebrow-less monster trying to hide her face in the shadows of the corridors). My lips were too full, and always parted, and unfortunately that showed off my crooked tooth. My hair was too frizzy to properly tame into any style and stuck out from whatever was used to hold it down, an untidy frame to that imperfect face.

My body was not formed yet, not into its final shape, but it was starting to get there – and once the changes began they too had been fair game. My ankles were too thick. My waist was too large. One of my breasts grew faster, was bigger, than the other. My fingernails were short and stubby, and wasn't it a *pity* I chewed them so much.

My mother might have loved me the way I was, maybe. But I

didn't remember my mother. *She* told me that I had killed my mother, in fact. The woman who took my mother's place told me that it was my fault that my mother was dead. It never occurred to me to think that might have been an expression of thanks (else *she* couldn't have been here in the first place). But by the time she came I was at an age where everything I was told I took as being the truth, because it came handed down from an adult. And if that held, as a rule, then I was an ugly, black-haired, snaggle-toothed, squint-eyed, big-nosed, flapper-footed, thickly built, unloved and unlovely girl growing into what would undoubtedly be a problematic unmanageable unmarriageable (except through great cost, which the family was unable to consider affording, as I was subtly given to understand), and thoroughly useless woman.

There might be a place for me in *her* household, as some sort of servant, maybe. I might have been nanny, but she could not seem to carry any of her pregnancies to term – and after the third one that too became my fault, somehow. It was my ugly face that was scaring her children away before they could be born. Before she could give my father the son he so wanted. It was all my fault.

The mirrors told me that, when she wasn't sniping at me. The mirrors told me so subtly, in whispers, echoing her words. *You are ugly. You are unwholesome. You are fat. You are useless. You killed your own mother when you were born.*

They sang a different song for *her*, though. I lingered by her rooms when she was being readied for bed, a maid ministering to her needs, brushing the long silky hair of which she was so proud, so unlike my own – so like any that that her own children might be graced with. I heard the maid praise the hair, and I heard *her* answer, my stepmother, her voice gentle, satisfied, proud.

I am beautiful, that voice said. *She is beautiful*, the mirrors agreed, in whispers.

I was not asked for an opinion.

It was after the third miscarriage that her dislike for me turned into an outright cold and implacable hatred. I'm not sure exactly when that happened, but I became aware that she was looking at me in a different way, speculatively, the thoughts written on her face becoming frightening. She was looking at me, and seeing a world without me in it, and wondering how much better such a world might be for her.

It did not surprise me when, not long after that change became noticeable, one of the kitchen maids, who seemed to if not like me then at least feel sorry for me, whispered to me one morning,

"Be careful about your food."

I thought about that. But if this was the way *she* wanted me gone, there was little I could do about it. Our food was served to us as we sat at table as a family, and I was still part of that family, eating the food that others put down in front of me. If only one plate, one cup, were to be poisoned... it was easily enough done. I could not insist on switching plates every night and eating off someone else's, to protect myself. She would not have stood for it, and I would have been revealed to be without manners as well as ugly and unwholesome. So I picked at my food, after that, at our mealtimes, and when everyone was abed I would creep down to the kitchen and eat what I could find, just to stay alive.

She was told about the strange things going on in the kitchen at night, though, soon enough. And after the first night I nearly ran afoul of the servant who lingered late with lights to see if she could either catch a culprit or see where the mice were coming from even that was not really an option any more.

Run, the mirrors said. *Run, to some place where your ugliness will not cause such grief, such harm. Run.*

Run, the gentler mirrors said. Or the crueler ones, I don't know. *Run, before you die.*

So I packed a small carpetbag, with those small white hands with the thin fingers and the bitten nails, and it was a pathetic enough bundle of possessions to mark the short years I'd been on this earth. I took a spare set of clothes, a couple of favorite books, my slippers, my hairbrush, the earrings which had come down to me from the mother I had never known, given to me by my father one day without any word other than an attestation of their origin after which their existence was never mentioned again). I took some bread, a wheel of cheese. I took no mirrors.

I have no idea if they even pursued me or if my sudden absence at breakfast the next morning – and at dinner that night – and at breakfast the day after that – was greeted by nothing except relief, and perhaps a double check of whether any of the silver was missing. By that stage I was deep into the woods – alone, on foot, dragging the bag that despite its negligible contents was almost too heavy to hold after an hour of carrying it, without any idea of where I was going or how I was going to get there. And fall was already biting in the air, and winter was coming, soon now.

I walked for three days. The remains of the bread I had taken were stale and hard. The cheese was beginning to make me feel nauseous. I had no idea what I would eat, after these things were gone. I drank recklessly from a forest stream that I found, and worried that I hadn't brought a container to carry water with me. This had been badly planned – but then, I hadn't really planned it. The mirrors told me I had to go and I went. Ran. A refugee from hate and from malice.

I slept where I dropped, each night, shivering, wrapping myself in loving overhanging roots when I could (where it was warmer) and then shaking the leaves and the dirt down from my dress in the morning, like a human hedgehog getting uncomfortably rid of stuff stuck on its quills. On the fourth night, cold, exhausted, hungry, and increasingly thirsty (I had found no friendly stream that day), I collapsed heedlessly underneath a tall ash, too tired and too dispirited to go any further. Eventually, I slept.

When I woke, it was to three short, ugly little men who stood above me, eyeing me contemplatively. Two of them carried woodsmen's axes. Another carried a large dagger, almost long enough (on him) to be called a short sword. They wore badly handmade felt hats, the stitching uneven and coming apart where the seams were, with signs that those seams had been re-stitched before. Possibly many times. They also wore almost identical trousers, leather jerkins, and boots which looked as though they has seen better days.

Their eyebrows were huge and furry, their lips I couldn't see (but at least one showed a crooked tooth through a thicket of beard), and their eyes were small and close-set on either side of noses which looked, to a man-jack of them, as though they'd been broken in several close-quarters fisticuff fights and re-set badly.

For some reason, I warmed to them immediately.

"What are you doing out here, on your own?" one of them asked, frowning, wrinkling his features into an even more frightening formation than before.

"I'm running away," I said. And then, for no reason that I could think of, added, "Because I am too ugly."

Their expressions were interesting, for a moment. And then one of them said gently,

"Are you hungry? You don't have to be afraid – but our cottage is not too far away, and at least one of our brothers is home, cooking. It won't be pretty and it won't be nearly enough – but we'll share."

I thought about stale bread and the remains of that increasingly iffy cheese, and I said, "Thank you. That would be very nice."

Well, I was ugly. But I wasn't stupid, and nobody had ever said I had bad manners.

The cottage was sturdy but it definitely showed that a gaggle of men lived here with no woman's touch to the place. Axes stood leaning on walls, or fallen down beside them; there was a layer of dust on things not touched regularly; the kitchen was a mess of dirty dishes, many of which were doing second-go-around duty as manhandled by the brother who had been designated as cook. He looked surprised when the three who had escorted me there ushered me into the house, but not put out. He simply wiped another plate down with a (none too clean) cloth and set it at the table, scootching the others closer together.

I was welcome here. It was a strange feeling.

And there were no mirrors in that house. Not one. There was a blessed silence from whispers.

There were three beds in that house, and it seemed as though they were all shared, by a changing cast of the seven brothers who lived here – seven small, ugly men who eked out a small living as woodsmen and hunters and sometimes builders, if someone would hire them to raise a barn or a small house. I was given one bed, and they all piled into the other two, when night came – there was no question of them turning me out again to go on my way, not until I chose to go.

And I stayed for a day, and then another. And another. And then one day I found myself alone in the house, all the brothers away at work somewhere, and I rolled up my sleeves and repaid their kindnesses. I fetched water, and scrubbed all their dishes to a state of cleanliness which they probably hadn't seen since they had been new. I put everything away in its own tidy and accessible place. I cleaned out the fireplace. I swept the floors. I made the beds with clean linens – they didn't seem to have much of those and what they had was not always free from rips and holes, and I repaired what I could with needle and thread I found in the cottage. I even tackled one of the coming-apart hats which I had found tossed into a dark corner, apparently as unredeemable.

They returned, the brothers, as the light began to fail and a thin snow began to fall, in twos and threes, from they had all been. They noticed the place was different. They raised their eyebrows, but said nothing. Neither did I. After the evening meal I sat in front of the fire working on the rest of the hats. They said nothing. Neither did I.

But the day after that two of them stayed behind at home when the others went away, and began sawing and hammering at something at the back of the house. An extension quickly took shape there; they raised the walls and had the roof on before the real snows came, and by that stage it had its own hand-made wooden bed with a straw mattress, its own pillow, its own little pot-bellied iron stove which two of them had carted up from somewhere on a wagon and whisked off into the new addition without a word. It even had attempts at crude comfort, like a small rug beside the bed, an oil lantern which gave a good light, for sewing, perhaps. I moved in there, without a word spoken. Everything was understood. I learned to cook better than the itinerant brother who happened to be in charge of the kitchen managed; I even, when the spring came, asked one of them for seeds and seedlings and started a small garden out back where my extension was. And we had fresh carrots and beans and pumpkins that year, and there was even apple pie (when they brought me the apples, and the flour, and the butter).

Only once was our first meeting ever referenced again.

It came weeks, maybe months, after I had been living there, a part of their household, a part of their lives.

"You are not ugly," the oldest brother said to me, abruptly, one evening as I stood outside the cottage's front door to greet him as he came home. "You said that to us, that time, in the forest. You are the loveliest thing any of us have ever seen and we are grateful for your presence here."

"The mirrors told me," I said faintly.

He held my gaze with his own, and said, his voice level and flat, "Mirrors *lie*."

He was right. Mirrors of glass and silver lie all the time, because they only see the outer skin. But I was looking in a mirror even as he spoke, in the mirror of his eyes, and I could see myself reflected back at me.

No, not ugly. Not ugly any more. Snow-white, and dark-haired, and smiling with those full lips and showing a crooked tooth.

I ran, from hate and rage and malice and evil – and somehow a refuge was waiting after all. A place where there were no mirrors, and I would always be loved. And treasured. And respected. And beautiful.

tales re-told

Rum Pelt Stilt's Skin

There is a rot at the heart of the Kingdom.
There is a curse that can't be broken.

There used to be a formal garden behind the White Palace, a place where a green sward and a carefully cultivated riot of flowers surrounded a marble fountain. Now they had taken to calling it the Walk of Queens, because the statues raised beside its paved walkway were not just beautiful works of art. They marked the graves of five women who had tried and failed to remove that curse. Six, now – but the sixth was too new, too raw, for the statue to have been raised yet.

And the curse was still there.

And the word was out that the King was looking for a new wife.

The man who sat brooding in the corner of a wayside inn nursing a half-drunk tankard of ale was one of the King's Ministers, although his shabby and travel-worn clothing certainly did not mark him as any sort of dignitary. But that was all right – he was hardly bound for a foreign court. They were all out of foreign Princesses for the King to carry off to the White Palace on the hill above the city – all out of willing ones, anyway. The Minister could hardly blame them. Marriage to this King seemed to carry an automatic death sentence after only seven days – and seven days as a Queen was proving to be less than enticing for a prospective bride. The handful of ministers had been sent out into the countryside, to scour the houses of the aristocracy for suitable daughters – but this man, at least, had found slim pickings.

He had found only one young woman of marriageable age, and he suspected even that was because he had arrived earlier than he had been expected and had caught the family by surprise; even this young woman was hastily put beyond his reach by a sudden and (the Minister was certain) rather unexpected announcement of her impending nuptials by her father. She had looked rather astonished as she had gazed on the man who had been named as her future husband – and so had that man. The Minister could hardly stand up in the house that did, after all, offer him hospitality and accuse his hosts of lying. However, by the time he could extract himself from that situation word of his errand had gone out before him and every other house that he had visited had been distinguished by its lack of any females of childbearing age. He was on his way back to the White Palace, to the King, empty-handed and heavy-hearted.

He had not meant to enter into a conversation on this matter with any he met on the road – it was the King's business, after all – but somehow despondency and the ale had loosened his tongue at this particular hostelry. He was not quite sure how it had come about but he found himself discussing the daughter of a local tanner and leather-worker with a brace of drinking companions whose beer he appeared to have purchased for them as payment for this information. The young woman in question was certainly not of noble blood, and was probably, judging by certain turns of phrase and eloquent expressions on the faces of the minister's informants, at best... homely. But she was of the right age, if only just barely, she was not promised to anybody, and best of all she had a reputation of being a good weaver... something that the Minister could, if all else failed, present as his reason for bringing this girl to the Palace. Because a weaver is what the King needed. The unfinished tapestry which stood mocking them all in the golden room at the top of the palace tower – the tapestry which was prophesied, when completed, to reveal the name of the evil spirit which bedeviled the King and his Kingdom – needed a woman's hand to work it. Six Queens had tried, and failed. Perhaps, this time, the King could use the glittering lure of a crown as a lure and a reward rather than a pre-requisite – perhaps his mistake had been marrying the women first, before he had brought them here to finish the tapestry and remove the curse. Perhaps only a woman whose head had not yet felt the weight of that crown could accomplish the task. And besides... if this one failed, as the others had failed, there would be no seventh Queen to lay beside the six who already slept the eternal sleep on Walk of Queens. The woman who failed could be buried quietly somewhere out in an unknown corner, in an unmarked grave...

This girl's father might not be too eager to hand her over to such a potential fate – but on the other hand, he was, by all the accounts the Minister had heard, poor enough to let her go for a small discreet purse of gold... and besides, there was always the chance, the *chance*, that she could do this thing, and actually become the next Queen. In which case, of course, the purse of gold would be multiplied, a thou-sandfold, by virtue of having his beloved daughter sit in a golden throne by the side of the King of the land. As for her not being the most appropriate of brides for a king – well – the Minister could, he found himself thinking, gild the lily as best he could during the remainder of the journey back to the White Palace, and present his King with – if not an ideal prospect – at least an opportunity.

He thought better of seeking out the tanner's house that night, having himself imbibed more than he thought was entirely advisable and feeling distinctly light-headed with it. But he fought down an incipient hangover headache the next morning, and presented himself at a decent hour on the doorstep of the tanner's workshop.

The man who came to the door at his knock looked promising – he appeared thin and tired, and his eyes were bloodshot and bleak. He had not had much sleep of late.

"I am looking for Geerd, the leather worker," the Minister said, knowing full well that the man stood before him. "I come from... the King."

That had less of an effect that the Minister had expected, or hoped for. Geerd simply nodded, wiping his hands on the sides of his trews.

"I am Geerd," he said. "What does the King want with the likes of me?"

"Your daughter," the Minister said.

Geerd straightened, his gaze sharpening a little. "My *daughter?*" he said, his voice wary. "What has my daughter to do with the King?"

"She is by reputation a skilled weaver," the Minister said, repeating gossip he had only heard for the first time the previous night over beer in a voice of such conviction and authority that Geerd actually stepped back in the face of it. "As even you will know, there is a tapestry in the heart of the White Palace that desperately needs to be completed..."

"Yes," Geerd said. "I know. I also know that every hand that was laid to the task belongs to a dead woman. What, the King has run out of Princesses and grand ladies to marry, that now he needs to kill my child?"

"If she succeeds, he will make her Queen," the Minister said.

"They were all Queens, before they began, all the ones who died," Geerd said. "And they are all just as dead."

"I am authorised to offer you this," the Minister said, hefting a small leather purse in the palm of his hand. He was, of course, authorised to do no such thing – but he had every hope of this small investment bearing rich dividends if his scheme came to fruition. "The girl comes with me, today."

"My last apprentice left me, four days ago," Geerd said. "My wife has been dead these ten years. My younger daughter is sick, and like as not will not live to see the next summer. This shop... and Antje... are all that I have. I do not believe that you can offer me enough gold to sell my..."

"Papa," said a clear high voice from inside the shop. "With the gold you can hire another apprentice, buy medicine for Caja. I will go to the King."

"Anouk... my Antje..."

"I *am* a good weaver, Papa." Apparently she had been listening in to the conversation, from within. She had heard enough.

"So were they, the others, the rest. The Queens. I cannot send you to your death..."

"You are not sending me, Papa. I choose to go."

She came out of the house as she spoke, into the Minister's sight. He gave her a long apprising look and hid a small sigh – he had not been far wrong. The girl was tall, rangy, almost bony; her hands were long-fingered and well enough shaped but perhaps a little on the large side, and raw from the work she had been doing in the house and in the tanner's shop; her ankles were thin, red from the cold, and her bare feet were thrust into a pair of wooden clogs. She wore a none-too-clean white cap on her head, and from underneath it a few strands of lanky hair of a non-descript colour escaped to fall over her face. She had a somewhat prominent nose, and direct blue eyes – she would have to be taught not to hold and challenge a man's gaze like she was doing right at that moment, before she was presented to the King.

It was Anouk who reached out and plucked the purse from the Minister's hand, and closed her own father's hands around it. As she was doing so, she leaned in and kissed him lightly on one weathered cheek. Her only gesture of farewell. She hesitated for just a moment, as though she was considering going back in to take her leave of her sick younger sister, but appeared to decide against it, and turned to the Minister instead.

"I am ready," she said simply.

The Minister found himself a little disconcerted, but this was what he had come for, after all – at least he would not return to the Palace empty-handed. He nodded at Geerd, and turned on his heel to walk away. Anouk followed.

"We had better," he muttered unwillingly, without glancing back but very aware of her appearance at his back, "find you some halfway appropriate clothes."

He handed the girl over to the wife of the innkeeper when he returned to the hostelry, giving the woman the rest of that day and that night to make the girl remotely presentable. He was planning to leave early the next morning.

It took him a moment to recognise Anouk when he emerged into the courtyard of the hostelry in the grey light of the morning after. She was still wearing her wooden clogs but she had been given a pair of clean worsted stockings which he caught a glimpse of underneath the hem of a not entirely new but clean and well-made dress which might have belonged to the innkeeper's wife herself. The cap had vanished, and her hair had been braided into a neat crown about her head – it must have been washed, perhaps with chamomile, because it seemed blonder than the minister thought it had been the day before. She was still as long-limbed and angular as a young colt, but that could not be helped – and the new dress did seem to give a hint of the fact that with the right seamstress a womanly figure could well emerge from underneath the shapeless garments she wore. She met the Minister's gaze squarely, with full understanding; her hands were folded together against her ribcage with a strange serenity as she waited for him to more or speak.

When he finally did, it was brief.

"You clean up better than I thought," he said brusquely. "Come. We should be on our way."

The Minister wondered how the others had fared, his colleagues sent out in other directions to find the King a new wife. When he and Anouk arrived at the White Palace he sent her into a quiet anteroom to wait, with a footman on duty at the door just in case she should decide to bolt after all, and went to speak to the King alone; he was not away for long, and when he came back it was to crook a finger at Anouk, who had been quietly sitting on a chair upholstered in dark brocade, to follow him.

They crossed empty halls, passed along colonnades flanking cold winter courtyards, and finally climbed a long, endless, winding stair. Right at the top, a single door opened off a small landing. The Minister turned a large iron key which stood in the door, and pushed it open, gesturing for Anouk to go inside. She obeyed, and found herself in an eyrie. The room was many-sided, and every side had a window, and the windows looked out over the Palace, and the grounds, and out into the countryside. A long way away to the horizon a line of blue mountains was visible against the sky; in another direction, there was the hint of water as the light reflected off the lake to the south of the Palace; another view showed a wide and dense wood, partly bare of foliage now that it was winter but enough of it evergreen to give a sense of its depth and scope.

The inside walls of the room, in between the windows, were gilded – and shone with a soft golden glow.

"Oh," Anouk breathed. "How beautiful."

"Never mind that," the Minister said. "Look, here – this is all you need to pay attention to."

Anouk brought her gaze back to the center of the room where a loom was set up, a half-finished tapestry upon it. At its foot was a basket containing a pile of yarn; in front of it, a small three-legged stool.

"This is what my lord the King bade me tell you," the Minister said. "Your task, which begins right now, is to weave that tapestry until it is done. You have seven days to accomplish this. You will see nobody from the moment you set your hand to the loom to the moment those seven days are up and the King himself will climb up here to inspect your work. If you succeed, you will be wed to the King the very next morning, and become the Queen of the land. If you do not succeed..." He did not finish. He did not have to. Anouk already well knew the price of failure. Six Queens lay in their graves, somewhere in the gardens below – six Queens who had paid the price of failure.

She realised that a part of her should be afraid, but somehow she could not quite seem to summon up fear.

"What is the tapestry's design?" she asked, instead. "How am I supposed to finish something of whose final form I have been given no hints?"

"The tapestry knows," said the Minister. "It needs a woman's hand, to weave – but the design is already within it. Because the word is... that when it is done it will hold the true name of the demon who is the canker at the root of this realm – and once we call him by that true name, he will be vanquished, and he will be gone forever. Show some sense, girl. If we already knew that name, then we would not need the tapestry. That is why you are here. To find this secret out."

"But how will I know..." the practical Anouk began, but the Minister raised his hand for silence.

"Enough," he said. "It is done. Your seven days have begun."

69

He hesitated, as though he considered wishing her luck – but decided against it. Instead, he gave her a small sharp bow, and backed out of the room, closing the door behind him. Anouk heard the key turn in the lock. She was alone with the magic, alone what felt as though it was the heart of the kingdom; she felt as though this room had been designed for the single purpose as to allow somebody who loved this land to come up here and gaze out and see every hidden nook and cranny of it all, water and wood, hill and dale, village and town...

The light was starting to fade, the views vanishing into shadows and twilight, and she finally investigated the rest of the room she had been locked into. She discovered that she had a lamp, and a supply of oil – and she lit it, and hung it from a hook set beside the door. The lamp was a small one and looked barely adequate, but the golden walls picked up the light and reflected it, and the room was suffused with a soft, bright glow. The only other things in the room, aside from the loom and the skeins of yarn and the three-legged stool, were a thin straw pallet and a woolen blanket folded upon it. None of the windows had glass or coverings upon them, and this room looked as though it got cold enough on winter nights to freeze the marrow in a living being; the blanket looked woefully inadequate against this. But oddly enough, Anouk was not cold. She completed the circuit of the room to find nothing more than another tiny door that opened into what looked to be a privy. That was all.

She crossed to the loom and inspected the tapestry. It showed no obvious pattern or design that she could immediately discern, nothing that she could use as a starting point to continuing where it had been left off, but there was a thread still attached which looked as though it had been abandoned mid-weft – and she sat down and reached for it.

It seemed to... vibrate... gently underneath her hand. As though... it was breathing.

Anouk gentled it, whispering softly to it as she might have whispered to her feverish little sister, soothing, gentling. Before long the whisper had turned into a soft tune, into something almost like a lullaby. And somewhere underneath it all she sensed the others who had been here, the restless ghosts of the dead Queens. Their presence. Their frustration. Their... their fear.

She heard their names, shivering like a breath of wind through dry autumn leaves. The names carved under the statues on the Walk of Queens – five, and a sixth yet to rise.

Gisela. Hedwych. Katryn. Mirthe. Stefana. Viona.

Her hands found a rhythm. Beneath her fingers, the threads wove together, knit, began to find a pattern born in her soft, hummed lullaby.

Why did they die? How did they die...?

"They were easily distracted..."

A voice, from nowhere, as if in answer to her question. Anouk kept her eyes on her work, kept on humming.

"...are you easily distracted...?"

Anouk did not respond.

"...are you afraid...?"

"No," Anouk said softly, "I am not afraid."

"You will be," the voice said, and she almost felt lips moving against her ear, the words poured into its shell like secrets.

"What is your name?" Anouk asked.

"That is what they brought you here to find," the voice said. "When you have finished the tapestry, you will know."

"And I will finish it," Anouk said.

"Then you will have to work without stopping," the voice said. "Because let me tell you the rest of the story, the part that they tell none of the Queens before they are brought here. I am under a geas to stop you from completing this task, at any cost. What they did not tell you that whatever work you do on that tapestry, I will begin to unravel, the moment your hand leaves the thread. As fast as you do, I will undo. And when they come for you at the end of your seven days... you will die. As all of the others died before you."

Gisela. Hedwych. Katryn. Mirthe. Stefana. Viona.

Anouk bent her head, and focused on her hands, on their steady, constant motion. And all the while the whispering voice was all around her, wrapping itself around her fingers until it took a conscious effort to move them, tangling in her hair, echoing in her mind. There was nothing coherent about the stories that it told, and it seemed to trip easily between one dead Queen and the next, but it told of them all – about all the women who had come here to find out the name of the spirit who haunted this place, and died trying. One of the Queens had been driven mad by that voice, apparently, and had jumped from the high windows to her death. At least two of the others had been found here sitting quiet and idle and quite mad before the half-unravelled tapestry, with no trace left that they had done any work on it at all, and had died quietly before the sun had set on the day after they had been taken from this room.

"I showed myself to all of them, in the end," the voice said, whispered, hinted, quietly threatened. "And when I did they all went mad. Every Queen. And then they died."

"I am not a Queen," Anouk said.

She had glanced up and out of the windows, every so often, at the beginning. After a while, she stopped doing that. She lost track of time. All that existed was the tapestry, and the prophecy – and the more she worked, the more the tapestry revealed, and the more she understood. And the greater her pity grew, because she understood more than any of the other women had done; she had got furthest in, had seen the pattern almost complete.

"He stole my skin... he stole my love... he stole my life... and thought I was done," the voice said into Anouk's ear.

"Who did?" she asked quietly, her hands working the loom. She had not slept, had not eaten, in she could not remember how long. Her fingernails were ragged, her fingertips raw and bloody, leaving small smears of her blood on the tapestry.

"A war of mages. A war of mages. And Gisela paid the price first because she did not understand – ah, she, she made me – and I..."

The first of the Queens. The one who had jumped, apparently. The one who *did* know too much.

"What happens," Anouk asked, "if I find the true name?"

"Then I am free," the voice whispered.

"So why then are you killing the women who were sent here to complete this tapestry? If you had allowed them to complete their work – any one of them – you could have been free a long time ago."

"I set up the tapestry. It was to be my key, my release. But then *he* set the doom upon me, that I must unravel every night the work that was put in during the day. A war of mages."

"Who is he, then? And who are you?"

"I... I am.... I am the King..." the voice was barely there now, just an echo in her mind. "And he is... he is... he is..."

"His is the name which is revealed by this tapestry, is it not...?" Anouk said, her own voice dropping into a whisper.

She was close. So close. The tapestry was almost done. The basket of yarn was almost empty. The sun had risen and set several times, she was aware of that, but had lost count of how many. Soon, now, they would come for her. Soon.

"It is a skin," the voice inside her head said, softly, softly. "It is a skin. Do you understand?"

"Yes," said the tanner's daughter, who had seen many skins stripped from the bodies which they had contained. Who was not a gently-reared maiden, nor yet a Queen. "I understand."

"Then see," the voice said. "Look, and see."

Anouk, without stilling her hands, allowed her eyes to slide off her work for just a moment and light on the vision she was being offered. She said nothing, allowing her gaze to linger there only for a moment before bringing it back to the almost-completed tapestry. But that one glimpse had been more than enough – she knew what had driven the other women out of their minds. The shape of a naked man's body, losing cohesion, writhing muscle and bone, dripping blood, bulging eyeballs in lidless sockets, bared teeth in a lipless face.

She was weaving a skin. A skin woven of magic and revenge. A skin that would reveal the name of the ghoul who had stolen a King's face to wear as his own.

"Do you know," the skinless man said, hanging in mid-air before her just beyond the tapestry, just beyond her range of vision, "what you need to do?"

"Yes," Anouk said. "I know."

"It is the morning of the eighth day," the wraith said. "He comes."

And Anouk pulled the last thread across, and made it tight, and tied it off.

"I am done," she said.

With aching and bloody hands she struggled to release the finished tapestry from the loom, scrabbling at knots – it was loose but she was still holding it on to the frame when she heard the key turn in the lock and the footstep that came into the room, and then stopped.

"Your Majesty," she said, without turning.

"You... are done," said a man's voice behind her. If she had not understood this game before now, she might have been puzzled, even distracted, by its joyless inflexion – she would have thought that this outcome would have been the pinnacle of the King's expectations, finding the woman locked into the tower alive and sane after her seven days incarceration, the tapestry of the prophecy finally completed, everything about to turn out well.

But things were never as they seemed.

There is a rot at the heart of the Kingdom.

There is a curse that can't be broken.

"I am done," Anouk said. And turned, with the tapestry in her hands, staggering a little in her exhaustion but still steady enough to accomplish her purpose, flinging out the tapestry before her, high and wide, so that it fell and settled over the shoulders of the figure of the man who called himself the King. He saw it coming, too late, and tried to scramble back – but the room was too small to allow him to run. He screamed as the tapestry touched him, crumpling to the floor as it curled around him, wrapping him inside it, bigger than it had seemed to be in Anouk's hands, growing where it needed in order to stretch everywhere it was required, enfolding the man and as it did so turning him into something else, something different, something twisted and malignant and evil and hideous to look at as it crouched hissing and snarling on the floor just inside the door of the golden room.

"Your true name is Rum Pelt Stilt," Anouk said. "And this is Rum Pelt Stilt's skin, woven of enchantment, the thing that shows you in your true shape."

"I... laid... a spell... on it," the creature on the floor hissed and wheezed, writhing. "It could never be completed by a Queen who laid her hand to it..."

"I am *not* a Queen," Anouk said. "I am a tanner's daughter. And I know a thing or two about the skin of a living creature."

"But I will make you a Queen," said a voice behind her, not a whisper any more but real and solid and belonging to a man made of flesh and blood... and his own proper skin. "If you will it. Today you have given me back my life, and my Kingdom – and I am forever in your debt, Anouk, tanner's daughter."

Anouk, too weary to move, barely turned her head enough to look.

A man wearing the face of the King she had just reduced to the gargoyle on the floor stood beside the empty loom, the blanket from the pallet she had not slept on now wrapped around him like a toga, and looking every bit as royal as the one whom she had destroyed. "I am Floris, and this day you have freed me from the evil spell that had kept me trapped here – a malevolent spirit doomed to prevent my own freedom, by destroying those whom I had hoped would be able to release me. He... wanted my life, that creature there. He wanted Gisela, the woman I loved, for his own. So he laid his plans, and he worked his spells, and seven days before Gisela and I were to be wed he came to this place, and we fought in this high room, and he took what he wanted from me. I remained here, helpless, bound by his words – and yet... and yet... I managed to keep enough of my own magic woven into his to lay the path to my redemption for one who understood."

"He married Gisela," Anouk said. "And he sent her here, because he had to, because that was a part of your own counterspell. The woman he made his Queen had to lay her hand to this tapestry."

"Yes," Floris said. "But she was not strong enough, or else seeing me in the shape which I showed you earlier... broke hear heart, destroyed her mind. Perhaps she loved me too much to bear the knowledge of the truth. Her blood is as much on my hands as it is on his – I, who loved her, helped destroy her. Her, and all the other Queens who came in her wake. Until you came."

"But I was not a Queen."

"They told him it was too soon," Floris said gently. "Too soon to add another to the Walk of Queens. And enough of humanity had bitten into him that he bowed to that, and chose to offer the crown as a reward, this time, and not sacrifice yet another Queen to the game. And you... you came up here, up from the land, rooted in the soil of the realm, and you looked out of the windows of the high room, and you were not afraid – you said it was beautiful. And for the first time, I heard not fear... but courage, and humility, and hope."

He reached a hand out to her, but she bowed her head, hiding her own hands in her skirts.

"No," she said, "my hands are..."

But he took one of her hands, and held it very gently in both of his own, and brought it up to his lips to kiss her ruined fingers.

"Your hands are a miracle," he said. "I will honour every cut and score and scar that you have put on them for my sake. And in those hands I place it all – this land, which you called beautiful, and the King whose soul you just saved."

From the windows of the golden room in the highest tower of the castle, standing side by side, they watched the winter sun spill over the land, and all was sharp and new and clean again in that cold clear light of a brand new day.

The Butterfly Collection of Miss
Letitia Willoughby Forbes

❧☙

The house on the corner of Fifth and Amaryllis was not a house. Not really. It was a mansion.

It was a small castle.

The "corner of Fifth and Amaryllis" was a little misleading, in fact, because the house stood on a tract of land which took up all of the south side of Amaryllis, all the way up to Sixth Avenue—and on the far side from Amaryllis street the grounds of this particular estate abutted onto a public park which gave onto Iris Street on the far side. So this house was the only house on that block, really.

Built of stone, it was set back from the street. A dark, shoulder-high, manicured hedge, kept trimmed and immaculate and absolutely impenetrable, hid most of the garden from sight—only two gaps were allowed in this, a wider one which opened onto a driveway which curved beside and behind the house (no street-facing blind garage door for this house—if there was a garage it was decorously out of sight), and a narrower arch which bore a low wooden gate, always closed and latched, and which opened onto a stone-flagged walkway stretching from the sidewalk of Fifth Avenue to an imposing front door. The walkway was bordered on either side by rose bushes gnarled with venerable age and bearing blooms, seemingly regardless of season except in the deepest of mid-winter, of unusual size and richness of colour and an absolutely bewitching perfume. The front door itself was set between two large bay windows in which lace curtains were always drawn, the only windows on the ground floor of the house on the front side, giving an impression of rooms of prodigious size within and beyond them. The second storey consisted of a row of Colonial sash windows painted an immaculate gleaming white, glowing against the dark stone—serried ranks of decorous bedrooms and boudoirs, no doubt. Above that, a third storey, mansard windows set into the dark roof, possibly servants' quarters in the days that well-off gentry like the kind of folk who would reside in a house like this still had live-in servants as a matter of course – and for all anyone knew this house still had them.

Above and behind all of this, mysterious and improbable, a glass cupola rose over the heart of the house from within a surrounding thicket of chimneys. It was built out of hexagonal panes, giving the cupola an air of being a diamond cut and carved by a master jeweller; on summer days the cupola glittered in the sunlight, both beautiful and somehow forbidding, as though it was whispering, through its reflected scintillae of light, *I am not for you. I am not for the likes of you.*

But also, for a certain class of man, an irresistible *I am yours, come and claim me.*

"So, there it is," Darius Green said, lounging on the other side of Amaryllis and leaning with a studied nonchallance against the fence of one of the more ordinary homes on that side of the street. He had changed his name, legally, years before—but although he might have been formally registered as Darius Green there was a lilt in his accent which still betrayed the boy who had once been Adario Verdi, a stow-away urchin new-come from the back streets of Napoli with little knowledge and ability other than cut-pursing and thieving, things he had dutifully practiced and improved on during his years in London. "You would have me believe this is the abandoned Willoughby Forbes mansion, Charlie? Doesn't look very abandoned to me."

Charlie O'Leary, reaching up to straighten his cloth cap, tilted his head as if he had been planning to spit sideways out of the corner of his mouth – but changed his mind under the withering gaze of a matron who chose that moment to walk down the street, clad in a severely respectable black bombazine gown featuring a truly stupendous bustle. "Abandoned is as abandoned does," he said instead, turning back to his companion. "Her ladyship – Letitia, her name was, or Lucrezia, something like that–lit out almost a year ago for destinations unknown, hunting for her father who had been missing for a good couple of year before that. No other known living family – her mother snuffed it years ago. So far as anyone can tell, nobody's actually *lived* in the place since. It's just been sitting there, locked down, just like you see it."

"Looks cared for," Darius said, hauling out his heavy pocket watch and consulting it, giving every impression of politely concealed but nevertheless very definite skepticism and impatience. "Somebody's living there."

"No live-in," Charlie said. "That I can see. I've been watchin' this place. A housekeeper type comes in once a week. A gardener is in there maybe twice a month or so, doing lawns, saying how-de-do to the topiaries, puttin' down fertilizer for those monster roses. 'S all."

"And how do you know that it isn't just empty inside? A hollow shell?"

"Nobody cares for a hollow shell like this thing's cared for," Charlie said. "There's gotta be something worth picking. An' what's more I know what."

Darius raised an eyebrow. "Oh?"

"Papa Willoughby Forbes was a lappy... a lep... a leaping..."

By now Darius was tapping his foot, letting a little more of that impatience show, and Charlie abandoned his attempts at being highfaluting.

"He's a butterfly collector," he said at last, scowling. "I do believe that's where he went and vanished at, someplace exotic, chasin' more butterflies."

"A butterfly collector," Darius repeated. "So what are you planning on stealing–butterflies?"

"You don't got any idea how much them's worth," Charlie said passionately. "I asked, I did, at the museum – the girl who sells tickets out front is a friend of mine, and she found out for me. Some of the rare butterflies are worth a flipping fortune."

"Uh huh," Darius said, unconvinced. Another lady, this one glancing over from under a lilac-coloured parasol, gave the two men a guarded appraisal – but was disarmed by Darius reaching up to touch the brim of his bowler while giving her a light social bow. "And how are you going to convince somebody that you own some rare butterfly from some tropic paradise?" he said to Charlie, not taking his eyes off the woman until she had given him a half-smile, convinced that he was in fact the gentleman he appeared to be, and walked on by.

Charlie bared his teeth in a grin—and it was not an altogether pleasant one. "I can sell anything," he said, the words a statement of fact, not remotely braggadocio or hubris. "You just got to help me get my hands on it."

Darius bent his gaze on the mansion. "We'd better have a lot of time to look," he said. "A house that size... and it could be anywhere..."

"Oh no, not anywhere," Charlie said. His eyes glided upwards and Darius followed them until they lit on the glass cupola.

"Up there?" Darius asked. "What makes you think so?"

"It's a greenhouse, innit?" Charlie said. "A nice little hot house garden."

"Are you telling me we got to go chasing after these butterflies with nets? They're all loose up there?" Darius asked, suddenly less eager to attempt to glean the Willoughby Forbes lepidopterist riches.

"Not *alive*," Charlie said.

He was starting to sound insufferably smug, and Darius told him so – but something about the whole caper had caught Darius's sense of whimsy and if half of what Charlie was saying was true, dammit, this might be rather more fun than most jobs he found himself involved in.

After he had vented his annoyance at the little Irishman, Darius settled back against the fence of the other house and crossed his arms, staring up at the dark mansion across the street.

"All right," he said, "I'm in."

Charlie pumped his fist in the air, discreetly, in a brief display of triumph, and then controlled his enthusiasm, the consummate professional.

"I figured, two days from now would be good," he said. "The house-keeper-biddy comes in tomorrow—and then the gardener isn't due until the middle of next week. We have a window."

"I'll case it," Darius said. "Make it three days. I want to know everything I can about this place—and three days is cutting it pretty fine."

"But I've already spent weeks watching the place..."

"My way," Darius said calmly.

"Fine," Charlie said, with a rush of annoyance. "I'll come get you..."

Darius pushed himself off the fence, tipped his hat at Charlie as though they had just been two random blokes talking of nothing of consequence at all, and turned away, back up Amaryllis Street towards Sixth Avenue.

"I'll call *you*," Darius flung back over his shoulder. "And don't stick your nose above the parapet until then if you can help it. Disappear off the streets."

"Yes, *sir*," Charlie said sarcastically, tipping his own cap in response—but he had done it to Darius's retreating back. Somehow it had all slipped from being his own grand idea to being controlled by Darius the Mastermind, in the space of a heartbeat. "Disappear," he muttered darkly. "Right. With my luck he'll just go it alone and cut me right out of it..."

But two nights later there was a quiet knock on Charlie's door and when he opened up there was Darius, slouching with his hands in the pockets of his overcoat.

"Tonight," he said, without preamble, "if you're still up to it."

"Tonight? You mean right now?" Charlie squawked, taken entirely by surprise.

Darius shrugged. "Now, or you're on your own. I'm out."

"All right, all right, let me get my coat," Charlie grumbled, ducking back inside. It was the second week of September, and although the days were still warm with the remnants of August, early mornings and evenings were harbingers of October that was on its way.

"Something is strange inside that house, and that is the truth of it,"

Darius said quietly as the two of them made their quick and quiet way back to the corner of Fifth and Amaryllis. The gas lights had been lit along both Fifth Avenue and Sixth Avenue, but Amaryllis Street was dark, its lamps brooding black silhouettes. It seemed as though the lamp man was wary of this side street, and seldom ventured down it. And yet there was something there that wasn't quite gaslight, something that might have been weird ghostlight from the cupola of the old house which always seemed to give off a faint luminescence of its own, a strange white light with a greenish tinge. If he had been given to fancies or prone to dwelling in his memories Darius would have compared it to moonlight through water, like he had seen it once back in his native land, diving in the shallows on a moonlit night.

"Eh... *inside?*" Charlie asked, faltering mid-step. "You've actually been inside?"

"That's what's strange," Darius said. "I actually took the trouble to look around–I watched your 'housekeeper biddy' when she arrived, and I actually knocked on the back door while she was there, pretending to be selling something – she told me smartly to get myself off the premises, to be sure, but before that I was able to see a few things – that garage in the back, that's a later addition to the house, it's wood not stone, and I could see that there was a door leading from the kitchen straight into that space. I could not see a lock on it, and there was only an old iron padlock on the garage door, the work of minutes to deal with. So the next day, I did just that – the gardener wasn't due for another day or two anyway, the garage is out of sight of the street, and, well, it did occur to me that it was unlikely that nobody else had noticed these happy coincidences before you did, Charlie. This isn't a house that's exactly... secured."

"So?"

"So it did occur to me that we might be wasting our time altogether," Darius murmured. "But then when I got inside... things got... weird. First off, there was no lock because there is... a mechanism instead. Gears and levers and things. Wheels. You turn a handle on the outer side of that garage door and there are clicks and groans and rattling and the thing... swings open. By itself. And then, once you get inside – it's as though that house doesn't mind in the least that people

82

get into it, or how they get into it. It does seem to have an opinion about people getting *out* though. Particularly if they are carrying something that belongs to the house. There was a fine little horse head statue that looked small enough to carry and valuable enough to matter–and I was going to take it as a souvenir–but I was given... a certain sense... of it not being advisable for me to try and remove it from the premises. Twice I found myself at the back door empty-handed with no clear memory of having put the horse statuette down– twice I found it back where I first saw it, gracing the mantel. And I knew, I clearly remembered, taking it down from that mantel and holding it in my hand. *Twice*. Second time it happened, I just looked at it, and I left it there, where it was. And I went away empty-handed. And I never even went up the stairs to the upper floors at all. There the stairs were, going right up, starting right at the toes of my shoes, and yet somehow I never managed to set foot on them. I was in there for two hours according to my watch – and according to this massive old clock out in the hall, you could see its workings through the glass door and it was more cogs and wheels and polished brass – and yet I do not remember two hours passing, nor what I did with them other than taking a horse head figurine from its place and putting it back twice. I think the house has been left well enough alone because it's simply... *guarded*."

Charlie, superstitious by nature, began to slow down, lagging behind Darius. "You mean... haunted?"

"Maybe it'll dilute for two men," Darius said. "Come on, you big baby, it didn't *hurt* me, whatever it was, and besides this whole caper was your idea anyway. I wouldn't know where to look for a butterfly collection nor what to do with one if I had it. And perhaps the spells and charms work only for horse heads and not rare butterflies."

Charlie was of the sudden opinion that any such spells and charms might work on any unsanctioned hand which tried to lift things that the house knew belonged to it, rather than protecting individual objects – and he was now just as loath to penetrate this 'abandoned' mansion as he had been enthusiastic to do so only a few days before. But Darius seemed to have something to prove and Charlie somehow found his unwilling feet had dragged him to the last place that he wanted to be, the gravelled drive that widened into a narrow courtyard around the back of the Willoughby Forbes mansion. He heard his own teeth chattering as Darius suddenly made a small light flare in a tiny hand-held lantern which Charlie had not seen him carrying–he must have left it secreted here, against tonight's need.

"Hold this," Mathew said tersely. "Give me a little light, here."

Darius's fingers swiftly teased open the padlock on the barn or garage door, under the light that Charlie shook down on his hands from the lantern trembling in Charlie's own – this was the padlock with which Darius had already made the acquaintance of a few days before, by his own story, and had been merely put back in a semblance of wholeness, easily pulled apart again.

"Come on," Darius said, pushing the garage door open a crack. "Bring that light in, and stop looking like you'll run like a rabbit if I turn my back for one instant. This way. Careful, the floor's uneven, and there's a step before the door."

He said the last just as Charlie stubbed a toe painfully against the riser, and he mumbled a curse under his breath just as Darius laughed softly and said, "Yeah. That one. Now come on up, give me some light over here while I work this contraption."

Charlie obligingly lifted the lantern, and Darius bent over a lever or handle, brass polished to a golden glow, and gently pushed it down. After a series of whirring noises there was a soft click, and the door sprang open, just a crack. Darius eased it the rest of the way and turned to beckon.

"Come inside."

Charlie stepped over the threshold gingerly, as though he expected demonic voices to whisper maledictions into his ears – but he heard nothing other than a quiet creak as Darius pulled the door open and then the sound of soft footfalls on the blue and white tiles on the kitchen floor, revealed by a shaft of the lantern light. Charlie paused, lifted the lantern, tried to squint at his surroundings and make a closer inspection of the clockwork contraption which graced the inside of the door, but Darius's impatient voice from the shadows made him tuck his head defensively between his shoulders as he took another step forward.

"It's just a kitchen. Nothing that interesting in here."

"But the door..." Charlie began, and Darius made an impatient click of his tongue against the roof of his mouth.

"Yes. Undoubtedly fascinating. I don't have the first idea why they went to such lengths, on simple door – but come on, now, if you want to get anything done. We don't have all night."

Charlie followed Darius out of the kitchen and into an ornately furnished dining room panelled in dark wood, porcelain plates and cups glinting in the lantern-light from behind glass-fronted cabinet doors. The dining table was huge and solid, with enormous clawed feet, surrounded by eight chairs, each of which looked like it weighed more than a couple of Charlies put together. It did not seem possible that such things could have been brought here from someplace else; it would have taken a team of elephants to deliver them and dozens of burly, bare-chested, turbaned slaves to bring them inside. The furniture looked like it had been hewn in place, right here, from some giant mahogany tree which had mistakenly sprouted from between cracks in the stone-flagged floor.

But Darius was uninterested in this room, too, at least for now. He was beckoning from the far doorway and Charlie followed with the lantern.

"There," Darius said, once they had entered the main parlour. "On the mantel. The horse head. That's the one that wouldn't leave."

Charlie brought the lantern closer and obediently examined the small sculpture, but an examination by lantern light brought forth no obvious curious properties.

"You want to try taking it again?" Charlie said dubiously.

"Maybe later. Bring that thing. Come look at the stairs."

The stairwell to the upper storey, centered in the entrance hall, so as to be viewed to best advantage from the front door which it faced, swept elegantly upward in a gleaming curve of polished wood. There was a narrow strip of lush oriental-patterned carpet runner fastened in the middle of the stairs by means of a thin brass rod holding the carpet flush against the bottom of every riser.

"Odd," Charlie said as they padded to the bottom of the stairs.

"What is?"

"No dustcovers on anything, like you'd expect in a house not lived in this long. And no *dust*. Look at this floor. Look at the stairs. And you'd think that the trinkets like your horse head would have been put away, seein' as there ain't nobody here to actually set eyes on it – and same with the china, in the dining room. It's all left... ready... as though the master's expected any moment..."

"Perhaps he is, for all you know," Darius said. "Maybe it's all been cleaned up for the triumphant return of the Willoughby Forbes family next week."

"Maybe," Charlie said, unconvinced.

He came to the bottom of the stairs, fully intent on climbing them; it was a few moments later, apparently, that Darius said, "Well? Aren't you going to go up?"

Charlie found himself standing with his feet a respectful pace from the stairs, holding out his lantern.

"Oh, right," he said, and prepared to take that step forward.

A few moments later, Darius laughed softly.

"You see what I mean?"

Charlie growled, deep in the back of his throat. "I'm beginnin' to think that this was a whole lot of a bad idea," he said sullenly.

"Ah, but I think I have it kind of figured," Darius said. "We both aimed for the center. For the carpet. But if I go off along the edge there..."

He padded up to the staircase and put a foot carefully on the couple of inches of polished bare wood between the center carpet and the edge of the stair. Nothing untoward happened, except that now, and it seemed miraculous under the circumstances, he was able to slowly and carefully climb the stair.

"So long as I touch only this part of the stair, and neither the carpet nor the banister," Darius said. "It was like somebody had a blind spot–someone who only saw one person climbing the stair, and that person did it sweeping up the middle of the stairwell with one arm on the banister–just like you and I would do it if left to our own devices–and assumed that that was the only way to do it. So carpet and banister were drenched in the 'do not go here' command."

"Such nonsense," Charlie said.

"Come on, trust me. Don't touch the carpet, don't touch the rail, and you'll be just fine. Try it."

Against his own better instincts at this point, Charlie did, and found that Darius was completely correct. Placing his feet with great care squarely in the bare-wood gap between carpet and stair edge, he was able to climb very slowly and warily, his balance oddly precarious given the need to also hold up the lantern so that it gave out useful light. He wound up doing most of that long twisting stair on the balls of his feet, and his calves were aching with the strain by the time he stepped out on the first landing.

He sucked in his breath as he stepped up on the last wooden gap, and saw Darius standing in the second floor corridor, squarely in the middle of the carpet runner laid there. Darius laughed softly as the lantern light illumined Charlie's stricken face.

"No, apparently the carpet hasn't all been hexed," Darius said. "This particular one doesn't make you want to march back down there in a hurry. Looks like once you're up here at least the first round of the booby traps is sprung."

"And what's up here?" Charlie asked.

"We'll find out, I am sure," Darius said. "Maybe even your butterflies."

"I'm not for sure certain they're worth enough for *this*," Charlie muttered darkly, but lifted his lantern, took a deep breath, and stepped off the bare stair onto the hallway carpet.

Nothing remotely unusual happened, and he let out the breath he had been holding.

"Okay, then," Charlie said, lowering the lantern a fraction and looking around into the deep shadows that surrounded the two of them on the landing. "What now? Door to door?"

"I think I'd rather like to take a look at that rooftop butterfly house of yours first," Darius said slowly. "These will all be here on our way back. Let's look for a second stair."

The second stair led off the far right-hand end of the second floor corridor, a wrought-iron spiral in a matte black that sucked in the lantern light and made it look like they climbed on shadows instead of solid treads, but other than that it was free of the sort of enchantments that barred the entrance to the main stairwell in the hall. They climbed slowly and carefully. At the top of the stair they emerged through an archway into a little tiled anteroom which in its turn opened out into another corridor, narrower than the one below but covered in a plain and utilitarian runner rug along its length. It was very dark; in the pool of lantern-light. They could see wall sconces where lamps or other lighting fixtures used to be, but were no longer. The guttering lantern was the only light they had.

A number of undistinguished and very ordinary doors opened on the one side of the corridor, the side that faced to the front of the house—these would no doubt be the rooms behind the mansard windows visible from the street. On the other side, there was only one door – a big double door that looked like it was made of solid oak, held by wrought-iron hinges – the kind of door that looked as though it was built to stand up to a battering ram. It was oddly incongruous, facing out into this narrow corridor, even if it weren't for the elaborate mass of interlocking cogs and wheels, as well as a gleaming brass bar off to one side which looked as though it could be slid into place across the double doors as a formidable barrier. It looked a little like the contraption that had graced the inside of the kitchen back door, but an order of magnitude more complicated and businesslike. There was something about it that made Charlie feel very uncomfortable, but then he was crawling around an empty house in the middle of the night with evil intentions and it was hard to separate this niggling feeling that he had that he was missing something obvious from a general wariness of the burglar going about his natural business.

Only a few steps beyond, the corridor ended in a bare wall, its length less than half of the corridor below.

"What a very odd arrangement." Darius murmured. "That door—it must open inward, each side is almost the width of this corridor, if you opened it out you'd be stuck inside the doors like a cage. But the hinges are on this side, and so is all of *this* stuff. All the mechanics. A very strange thing to install up here."

Charlie caught himself thinking that the doors were alike in some fundamental way to the massive dining room furniture downstairs—both looking as though they had blossomed into their final shapes here, inside the house, growing into their form and function rather than having been brought in or built into this structure by human hand.

Organic, kind of. *Alive.* Charlie was certain that he would have felt rather strange climbing into one of those mahogany dining chairs – he had the strangest feeling that they ought to either rise and serve him his dinner, or else eat him whole for *theirs.* Here, he felt a distinct reluctance to lay his hand on those double doors. It was not the same 'do not touch' air from the stairwell in the hallway, but something... different... something... deeper.

Charlie cleared his throat.

"Let's get out of here," he said.

Darius's teeth flashed in the lantern-light. "What, having gone this far? Some thief you make. No wonder you never did a big job on your own."

"I know when to run," Charlie said, realising his teeth were beginning to chatter even though the corridor was not cold at all. "I know when the best thing to take with me from a job is me own skin."

"Your valuable skin notwithstanding, nothing ventured, nothing gained. I think what we might be looking for–and more besides–is right behind these doors. Skedaddle, if you must. But give me the lantern."

Charlie considered his alternatives. Given the choice between following Darius into a place the very thought of which was beginning to actively frighten him, or making his way back downstairs through this eerie empty house in the dark down long empty corridors and two sets of stairs, he decided that at the very least he would not die alone. He clenched his teeth, locking his chattering jaw.

"Go on, then," he managed to squeeze through the gap between his two front teeth, lifting the lantern higher. "I'm right behind you."

He saw Darius's eyebrow rise at that, but he said nothing, simply turned back to the double doors and laid his hand on the latch.

There had been no sign of an actual lock, other than the interlocking wheels, but they seemed to be disengaged and one of the wings of the double door gave freely under the tug of Darius's hand and swung outwards, smooth and silent, on oiled hinges. Darius stepped aside to let it open through; Charlie followed, with the light.

They found themselves in a small anteroom, with a glass door on the far side which opened onto what amounted to another corridor – or, more precisely, more of a cloister, with its inside 'wall' nothing more than a series of archways leading through into the central atrium– which was the garden underneath the glass dome on the roof of the house. The moon was only a waning sliver that night but somehow the glass panes took what light there was, fractured it and focused it so that there seemed to be rather more moonlight in the garden than there should have been, and almost no further need for the lantern Charlie carried.

While Charlie gaped at the lush garden awash in magical moon-light, Darius was looking around with a more practical eye. He finally nudged Charlie in the ribs.

"Over there," he said, pointing.

Charlie followed the finger with his dazzled eyes, seeing nothing. "What?"

"Just follow me," Darius said. "Come on. Bring that thing."

They followed the open colonnade down to where it was closed off by a glass door. It was not locked, and Darius opened it and stepped into what looked like a large study, or a small library. A desk was tucked into one of the mansard windows that jutted out of the house roof; the walls surrounding it appeared to be built of books. Wherever there were not bookshelf-festooned walls, the rest of the place was a glass cage consisting of the window facing out to the street, on the one side, and three sets of doors – the one through which they had just entered, an identical door which led out of the study on the far end and presumably let into the cloister on the other side, and a double French door which faced into the conservatory.

Charlie had gone over to inspect the bookshelves, shading the lantern with his hand and keeping the light from the mansard window (it would not do for somebody from the street to see a burglar's light dancing in the window up here).

Darius had turned his back on the shelves and stood staring out into the garden, lit with that eerie bone-white light.

"I think I found our butterflies," Charlie said in a low voice. "There's drawers down here underneath the shelves. And they're full of specimens."

"Damn the specimens," Darius said, without turning around. "They're out *there*. In the garden. Look."

"At *night?*" Charlie said, as he turned to cross to the inward-facing glass door. "That can't be right. Maybe they're moths..."

But they weren't moths.

Something had stirred up and disturbed what had looked like an empty and quiescent conservatory, and it was now full of fluttering shapes. The set of the wings said butterfly, not moth, and even in the strange light the two of them could see that there was more colour out there than was generally known to occur in nocturnal moths.

"I'm going out to take a closer look," Darius said. His voice was strange, slow, almost slurred—as if he had been hypnotised, or enchanted, as though he was no longer guided by his own will.

"I have a very bad feeling..." Charlie began, but before he could finish his sentence Darius had pushed open the French doors and stepped out into the night garden. He did not close the door behind him.

"This is a bad idea," Charlie muttered, even though Darius seemed bent on ignoring him, setting the lantern down on the floor by his feet and reaching for the door.

"A very bad idea indeed," said another voice. Not Darius. Dry and high and leathery, an aged female voice. Somewhere in the garden right beside the open glass door.

Charlie froze in mid-motion, his hand outstretched. "*Who's there?*"

A strange creature stepped into the light. It was shrouded, dressed in what looked like a beekeeper's outfit—throat-to-ankle robe; long gracile gloves reaching up to its elbows, with thin sensitive finger-sheaths which permitted easy manipulation of objects; a hat draped with a veil which rested in folds on its shoulders and breast. All in black. A black ghost in the bone-white garden.

Something tickled Charlie's wrist, and he shook it off, instinctively; a beautiful butterfly with large dark wings rose and fluttered off into the garden. Two more followed it into the office through the half-open door, alighting on Charlie's hair, his shoulder. He batted them off with his hands; one of them clung briefly to his finger with tiny, delicate butterfly feet before fluttering off. His finger stung where it had touched him. His wrist was beginning to throb, where the other had landed; looking down, Charlie could see a discoloration starting to form there, like a dark bruise.

More of them fluttered in, swarmed around him. He backed away, swatting at them; from somewhere inside the garden he thought he heard a shouted curse, a cry, a low moan of pain.

"Darius?" Charlie tried to shout in a whisper, but the name didn't carry very far.

"It's too late for your friend," the black ghost said. "It's too late for you too. They've tasted you. You might as well come out here with your friend or they'll break this glass door to get at you if you try to shut them out. And they can do it."

"Who are you? How do you know? What are these things?" Charlie was panicking now, seriously panicking, and the butterflies were everywhere. He had taken off his cap when they had come into the house, and now several of the butterflies had tangled into his hair. He tried pulling at them and yelped with pain as he seemed to accomplish nothing more except trying to pull out his own hair; they weren't letting go. When he brought his hands back down they were coated with a strange oily residue.

"Are you the housekeeper?" Charlie asked. "Get them off me–get them *off*..."

The black ghost reached down and removed the lantern before Charlie could kick it over. Charlie actually heard her voice break open into the dry husk of a laugh, a wry chuckle.

"Best thing in the world, if the whole thing went up in flames," she said, apparently to herself. "Best thing in the world. But they wouldn't let that happen anyway. Come out into the garden, do. It'll be a mess, cleaning out the study tomorrow. No, I am not the housekeeper." She paused, letting Charlie try and figure out why there would be a mess in the study the next day and watching him come to the possibly exaggerated but largely correct conclusions. "Trust me when I tell you that it is already too late. They have you. They are mine. I know them. I made them. That is my sin, and I live with it. I am Letitia Willoughby Forbes and this... this is my butterfly collection."

The tiny butterfly feet were like acid on Charlie's skin. His scalp began to burn. One of the butterflies' wings had brushed across his face as it fluttered past, barely touching his cheek just underneath his right eye, and the eye had already started to swell shut–he could barely see through the slit any more. It hurt. It *hurt*.

Charlie actually whimpered. "It feels like acid."

"It may be. They certainly added a few... refinements since I made them." The old woman was very calm, very matter-of-fact about it all–distant, even detached, as though all of it was an interesting problem that had nothing at all to do with her... even while she was taking ownership of it all.

"They're butterflies–they aren't wasps–how can they–"

"Oh, they're worse, they're much much worse. They're not stinging. They are feeding." Letitia's voice was calm, almost soothing, as though she were talking about something a million miles away and not right here, right now, trying to eat Charlie alive.

Charlie actually swatted one of the insects, hard, and it splayed against his shoulder where he had slapped it with one rapidly numbing hand. In the white light of the garden, he glanced over and thought he saw... tiny cogs and wheels, like delicate clockwork, instead of the smeared insect flesh he was expecting. And as if to confirm his suspicions, the creature he thought he had killed shivered its wings after a moment, in an oddly awkward motion, like a broken clockwork toy. Then it actually managed to lift its badly damaged self and fly jerkily, listing to one side, back out into the garden.

"You can't kill them," Letitia said. "Not like that, at least. It's gone back to repair itself. It'll be back. Perhaps even tonight."

"What are these things?"

"I made them," Letitia said. "To prove something to my father. To prove something to my mother, who was already long gone and needed no proofs from me. To prove that I was better than either of them. Instead, it turns out... Oh, *do* come out of there, there's a love. I really don't want the extra work, it'll be easier here in the garden."

Dazed with confusion and now pain, Charlie finally obliged her and stepped out into the garden. He might have reconsidered, had he been in his normal mind, because a cloud of butterflies bore down on him the moment he stepped out into the white light, covered his arms, his torso, his head, his face. But Letitia had pulled the door closed behind him as he had left the little study and now he was out here, exposed, voraciously gnawed on.

He fell to one knee, then both, then to his hands and knees. His breathing was shallow, rapid.

"*You* made them?" he kept repeating. "You?"

"My father was walking in the country hedgerows one day and he saw a young barefoot girl singing a briar into a wall of full glorious pink roses," Letitia said, apparently to nobody at all, her voice oddly dreamy as though she were telling a fairy story to a child at bedtime. A story she knew well, that she had told many times before. "He fell in love with the magic of her, and he married her. But he was a scientist, and his world was made out of things fashioned from clockwork and brass and oil and steam; his dream was to fashion a creature every bit as good as man but unencumbered by the weight of a soul. *Her* world was spells and cantrips, herbs for healing and for mischief, songs and stories, the magic of the earth and the sky, the water and the garden and the growing things, like any good hedge witch's should be – her dream was to keep her spirit free, and her hands flowing with magic. They fell in love but they stood in each other's way—because she did not believe in life without a spirit, and he scorned and wished to shore up the fragility of life which depended on such non-empirical spirits to exist. So they loved each other, and they fought, and they had a child. Me. And each tried to win me for their side of the war. So I learned at my father's side – there is a laboratory on the far side of this garden, he lacked for nothing there – how to make a creature out of cogs and wheels. He collected butterflies from all over the world, and I loved seeing his specimens so carefully laid out and meticulously annotated, but they were dead things in their glass cases, and so I made a clock-work butterfly, and another, and another, replicating his collection by mimicking the specimens in his cases. I learned from my mother down in the kitchen garden how to take one of these clockwork butterflies and somehow, while winding one up for the first time, give it the breath of life itself. I let them loose up here, in the roof garden, in the conservatory. And that's where they eventually killed my father."

"He never... went away..." Charlie managed, his mouth almost full of butterflies, his lips burning with the gentle touch of their acid feet.

"He died in that very study behind you," Letitia said. "My mother had been gone for some time by then—she died when I was no older than seven or eight. Maybe nine. That was about the age I made my first butterfly. Mother is actually buried down in the garden—there's a grotto, with an angel. It is her magic that lives down there – you noticed the roses? The scent of the roses? That is her – that is my mother's presence, the hedge witch's touch. My father... well, he helped too, in his own way, I guess. We poured what was left of *him* out onto the rose beds that my mother had loved. His ashes seemed to do them good. And after him, the rest..."

"Rest...?" Charlie said. It was the last word he spoke, and his eyes, open under half a dozen butterflies each, no longer saw anything at all. But Letitia didn't appear to notice.

"The burglars who came for the easy pickings, just like you," she said dreamily, sitting cross-legged on the white-gravelled path in the conservatory, beside Charlie's body. "I laid a few easy spells on the lower floor but they always found their way up here somehow. And their ashes went into the roses, some of them... and now, most go into the hedge of thorns. I'm growing it high, you know—high, and all around, closing in the pathway gate, and the driveway. We don't use those any more, anyway, we don't need them. And the house shall be surrounded by it, by a hedge of thorns that is going to be too high to climb and too thick to hack through. And perhaps in time they will forget about us, here in our little castle. And in a hundred years, two hundred, maybe the butterflies will have worn down, and worn out. And it will be safe again. And some day some hero will come hacking in with a blade, expecting to find a sleeping princess, maybe." She cackled to herself, softly, as butterflies landed on her and then fluttered off again defeated by her gloves and her veils. "Perhaps I shall still be sleeping," she murmured. "For them to find. Or perhaps there will only be a lot of dead butterflies, clockwork worn away by the centuries..."

She looked down at Charlie one last time, to where he lay at her feet, not moving. Then she sighed, and struggled up, brushing butter-flies off her arms and legs as she unfolded her frame, slowly and painfully.

"I have to remember to let the gardener know there will be fresh fertiliser next week," she muttered under her breath.

The roof garden was quiet, awash with ghostly white light, the only sound a susurrus of fluttering shadowy butterflies. Letitia made her way back into the cloister, back to the double doors, took meticulous care to brush off every last butterfly from her head and hands before she allowed herself to open the door and step out into the corridor, closing the door behind her. She was careful to inspect the locking mechanism as the door closed, and then turned a brass key in the midst of it all, and the cogs and wheels whirred and turned until the brass bar slid slowly across the double doors into place.

Charlie had been right to be wary of this door – and it was now obvious why. It had not been designed to keep anyone out of the conservatory. It had been built to keep whatever already *was* in the conservatory from escaping the place and finding its way into the house.

"Did I do well, Mama? Did I do well, Papa?" she whispered, as she walked down the corridor, drifted town the iron stair, made her way down the wider corridor on the second floor to a white door on the far side of the house, and finally let herself into a bedroom furnished only with a single white-painted four-poster bed with red velvet curtains draped on its sides. Shedding her beekeeper costume like a chrysalis she emerged as a slender-limbed, fragile-built creature, white hair cropped short and standing around her face like the halo of a dande-lion puff, her eyes wide and dark blue, her mouth generous, her nose a little sharp but not unattractive. Long ago when she was young she might have made a passable sleeping princess in a castle behind high walls of thorn; now, she was just an old woman, moving with the slow dreamy motions of a memory of forgotten youth.

"Must remember... tell the gardener..." she murmured, as she climbed into the bed, laid down on it upon her back with her arms crossed over her chest and a small secret smile on her face. Her eyes closed, the smile lingering, her lips curving and parting to reveal tiny perfect teeth.

"Time to sleep now," a voice that was barely hers, barely audible, came from between those smiling lips like a ghost.

Above her head, as though they heard, the rustle of wings stilled as the butterflies settled back into the trees.

The big stone house on the corner of Fifth and Amaryllis was different from the rest of the houses which surrounded it.

The house on the corner of Fifth and Amaryllis was not a house. Not really. It was a place where a cloud of tiny, perfect, deadly butterflies made from brass clockwork and silk guarded the sleep of an aged princess waiting behind a hedge of thorns for a rescue that never came.

Glowstick Girl

The days ran together at the Center, and after the first couple of weeks Luz had stopped counting them. She had milestones — there was the day they were taken, Papa and Alejandro and Valentina and Luz; there was the time that they separated them, and they took Papa and Alejandro away to some other place, leaving fourteen-year-old Valentina to look after her nine-year-old sister; there was the time that one of the health workers who did the rounds in the pens had paused and said something in a tone of voice that had immediately triggered Luz's every instinct of fear and dread although she had not immediately understood what 'infirmary' meant — it was another worker who gently explained to her later that Valentina had been taken away to a hospital bed, where her cough and her 'bad color' could be treated (except that she had never come back. Luz's older sister vanished from her side like a ghost and became a memory). After that, Luz was alone, just one amongst many who were alone, trying to sleep at night on hard mattresses under thin blankets, waiting for... none of them knew what they were waiting for. Some were younger than Luz; she heard the little girls whimpering for their Mama, hiding their faces in shadows, but she had lost hers before she had ever known her (she herself had been the cause – the late, unlooked for, unexpected child who had caused sepsis and death in the wake of childbirth leaving both the newborn mite and her brother and sisters motherless) and she could not reach out to them, she did not know how. She herself missed the rest of her family. Her sisters – the imperious Maria, her mother's namesake, the eldest, married and with a family of her own, who had not accompanied them on this fatal journey; Isabella, safe in her convent and her faith, the child the family had given to God; Valentina, bossy and sometimes a bully but nonetheless the sister closest to Luz in age and a protector who was sorely missed in Luz's current circumstances. Her only brother, Alejandro, of whose great and wondrous destiny everyone in the family was so absolutely certain. Her Papa, who treasured her, as the last memory of his beloved wife. Her aunts and uncles, who doted on her. Her beloved Abuela, who surrounded Luz with the kind of unconditional love that she had always taken for granted, had always believed utterly that it would always be there, and now, in its absence, Luz often found herself shivering even when she was not physically cold. Her soul was iced. One by one they had been taken from her – her mother, her father and brother, her sisters, her grandmother – and she was alone. She was nine years old and she was completely alone, in a land of strangers who often did not even speak her own language and understood nothing of who Luz was, of what she needed, what she thought, what she believed.

It had been summer when they had been taken – and Luz had stopped counting the days. It was with a sense of shock that she woke one day and realized that somebody had tried to be festive, and had put up a somewhat scrawny three-foot-tall miniature indoor evergreen in a terracotta planter, a shrub-sized plant almost violently determined to be a Christmas tree. Its handful of ornaments – some quite inventive – and a dogged sprinkling of tinsel insisted on a 'Feliz Navidad' – but there was nothing about the place Luz was in, or the people that she shared it with, that spoke of Christmas to her. Some of the younger children smiled when they saw the tree. Luz just withdrew further into herself.

It was wrong. It was so wrong. Everything was wrong.

They handed out glowsticks to the children, the workers who were in charge of them, and to Luz this was almost the final insult – the garish plastic things being the very symbol of everything that this place represented or the 'Christmas' joy it tried so hard to foster. But she took the glowsticks – she ended up with five of them, in the end. The others lit theirs immediately, as soon as they received them, and some closed them into circles which they wore as necklaces or as bright neon halo-crowns tangled into their stringy dark hair. Luz tucked hers away in a fold of her blanket. They were foreign. They were bitter. They were a reminder of everything that she had lost, just a fake and garish imitation of things she had loved. She could not bring herself to give them a moment of joy.

But they burned in her mind, and it was later, much later, when everyone else around her had stopped whispering and whimpering and had dropped into the deeper breathing of sleep, that Luz pulled out her glowsticks and stared at them. And then, slowly, almost against her will, she took one, and snapped it into garish green life.

The pen faded from around her, its wire walls, its hard floors, the other children curled up under their thin blankets. And in the green light, Dia de las Velitas, the Day of the Little Candles, rose around her.

That day that they always waited for, when the Christmas celebrations truly began – when hundreds of candles spilled into homes and then out of them and into the streets, entire neighborhoods flickering with star-like lights. The young Luz skipping down her street, holding onto her Abuela's hand, being told the story – how the candles were there to light the way for the Virgin Mary, bearing the child that would become Baby Jesus, the Son of God. The family would send word to Sister Isabella at her convent, together with a special rosary, asking for a special novena – for prayers – for intercessions with the Mother of God in the advent of this, the holiest of days. The cloak of God's love and protection would be spread around them in return. It was so, it had always been so.

"She speaks to God, on our behalf," Abuela had said. She had always had a special pride in Isabella's vocation.

"But I thought Mama did," Luz had responded, having overheard intercessions addressed to her dear departed mother now part of the heavenly host at God's feet.

"But your dear Mama is there," Abuela had said. "Your Mama, who shares the same name that graces the mother of Baby Jesus, our Maria of blessed memory – she lives there now, and we are sundered until the day we are all called before God in Heaven. Isabella, she is still here. She is here, with us, in body, while her soul gets to visit Heaven because it is holy, and she is a bridge for us, living at once in the kingdom of God and the kingdom of Man, able to intercede because the saints hear her clearly."

It was often confusing, and Abuela's religious dogma was often idiosyncratic enough for her own children to smile when she went on her wilder flights of fancy – but she built a castle for Luz to live in, a castle full of saints and angels and people who could speak directly to God, and full of light.

Luz bathed in that light – it was like the light of her grandmother's love, surrounding her, protecting her. The light of faith. The light of security. The light of a joyous time. There was a promise here – things would never be so tough that they would be insurmountable, because the candles were there, and the candles meant everything would be all right...

The glowstick began to fade, and the flickering candles of the Dia de las Velitas began to gutter in Luz's memory. She gasped, bereft, unwilling to let go of the glow that had once brought her such joy, reaching out for a second glowstick, bringing it to life.

The little candles faded away anyway, but now Luz saw the ubiquitous nativity scenes of her childhood, which were springing up everywhere – the nativities with their empty cradle, waiting for the hour in which it would be filled with the promise of the season. Big and elaborate ones with life-sized figures, like the ones before churches, or in public squares. Little ones before people's houses, or tiny ones inside people's homes, small enough to set under a Christmas tree, or on a mantle – some disastrously and delightfully made by the small hands of young children. Joseph, Mary, the Wise Men, the shepherds, the angels

– some of the scenes with all the animals, like the sheep and the camels and the donkeys and the cattle from the story of the birth of Christ. It was the run-up to Christmas, the nine days before, the days which Luz's Abuela had called the *Novena de Navidad*, the special songs and prayers were said.

People gathering around the Nativities, to sing and to pray. Luz laughing as she recognized her Tia Gabriella, perched precariously on a patient donkey with a blue veil draped over her dark hair and steadied there by her Tio Matias's hand, Mary and Joseph setting out on their fateful night to seek shelter as the story told, as they set out on their *posada*, knocking on doors and singing for admittance accompanied by companions playing guitars, being beckoned inside to gather around whatever nativity scene had pride of place inside that house and to share song and prayer with their hosts.

Fading again, into a paler and paler light. Luz struck a third glow-stick. It was red, and in that rich red light she saw the open doors of the church, glowing, people stepping in with humility and joy for the *Missa do Galo* – the ruby lights of the votive light racks and pyramids, the silver-grey smoke from the swung thurifers, the starched whites and dark purples and vivid reds of the liturgical garb. The first time she had accompanied her family to the Midnight Mass on Christmas Eve Luz had been seven – could it really have been only two years before? – and the experience had seared itself into her soul. She had fallen asleep at one point, and then woke with her head leaning on her Abuela's shoulder, her eyes suddenly wide with guilt and fear – had she slighted God by falling asleep in His house on the holiest night of the year? Should she have fought to stay awake? But the roosters were beginning to crow in a harbinger of dawn, and she was only a little girl after all and maybe she hadn't really been asleep she had merely closed her eyes for a moment. She certainly remembered the glorious Mass, and the richness and panoply of the of moment, the voices lifted in song, the incense drifting in scented clouds in the aisles and between the pews.

And then the magical experience when she had been allowed, when they returned home from the Mass, to place the figure of Baby Jesus in his rightful place in the cradle of their nativity scene. All was right with the world. The Son of God was here, had been born. It was Christmas Day.

He would have brought presents. Baby Jesus, not the jolly old man with a white beard and a red suit. "Father Christmas" was nearly invisible, irrelevant, in Luz's world.

The presents which Baby Jesus had brought glimmered, shimmered, faded into a glowstick ghost.

Whimpering, Luz scrambled for another. She only had two more, but trying to capture the images she was losing was far more important than thinking about nursing her inadequate supply.

The new one lit green, and then it took Luz through that green veil into white light, and the memory of the last Christmas feast back home, surrounded by her family.

The last feast Abuela had prepared.

All the traditional favourites were there. Abuela had made *panetón*, and the children had helped with it – Luz herself had been allowed to put the dried fruit into the mix. They had also been allowed to 'help' with making the *buñuelos* before Abuela fried them up; she had also made *tamales de Navidad*, wrapped in plantain leaves, and *natilla* for desert; she had made her own special version of *canelazo*, which Valentina had been allowed to sip but Luz was not, considered too young for the alcohol that spiked the hot spiced drink. Roast pig, and fried chicken, and best of all Abuela's special *arroz con leche*, redolent with cinnamon, something that Luz was perfectly certain came straight from that Heaven that Abuela was so closely on speaking terms with. The smells and the tastes of that family Christmas feast exploded in Luz's senses – the rich aroma of gravy and roast meat juices, the sweetness of plantains and sugar and sweet rice, the spiciness of cinnamon and vanilla.

All memory now, and never to be repeated. Abuela had died that spring, in May of 2019. It had been the last *arroz con leche* she had ever made for her grandchildren on Christmas day.

As the glowstick faded, taking the feast with it, a ghost of a conversation that Luz had overheard only weeks before Abuela had died arose like a haunted whisper in the back of her mind – it was a horrible night, one where she was supposed to be asleep, but both she and

Valentina had been wakened by noises – they did not understand what had happened, but they were aware that it was something to do with Alejandro, their brother. There had been danger. There had been blood. There had been a lot of sibilant whispered conversations, and whimpers, and moans. Pain. Mystery and pain.

All Luz would remember was Abuela's voice, trembling in a way that she had never heard that voice tremble before, saying something that Luz could not bring herself to understand.

"Save the children. You must save the children. Take them, take them now. It may already be too late for Alejandro but if he stays here there is no hope, and the girls... Maria is married now and she is her husband's responsibility, and Isabella is in God's hands, but Alejandro, Valentina, Luz, they are yours. Take them. Save them. Go now. Don't worry about me, I will be with God sooner than you know – but save the children, Nicolas, save the children, take the children, now..."

The days had darkened, just like the glowstick had done. Their lives became difficult, their father became sharp and distant and worried, Alejandro became oddly defiant while suddenly seeming more vulnerable than ever in Luz's eyes, Valentina turned sullen and secretive, and Luz, after Abuela's prophecy came true and they buried her on a much too bright and beautiful day in May, was quite alone. She was the child, the baby, nobody told her anything or consulted her about anything. When her father gathered up the small family and they set out on the precarious journey to a place called 'America', Luz followed, in silent terror, leaving everything she had ever known behind.

The journey was harrowing, and its end was a catastrophe. Hunted, and then caught like prey, the girls were separated from their father and their brother... and then Valentina had sickened... and now...

Luz tried to stop the gulping sobs that rose to her throat, covering her mouth with both her hands. She squeezed her eyes shut, tight, but hot tears still forced their way out between her lashes, spilling onto her cheeks.

She wondered why Isabella, whom Abuela had called their bridge to God, had failed to intercede with Him on her family's behalf – why her Mama, in Heaven, and now her Abuela, up there, had not helped them, had not saved them... saved her.

Alone, now.

At this time of the year, at the turning of the year.

Feliz Navidad.

A sob tore free and tumbled out through Luz's fingers; she opened her eyes and through a haze of tears sought the last glowstick, shaking it into life with something that was at once terror and defiance. A golden light spilled out, and in that light Luz suddenly saw something beloved, something familiar – the figure of her Abuela, climbing down as though on steps that Luz could not see, smiling, her arms held out to the cowering child.

"Abuela...?"

"Come," Abuela's soft voice said. "Come, now. Come to me. I will keep you safe."

"Is there *arroz con leche...*?"

"There is always *arroz con leche* in Heaven," Abuela said.

Luz felt soft hands smooth away her tangled curls, wet with her tears, away from her face.

She looked up, into Abuela's face, and smiled. Her smile was a light, a greater light than the glowstick could have ever made, and Luz dropped it at her side. She no longer needed it to see. Abuela's hand was out to her, an invitation, and Luz reached out and took it, with a soft sigh. And she climbed away, at her grandmother's side, up the steps that were not there, into the sky.

They found Luz Garcia on Christmas morning, curled up in a ball, her eyes closed and her face tear-streaked but a soft smile curling the corners of her mouth. She had been dead for hours. Beside her, in a pathetic little heap by her hand under her thin blanket, lay the spent ghosts of five glowsticks.

"Was she trying to keep warm?" one of the women who found her said, her voice oddly muffled. "Having a party...?"

They would never know. They would never follow her into the memory and the light, into a place that smelled of cinnamon and incense – they would never know the bittersweet gift that the Baby Jesus had brought to Luz Garcia that Christmas – the gift of the gentle passage for a lost and frightened child, a child who had lost everything but love. The gift of a grandmother's hand to lead her higher, to dissolve into the brightness of Christmas Day.

The gift of five glowsticks, to light her way.

Hunting the Wolf

I t was the day before Christmas Eve, and I was sitting by the window in my third floor apartment, a half-drunk glass of the last of my good brandy in my hand, staring out into the street. It was starting to snow, but there were still people scurrying up and down the pavements, bundled into improbable silhouettes only vaguely human-shaped, bent over double with their chins, underneath their mandated Plague Year masks, tucked into their scarves and collars to preserve whatever warmth there was to be had. The temperatures had dipped below freezing an hour ago. What slush there was on the roads had hardened into icy ridges; there was little traffic, but somewhere not too far away there were sirens – the hidden wailing that was the backdrop for the city, the indication that someone somewhere was having a bad time, a worse time than me.

I was just... alone. On the day before the day before Christmas Eve.

The Ghost of Christmas Past was whispering poison into my ear. Memories. A time when I was a little girl, and waking up eagerly on Christmas morning to race down to the living room and see what Santa had left under the tree; a time when I was young and thought I would live forever and partied until pale dawns painted the sky red and gold; the new wife sharing the first magical Christmas with a husband whose shine had not worn off yet and whose smile could still send me swooning when he aimed its high-voltage power in my direction; the first Christmas after I walked out on that marriage, which had gone gray and withered; this Christmas, two years after that, still alone.

Well… maybe not… I turned as I heard a particular kind of knock on the door. I thought I recognized it, and I was right – when I padded over in stocking feet, nursing my brandy glass against my bosom, and worked the three locks I needed to undo to get the door opened, it was Hunter who stood there, dressed with his usual disregard for the weather. The only concession he made to the temperatures outside was a sorry-looking felted muffler he wore wrapped around his neck and halfway up his ears; other than that, he was coatless, dressed in a flannel shirt, ratty jeans, and shoes that looked woefully inadequate to the conditions.

"Hey," he said, helplessly.

"You've got to be frozen, you idiot," I said, moving aside. "Come in."

He did, slipping the loops of his mask off his ears, peeling off the shoes in the hallway as he did so, pressing down on the heel of the shoe with one foot as he slid the other out. The socks thus revealed looked almost worn through in places but were still mercifully whole enough not to show me bare toes poking out.

"You want coffee?" I asked. "Something hot to drink?"

He nodded. I tossed my head in the direction of the kitchen nook.

"There's some in the pot. You may have to nuke it."

I didn't offer him any of the brandy. That was for me. As he went in search of the coffee, I returned to the window, and continued to watch the night falling, the shadows creeping out of dark corners and stairwells and doorways and spilling out onto the pavement. Lights were coming on in windows. I watched them, nursing the brandy. So many strangers. So many lives. I wondered how many of them were basking in the smile of a new spouse this year, like I once did. Someone had to be. It was simple statistics.

"So what brings you round?" I said, over my shoulder, as I heard him approaching.

There was something in the quality of the silence that met that relatively innocuous question that made me suddenly turn sharply, seeking his gaze with my own. He met it, mutely. He said nothing. He didn't need to. I tried to stop my hand from shaking but the brandy in the glass told its own story, and I put the glass down, very deliberately.

"Again?" I asked, quietly.

"Yes. Last night. They found the victim this morning, when her daughter and granddaughter came to see her, and found her... in her bed..."

"Witnesses?"

"Not this time," he said.

Not *this* time.

There had only been one witness to the act of the killer whom I had dubbed the Wolf. Myself. I had seen the man slipping from my own grandmother's house, leaving the door ajar behind him, as I approached. He had turned, and he'd met my eyes from across the top of a plain black mask, and held them. The edge of the mask underlined those eyes and focused me on them, and I would never forget them – they had been light brown, almost golden, a wolf's eyes. For a long moment we stared at one another and I could almost feel the weight of thought, of consideration, of possibility – should he remove the one who could potentially identify him? But then the eternal moment passed, far quicker than it had been perceived to have lasted. We were both masked, after all, and there was a certain anonymity in that. He had chosen to turn and melt away into the shadows. I had gone inside, and found my ninety-year-old grandmother, her eyes wide open behind the round glasses still perched on her nose and the expression on her face one of an almost ludicrous open-mouthed surprise, the knife that had taken her life lying on the blood-smeared hand-made quilt covering her where she lay in her bed.

Somehow I had passed through shock directly into a white-hot vengeance. I would find the Wolf. I would make him pay for what he had done.

Then a second old woman had been killed. And now, Hunter brought word of another.

I knew why he was here. He was broken, himself – he was a veteran with PTSD who flinched at loud noises but he had appointed himself as my paladin, deeming it his duty to protect me even while flinching from the loud noises which might have threatened me in the first place. He knew that I'd get wind of the latest killing, sooner or later, and he didn't want me to hear it on the news, and he didn't want me to hear it alone.

He stood – all six foot five of him – cradling a coffee mug in his big hands, hunched over in a posture of what was almost helplessness, staring at me out of eloquent eyes.

"Right," I said.

"What?"

"He isn't going to stop. I'm going to find him."

"Lett..."

I was halfway to the door, gathering up my purse and coat as I went. I turned at the sound of my name, a version of it that only Hunter used, raising one questioning eyebrow.

"Where are you going?" he asked.

"To set a trap," I said, and to those who did not know me the smile that accompanied those words was sweet.

Hunter winced at it.

"You're going to get hurt," he said.

"Somebody is," I said firmly, shrugging into my coat and striding out of the front door which I had dramatically flung open.

I left him there, him and the coffee.

And, I suppose, the abandoned brandy.

I made some necessary purchases, paid some necessary visits, signed some necessary papers. At the end of it all I presented as somebody else entirely – a modest furnished apartment in a shabbily genteel quarter now had a little old lady as a tenant, silver white hair scraped back into a ballerina bun at the back of my head, wearing spectacles much like the ones my grandmother had worn – in fact they were the selfsame ones that had belonged to her, that had still been perched on her face when she had been murdered in her bed. Where a million women pursued creams to smooth out wrinkles, I sought out stage make up with which to enhance mine; I affected rheumatism gloves, to camouflage my youthful hands. I had even petitioned my new landlord about a cat (what self-respecting little old lady didn't have a cat?) even though the lease I had signed specifically stated 'no pets'. Well, one could wheedle and cajole and perhaps bake cookies as bribes. What were little old ladies for, anyway?

I moved into the furnished apartment, made chatty acquaintance with a neighbor or two, made absolutely certain that everybody (and their cat) knew that I had just moved to the city from the farm I could no longer afford to keep or run after my dear departed husband had passed – newcomer, without friends or family, temporarily even catless, living alone in an unfamiliar place. I made it a point to get lost three or four times on my way home to my apartment from places I had gone to, and even got escorted back once by a friendly police officer, delivered to the doorstep of my home like an errant parcel, him standing there and grinning while I thanked him profusely and publicly out on the street and told him that yes, I would get a map, and to maybe drop by next week for some chocolate chip cookies. I made it my business to be obvious, and old, and genial, and trusting, and friendly. I painted a metaphorical target on my forehead and on my back, and waited for the Wolf to notice.

The old-lady me didn't know Hunter so I told him to watch over me if he needed to but from a distance, so as not to blow my cover. But he found ways of staying near me. One time, about a week and a half into the charade, he stepped up beside me in the supermarket produce section as I reached for a bag of potatoes.

"It isn't going to work," he said in a low voice, not looking at me.

"It will," I said.

"Just exactly what do you think you are going to do if he…"

I knocked over a supporting potato, starting a small avalanche; he instinctively dived to stop it, distracted, and I stepped away while he was busy.

"I'll know what to do," I said softly as I began to walk away. He heard me; I saw the quick glance that came my way, wrenched from the cascading spuds. It was entreating, apprehensive, concerned. But I couldn't have him hovering. Wolf would notice a bodyguard and all this would be for nothing.

Don't ask me how I knew that Wolf would come. I knew. I got his vibration, that night, and I was attuned to it in some way – not so much as I could tell you where he was or what he was doing but I could... sense him... I knew his intent. And I was going to be the one to stop him.

And come he did.

It took longer than I wanted or might have liked – particularly since I didn't step out of character even if I was on my own inside my new trap-nest apartment, the disguise staying on and being renewed when necessary, to be in place if required, simply because I could not possibly know when precisely the Wolf would arrive. It took just over three weeks, but it was just about bedtime one night, as I was about to turn off the lights, when I was alerted by the smallest of noises. If I'd ever got that cat, it might have been the pad of a cat's paw on the floor. But there was no cat, only me... and, now, a presence in the apartment that electrified the air around me. I turned around to ostensibly plump up my pillows (and curl my fingers around something tucked away in between my bed and the bedside table, drawing it inconspicuously underneath my quilt and out of sight). When I looked around again, he was there, barely a step away from the edge of the bed; if he'd been wearing a coat he'd shed it, and I noted that he was now clad in a blue flannel shirt with a hint of a t-shirt underneath. It seemed almost ludicrous under the circumstances, given that masks were now so ubiquitous everywhere for all the wrong reasons, that he was wearing one for the purpose for which it might have been originally intended – concealment. Above the mask's edge his eyes gleamed at me, the remembered gold.

One of my bare feet – my own, showing my own (relatively) young age and not that of the crone who I was impersonating – was showing from underneath my covers and I was suddenly very aware of it, appalled that one small detail I had neglected to properly 'age' might betray me completely, all being in vain. I held Wolf's gaze while I shifted unobtrusively curling myself up completely under the covers, hoping that he hadn't paid attention, that he hadn't noticed.

And then he spoke, and the hope was gone.

"What lovely smooth feet you have, Grandma."

The voice was soft, cultured, almost gentle. And cold as glacier ice.

It was already over. I don't know what my real plans might have been or if they would have worked at all, but I was out of any of those options.

"The better to run you down with," I said, instead, and smiled at him – the same smile that I had shown Hunter back when I had started to put this plan together.

And then I flung back the covers and tasered him, point blank, right over his heart.

He jerked back, flinging his arms to the side, staggered, tangled his feet, and went over like a poleaxed ox, uttering a guttural cry. For a moment, holding my breath, I sat there in the bed, twitching, and then, realizing I had no time to waste, slid out of bed, pulling open the drawer of my bedside cabinet as I did so to retrieve and dangle two sets of sturdy police-issue handcuffs from my fingers. Wolf didn't give me trouble as I slipped one of them around his left wrist and manacled him to the leg of the very solid mahogany bedframe; he was starting to stir and struggle feebly as I locked one bracelet of the second handcuffs around his other wrist, and dragged him around to spread his arms, attaching it to the bedstead's other leg, leaving him lying spreadeagled and face down on the floor.

He was gulping air as I came down on one knee beside him, still clad in my modest granny nightshift which pooled around me on the floor. I slipped his mask off, taking a good long look at his face, committing it to memory. It was not a bad face; if you met it in the street and it greeted you with a smile you might have trusted it. A manly chiseled jaw, and a cleft chin, and a straight nose, and good strong cheekbones, and would have probably showed white even teeth if it offered that smile. But the eyes would have spoken to you above it all and told their own tale. It was a wolf, still a wolf, wearing a man's guise.

I bent closer and spoke in a soft voice, just loud enough for him to hear – to be sure, I was far from certain that he heard and understood but I wanted to hear myself say it.

"You left the knife," I whispered. "When you killed that old woman whom I loved. You left the knife behind. That was stupid of you. Were you disturbed? Did you hear me coming? You know I saw you. And I kept two things from that scene. I kept her glasses. I kept the knife. It's lived in a carefully sealed baggie since that day, waiting. I'll leave it and a witness statement right here beside you, for when they come to get you – and I'm going to call them to come and get you, right now. What a big knife you had. All the better to tie you to her, to what you did to her. Someday they might find out why you did it. I don't care. You did it. That's enough. I swore I would find you, and I knew that I would. I hope they lock you up and lose the key but if they don't... remember I will still be out there. And the next time I find you I will not wait for the wheels of justice to turn."

He'd turned his head, was clearly listening, but his eyes were still dazed and unfocused. I could not know what he heard, how much he understood.

No matter. That witness statement, ready and prepared years ago and just waiting for this moment, which I now laid on the pillow of the bed which I had vacated, the baggie with the bloody knife beside it, would have to suffice to tell the tale.

I took off the nightshift, leaving it folded neatly underneath the pillow. I could hear him groaning as I got dressed, heard him twitching, learning that he was bound, the groans turning to low growls, but I did not pay any further attention to him. I was dialing 911 on my cellphone as I slipped out of the apartment, the grey wig off, my own hair blowing in the cold wind, my voice into the phone muffled from behind my mask.

They would get him.

My work was done.

I called Hunter from my own apartment after I got back there to tell him it was over, and to tell him something else, too. I invited him to meet me at a specified address on the following morning, and he dutifully turned up there, carrying three different newspapers under his arm.

"Headlines, in all of them," he said, taking the folded papers out to wave at me. "He's in custody. Will be arraigned for several murders very shortly." He paused. "Are you sure you're all right? This wasn't exactly something that a young lady ought to be..."

I raised a hand to silence him. "This," I said, "is what needed doing. And continues to need doing. There is more than one Wolf in the world." I stepped away from the office door – with frosted glass in the upper panel – in front of which I had been standing, concealing it from his sight, and was rewarded by the double take as he took in the name painted on the glass and the other thing, underneath that.

"You can't be serious," he blurted.

"Oh but I am," I said, turning to push in a key and then to nudge the door open, inviting him inside with a toss of my head. "And I could use a – well, call it what you will. A secretary. An assistant. Want a job?"

He was still staring at me as he followed me inside, and then I could see the corner of his mouth start to lift as he shook his head slightly in a gesture that was partly bewilderment and disbelief but also, I hoped, a dawning of acceptance.

Behind him, the door to the new office slowly swung closed again, and then snicked shut.

The sign on the glass panel, in gilded and deliberately old-fashioned lettering, faced back into the somewhat dim corridor, inviting clients to knock on the door and engage the services...

...of Scarlett Smallcowle, PI.

new tales

Spiderhair

Mila's hair had never been cut.

By the time she was ten, her wavy mahogany-coloured hair fell to the small of her back. At thirteen, she could fold an inch under her rear and sit on it. On the day she turned sixteen, if she braided it up in two long braids they would brush the back of her knees; unbraided, the ends fell to mid-calf.

She usually wore it plaited up out of the way and coiled around her head like a crown. But when she let it down, to wash the great mass of it and then combed the tangles out and let it dry as it hung loose around her like a cloak, there were always people who found business with her house, just so that they could come by and gaze on Mila's hair.

"It's witchery," the women would murmur. "No good will come of it. It's Fae hair and it will call to the place where it came from sooner or later."

If anybody thought Mila's hair would bring her luck, that didn't happen. In fact, exactly the opposite. She lost her mother - in childbirth, with the woman's seventh child - when she was only twelve years old; her father remarried a year later and brought an evil stepmother into the house with the seven motherless children. The second wife very soon bore her own son to her husband, and it became very clear that it was this boy who was the prince of the house now, and not the children of the first family. Mila was the eldest, and did what she could to help and protect her younger siblings, particularly her youngest brother, who had never known a mother's love and was growing up mute, wrapping himself in silence like a shield. Mila was terrified that her stepmother would find a way to get rid of her somehow - to marry her off as fast as possible, to no matter whom, just so that she was out of the house - and that she would have to leave her brothers and sisters to the stepmother's mercies. Mila knew that the fact that she would have little in the way of dowry was a stumbling block in that plan (the stepmother wanted to get rid of a potential rival, not dilute what she saw as her own son's inheritance) - that, and the fact that she considered herself to be no beauty. Aside from the glory, justly famous in their village, of that hair.

She used to braid it up into one long braid and flip it over the top edge of her hard, lumpy pillow when she slept at night - letting it pool between the pillow, falling behind the thin mattress and hanging down into the space below her narrow bed like a fishing line. Sometimes she would dream about monsters under the bed, their eyes gleaming in the shadows, their sharp teeth nibbling at the ends of the braid. On the mornings after those nights, she might wake to the sight of a spider skittering from the side of her braid, up which it had scrambled, and across the side of the bed and away. She was so lonely that she began to name the spiders, giving them personalities, making them her friends. She'd have to get up early, with the dawn, to do the chores her stepmother demanded - but she always found time, if she woke and noticed one, to exchange a pleasant good morning with the spider of the day. They always seemed to pause and acknowledge her whispered words to them, as though they understood, and graciously returned the greeting before they disappeared off into some sheltered corner out of sight.

On a cold winter morning Mila woke sick and shivering, and her wrist felt hot to the touch when she brought it to her lips. She knew she was running a fever; even so, the spider that morning seemed to linger a little longer, watching her, as she turned her head and the creature scuttled from the folds of her braid.

"Sorry," she murmured, "I don't feel so well... good morning..."

She did not see the stemother sweep in imperiously, not until a slipper came down hard on the spider on the bed before it had a chance to scuttle away. Mila let out a small cry of distress, and then another of pain as the stepmother yanked the hair out from behind the pillow and sharply upwards until Mila's head jerked with the motion.

"Lazy girl," the stepmother said, "lying in like a queen - when there's work to be done - lazy and filthy - you have spiders in your hair! How horrid! Your precious hair - it's full of cobwebs and dust!" She dropped the braid like it disgusted her. "Up! And don't let me ask you twice again!"

Mila coughed, a sharp, deep cough that scraped her chest. "I don't..."

"Do you want me to get your sisters to scrub the kitchen floors for you?" the stepmother asked nastily.

Mila's sisters were nine and seven years old. They were children, and they were Mila's to protect. She dragged herself upright in the bed.

"No. I'll... I'll do it."

"If I don't see you with a scrubbing brush in ten minutes it's going to be your sisters out there," the stepmother threatened, and swept out of the room again.

Mila struggled upright, sobbing quietly, fighting for breath.

"I'm sorry," she whispered into the cold air, to nobody in particular, to the spirit of the slain spider. "I'm sorry, I could not stop her..."

She felt a tickle on the side of her neck, and lifted a hand to brush at it - when it came back down, she realised she was holding a spider perched on her fingertips. They looked at each other, the spider and the girl, and then the spider whispered,

"We will help."

And then it scrambled down the back of Mila's hand, dropped into her lap and then sideways onto the bed and away.

"...how?" Mila asked her empty hand.

By the time she reached the kitchen, sloppily dressed in haste and without having brushed out her hair, she stopped astonished as she reached the kitchen. The entire floor was covered in a thin layer of cobweb, trapping every last piece of dirt on the kitchen floor; it was not a matter of scrubbing any more, it was merely a matter of sweeping up the cobweb mass and its gathered-in specks and morsels, and bundling the entire mess into a ball to be thrown out onto the midden.

The entire process took less than ten minutes. Coughing, Mila retired to the corner where her bed was, to finish getting dressed properly, to... but she stopped short of unbraiding and combing out her hair. She had been reaching for it before she dropped her hands, thoughtfully, and let it be. She simply wound the long braid into a crown on top of her head and pinned it up.

That seemed to be the covenant. Every morning, still sick, she dragged herself out of bed and found the cobwebbed kitchen waiting for her. She's sweep it up, the kitchen would be left clean enough even for the stepmother's inspection, and Mila retreated to nurse her cough.

The winter was long that year, and cold, ever colder. The stepmother's son had a fine woollen blanket to cover him, and slept warm in a soft bed. The first wife's children huddled under thin threadbare quilts, and shivered. Mila's cough grew worse.

She woke one morning, warm, unexpectedly warm, and opened her eyes to see a blanket of shimmery spider silk laid across her coverlet. A spider slipped out of her hair, lingering briefly on the pillow beside her.

"We will help," it said.

"My brothers and sisters..." Mila began, and the spider shifted a little to the side.

"We have helped," it said.

The stepmother did not find out about the spidersilk quilts until maybe a week later, when she stumbled into one before the spiders had a chance to vanish them away in the mornings as they usually did. The woman screeched in horror, backing away from Mila's bed, covered in the spidersilk web.

"Filthy girl! FIlthy! Look at you, sleeping in the filth - under cobwebs! Who'll marry you now? Look at you - spiders all over your hair - Spiderhair! Dirty, filthy girl! Get out of my house!"

"Not without my brothers and my sisters," Mila said.

"All of you, then! Children of spiders and flies! Filthy children! Get out, before your wretchedness ruins my precious boy!"

There wasn't much to pack. What there was, the spiders took care of. "We will help," they said, the spiders that came out of Mila's hair. They wove cloaks for the children and bags to carry their meager belongings in, they wove warmth for the children's feet. The seven children, Mila at their head, trudged down a frozen country road until they were out of the village and into open fields and then into the woods - and the spiders whispers stopped them there. Mila told her brothers to set up branches, like the spiders instructed her, and then the spiders wove walls between them, and a roof above, and the children slept snugly in sleeping bags of spider silk, warm and safe.

They wove clothes for Mila, and they wove a silver diadem for her which was part of her glorius hair - the stepmother had called her Spiderhair, to insult her, but now it had become her name, her identity. In the warm springtime, her feet bare and her clothes made of spider silk and a silver crown in her hair, she walked the woods to gather the mushrooms and the berries for her brothers and sisters, and she walked barefoot in the dusty country roads, bearing blankets of the finest weave to sell - light and warm and strong, made of spidersilk. It was thus - barefoot, silver -crowned, carrying spiderspun - that the King's son saw her on a spring morning, riding down the road back to the castle, and reined in his horse, bewitched. The mahogany hair that almost swept the dust of the road in a long sleepily tangled braid, the silver dress, the silver crown, and asked her name.

"Spiderhair," she said, and he laughed, with wonder, with joy.

"You are beautiful," the Prince said. "Come with me, and I will put a crown of real silver on your head."

"I have promises to keep," she said.

"And I will keep them with you," the Prince said.

"Go," said the spider who had slipped out of the braid and sat on Spiderhair's shoulder, "we will help."

"I have brothers and sisters," Spiderhair said.

"Bring them," said the Prince. "How came you to be out here by yourself like this?"

"My stepmother turned us out," Spiderhair said.

"Turned out children into the wild to fend for themselves? She should be punished for that," the Prince said.

The spider whispered something and Spiderhair smiled. "She has been," she said.

"Show me," said the Prince. "And then we will gather your family, and we will take you home."

He gathered her up before him on his horse, and they turned back towards the village.

It was not hard to spot Spiderhair's old home. It was the house that reeked; it was the house around which clouds of flies hung, from the foundations of which bugs and centipedes oozed, and angry armies of wasps buzzed from nests built under the eaves. It was a house from which the spiders had fled, leaving all the vermin behind to breed and flourish.

Spiderhair's stepmother stood on the top step of her house, swatting away flies, her hair straggly, her arms fleabitten, her eyes wild. She saw Spiderhair before the Prince on the pale horse, and would have shouted but for the fact that she seemed to have lost her voice, her eyes round and full of malice and hatefulness.

"You have cursed us!" she screeched at last, finding the words somewhere. "Ever since you set foot outside this place it's been nothing but... but... this..."

"Yes," Spiderhair said. "We left. You drove us out."

"Bring them back!" the woman said, and this time her voice actually broke. She scratched at her arms.

"You killed," Spiderhair said. "It is not up to me to send them back to you."

"We will help," said a spider by Spiderhair's ear. She had not asked. But she had felt a pang - for her father, trapped inside with the vermin.

The spider let itself down on a length of silk, and scuttled towards the house. Spiderhair saw it pause for a moment, as though calling for reinforcements, before it vanished from her sight.

The spidersilk melted from her hair, and the braid unwound, cloaking her slender body in mahogany glory.

"Mila," she said to the Prince, smiling up at him. "My name is Mila."

Without further word, the Prince turned the horse and left the village house behind, with the blessing of its spiders once again. They stopped to pick up Mila's six sibilings, one on each horse before a member of the Prince's entourage, and they all went up together to the castle.

No spider was ever killed in the castle again.

For A Coin of Silver

"The *other* First and Last House," Phao Sarasin said, his face dark with rage. "The *other*. A traveler walks into my House, the one I build and nurtured, the one I made, and talks to me about the *other*? There cannot be another. I chose that name for the inn – right here, right at the edge of town, it's the first and last friendly house that a traveler will find here – and then somebody just... steals it? Just like that?"

"Well, *pawchuj*, if he is on the other edge of town..." Sarasin's grandson Hian began in a soothing tone of voice.

But Sarasin would not be mollified. "He's a thief, and a swindler," he declared, pouring the full fire of his fury on this competitor, whose name he didn't even know. "He is stealing *my* customers. The customers of the only First and Last House in the town."

Hian left it. There was no getting through to his *pawchuj* when he was in this kind of mood. And luckily another brace of travelers came through before the old man had a chance to work himself into a full apoplexy, and he donned the innkeeper's smile and went out to serve them, banking the flames of his resentment until such time as something could be done about it.

❧

"He said you stole his name, his idea," Sar Ngor said, highly indignant, as he busied himself over the wood-fired range where he was supervising that evening's meal for the tavern. "You stole it Father. Apparently that is what the old man said. As though he had a writ that ran on it – the First and Last House. As though the town had only one boundary, and there could be only one."

"To be fair," Sar Chhuon said placidly, "I did open this place very recently. And he has held that name for many years now, apparently. I did not set out to steal anything – but it is easy to have the same idea if it is a good one. And really, it was his own customers that brought it to me – the folks who came travelling from his end of town to this one, and telling me that I was the last house to his first – and then I said the same to some soul traveling in the other direction, and it stuck..."

"You are *justifying* yourself," Ngor said. "You ought not to have to. It was as you said – even so – other people brought the name over. And it is hardly as though either of you has a *sign*..."

"Oh," Chhuon said, "as for that, I am told that he does, in fact. Have a sign."

"Well, he could hardly say that you stole *that*, then," Ngor said. "You do not – "

Chhuon made a small helpless gesture, throwing both his hands into the air. "Well," he murmured, "it seemed like a good idea – and I – well, I – there is an order for a sign, in with the signmaker, for just such a sign. I did not think..."

Ngor made a frustrated face, scrunching his features into a scowling mask. "You just declared war, then," he said. "On your own head be it..."

❧

"I ought to go over there and knock his head against that new sign I am told he has just commissioned," Sarasin muttered, for the fourth time that morning, bustling around the back of the Tavern.

"Oh, *pawchuj*," his grandson said, exasperated. "Would you let it be?"

"He *stole* it," the old man said obstinately. "He *knew* I had such a sign. The signmaker would have told him so."

"Would he?" Hian said. "Whatever for? It would mean that he was out a commission, and after all it is no skin off his nose if you two mad old men had a brawl over it in the public square. The signmaker might have been hired to paint the signs telling people where to go to watch the fight, mayhap."

"But mine is the first tavern," Sarasin said, unwilling to let go so easily. "The best. I stint no expense for the food, even for the cheap meals. Nobody leaves here hungry, or thirsty, or sickened with something that I have provided."

"You don't know that anyone does so from his tavern, either," Hian pointed out.

"I am sure some do," the old man muttered. "And anyway, what is the thief's name?"

"You would think he invented the idea of a traveler's inn," Ngor said. "This... what is his name again?... Phao Sarasin...?"

"Well, he did invent this one," Chhuon said. "His one."

"But this is a big town now," Ngor said. "He cannot have expected to be the only hostelry..."

"No doubt," Chhuon said, raising a hand to calm his son. "But if he has been here for a long time, which I think he has, then he has some cause to resent those who came after. He may not be the only innkeeper in town – or at least not any more – but he does not have to like that. I can understand that. I do wonder, though, just what makes him think that his First and Last House is so superior to any other which might lay claim to the name."

"Perhaps I ought to go and pay him a visit, and find out," Ngor said.

Chhuon smiled. "You? If you go there it will be to start a war..."

"He already started *that*," Ngor pointed out.

"Not a *war*," Chhuon said. "Just a resentment. And he is welcome to wallow in it, but I will not join him there."

§♠

Perhaps it was just the incessant attempts of his grandson to keep him calm that finally spurred Sarasin to set out from his tavern, into the twisting alleys of the old town, over cobbles he had barely walked for years, buried as he was in the day-to-day business of running his inn. It was others he had sent out to buy supplies and to bring them back to him – that was not his duty, his own duty was to make sure that the traveler who laid down his load at Sarasin's inn left rested and satisfied when the time came to pick up his journey again, and Sarasin took that duty very seriously. If a traveler had the smallest complaint as his sojourn at the tavern came to an end – if his rice was cold , or his bed was hard – it was something Sarasin felt to be his own personal failing. He would be – he always was – the best innkeeper in his street. In his neighborhood. In the world. Certainly in his own town.

It would not have burned him so much that another tavern had opened in that town if that tavern hadn't picked up the name he had been so proud of, he had cultivated, he had made into his own personal banner. This... it just felt personal. Not so much another tavern filling a vacant niche but someone who had come to this town for the express purpose of ruining Sarasin's life.

And that, at the very least, was his bounden duty to go and see for himself.

He set out in good time to arrive at the rival tavern at its busiest hour – and he had judged well, because the place was bustling when he got there. He could see that its benches were filled, and that its patrons were being treated well. An utterly irrational resentment at this rose like bile at the back of his throat, and he bared his teeth as he stood on the path to the front door of the place. This... this was the spirit of *his own place*. Except that, here, it belonged to another.

Well. He had come all this way, and he would go the distance.

Taking another step, his foot touched something solid on the ground, and he glanced down – and saw a silver coin lying in the path, something that some careless patron must have dropped as they were on their way in or out of this place. Sarasin bent and picked it up, turning it over in his fingers, and the beginnings of a smile began to play around his lips. He would taste the food and the wine of this place, but it would not be his own coin that bought it.

Chhuon knew immediately who it was that entered his establishment and stood for a moment looking around the room. Ngor had reached the same conclusion, and had already made an instinctive motion towards the old man – but Chhuon waved him back and himself approached the new guest.

"Welcome," he said, bowing politely. "I am Sar Chhuon, the owner of the First and Last House on the West Side of Town. How can I serve you?"

Sarasin's lips twitched. It was elegantly done, claiming the name… but only on the *west* side of town. He took the seat to which he had been shown, and laid down the dusty silver coin on the table. "Give me your best," he said.

Chhuon smiled, and took the coin, stepping back with another small bow. "It will be my pleasure," he said.

"It was not bad," Sarasin had to admit when he returned home to his grandson. "Not as good as ours here, mind you, but not *bad*. Expensive, though."

"Why, how much did he want?"

Sarasin grinned. "A silver coin, boy. But it was not mine – it was found on the steps of his own house. So I paid him with what was probably his own money."

"My turn," Chhuon said, setting his cap straight on his head. "He came to me, and therefore I will go to him. It is time I found out what the other inn has to offer."

"You would not let me go, and yet now you..." Ngor began, but Chhuon waved him down.

"Like I said, boy, you would start a war. I... go to see a man who broke bread in *this* house. At the very least I owe him that."

"You are going to go and spend good money..."

"As for that, have no fear," Chhuon said with a small enigmatic smile. He put a hand into his pocket and brought out the silver coin, turning it between his fingers as he showed it to Ngor. "I will pay him with this. It is what he paid me – and surely what he has to offer will not cost more than that which he received."

Sarasin was somehow less than surprised to see Chhuon push open the door of his hostelry and step inside, three days after he himself had returned from Chhuon's own. He nudged Hian in the ribs.

"Look who is here," he said. "The very man."

"You mean that is...?"

"The proprietor of the First And Last House on the West Side of Town, yes," Sarasin said, grinning wolfishly. "Well, but it may be that he has come to learn about hospitality, from the one who was here long before he came."

"Should I serve him?" Hian asked, a little nervously.

"I will do it myself," Sarasin said.

Chhuon had taken an unoccupied seat and waited there patiently to be noticed. He smiled as Sarasin came over, tilting his head in greeting.

"Welcome to the First and Last House," Sarasin said.

"On the *east* side of town, at least" Chhuon said, sincerely and politely, but with an exquisite edge of emphasis nonetheless.

Sarasin's smile, despite himself, widened just a notch. "And how may I serve you?" he inquired.

Chhuon produced the silver coin. "Your best," he said. "Of course."

"The same coin. The man paid me with the self-same coin."

"How can you possibly tell?"

"I do not know, boy, perhaps I could smell it," Sarasin snapped. "All I know is that I *know*. The man steals my house's name and then he pays me with the self-same coin that I used to pay him first. That means no profit – "

"For *either* of you," Hian felt compelled to point out.

"Yes, yes," Sarasin said impatiently. "But he will not get the better of me. I have been here for too long to fall for those tricks. Tomorrow I shall go back to his house, and I will take the exact same coin with me. Then we shall see."

"It's the same coin!" Ngor said, outraged.

"Well, and if it is?" Chhuon said, hefting the silver coin in his palm and smiling down at it. "I have to admit, the man has style. But this cannot be allowed to stand – I will not have him have the last word. It goes back, tomorrow."

"What, the coin?"

"Oh yes," Chhuon said. "I will return to his house and buy his best drink with it."

"Do you think that he realizes...?"

"He will," Chhuon said. "Eventually. Probably. But we shall see who is left holding the coin, at that moment."

Chhuon took the coin back to Sarasin's house.

Sarasin returned it to Chhuon's house two days after that.

It came right back to Sarasin before the week was out.

And was tossed onto Chhuon's table the week after that.

Sarasin's, the day after.

Chhuon's the day after that.

There came a time that the two innkeepers began to keep an eye out on their front door, for the inevitable appearance of the other man bearing the coin of silver. They began exchanging that coin with knowing smiles at one another, although neither ever said a word about it – they both knew very well what they did, but the tacit unspoken secret of it was part of the payment that passed between them. It had almost begun in meanness, an unwillingness to allow either to show a profit on the enterprise of entertaining the other, but it passed beyond that – into complicity, and then, slowly, almost without either man being truly aware of it, into companionship, and from that into friendship.

They began to look forward to one another's visits, catching up with gossip from the east or the west side of town, comparing travelers, commiserating about prices, letting one another into minor bargains to be had in town.

It was Chhuon who stepped into Sarasin's place on the day that made up the count of ten years having passed, and he lingered after closing time, after everyone else except the two innkeepers had left the front room of the inn. The fires were banked down, everyone else's chores were done and they had left for the night, and the two men sat nursing their drinks across a scarred wooden table in companionable silence.

Chhuon pulled the silver coin that had settled their debts for a decade out of his pocket, and placed it on the table between them.

"How long," he said conversationally, "are we going to play this game? Should we retire the eternal coin – you know, of course, that you are welcome at my table on any night of the year and it does not require a silver coin to pay for your presence there?"

Sarasin, unaccustomed to sentiment, cleared his throat and scowled. "Well, likewise, you, here, you know."

"I have known for a long time, my friend," Chhuon said. "Here is what I suggest. Let us take the coin to the square, and find a loose cobble, and put the coin underneath it – that way, it is halfway between the First House and the Last, always, and we can just take it as understood that our bills are paid at both. It will save us from carrying the thing around, back and forth, for another ten years, at least."

"Gods willing," Sarasin said automatically. He was not a young man any more and another ten years sounded like a long time for him now.

But he found himself liking this idea – whether he was given ten years more, or less, or longer. "Very well. Let us do this thing, then."

"Now?"

"Tonight," Sarasin said. "There is never any time like the present."

❧

More years flowed by after the night the two men buried the silver coin in the midst of the cobbled town square – one, five, seven. But Sarasin might have had a touch of prescience on the night that they had done this thing, because he was not given the full ten years that Chhuon had so blithely predicted lay before them both. In the winter of that seventh year, Sarasin sickened, and then took to his bed, and before the week was out he was dead.

That, in itself, was not surprising – because he was getting on in years, and it was not unexpected that he would meet his gods sooner rather than later.

But what followed, might not have been seen as quite so inevitable. Chhuon was fully twelve years younger than his friend, the innkeeper of the First and Last House of the East. And yet, not two days after Sarasin's death, Chhuon himself took ill – with an illness that was eerily similar to the one that took Sarasin's life. And before that week was out, he, too, was dead.

The heirs to the two Houses, First and Last, at either end of town, sat down together after Chhuon was laid to rest, sharing a bowl of rice between them. They did not talk much – the sorrows were still a little too fresh. But there were some reminiscences that were shared, and the foremost amongst them was the silver coin of legend that their elders had passed back and forth between them for so long. They could not recall, afterward, which of them it had been who had had the idea that they should go back and find the place where the old men had buried the treasure, and take it out again, and have the silver coin cut into two halves so that they could each keep one in memory of the strange friendship that had grown between the two men, so very different from one another, so very much alike.

Neither had been paying that much attention to the center of the

134

town, being all too concerned with their own ends of it, but it was only after they arrived at the central square that it began to dawn on both the heirs that this was not the same square that their father and their grandfather had walked. It had been built, and re-built, and rearranged, and most importantly... re-paved. In fact, it was still freshly dug up and men were still finishing up the work on the new paving, cleaning up, too busy to pay the two visitors more than the cursory amount of attention required to ask them politely to move out of the way when they found themselves obstructing the workmen in their purpose.

The coin, of course, was gone.

It had held the souls of two men, in the end, but whoever had taken it would have been happy to have found treasure and would not have known about that, nor given any thought to it. The coin had gone into some strange purse, and would eventually, no doubt, be paid out at last for a legitimate reason, buying something solid and real, something measurable and empirical, be it goods or services, that the one who had paid the coin would have considered to be a fair exchange for his money. But the anchor had been taken, lifted, and it would have been futile trying to find out which one of the men who worked on the square had been the one to find that coin. The two souls which had been bound by it had been set adrift again – and the men had died, both, even while the town square was still in the process of being re-paved with new stones.

Phao Hian and Sar Ngor, innkeepers now of the First and Last Houses of the East and West of town, stood over the place where the silver coin should have lain, and felt a deeper sorrow still than they ought to have done at the loss of those whom they had loved.

"It stands, though, the old bargain," Hian said, speaking first. "The one they made. For my part, it stands. And it will stand for as long as my House stands."

"My best," Ngor said, nodding. "For a silver coin."

He took one out of his purse as they stood over the cobbles, and held it out part-way to Hian. Hian's fingertips brushed it lightly, and then his hand dropped.

"We bury it?"

"Like they did."

"Tonight, after the men are gone...?"

But Ngor suddenly hesitated.

"But if we do... and they move the stones again..."

They stood in silence, staring at one another, wondering if they were setting the term of their own mortal days by this act. In the end, it was Hian who stirred.

"It does not matter if this is here or not, ten years from now," Hian said. "It does not matter if is there now, for that matter. Not physically."

"No," Ngor agreed, after taking a moment to think it over. He put out his right hand. Hian clasped it with his own.

"It does not need to be here for the vow to be valid," Hian said. "For a silver coin. My best. Always."

Ngor nodded. "The same."

Ngor still held the coin that they might have buried; instead, their fingers touched briefly across it, and then Ngor returned it to his purse. They no longer needed the physical object as proof of their vow, after all; the spirit of a silver coin spun above the new-cobbled square like a light, and they could both see it clearly from where they stood although the workmen seemed to have no problem at all in ignoring its existence.

They watched it, for a moment, and then they turned and walked in opposite directions, each to light the lights of welcome for travelers who stopped to rest... at the First and Last House at the edges of their town.

Safe House

The cottage on the corner of our street was a pretty place. It had a garden just sufficiently unkempt to invite pleasurable speculation and daydreams about what went on behind that tangle of bushy lilacs, old-fashioned roses, holly, rowan, hazel and, in high summer, a bunch of colourful flowers for which there were no real names – they were just splashes of scarlet or blue or gold amongst the green.

We had no real idea of who lived there, but we would occasionally catch glimpses of a woman drifting through the greenery with a pair of pruning shears in her hand. Her hair was silver-gray, pulled neatly back into a braided bun at the back of her head, but her face , from the quick glances which we were vouchsafed, didn't really match – it was a youthful face free of wrinkles or lines, smooth and fair-skinned beneath its halo of silver hair.

She had butterflies. And humming birds. And a stork had a nest on the chimney pot. And in summer there were swallows' nests in the eaves.

She had bees. There was a quiet heady hum to her flowers in the dog days of summer, when we passed outside her white picket fence. Something somnolent and sweet, lulling, inviting, as though to step through her gate – never quite closed, always a little ajar – would mean stepping into a small piece of heaven, apart from the rush and tumble of the real-life world.

We also knew that she had cats – sometimes we saw a silver tabby, other times a sleek black cat, or a streak of marmalade, or a glimpse of tortoiseshell – sometimes they seemed to be hurt, and we'd spot them slinking into the garden, limping, looking like they had been in a fight, with scratched noses or shredded ears. How many cats there were, or if they all belonged to her, we could not tell.

But that was all we really knew. She never got mail. She never stepped out of that gate herself. If her immediate neighbours had ever met her, they never said so; we never even knew her name. She was just there, at the end of the street, the back of her house spilling into an old abandoned orchard and then an open field. She was present, but not really accounted for – she had no real purpose in the neighbourhood.

Or so we thought, then.

I found out different, that summer I turned thirteen.

We all knew about Janey and William – they lived at the other end of our street, in a house which was also untidy and unkempt but with an air of abandoment and despair rather than pleasant and tranquil informality which wreathed the mystery cottage. The neighbourhood rumours had it that their mother had died of complications after William was born; Janey, who was only seven at the time, more or less got handed the baby by her widowed father who then retreated into his own little world and appeared to forget all about his children.

Except for when he remembered, for when he emerged from his gray melancholy and traded it for one of his incandescent and irrational rages, and screamed abuse at his children; once he went after Janey with a bread knife. At such times she would gather up her brother and flee, seeking sanctuary out in the street – or, if one of the mothers on the street happened to notice the two forlorn kids loitering on the sidewalk, temporary refuge in one of the neighbourhood houses. Ours was only two houses down from theirs – we always knew when their Pa went berserk, and my mother would often look out for them when they came slouching down the street looking lost and miserable and beckon them inside for a glass of lemonade or hot cocoa, depending on the season, and an invitation to stay until things calmed down back home.

That's how I got to know them. Janey was only a year older than me, and William was quiet and shy enough not to be a nuisance; Janey was close-mouthed about her home life but not completely closed off; she said just enough so that I caught a glimpse of her hell over the years, trying to keep her brother out of her father's way, trying to figure out how to feed and clothe the both of them when her father didn't seem to care all that much. It was bad – but it all came to a head, and became much worse, in my thirteenth summer.

Janey had just turned fourteen, and she was ripening fast – she had long wheat-blond hair and wide eyes the colour of forget-me-nots, and that summer the leggy child had started to curve into a woman's body, and her father had started to notice how much she resembled her mother, now years gone, and had taken to watching her with a strange new gleam in his eyes. She never told us this, not directly, but her voice changed when she talked about her father now, dropped into a lower register, and the things that she didn't say were present like ghosts in what she did tell us about. We could all hear the undertone of fear in her voice. But her Pa had not done anything, yet, and we could do nothing to come between a father and his children. It was not our place.

Until William came running round to our fence one afternoon, tears streaking his face, and tried to tell us incoherently that some-thing had happened, that Janey was gone.

"Gone? Gone where?" my mother asked, gently but urgently. "Sit down there, good lad, do you want a drink of water? Can I call some-body? Take a few deep breaths and then tell me..."

But I was out the back door already, and then down the street, scouring the neighbourhood for Janey. William didn't say where she had gone, but it couldn't have been far...

...And I was right, because I was just in time to see her stop briefly beside the half-open gate of the cottage at the end of the street, pausing as though somebody had called her name. She turned her head briefly, tilting it, listening, and then she turned into the gate, stepping under the trellis arch that framed it, and vanished out of sight behind the greenery.

I followed.

I hesitated for just a moment before stepping across the threshold, but a sense of urgency, as well as an unwilling curiosity vanquished that quickly enough. The garden beyond the gate was not a wilderness but neither was it neat, its patch of lawn dotted with dandelions and small white flowers like stars nestling in the greensward; the scent of roses was powerful, and sweet. And then I saw that the door of the house was open, and that Janey was standing on the threshold, and that the silver-haired woman was beckoning her inside.

"Wait!" I said, and hurried forward. "She's my friend," I said, when I reached Janey's side. "She isn't alone."

"That is good," the woman said, her voice soft and pleasant. Her eyes crinkled a little at the corners as she spoke, a hint of a smile. "Everyone needs a friend. Come inside, both of you – you will be safe here. This is a safe house, and no harm can come to you here."

The big orange tabby cat was stretched out on a cushion in a bay window as we stepped inside, Janey and I, and yawned at us lazily. There was a kettle on the range, starting to whistle, and our hostess glanced in that direction.

"I expect you would like some tea," she said. "Why don't you go and make friends with Saffie, and I'll bring a tray in when it's ready?"

The cat purred gently as we came closer and suffered us to stroke his lustrous fur, his narrowed eyes only flashes of emerald green in the tiger-striped shadows of his face. While Janey baby-talked to the cat, crouched beside the window seat, I found my own attention caught by the bookshelves against the wall. The books in it were quite old, some of them, with the binding coming apart – and they seemed to be in a language I could not recognise. I was starting to reach for one of them, for a closer look, when the silver-haired woman's voice stopped me.

"Come and have some tea," she said. "I have made cookies this afternoon, too."

Saffie yawned again, let out an odd sound somewhere between a meow and a canary chirp, and jumped off his window seat, stalking out of the room with his tail in the air as though mention of tea had offended him in some way.

"Where's all your other cats?" I dared to ask, my voice sounding thin and reedy with an odd sort of apprehension.

"They come and go," she said. "Saffron and I, Saffie as I call him much to his indignation, we are the only ones that live here. The others come when they need me. This is a safe house."

That was the second time she had said that, but I was not understanding them yet, not really, not properly. Janey, her eyes still red and swollen from recent weeping, reached out for a cookie with one trembling hand.

"Thank you," she whispered..

I felt an odd aversion to the offering. "No, thanks," I said. "None for me."

"Tea?"

Janey accepted a porcelain cup with pink roses on the side, with milky tea swirling in it from having sugar stirred into it with a silver spoon. I, again, declined; this cottage felt like fairy country, and accepting food would have meant... something that I only barely understood, an acceptance of a contract, coming into a strange place and suffering the door to be closed behind you with no guarantee that it would be opened again if you wished to leave.

But Janey had already bitten into her cookie, her eyes dreamy now, calming down.

"What kind of cookies are they?" she asked.

"Chocolate chips, of course, everything tastes best with chocolate," the silver-haired woman said. "And my own honey, for sweetening, instead of sugar. And a few secret ingredients of my own. Don't worry, sweet girl. You will always be safe here."

We didn't stay long, after that. I was getting nervous, and I managed to convince Janey that we'd best leave – but not before she told us one more time, the woman from the cottage, that it was a safe house, and that we were always welcome there.

. . .

It was two days after this that I first saw the strange cat, fluffy and biscuit-coloured, streaking through our garden. I thought I could see it limping, a little, as it ran – but it was gone before I could be certain, and the only thing that I *was* perfectly convinced that I saw as the cat turned momentarily to look at me were two blue eyes. The same colour as Janey's.

We all saw the cat after that, several times; my mother agreed with me that it seemed to be hurt, its fur occasionally matted, its ears flat as though it was angry or afraid – my mother tried to lure it onto our porch with a milk saucer but it wouldn't come anywhere near any of us, only using the bottom of our garden as a passage to wherever it was so intent on going in such a hurry.

I don't know why I followed it, finally, one day. It was just a cat, after all – but I could not forget those eyes, and I had not seen Janey for almost a week now. When I saw the tawny cat streak past our fence in the gathering twilight, I trotted after, keeping it in sight as it wove in and out of the shadows, catching sight of it again just as I thought I had lost it... until I saw it flatten itself against the ground and slide under the picket fence into the garden of the cottage on the corner.

This is a safe house. The silver-haired woman's words suddenly smacked me in the face, but they could not possibly mean what I thought they meant. That cat, so nearly the colour of Janey's hair, with Janey's eyes, could not possibly be what I suddenly thought it had to be.

I crept up to the fence, peered through the gate into the garden. The tawny cat was nowhere to be seen, but the tabby was sitting in the middle of the dandelions in the postage-stamp-sized lawn, washing its face. It paused for a moment as I looked inside, glancing back towards the gate, meeting my own eyes squarely, its gaze feline and serene, giving me nothing. Then it flicked its tail and continued with its ablutions.

I noticed that its ear was bloody, as though it too had been in a fight. And the paw it was licking with which it then washed its whiskers looked scabbed, as though somebody had stepped on its foot with hobnailed boots.

It got up and stretched, yawning lazily in my direction, showing me sharp white teeth.

You do not belong here. Not yet. Go.

I obeyed the unspoken command. That time.

But that lingering sense of 'not yet' stayed with me, binding me to the cottage like an invisible chain. The next time I followed the strange new cat to the cottage there was no tabby on the lawn, and I crossed the threshold of the garden gate and crept up to the window, using the geraniums in the window box to conceal myself as I peered inside.

The silver-haired woman sat in her rocking chair, a basin of water at her right hand, using a clean wetted cloth to dab at the face of my friend, Janey, who huddled at her feet, crying.

"But I don't *want* him to get hurt," Janey said, hesitating over every word, sounding anguished and conflicted. "He's my father. And he can be sweet. And I know he loves us, really. It's just..."

"Hush, sweet," the silver-haired woman said, dabbing gently at Janey's temple. "All will be as it must."

And then she looked up, and straight at me – straight at me as though the concealing geraniums weren't there at all.

I tensed to flee, turned to run, but before I could move the silver tabby was out on the lawn again... and then it wasn't any more, and it was the silver-haired woman who stood there, a slight smile on her face.

"So," she said. "It's to be you after all."

"I'm... I'm sorry..." I stammered, bereft of any other words. I should have been promising that I would tell nobody about this, ever, if only she would let me go. But I couldn't seem to utter that out loud.

I froze as she came towards me, reached out a hand, lifted my face by the chin to look into my eyes.

"You do not belong here, but you know, and you understand," she murmured. "This is not your house. That is still coming."

"What do you mean?" I stammered, rooted to the spot.

"Your friend comes here for protection, for healing. Here, she is safe. I told her it was a safe house – that is what I do, I take in the wounded of this world and this house, this garden, can make them whole again. You, my child, are not wounded – but you are what comes after me. There are only a handful of us in this world at any one time – the healers, the ones who make a safe haven and who guard it, sometimes by a word or an invitation inside for a cup of tea, sometimes with our own blood and tears."

"You're the tabby cat," I said.

"Sometimes," she said, smiling. "And yes, you've seen me here at least once in the aftermath of a battle with some demon out of shadow. Human stupidity, or arrogance, or greed – something that comes out of the dark and has the power to hurt the innocents in its way. I Protect."

"How...?"

"It will come to you, " she said gently. "It is given to all of us to find the one who will succeed us eventually – and I can see that some day you will take my place. Not here – this is my house – but somewhere else, in a safe house of your own, in some other corner of the world where there is a need for healing magic and a healer to wield it." She paused, hesitated slightly as though she were weighing something in her mind, and then came to a decision and reached to lift a slender silver chain over her head. It bore a pendant, a single round stone, golden except for a dark vertical streak in the middle, looking like lion's eye. Before I had a chance to protest, to refuse, the chain had slipped over my own head, the pendant coming to rest over my heart. "This will tell you when," she said. "You will make a safe house one day, and it will grow old roses in the garden and call to the sick and the wounded and the ones who need protection. And in that stone lies the spirit and the wisdom that I myself inherited once from all the ones who came before me. It's yours now. You are the Protector. Those who have come to me before now – your friend, Janey, is the last of them – it is still given to me to shelter and to protect. But from now on, until you make one, there will be no safe house for the wounded of this corner of the world. It will take as long as it must... but make it fast, because every day that you delay you prolong their suffering." She leaned over and actually kissed me on the forehead, as though in benediction. "Go, now. And remember."

.   .   .

The cottage had a "For Sale" sign in the front only two days after that. I don't know who eventually bought it, because it remained unsold until my own family sold up and moved away that winter.

I never saw Janey again. But I remembered her – and I would often turn reflexively after a head of wheat-blond hair while walking in the street, wondering if it was her, if it could be her, what had become of her in the summer that she disappeared. But it was always a stranger, and the eyes were never quite the same shade as forget-me-nots. No, she was gone. Gone forever.

I was only seventeen when I heard the call, when it began.

First it was the stray cats of the neighbourhood who came, and I didn't realise what I was starting the first time I gathered up one of them in my arms, crooning, and washed up its poor scars and weals and welts. I don't remember exactly when it was that I dug out the cat's-eye pendant, which I had taken off when I left the silver-haired protector-witch's garden and had never worn again after that day, and hung it around my neck – or the first time I realised that my hair had somehow turned silver overnight, or that I could trot around the neighbourhood in the shape of a silver tabby cat, or the first time I fed a crying child the special cookies that allowed it to come running to me in the guise of a kitten when it was hurt or scared. But somewhere along the line I realised that I was living on my own, as though the rest of my life had been a dream – and I could smell the old roses in the garden of a cottage at the end of a suburban street.

And that was the day I saw a wary, rangy teenager poised ready to flee on my doorstep, staring at me with huge dark eyes so much like mine had once been, and I understood. And I smiled.

"Come in," I said softly, beckoning with one hand while the other closed around the eye of the cat on my breast. "This is a safe house."

&

Color

He had come to give back what he had once begged for. To return the gift. To plead and grovel, if that was what it took, because it would mean a return to innocence.

"I cannot," she had said. "what I have given... cannot be taken away." She had reached out, traced a finger down the curve of his cheek, and then showed it to him, the fingertip damp with the tears that had streaked down his face when he had come into her presence. "This," she said. "I gave you this. You cannot unlearn to weep."

He remembered coming to this house – it wasn't as long as ago as it now seemed to him, his days had been lengthened by his anguish. But the thing that had led him here, that had been building, for a while; it was as though he had been living on the edge of something for what seemed like several lifetimes, seeing something out of the corner of his eye, feeling a yearning he could not quite understand, overhearing conversations he could not make sense of.

Mahoud and Lila, it had been – the two human changelings – who had pushed him into it at last.

The humans stayed the age at which they had been taken, never growing older in the woods of Fae. Sometimes the reason why was obvious – the King or the Queen had a sudden hankering for nubile mortal flesh and they would turn up, the young knights or the girls barely stepping into the full flower of their womanhood, doomed to smile and to dance forever in the courts of the Fae, never to return to their homes and their families again even after the ones who had plucked them away from it all had long lost interest in them and had moved on to new favorites. But Fae could be random, or simply curi-ous, or acting on geas, or occasionally just plain malicious. Sometimes the humans taken were older people, grandmothers snatched from hearthsides and condemned to an eternity of the aches and pains of old age or old men who hobbled through the woodland paths of the Fae kingdom with canes and walking sticks and used them, when taking a moment to rest from their exertions, to swat the nodding flower heads off their stems or to swipe at a passing doe, or dove, or butterfly.

And sometimes they were younger – much younger – than the ones chosen for reasons of physical infatuation alone. If they were babies, then the Fae allowed them to grow up – to a point – and then get stuck at whatever age the whim of the Fae had decreed. But if they were older than a handful of years – if taken at age five, or six, or seven – they would stay children of that age. The Fae didn't seem interested in allowing these to grow up and into young adults. After all, if the Fae wanted more young men and women there were more in the human kingdoms that were ripe for the taking, without waiting for the incon-venient years to pass until the children already underfoot grew up enough to become interesting.

Lila had been six years old when the Fae had stolen her away. She was a fragile pale child of sunny disposition and endless curiosity, and most of the Fae had time for her, to smile at her, to answer a question or two, to offer her the magic of a bird landing on her small wrist or a mushroom that tasted like gingerbread. But there were times when she was left to fend for herself, alone and lonely, and it was the other changelings who cared for her then.

Mahoud was thirteen human years old, but he had been living in the world of Fae for longer than anyone cared to remember. He was a thin, wiry, brown-skinned boy with skinny limbs and calloused bare feet; in his face, his dark eyes burned like twin coals. He was old enough to remember his world and what it was like and what it had meant – he had been a pauper born into a family of paupers who made their living thieving in the bazaars. Before Mahoud was seven he had been an accomplished cutpurse, contributing to the kitty of his large and tumbling family – his wizened father who was old before his time, worn down by a life of unrelenting hardship; his regretfully fecund mother, who could be counted on to produce a new baby almost every year; his tribe of brothers and sisters, nine of them by the time he had been snatched, ranging in age from babes in arms to grown men and to full-bodied women capable of bearing children of their own, and another in his mother's belly already and on the way.

Mahoud had been payment for an ill-conceived debt his father had been conned into owing one of the Jinni. That was pretty much all he knew of the matter – that, and the fact that one night he had gone to sleep as usual surrounded by people and noise and the smells of the dregs of the bazaar and the places where the poor people slept... and woken up here, in the woods of the Fae, in a place that was strange and foreign to him, stranger than anything he could have ever imagined. He had been frightened, in the beginning, and for a little while he had been cosseted by a number of the Fae who found him intriguing; if the Jinni who held his father's debt was one of these, Mahoud never knew it. But in time they drifted away, as Fae do, to other entertainments – and Mahoud had appointed himself the protector of the younger and more bewildered of the changeling children, as lost and adrift as he himself had once been.

Mahoud was Lila's guardian shadow, protecting her fiercely from harm or even a harsh word. The pair of them were always together, Mahoud's dark curly head bent down to her pale ringlets as they walked the woods or shared their meals by the brookside or on the beach of the long lake where the water lapped gently at the shore. And he would keep her entertained, and stave off her sadness, by telling her stories, things he remembered from his own mortal days, things Lila had never seen or could barely imagine.

It was these that had drawn the attention – and eventually kindled an obsession – in the mind of a Fae who once overheard Mahoud's stories purely by accident, and then found he could not stay away from that hypnotic voice and the images it conjured up.

"...busy paved courtyard," Mahoud would say, in his singsong voice and the exotic accent he had never lost, lying back against a piece of driftwood with Lila's small hand in his own and her head pillowed on his chest. "They sold herbs and potions and spices and incense over in the far corner, and you could tell, because the scents rose and mingled like spirits, and you could smell rose, and cinnamon, and patchouli, and cardamom and nutmeg, and sesame. And there would be honey sold in the stalls beside those, rich and fragrant and golden, and sesame cakes, and a man who roasted green berries right there in the market place filling the air with a heady aroma."

But Lila was a girl. "And the clothes?"

"Oh, the clothes," Mahoud said. "Over in the eastern quarter, they sold silks – scarlet silks, and sky blue, and golden, and even the most expensive of all, the purple, although it was supposed to be reserved for those in whose veins the blood ran royal... but you could buy it if you had enough gold, or you knew somebody, or you knew the right questions to ask. And next to that an old woman sold sheer veils in jewel hues, and next to her, the cobbler sat out in the streets and you could see how he made the shoes – the simple leather sandals for the poor folk, and the elaborate ones with long curved toes for the highborn ones in their halls of pale marble and porphyry and soft carpets."

"And the carpets?"

"You could buy them too, not far away, and behind them there were stalls which sold the skeins from which they were woven – the silk and the wool, dyed all the colors of the world."

"And what did the rich people buy?"

"They bought the best – they bought the carpets which they believed could fly, little girl – the most expensive ones of all, the ones woven from the finest wools, with intricate patterns of dark blue, and gold, and rose madder. And they bought hats and turbans out of golden silk, and jewelled hat pins with gems like blood-red rubies and sapphires, blue like a summer sky or the dark ones the color of midnight with bright stars swimming in their depths, jewels as big as your fist. And ropes of pearls, white like the teeth of maidens or flushed with a faint tinge of pink, like a dawn across the ocean, or pale blue, like the birds' eggs that they sold over in the part of the *souk* where the animals flapped and squawked and screamed and roared all together..."

"And what kind of animals?"

"Oh, all kinds! They sold monkeys with scarlet leather collars and leashes, and tawny lions captured far to the south, and blooded horses, midnight black or pure white or roan with four white socks. And also peacocks, with their magnificent tails and the plumes winking purple and green in the fall of blue feathers. And birds of paradise, red and white and golden and green and blue, and the lyre birds with the strange tails, and then also..."

"The tigers?" Lila would murmured, growing sleepy, her long-lashed eyes fluttering closed against the silk of his vest.

"The tigers," Mahoud said, his voice slipping into a whisper that was a lullaby. "The great tigers with their black-and-orange striped fur, and their glowing jewelled eyes..."

Other times, Lila would be the one telling the story – describing in vivid and childlike detail the gardens she remembered from her days in the human world, where she had been left to kick her heels on the green lawns of her mother's garden, watched over by a yawning nurse-maid drifting off into a quiet nap on a summer afternoon... a nap which had allowed Lila to be snatched away... and that was the point in the story where she would always falter, and look sad, and then speak no more until Mahoud cajoled her into a smile many hours later. But until she got there, she would describe the flowers the grew in that garden as though they were still growing in ghostly profusion all around her.

"Mama told me all the names and I could never remember which was which," she explained earnestly to Mahoud. "There were foxgloves, and hollyhocks, and daisies, and poppies, and bluebells and things that smelled good, like hyacinth or lily of the valley. Lily of the valley was always white, but the others, there was blue, dark blue, like nanny's stockings – and there was pink – and there was yellow – oh, those were my favorites, the yellow! – and there were red ones, too. And she grew roses, I remember those, and they could be any color at all, white like the lily of the valley... and they could be yellow too... or dark, dark, dark red..."

"Like the Queen's rubies," Mahoud said.

"Redder," Lila said staunchly.

Such were their conversations, and their memories. They would talk of silks or flowers, and it would all come back to color and hue. Or Mahoud would start talking about the sky and the sea and how the color of the sky could change the color of the sea – or Lila would start asking him if where he came from the sky was a different color in spring and in summer and he would explain patiently that what she would call 'spring' was not a season in his own country, and no snow fell in what she would call 'winter'. And the one who lingered in the woods just out of their sight would listen, and he found himself fiercely missing... something that he had never, before that moment, realised that he had lacked.

The Fae never noticed color. They never saw it. They saw shape, and form, and light; to them, the adornments they wore, the jewels that gleamed on their clothes or in their hair, were chosen not by virtue of their color but by how bright they were, and how the internal facets in their depths where the light was caught and broken and reflected back changed the quality of that light.

The one who listened to the two human children talk of color would rise from his place of hiding, and walk out on his own, and stare hard at the sky above his head or at the waters of the lake to see if he could glimpse what the children had been talking about. He began to spend his time painfully trying to compare the quality and – yes – the color of the light which broke into a summer's day, or wound down a winter twilight; he would sense that the quality of the light was different at different seasons or at different times of day or in the depths of the wood as compared to out in the middle of the lake, but he could only begin to glimpse it, to realise that there was something different, that it might have something to do with all that color that the children always talked about, the color of jewels and of living things and of the earth and the sky. But if he turned his head and took his focus away he saw again as the Fae saw, no more than that, no less – and no vivid colors to put hue and nuance into his world.

It was *not* his world.

But he could not let it go.

He even cornered Mahoud once, demanding that he explain the way he saw things, but only succeeded in frightening the boy and frustrating himself even further.

"It's no use," he said, throwing his hands up in resignation. "I don't understand."

"The witch in the garden of statues does," Mahoud said, after a small pause.

"What was that? How do you know?"

"Because I talked to her, and told her of things I had seen, and she could see it," Mahoud said.

"Why do you call her the witch?" The question was almost an afterthought, but the tone of Mahoud's voice had been one of respect, and awe, and not a little fear.

"They told me... when I first got here... that she had powers," Mahoud said, almost unwillingly, as though he was betraying a secret. "That she had walked in the human world. That she might be able to return a human child to the place from where he had been taken."

"I listened to your stories," the Fae said slowly, staring at the human boy. "Your life was not easy. But here, you are not hungry and you do not need to steal for your food – here, you have a place to sleep and no vermin nibble on you in the night – here, you have the freedom to go where you please and do what you wish..."

'And here, nobody loves me," Mahoud said softly.

The words fell into a silence. And then, after a long pause, after it became obvious that Mahoud had said everything that he had wanted to say, the Fae sighed.

"And could she help you?" he asked.

"She said that for those like me the road leads only in one direction," Mahoud said. "When I spoke to her she told me that most of the people I had known and loved would already be dust and ashes.

She could not take me back, not to the moment in which the Jinni took me in place of my father's debt, not to the warmth of my mother's love, or my sisters' affection – and those were the things I wanted to go back *to*."

"Human emotion," the Fae said. "Ephemeral and passing."

"And eternal," Mahoud said. "*She* understands."

He had never thought of the one who dwelled in the garden of statues as a witch of any sort. She was Fae, like himself, and that was enough. But Mahoud's words lingered with him, and finally he found himself loitering on the path that led to her garden, the blind stone eyes of two of her statues staring unseeingly at him from either side of the carved wooden gate which stood ajar. If Lila had been there, she might have explained where all the flowers were supposed to go – but there were no flowers here, that the visitor could see, even though he glimpsed what might have been rose bushes allowed to go to twisted briar and tangling against the side of the house that stood there in the middle of the garden. The garden itself was a maze of paths, laid out in crumbled white stone or perhaps shell, winding their way like a labyrinth between green hedges, and statue after statue after statue brooding where the paths crossed and recrossed.

She had been waiting for him on her doorstep, the one he had come to see, leaning against the doorjamb, watching him approach slowly, almost unwillingly, but drawn to this place by something he could no longer hold down.

"I know why you have come," she had told him.

"I want to see," he said. "Never in my existence in this place have I thought of myself as blind – but I am, I *am*, and those children with their mortal eyes see the world far better and far brighter than me. I want to see the way they do. Just *once*, I want to see the way they do. To feel the colors on my skin."

"I can do this for you," she said. "Are you certain?"

"More certain than I have ever been of anything," he said, and he meant it. Then.

She lifted a small crystal phial, dangling it by the narrow neck between two fingers of her left hand. "This will open your eyes," she said. "A drop in each eye, that will be enough. I ask you again, are you sure?"

"I am," he said.

"Three times I must ask, and three times you must affirm it. Do you truly wish this to be done?"

"Yes," he said. "I wish it done."

"Kneel," she said, "and look up, and do not blink or close your eyes until I tell you to."

He did as he was bid, kneeling on the white path at her feet, feeling the sharp shards of whatever had been strewn upon it cut into his legs. She opened the phial and carefully allowed a single drop of the liquid within to fall into each eye. It burned, like acid, like fire, but she had told him to keep his eyes open and so he did it, concentrating on the points of pain on his knees and shins rather than on what his eyes had to endure. Only one small gasp of pain was permitted to escape.

It was she who reached out at last to fold his eyelids closed over the thing she had put into his eyes.

"It is done," she said. "Go, then, and see the things you wanted to see."

"And the price...?" he asked, after a moment, opening his eyes to stare at her.

"Oh, you will pay it," she said softly. "But not, perhaps, to me..."

He wandered for a while in the Fae woods, afterwards, feeling a little lost, a little afraid – but the obsession was upon him in full strength and power now, and he physically ached to experience that human sight that he had bought... for a price he still did not know the nature of.

And so he crossed the boundary, through the Shadowlands, into the world where the humans teemed and laughed and ran and loved and dreamed.

And for a little while, everything took his breath away. Everything was richer and brighter and more vivid than even Mahoud had managed to paint with his stories. He wandered the world that was open to him, from the *souks* and bazaars which still existed in the place where Mahoud's family had once walked, quite probably not greatly changed from his day – to the cottage gardens that little Lila had brought the memory of into the woods of the Fae – to rivers where light scintillated on the muddy brown waters and fishermen pulled out writhing fish from the deeps, impaled on cruel hooks and twisting iridescent in the sunshine – to the spread of wings of the scarab beetle, and the ladybird, and a kingfisher – to a bruise-colored sky brooding over a field of golden grain studded with scarlet heads of poppies – to the flower markets of the old cities, where tier upon tier of vibrant hues cascaded one upon another until his eyes hurt from the blaze of glory...

And then, slowly, he began to realise what he had done.

The colors were not just on the surface of things. They had roots deeper than that, sunk into the minds and souls of the creatures that his gaze touched, and he could see it all now. There was no hiding from any of it now. The veils had all been torn away, and the world was naked to him, and raw, and the colors had edges like sharp knives.

For every mysterious or serene blue, there was also a curling tendril of the blue of pain – of bruising, of enduring loss and sadness.

For every warm shade of yellow or gold, there was an amber-hued shadow lying on people's faces, huddling in the depths of their eyes – shadows of cowardice, or of malice.

For every green of leaf and bough that rested the eyes and healed the soul, there was a green wraith of envy and jealousy and possessive greed that lurked in the deep shadows of people's homes.

For every vivid scarlet and ruby red, there was an explosion of fury somewhere, tongues of flame – of anger and terror and cruelty, the fires that burned heretics, the fire that came out of the mouth of a gun, delivering death.

For every color, there was a dark twin, a shadow, and it came to him in hues and nuances, just as he had dreamed, but he could not close his eyes to any of this, could not unsee, and when he tried... his eyes leaked, and burned with the same burning that he had felt when the witch from the garden of stone statues had put a drop from her phial into each of his trusting eyes.

He recoiled from it all, in the end – and ran back, to the things that he knew, to the quiet woods of the Fae. But the colors followed him there, the memory of it all, and it was as if they had lodged deep inside of him, a slow poison in his soul, and were never going to let him turn away again.

He endured – but before long they noticed, the others. He was the only one with eyes that ran water, and sometimes they would do that at a mere memory of something that he now carried within him. He began to avoid the other Fae, avoided the changelings altogether, drifted alone and wretched through the woods for a little while until he could take it no longer and made his unwilling way back to the garden of the statues and the witch who dwelled within.

To beg for it to be taken away.

Believing that it would be. Might be. Could be.

Right until the moment she shook her head and told him no.

"Mahoud said you understood – that you can see – if he speaks the truth then how do you bear it?"

"I ripped my own heart out and ate it dressed with saffron and cinnamon...but I would not do that to another... and it's already far too late for that, with you.," she said. "I could have offered you the same bargain, right at the beginning of it all, but, like all those who came here before you begging for the thing that you wanted, you would not have taken it, you would never have accepted the simple truth that the clarity of vision you demanded would shatter your own heart in your breast. For you... I only have three choices. I can take your eyes and leave you in darkness for ever more; I can take your memory and send you back into the world a drooling idiot who will spend his days wrestling with a regret and a sorrow that he knows no reason for; or I can turn you to stone and take it all, so you have neither soul nor memory and will feel nothing more ever again."

"What was in that phial?" he asked at last, his hands twisted into fists of fear, of fury, of shame.

"Tears," she said softly. "Human tears. And once you've seen through human tears, you can never unsee that world again, gift and curse, yours to bear, now and until the end of time. Now choose – your eyes, your memory, or the stone."

In the end, it was no choice at all. His eyes, brimming with the human tears which she had put there, followed where she pointed – into her garden where all the paths led, where brooding statues lined the labyrinth. There was a place out there, waiting for another.

witches

The Wedding of the Weed Witch

The thin scratch at the door came very late, but Sibella was still up. There was little sleep in their cottage in those waning days of her mother's dying; the woman about to enter her last sleep fought with astonishing strength against slipping into lesser slumber, and only permitted herself an occasional snatched catnap before waking and demanding that Sibella talk to her, or feed her, or sponge her down, or otherwise remain within earshot and arm's reach and awake and alert. Sibella's mother was dying, but it was Sibella who was pale and exhausted, dark shadows under her eyes, the skin on her face drawn too tight over her sharp cheekbones.

Her mother had finally drifted off, when Sibella became aware of the noise at the cottage door, and she almost considered ignoring the quiet summons completely and trying to close her own eyes for a few precious moments. But there was something insistent and urgent about it, and Sibella finally sighed and gathered her skirts and walked over to the door, to crack it open a little.

"Who is there?"

"Sibella. Can you run?"

The voice was a whisper, but Sibella recognized it — she didn't have many friends, but she counted Marian as one of them, and it was

Marian out there in the night, wrapped in a dark shawl, cradling a travelling bundle in her arms.

Sibella stole a glance back into the room. Her mother still sat with her eyes closed, breathing shallowly.

"Run?" Sibella questioned bleakly. "How? Why? Where?"

"The black banners are up on the towers," Marian said. Only that.

The tenth wife was dead, then. They will be coming for the next one.

"Jenessa and Saira and Lyd have gone already," Marian said urgently. "The roads won't stay open for long, now. And if you stay too long..."

"I may be the only one left here, when they come," Sibella said, more to herself than to Marian.

"Will you come?"

"And abandon *her?*" Sibella said, with a quick tilt of her head in her mother's direction.

"You owe her much, but do you owe her that much?" Marian asked.

Sibella hesitated. It sounded very sweet all of a sudden – she had a *reason* to go, to leave the cranky dying old woman to her own devices and to flee, before the Keep sent out to gather in the next wife for the dark king who brooded on the throne carved from a single bone torn from a creature long since lost to this world. The dark king who had now taken and devoured ten women from his realm. Women who had been spirited off into the Keep, and used, and burned up, and when each had been destroyed in the crucible of the king's power and his passion the black banners had been flown from the high towers to mark her death... and the need for a replacement.

"If you stay, and they take you, then you will leave her anyway," Marian said, her voice urgent.

"I know," Sibella said. "And I... I wish I could..."

"I cannot linger," Marian said.

"I know," Sibella said again. "Go. May the Gods give you grace."

"And you, my friend," Marian said.

And then she was gone.

Sibella closed the door against the night, very quietly, but it was loud enough to wake the sleeping old woman from the cobwebs of her nap.

"Sibella...?" The querulous old voice rose, demanding, and a hand freed itself from her coverlet, to reach out towards her daughter.

Sibella sighed. "I am here."

Sibella stepped out, very carefully, the next morning, to see to the chickens out the back and gather in what eggs there may have been – and already there was a sense of waiting in the air, even though the road that ran by their cottage was still empty of any movement. The silver white puff of a ripe dandelion nodded beside the path, and Sibella snapped the green stem, lifting the thing to her lips and blowing on it like she had done so often as a girl. The dandelion exploded, with the feathery fragments scattering into the air against the bright sky.

Because this was *her* garden, this wasn't an ordinary dandelion. Nothing in her garden was ordinary. She regretted her impulse almost

before she had finished expelling her breath – anything might happen when the floating pieces of the dandelion ghost found a landing place. She reached out a hand and closed it in the dandelion cloud, while it was still airborne, gathered a handful of the seeds, stuffed them unthinking into her pockets, watched others float away free, spared a brief moment to wonder where they might alight, what might happen there, how they would try to explain it. The people who had to deal with it could not know that this particular plant had grown from a seed which had been born in a weed witch's garden.

She was supposed to make a wish, she knew – that was the accepted wisdom. But that was for ordinary dandelions, not one of her own – and anyway, her wishes had withered, in the last year, at her mother's side. There were no words there, no dream to hang from them. Sibella knew that she was waiting, that she was only waiting for death...

...and now, perhaps, for worse.

Because they came, the men from the Keep, not too long after that. Empty handed, because all the young women who might have done as the king's next bride had seen the black banners and had gone into hiding, or ran headlong, as far and as fast as they could. The seekers who had been sent out in this direction had come up with nothing, no candidate – all the women who were left behind had been unsuitable, too young, or too old. They took Sibella when they found her, without asking for leave, without permitting protestations. The dying woman left behind to die alone was not their problem. Their problem was to find a bride for the King – and they had been left with few choices.

Sibella had never been past the iron gates of the outer walls of the Keep. When they took her underneath the great arch of stone and through the gates and into the first of the inner courts her heart beat so hard against her ribcage that it was a miracle that it did not burst through and escape her body – but she kept her head high, and her thin face from showing any fear or reluctance.

She would be a Queen.

For a while, at least.

There would be that.

There were stories, about the King. About how he wore gloves, all the time, because the touch of his bare hand burned human flesh. About his strange golden eyes, which had been described in whispers at country inns as being like a wolf's, or like looking directly into the sun. About his thin cruel mouth, and about how he kept his hair long and down over his ears so that he could hide the fact that they were pointed and elfcursed, and about how when he smiled his teeth were entirely too white and sharp to belong to a man.

Which was all strange because amongst all the people who repeated these stories in whispers over beers in taverns or across home hearths in winter evenings there was never any one of them who spoke from experience, from having seen any of it themselves. It was always something that was passed on from one teller to the next, spread like unchecked weeds into a tilled field, until it was impossible to tell any more where the weeds ended and the crop began.

All the same... there was no way of knowing how much of what was told and re-told was true. Sibella wondered if his first ten wives had felt those sharp storied teeth close on their flesh. If she would feel them.

There would be a wedding – all the wives had been given one. He gave them that, the king on the carved bone chair. He gave them that, and then they vanished into the Keep, and they were never seen or heard from – or about – again... until the black banners fluttered from the towers in time and a new woman was sent for, and a new wedding planned.

They took her to a tower room, up a winding stair, easily guarded – there was no way out except through the door at the bottom of that stair, or out through the window in the turret room seeking death.

"In seven days, the wedding," a grim-faced captain of the guard had informed her, before he left her there. "If there is anything you require, there will be runners at the door ready to go procure that for you. There will be people coming to prepare you for the ceremony."

"Actually," Sibella said, I would be obliged if you could provide me with flowerpots."

The captain looked at her as though she had taken leave of her senses. "Flowerpots?"

Access to real living earth, to a place where there was dirt on the ground in which to bury a seed, would have been preferable, but then it would be hard to keep her work from being seen. One worked with what one had.

"Yes," she said calmly. "I need seven. With good soil."

It was a bizarre thing to ask for, but there were no actual orders against flowerpots. The captain nodded. "I will see it done."

The pots arrived within hours, seven small pots with black garden loam inside. The captain had even sent a watering can to go with them, but Sibella put it aside. In the pocket of the dress she still wore, the dress she had been taken in, she found exactly seven dandelion seeds – of course there would be. Neither more nor less than the number she had specified. She was a weed witch after all.

She pushed each seed into its pot, set the seven pots beside the tower room's window, and lingered for a moment over each pot, her fingers touching lightly the dirt that covered her seeds. And then she sat back, and waited.

Because she was a weed witch, and because every seed she pushed into the ground grew into something, each pot had produced a seedling by the next morning. The seedlings grew as Sibella waited in her tower room, and a dressmaker came to measure her for her gown, and a man came with a casket of jewels for her to choose from to match the gown, and a shoe maker came to fit a pair of embroidered slippers in which she would never walk on bare ground, and a fragrant bath of herbs and flowers was set up for her on the night before her wedding, and a woman came to wash and dress her hair on the morning of the wedding day.

They tried to bring her flowers for a wedding bouquet, but she refused.

"I will have flowers," she said. No more than that. They pressed, but she stayed silent, and in the end other things needed to be done, and they pushed the flowers aside. She thought somebody would probably be waiting, as she was ushered into the sanctuary to be married, with a last-minute panicked posy because it had been ;forgotten'. But it hadn't been. It had never been forgotten. And the dandelion seeds had grown, and ripened, and they burst into bloom on the morning of her wedding, but only after everyone had scurried away and she had been left alone, just for a moment, in her tower room before she was to make her way down the stairs to be escorted to the sanctuary and the king who was waiting. It was in that moment of solitude that the flower buds opened, all of them.

White, lacy, with long dangling underpetals which looked like a delicate fringe, and in the midst a heart that was the palest, gentlest pink, shading into just a hint of something richer and stronger at the very center, a promise of something, but that something was distant, dreamed of, but not real, not yet, it was still to come. And that was the first flower.

Blue, dark blue, but streaked with paler blue on four petals overlapping and drooping, like an iris, the heart of the flower shading into indigo, almost into black. And that was the second flower.

Red, with scores of scarlet, as though someone had scored a living thing with claws and left traces of it, with what looked like way too many petals anxiously crowding one another around a heart of a red so deep that it looked like a pool of blood in the middle of the blossom. And that was the third flower.

Red again, but this time uniform, with four large petals around a black center round and tight like a button, fragile and veined like a poppy. And that was the fourth flower.

Golden orange, almost sepia-coloured, with strong waxy petals, shading into a pearly gold in the heart. And that was the fifth flower.

Blue, pale blue, with petals so thin and fragile as to be almost transparent, its heart a sapphire tangle of thin tendrils with golden fringes on the ends. And that was the sixth flower

White, simple, like a daisy, with slim narrow petals surrounding a pale yellow heart. And that was the seventh flower.

Sibella gathered them all into her hand, leaving the flower pots with only their memory and a few already wilting leaves, and walked down the stairs towards her wedding.

They noticed, of course. Everyone she passed looked, a long stare or a sideways glance, but they all saw the flowers she carried, each unique, each strange, unlikely to have been plucked from a common garden. But nobody said anything. Nobody asked. Not even the young woman waiting with the wedding posy which Sibella had been expecting, at the door of the king's throne hall. She waved those other flowers – those ordinary flowers – away, and they were taken away, without question. Because they simply could not match the glory of what she already carried.

The white, the blue, the red, the golden.

A man who had been standing just inside the throne hall doors turned, glancing at the flowers, to offer her his arm, and Sibella took it. They walked down the center of that great room, with fewer people present than Sibella might have thought would be there but still too many for her to single out or recognize individual faces. She did not try. After the first glance that swept those present, she turned her eyes towards the top of the stair which led to throne she had only heard spoken of in whispers, before... the pale throne carved from what had been living bone... and where he waited.

He sat tall and straight, dressed all in black except for the golden crown that sat on his head – but his hair, underneath, was hidden by a close-fitting cowl. And beneath the cowl and that crown... he wore a mask. A silver mask, with curling patterns beaten into it, the eyeholes too deeply cut and too camouflaged with the patterns for the eyes to be easily visible. She could not tell if they were the burning golden eyes that legend had them be. But he did wear gloves, just like the stories of him told. Black gloves, of leather which looked supple enough to be a second skin, which reached up to halfway up his forearms.

She saw him go very still for a moment, with those eyeholes squarely on the flowers in her hand. And then the mask lifted and she felt the weight of his gaze upon her.

There was no expression to read. She did not know what he was thinking or feeling. She had no idea what the next moment held for her, let alone the next day, or the next month, or the next year – or however long it would take for the black banners to be unfurled, for her. But she had what she held in her hands.

Because they all meant something, of course, the flowers. And she knew exactly what. And it was not a bridal bouquet, but it was a message, and the message was for him, for the king who was waiting.

She knew that he understood the presence of the message, but not its meaning. She knew that he would ask. And she would tell him.

There was a smaller carved chair for her, beside the throne of bone, and she walked to it, more regal than she had any right to be, and sat down, her back as straight as his own. He reached out one black-gloved hand, in silence; she freed one of her own from where her fingers had been curled around the flowers which she now held in her lap, and placed it on top of his. She had been right. The leather underneath her hand was supple, soft, warm to the touch. Like skin, but covering true skin. A hint of what lay underneath, but no glimpse of it.

They said the words over them. A man placed a golden circlet on Sibella's head, and pronounced her a wife. The knuckles of the king's hand lifted, beneath their leather sheath, and she understood the signal, and rose smoothly with him as he came to his own feet. There was no cheer from the people in the hall; Sibella and the black king walked by them, back the way she had been led to the throne, and out of the great doors.

He had not said a word.

They sat together at the high table at the wedding feast, the new queen beside the king in black. He sipped wine, from a cup specially molded so that he could drink through the mouth of the mask, but she did not see him eat anything, nor did she hear him break his silence, the hovering servitors running to do his bidding at the smallest gesture. She herself ate very little, her stomach in a tight knot, her crown like a ring of fire on her head, the seven flowers of her bridal bouquet laid on the table between the two of them. He never turned his head to look at them again, but she knew that he was aware of them, that he was careful not to let his hand brush them.

When he offered her his hand again, she gathered up the flowers with one hand and gave him the other, as before. Still in silence, he led her through the banquet hall where people had stood to mark their passing but Sibella knew that the wedding guests had fallen back to their victuals as soon as the royal pair had left the room, and that the party had been the merrier for their leaving.

They were preceded by two liveried servants who carried torches, and when the small procession reached the carved wooden gates of the inner chambers of the king – Sibella noted that the carvings on the door were the same as those on the mask he wore – the servants slid their torches into sconces, one on either side of the door, and took up positions beside them. The doors were opened from within for the king and his bride, they passed through, and a chamberlain who had dropped to one knee as they swept past him rose again and stepped out of the room and closed the doors behind him.

And they were alone, at last. The king dropped his arm and released Sibella's hand, and she, still in silence, stepped towards the great canopied bed and bent to lay her strange bouquet on the pillows.

"No."

It was the first word she heard him speak, and she turned to face him, and waited.

"Tell me," he said. "You will tell me now."

She could have dissembled and asked what it was that he wanted told, but the silver mask was angled so that she could see he was staring at the flowers. And that he understood perfectly well that their presence had been the beginnings of a message, but that the rest of the message still waited to be delivered.

And so she lifted them again, the blossoms, and held them in her arms.

"I grew these," she said softly. "In seven tiny flowerpots your guard captain provided for me. From dandelion seeds."

He made a noise that might have been disbelief, and the corners of her lips turned up in the beginnings of a small smile.

"A dandelion which once grew in my own garden," she said. "Where... many strange things might have been made to grow. They took me from that without asking, you know. They took me from my dying mother's side. Because an eleventh wife was needed."

"The need is great."

"And the price of it is high," she murmured. "So I grew them. I grew these. They are for you, as much as they have ever been for my bridal bouquet."

He said nothing, so she untangled the stems she held in her hand and lifted each flower in turn as she spoke.

"This is the first flower. It is the flower of innocence, the innocence you have taken from so many already – this time, from me. The innocence of women taken to be brides but not asked for their own choice, or their own desires. The innocence stolen, because you could; the innocence ravaged, and ruined."

She laid it on the brocade coverlet of the bed. He said nothing.

"This is the second flower. It is the flower of sorrow, the sorrow that comes with the knowledge that a woman is not given a time and place to choose what she was or what she wanted to be – with waking up on the first morning after a night before which had not been any of the woman's wish or doing. Of an understanding that a trap had closed, and a woman was inside it, and there would be no escape."

The second flower lay beside the first on the bed. She lifted the next one.

"This is the third flower. It is the flower of apprehension, of fear, of living from one blink of an eye to another, always wary of every word, every action, knowing that the smallest thing might be the death that was coming but not knowing which thing, or what kind of death, or anything at all... because it was not for any of your wives to know, it was not judged theirs to know."

The third flower followed the others. The fourth was lifted in her hand, and her voice became edged, like diamond.

"This is the fourth flower. It is the flower of defiance, of a moment when a woman's will rears up and screams, and a moment when a woman lays her hand upon the tiller of her own destiny. The moment when she made her life her own, and nobody else's; the moment in which even a death, if it comes, comes with meaning, and not just a passing thought on the vanishing of something ephemeral and replaceable. It is the defiance that knows that *this* woman is unique, and not like any other. If she is lost, through malice or carelessness, it might not be possible to find another to take her place, to walk up these same steps, to become wife number twelve. The defiance that said, *I am here. I am the last.*"

He moved, at that. Finally. It was to take a few steps back and sink into a chair by the hearth where a fire had been laid. As though the strength had suddenly gone from his legs.

Relentlessly, Sibella lifted the next blossom, but her voice had softened again.

"This is the fifth flower. It is the flower of wisdom, and it speaks of understanding I knew you would ask about the flowers because you knew that there was something to be told – you knew there was more to this, as soon as you laid eyes on them, and on me. I don't know what lies behind all that has gone before – but perhaps that the first ten wives had been a searching. But that the search ends now. I am here. I have come. No woman in your realm will ever flee their hearths in terror when the black banners are unfurled on the towers of your Keep, in fear of the unknown, of being dragged into the Keep, never to be seen again, never to be heard from or about again, until the black banners spoke of their passing. It was over. The flower of wisdom is the seal of that understanding. There will be no more."

The king's shoulders slumped forward, a little, and his head dropped forward. His mask was no longer turned to the flowers that she held.

But she did not stop. Only two remained.

"This is the sixth flower, and it is the flower of regret, because all of this is a sorrow, and I am to learn things, too – learn the truths that had been hidden from everyone for so long." Sibella crossed the room to where he sat, and sank to her knees beside him, laying the remaining two flowers on her lap as she reached up towards his face. "I will learn what you are underneath the mask, beneath the gloves. I will learn if you are human, just like me, or if you truly are no more than the scary stories told about you in the dark, about something fell and terrible from a world far from this one." His hands had come up to cover hers, to still them, to prevent her from taking the mask – but they were nerveless, strengthless, and they were no match for her will. The mask came off and then, slowly, he lifted his head to face her. What had been hidden had not been terrible – it was just a face, aged, lined, with traces of a life hard-lived imprinted on the features. The eyes weren't gold, they were blue – a pale, pale blue, like a sky just washed with rain. Sibella laid the mask on the floor beside her knee, and continued to speak, very sofltly now. "I will learn if it is true that you can truly destroy a human woman with a touch, or whether all those others had just withered because they hadn't been strong enough to face you. Did you ever remove this mask for any of your other queens?"

"Stop," he said. And he was a king, that should have been a command, one he knew would have been obeyed.

But not by this girl. Not by Sibella. Not by his last queen.

"I will learn, I will understand, and I will share. With that, we can change the world. I know that there is a secret at the heart of this kingdom, and this flower speaks of the regret that it is possible I will have if I learn it, or of the regret that would be yours if you let me. But hear this – by learning it, I take on its burden. That might mean many things – it might be a vow to keep silence on what I know, because that would be better for all – or it might be a vow to speak, and break the cocoon that had surrounded the Keep for so many years. I do not know yet. But I will."

He had covered her hands with his own, and now she freed one to pick up the last flower from her lap.

"This is the seventh flower, and it is the flower of acceptance," she said softly. "And that comes to both of us. Your acceptance, and mine. An acceptance that flows from truth, and from keeping no secrets from one another." She lifted up one of his hands and began to pull off the black glove. "I tell you this, I will find the wound that lies beneath, and I will heal it, or I will take its seed and plant it in myself, and die trying. And I tell you at the last, that I am a weed witch, and all the seeds I plant will grow."

But she was a queen, now, who was first a weed witch. And she would plant her seeds in the gardens in the heart of the Keep, and watch them bloom; she might plant one, who knew, in the hardened heart of a wounded king, and watch that ripen into a fruit that would be a release, and a blessing.

She rose from their shared bed, after he slept, after his touch had not burned her flesh but had instead ignited an unexpected flame of a shared passion. There was a door which led outside, through which they had entered this room, but there was another door, and it took her out to a balcony high on a tall tower, from which she could look out over the Keep, and then let her eyes travel to the far horizon beyond.

And then she looked up, and laughed softly, as a dandelion seed floated down and settled on her parted mouth – and then slipped inside, so that she felt the tickle of it on her tongue before she swallowed it.

And that, too, was a seed.

Twice Promised

"Honey?..." Margaret said, hesitating, watching Roland rock their newborn daughter's cradle with a distracted look on his face.

He looked up, managed a sickly sort of a half-smile, and then they both spoke in unison, in almost exactly the same tone of voice, filled with apprehension, with regret.

"*I have something I have to tell you...*"

They stopped, stared at one another, and then Roland smiled again, this time in a warmer, more encouraging fashion.

"Me first," he said. "I'm sorry, my love. I am really sorry. I screwed up."

Margaret blinked. "No," she said, "*I did...*"

There was an awkward silence, and then Margaret sighed. "Go on."

"Back... before we met... I was such a mess," Roland began haltingly. "Everything I touched – and I mean *everything* – it all just went straight to hell. If there was a job I wanted it would always go to the next guy. It went without saying that the only women I wanted to give the time of day to were way out of my league. Like... like you, for instance."

A ghost of a smile touched the edges of Margaret's mouth. "Right," she said.

"No, don't laugh," Roland said. "It's true. And until I met you... I didn't even know that there was anything to be done about it. It was just, kind of, the way things were. But then I *did* meet you, and it mattered – it mattered a great deal. So I... found a way."

"A way...?" she prompted, after a moment.

"For you, to... for us... for you to accept..."

"Right," she said again. "And what did you do?"

Roland swallowed. "There was... a woman," he said. "She came highly recommended. She was a thoroughly modern witch, they said, and you could go to her and you could ask for a favor and she would make it happen."

"And you did that?"

"I went to her... and I asked... I asked..."

"He asked for you," a voice said, and a shadow detached from the wall and stepped into the room. It was hard to resolve when the shadow became the person because they were both so dark – the shadow a deep absence of light, and the woman, the solid form who emerged, so deeply ebony black to be almost indistinguishable from the shadow itself.. The only thing that flashed light in the oval of her dark face was a bright flash of very white teeth as she smiled. "He asked for you, and I delivered. For a price "

Margaret sat up in bed. "Who are *you*? What do you want?"

"I am Shula, and I come to collect," the black woman said pleasantly enough.

Margaret turned back to her husband. "Roland, what did you promise her?"

Roland fought for the words, but Shula made the matter perfectly obvious by stepping forward and leaning over the cradle with the newborn baby girl.

"Hello, precious," she cooed at the child.

"The *baby*? You promised her the *baby*?"

Shula bared those magnificent teeth again. "His firstborn," she said. "And I have come..."

"Not. So. Fast."

Margaret covered her face as another woman stepped into the room, materializing out of what had been thin air. She was wearing untidy layers of tunics and skirts in ill-matched colors, a mane of wild henna-red hair streaming down her shoulders and over her ample bosom which she only emphasized by crossing her arms underneath her breasts and pushing them into prominence. Roland goggled, and Shula turned, with the smile turning into a pleasant snarl.

"Who, exactly, are you, and what are *you* doing here?" she asked the red-headed woman.

"Will you tell them, Alix dear, or shall I?"

"Tell them... tell us... what?" Roland asked.

"Roland... I'm sorry... your one can't have the baby. She's my first-born too. And I promised her... I made a bargain long ago... to give her to Ethelreda."

"You – *our* child – you did what?..."

"Made a bargain, a better one than yours, boy," Ethelreda said. "She got three wishes, at least, instead of your selfish puny little one. And she worked for it, too – she made the effort to come and seek me out, all the way out of her comfort zone and into the enchanted wood. Not like you looking up a name in a city phone book."

Shula snorted. "You've been living out in the middle of nowhere for far too long," she said. "Phone books are extinct, sweetie."

"What?" Roland said, ignoring them both, turning back to Margaret. "What did you sell our child for?"

"Sell her?" Margaret snapped. "You're a fine one to talk..."

Ethelreda began to count off the litany of Margaret's wishes by raising the fingers of her right hand. "To never know want. To forever be young... And to always be beautiful and irresistible to anyone whom she chose," she said. "And, well, I guess she chose your sorry ass."

"But *he* promised the child to *me*," Shula said.

"For one silly little wish," Ethelreda said. "I think mine is the superior claim. And probably the prior one."

"I was here first," Shula said obstinately.

"And I made an entrance," Ethelreda retorted. "This isn't finders keepers. There are rules about this. The child is mine."

"No, *mine!*"

"She's mine!" Margaret cried out. "I gave birth to her only hours ago! I never thought ... I never really expected..."

"Never expected me to collect? She wasn't yours the moment she separated from you," Shula said. "She was promised."

"Indeed," Ethelreda said. "Promised... to me."

They squared off, the two witches, glaring at each other. It was hard for them to do it eye to eye since Shula was a full foot shorter than the statuesque Ethelreda – but she more than made up for her lack of height in pure presence. The air in the room began to fairly crackle, with a faint smell of ozone building in the air. The ends of Ethelreda's hair began to lift and dance, as though in an invisible breeze.

"You aren't allowed to make a war of it," Roland said suddenly. "Not here, anyway. Not with mortals present. I know that much, I read about it. Before I got tangled up in... there are safeguards. There are *rules*. I know that much. You can't just do what you want. Shouldn't you – I don't know – get arbitration or something?"

Both witches turned to fix him with a gimlet stare and he shrank back into as small a physical package as he could make of himself, blanching.

"Just saying," he managed to squawk.

"He's right," Ethelreda spat out first. "The little twit is right. Under the Law we can't just duel for it. Not any more. We have to call in the Baba Yaga."

Shula's eyes flashed. "That hag."

"Hag or not. The arbitrator."

"*Fine*," Shula said, belligerently crossing her arms in an unconscious echo of Ethelreda's own earlier defiant gesture. "So go on then. Give her a call. Go on."

Ethelreda's lips thinned in disapproval at the challenging tone of that comment, but she didn't appear to deem it worthy of a response. Instead, she simply lifted her left hand and made an arcane motion in the air between herself and Shula. Her full lips formed a single word, but never did it audibly pass them – an almost subliminal whisper, a silvery vapor that spilled from her mouth, and the word she never spoke began to take form, the vapor turning into a pale grey smoke and the smoke into first the outline and then the firm shape of an unspeakably ugly old woman.

Margaret whimpered, and reached out to gather her newborn into her arms. The baby let out a sleepy protest as it was crushed against her mother's breast.

The new arrival sported a magnificent dowager's stoop, her straggly dirty gray hair piled on top of her head in an untidy mound held together with what appeared to be a chicken bone, and she bore the kind of preposterous nose which might have been the inspiration for every evil witch illustration ever made to a fairy story. It looked like it entered a room a full half a minute before the rest of her did, and sported a carbuncle of a large hairy mole right at the tip of it. Her deep-set eyes, of indeterminate color, were shadowed by unkempt brows, and there was a dark tattoo of some arcane symbol etched into her right temple. She materialized scowling, her gnarled ancient hands twisted into long-fingered, long-nailed claws.

"This had *better* be good," she snarled. "You just might have cost me a night's work, and I will take it out of your hide if I was summoned frivolously."

"That's for you to decide," Ethelreda said, speaking quickly, forestalling Shula who had opened her mouth but waited a moment too long to give tongue. "This is the matter. There is a firstborn, right there. And she's been twice promised. To me, in return for favors..."

"And to me, for same," Shula said.

"Whose firstborn?"

"Both of them. The mother and the father, apparently," Ethelreda said.

"So they both promised in good faith and with a right to do so?" The hag wrinkled her nose, and stared down the length of it at the two new parents. They both flushed guiltily and looked away.

"The child was promised to me," Shula said.

"And to me," Ethelreda said, equally firmly.

"I take it neither of you wishes to cede?" Baba Yaga said, turning her attention to the two embattled witches.

"A promise is a promise, and I have my rights," Ethelreda said. "And I have a legacy..."

"Oh, sure," Shula said sarcastically. "Always side with the generational ones. Just because you had a great great great great great great grandmother who was a witch before you doesn't make you a better witch than me."

"You know nothing of such heritage," Ethelreda said, lifting her head and giving Shula a haughty once-over. "Besides, you can barely call yourself a witch at all. You're nothing. You're barely here. You've more or less literally just been born yourself, so to speak – first generation. Pah. You haven't had time to figure out what your path is, never mind take the first steps on it."

"That's because your ilk won't give me the room," Shula snarled. "I've had to fight for every *inch* of space I occupy, battle for every step I took on that path of yours – and yet I'm here, and I'm just as good as you, and you are *no better*..."

"Enough," Baba Yaga snapped. "The answer is clear. Joint custody."

The two witches stopped arguing and brought their attention to the old woman, both looking aghast.

"Joint... custody?" What does that even mean?"

"I've never even heard of anything like that before. And I've been around for a long...."

Baba Yaga silenced them with a sharp gesture. "You called me to decide, I have decided. For six months of the year the child will live in the city. For six months, in the forest. You decide which six months where, it's immaterial to me."

"But that means there will be six months apart – how can she be trained if I can't – " Shula began to remonstrate, and Baba Yaga,s lipless mouth opened in a terrifying grin.

"I didn't say you could just shuttle the girl between you at your whim. I said joint custody and I meant it. You will ALL live six months in the city and six months in the forest The child, and both of you. Together. Until she is eighteen. Then her bond is up and she gets to decide what happens next, because you all made a mess of things."

"But that means..."

"But that doesn't work...."

"*Zhuzh-zhuzh-zhuzh*," said Baba Yaga, interrupting, holding one gnarled finger up. "You asked, I decided. Fiat. Now I am going to back to my own abandoned work. You can hammer out a deal between all of you."

"That is so unfair," Shula said.

"Who told you things would be fair?" Baba Yaga said, cackling. "I mean, you could always give up your claim. One of you, or both. Or else you have to abide by what I have said. Now go away and stop bothering me."

Her edges were already curling into smoke, and before she had fully finished the sentence in physical form she was gone, her last word just an echo in the smoke.

Shula and Ethelreda stared at each other.

"The *city*," Ethelreda spat out. "The dirt and the grime and the noise and the crowds and never a living thing growing that is wild and free. You are going to make her live that? You are really going to drag *me* here?"

"The city where you can find an ethnic restaurant on every corner, and where all the world is at your fingertips," Shula said. "You want to drag me to that stupid, stupid, stupid, stereotypical gingerbread house in the woods and...and... what do you *do* there all day? Is there even wi-fi?"

Ethelreda blinked. "What on earth would I need that for?"

Shula rolled her eyes expressively, and then, with some defiance, whipped out a cellphone from a pocket. "Right, then. I suppose we'd better get on with it. Here's a first lesson in the application of tech, you delightful backwoods hedge witch – this is a new contract and we need a record of it and I guess a picture is worth a thousand words." Her index finger began stabbing in various directions as she started barking orders at everyone in turn.

"You, let go of that child. Someone put a pillow in the crib. Put the child down. You, Roland, over here. Here's the phone. Put down the baby – yes, there, on the pillow – you hold one hand, Red, I've got the other, *take the picture already*, I don't have all day..."

They all instinctively obeyed, and Roland found himself holding the witch's cellphone and taking a photo of the two rival claimants, one on either side of the baby's crib, holding one hand each, staring fiercely into the camera. Shula reached out to whip the phone from his hand when he was done and peered onto the screen, frowning a little.

"It'll have to do," she muttered darkly, swiping her finger across the screen.

"And now?" Ethelreda said, frowning delicately.

"And now, nothing. I'll email you a copy...oh, wait, you don't really do email, do you. Fine. I'll print you a copy so you can have one for your own records. Well, that seems to cover..."

Margaret let out a wail. "But you can't just *take* her, not just like that – she's my *baby* – "

"Not any more, dear," said Ethelreda, cradling the child in her arms and rocking her gently. "Signed and sealed, and delivered."

"At least you get to have a picture," Margaret cried piteously.

"I guess we can let you have one, too," Ethelreda said, and turned back to Shula. "That gadget of yours, you can take another shot, leave them something to remember their own bargain by...?"

"Oh, sentimental claptrap," Shula snapped. "They don't need... besides, look at her. She hardly wants a picture of *that* face." This last was aimed, with a toss of her head, at Margaret, who did in fact present an unlovely vision of a blotchy face, eyes red from weeping, and bedhead hair sticking out at all angles around very pink ears.

"Well she did produce the child," Ethelreda said pragmatically. "And you forget part of my bargain. She mightn't be able to help herself right now – but you take a picture of her, even like this, and you see if my bargain doesn't hold true. She'll look like she's just stepped out of a salon. Take the picture, then. You, daddy, come over here and hover over her shoulder – here, hold onto the baby, just for a moment – hurry up about it, would you?"

Shula, still frowning, snapped another photo of the family never meant to be and then inspected the resulting picture with her head at a quizzical angle while Ethelreda gathered up the disputed child again, peeling away Margaret's clutching fingers.

"I'll be damned, you're right, she does look good," Shula said. "I'll email you a copy, Roland. Are we done now...?"

Margaret was crying again, great ugly sobs that were shaking her entire body, and Roland, looking equally bereft, reached out to awkwardly fold an arm about her shuddering shoulders. She looked for a moment as though she was contemplating shaking him off in bitter rejection, but then another wave of weeping took over and it was all she could do just to gulp air in between sobs.

"Can't we just keep her?" Roland said, bravely enough, his eyes never leaving the newborn daughter in Ethelreda's arms. "That way, neither of you would have to..."

"And she gets to choose when she's eighteen, anyway," Margaret said, managing to stuff a few brave words in between trying to remember how to breathe properly. "So whatever your plans are... there is absolutely no guarantee... and what if she chooses to be, well, mortal, to be ours, to be simply ours...?"

Roland's fingers squeezed Margaret's shoulders. "What if we appealed...?" he said. "What if we just said... that this joint custody thing... it's never been done before – what if we just made a case that it invalidates the bargain completely...?"

"There's no backsies," Shula said sharply. "You don't just get to rewrite your contract because you don't like what it stipulates. We accommodated, on our end – but you don't get to just nix things because you decide that you don't want to do what you promised."

"Twice promised," Ethelreda said grimly. "And twice claimed. We will all just have to make the best of it. Well, woman. Your place, or mine?"

❧

They had gone low-tech and ended up tossing a coin, in the end. Ethelreda had won the first six months of the mandated cohabitation, and Shula had had to make some swift accommodations to her lifestyle and her responsibilities in order to be here. She was far from happy about it – in fact, she was still in a blue funk of deep resentment. It wasn't just that she had to fundamentally alter her whole existence to be in a place which she had no particular desire to be in – it was a drain on her powers, as well, because this wasn't just a question of materializing in Ethelreda's cottage like she had done into the hospital room where she'd gone to claim her prize-child. No, this was more of a move than just making an appearance. And luggage necessitated a physical journey. And Ethelreda's woods didn't like the presence of her car. It had been a bit of a trip to get here, and Shula was still steamed about a completely unnecessary new scar from a scratch left on her paintwork by particularly feisty sharp branch which had taken exception to her trespassing in the forest. But that promised to be just the beginning of the insults that Ethelreda's world would pile upon her.

"Those the only shoes you got...?"

Shula had thought that she was alone in the quaint and rustic room – one which Ethelreda's cottage appeared to have added just for Shula's benefit, and which Ethelreda herself had remarked on earlier as not having existed at all until the moment the put-upon car had pulled up outside the cottage. She whirled with a scowl from unpacking the elegant suitcase open on the four-poster bed.

"*Yes*, they're the only shoes I got," she snapped. "There isn't much call for clodhoppers where I live."

"Not much call for heels out here, either," Ethelreda remarked, leaning against the doorjamb with her arms crossed in their characteristic way underneath her breasts. They curved gently out of the cord-gathered neckline of a peasant blouse, and Shula had to remind herself to take her gaze off the milky flesh and back to Ethelreda's face. Once there, however, her irritation with the face's owner returned in full measure.

"I packed flats!" she said, pointing to a pair of suede ballet flats currently parked neatly on the bed beside the suitcase.

"Those won't last you two days out in the woods," Ethelreda said conversationally.

"What am I supposed to do, buy an entire new wardrobe for this bucolic getaway of yours? It wasn't my idea, remember? Or what? Just go barefoot?"

Ethelreda, who *was* currently barefoot, wriggled her toes luxuriously. "Wouldn't do you harm to try," she said. "But I can understand that those precious feet probably wouldn't like it. Actually, you look like you could probably wear some of my shoes for the duration. We look like we wear a similar size."

Shula was about to retort something about her own feet being nothing like Ethelreda's paddles but she had to admit, at a cursory inspection of said feet, that they didn't look anything like the broad brown peasant feet she had been all too willing to ascribe to Ethelreda. They were pale, narrow, and surprisingly aristocratic. Shula had no problem imagining them in her Louboutins. In any event, the conversation was derailed by a high insistent wail from outside the room. The joint-custody baby was making its needs known.

"Your turn to change her," Ethelreda said, unfolding herself from the doorjamb.

"I changed her only a couple of hours ago!" Shula exclaimed.

"This morning, yeah. Don't know how much you know about babies but they do need that more than once a day," Ethelreda said, grinning. "I did it again, after, and I think she's letting us know it might be time for another. And I have dinner on the go. Your turn to change her."

Shula tossed the highly unsuitable skirt she had been unpacking on top of the unsuitable ballet flats and, muttering to herself, went in search of the child.

Shula had named her Shimmer. Ethelreda had begged to differ, and had settled on Rose. They both agreed that Rose Shimmer sounded preposterous, rather like a shade of lip gloss in a nice sweet pre-teen make-up cosmetics line. But they had to call her something – and in the manner of such things a totally unlooked-for result had emerged after Shula had exclaimed something about the baby being a disaster area, Ethelreda calling her "our tiny disaster" the next time she hefted the baby, and that had quickly degenerated into Dizzy. And it stuck.

"Hey, Dizzy," Shula said soothingly as she entered the baby's room. Dizzy, her cubby legs uncovered when she had kicked off a baby blanket off her tiny self in her hand-carved wooden cradle, stopped mid-whimper at the sound of her voice, and uttered a dove-like coo. Shula ran an experimental hand over the baby's diaper. "Right," she said, resigned. "Of course. Why does nobody warn you about this when you make bargains for firstborn children?"

It wasn't in fact supposed to be like this, at all. In Shula's mind's eye, when she had contracted for the child, she had kind of imagined herself riding off into the city dusk, in a cab, accompanied by a nebulous figure of a child who was... well... probably old enough to go club-bing. She hadn't really thought through the whole baby-in-diapers phase at all.

She changed the offending diaper – at least Ethelreda wasn't going to insist on the classical cloth diapers which needed washing and ironing and safety pins! – and tossed it into passed for a rubbish bin outside Ethelreda's back door, trying not to think too hard about who collected garbage around here and when. The baby settled happily into her cradle when Shula put her back down and stepped back out of the room. Sumptuous smells – a definite improvement on the odoriferous diaper – were wafting invitingly from out the kitchen where Ethelreda was fussing with herbs and spices, but Shula wasn't in the mood for small talk. She was, however, feeling twitchy and useless and at a loose end, and finally dragged herself into the kitchen clicking her tongue in frustration against her teeth.

"What is there to do here?" she demanded, and Ethelreda turned from stirring something in a pot to look the strange and incongruously, obstinately, elegant creature trapped in her house.

"Well," she said practically, watching Shula's restless fingers drum-ming on the kitchen table, "I'm not about to trust you with a sharp knife. The herb garden could do with weeding, if you want to put your back into something."

Shula looked down at her manicured hands, resigned. "I might have known it would involve actual dirt," she said. "I don't suppose you have gardening gloves or any such thing?"

Ethelreda made a quick dismissive gesture. "You know how to make the dirt go away," she said. "Or you ought to, if you're worth your weight in the craft."

"Fine," Shula snapped. "Where's the damn garden, then? I ought to tell you, I have a black thumb. No potted plants other than the occa-sional cactus have ever survived for long in my house."

"Noted," Ethelreda said. "Maybe it's just practice that you need. Back there, against the fence. Have at it, then."

The herb garden was just visible from the kitchen window, and shortly after this conversation Ethelreda was treated to the sight of Shula's wiry frame, clad in a pair of (admittedly designer) sweatpants and a tight pink tank top, kneeling by the herb bed which had been under discussion. Ethelreda was astonished and not a little annoyed to discover just how distracting the sight of Shula's bare, muscled arms pummeling the soil actually was – and it was with not a little regret that she sighed, a little while later, and emerged out into the back garden where Shula was working.

"Er, not that I want to be difficult, sweetie, but those are my chocolate mint plants that you're pulling out right there..."

Shula straightened, wiping at her forehead with one hand and leaving a fetching smear of dirt across her brow that Ethelreda suddenly found herself itching to reach out and wipe away.

"I told you I was awful at this," Shula said.

Ethelreda sighed. This had been too good to just abandon. "I'll show you which plants are the weeds," she said. "But you'd better stop, now, because I really don't want to lose the whole crop there..."

"Fine," Shula said, straightening. "I'm going for a walk, then."

Ethelreda glanced down at Shula's feet, currently clad in a pair of wedge-heeled backless thong sandals with diamanté detail. "Take the shoes by the door," she suggested practically.

Shula grimaced at the thought of someone else's shoes on her own pampered feet but had to admit that the suggestion was sound. Amazingly Ethelreda's shoes fit rather well, and she laced them up and set out along the path that led into the forest.

"Don't go too far," Ethelreda called out, as a parting shot. "The woods can be misleading, and you're hardly wood-wise..."

"I come from the concrete jungle," Shula muttered rebelliously. "Come and *get* me."

The path curved into the edge of the trees, and then led through filtered green light until it emerged onto a grassy slope which fell away towards a small vale with a creek running through it. The sun was warm, and the grass strangely inviting, even for a city girl who instinctively distrusted the idea of voluntarily allowing her rear end to come in contact with bare ground in unfamiliar territory. But, after all, she had just spent quite a while with her hands plunged into actual dirt, and at the very least the grass was not *that*. It was too much to resist in the end, and this was Ethelreda's country, and Shula decided to assume that it was all under Ethelreda's benevolent protection somehow. She settled down on the greensward, stretching luxuriously against a convenient smooth and sun-warmed rock which leaned back at just the right comfortable angle, and closed her eyes for just a moment against the golden afternoon sunlight.

When she opened them again, the sun was considerably lower, more burnt orange than golden, and the shadows were deep and long.

"*Dammit*," she muttered, annoyed at herself for being so easily seduced by the bucolic paradise and scrambling to her feet. For one panicky moment she could not really tell where it was that she had come out of the main woods, and grimly imagined Ethelreda's inevitable smug I-told-you-so if she managed to get herself lost on her first day she'd arrived here. But then she squinted at the trees, and an opening appeared vaguely more familiar than the others. She didn't pause to think about the reasons for that, deciding to trust instinct, and plunged into the deepening shadows.

There seemed to be something in front of her... something that she might have said, had she been so inclined, that was literally guiding her home. A moving shadow that wasn't of the trees, just far enough ahead of her for her not to be able to catch a clear identifying glimpse of it – and yet somehow she found herself trusting its guidance, following precisely where she saw it leading. And sure enough after a trudge that *almost* lasted long enough to give her a renewed panic attack, Ethelreda's cottage hove into view in its clearing.

Shula let out a deep breath she hadn't really been aware she was holding, and paused to contemplate it from where she had paused. It wasn't really a gingerbread cottage of course, not literally, but it had certainly been done up to look like one, mansard windows poking out through a thatched roof, cheerfully painted on the outside, with flower pots outside every window, and a chimney which emitted a gentle picture book ghost of white smoke. And when in the next instant its owner, her red hair spilling wildly over her shoulders, appeared on the doorstep, she was just a perfect match for it all.

"I was starting to wonder if I should go looking for you," Ethelreda said. "Come on in, dinner is ready." She allowed her eyes to slide down

Shula and linger for a moment on the sensible lace-up-shoe-clad feet, and then her lips curved into a smile. "Who's your friend?"

Shula looked down, suddenly aware that her guiding shadow had manifested itself into something more corporeal at her heel.

"I followed it home," she said. "I think."

"The usual line is, 'it followed *me* home, can I keep it'," Ethelreda said. "But leave it to you to pick your critter."

"What?" Shula said, frowning at the animal which stood looking back up at her out of intelligent bright black eyes.

"Honey," Ethelreda said, "your new familiar is a *skunk*. It can come in, if you think you can keep it under control."

"I don't have a familiar...!" Shula all but shrieked.

Well, now you do, the black eyed creature said straight into her mind, its tone every bit as sardonic as Ethelreda's could be.

How *inconvenient*. And how absolutely typical of the whole disaster. Shula stalked towards the cottage, the skunk trotting at her heel like a tiny dog. She had a horrible feeling that she would never be rid of the thing again.

The people in her condo complex already thought that she was weird enough. If she turned up with a pet skunk in tow, it might just be the final straw.

"I am starting to really regret this," she said conversationally, to the skunk, and then scowled fiercely when she caught herself doing it.

Life was knocking over dominoes fast. Shula wondered what the next surprise was going to be.

If the first six months, out in the woods, had been a trial for Shula, the plunge into the city was a disorienting onslaught on the senses for Ethelreda.

Ethelreda had been increasingly short and snippy as her six months drew to a close, and it was practically on a war footing that she arrived at Shula's sprawling penthouse condo. Shula had esoteric decorating tastes, and she had had absolutely nobody to answer to for any of them up until that moment, so she had indulged them to the fullest. The rooms were high-ceilinged, with large picture windows opening on a balcony whose horribly inadequate and non-baby-proof railing made Ethelreda clutch baby Dizzy protectively to her, and they were a riot of colors and patterns and shapes. Ethelreda tried to take it all in – the inlaid chess table in the corner of the living room, with hand-made chess pieces set out on it, the brightly patterned cushions strewn over the pale sofa, the esoteric artwork hanging on the walls, the hand-woven rugs strewn over hardwood floors, the statuary carved from exotic hardwoods or sandalwood or jade depicting African drummers or Japanese Buddha figures or exquisite delicate birds and animals.

"This is no place for a child!" Ethelreda gasped, seeing potential lethal danger for the baby everywhere.

Shula sighed.

"I didn't really think about that," she said. "I did prepare a room for her."

"Were you intending to lock Dizzy in there until she was fifteen?" Ethelreda demanded.

"I was hoping she would be trainable," Shula said, a little defensively. "You know. Like a cat."

"Just show me where to put her down," Ethelreda said. "And some of this stuff is simply going to have to *go*, Shula. At least for the time being."

"She's still a baby!" Shula said. "She's hardly likely to go stuffing her fingers into power outlets just yet."

"I haven't even started on those," Ethelreda muttered. "But yes, she'll start moving under her own steam *eventually*. And I'll not have her poking herself in the eye with some pointed stick you have in here that you thought looked good on the walls."

"Oh, she'll be fine," Shula said, with a touch of asperity. "This way. Her room is back here."

The baby's room was a lot more sensible, even a little drab compared to the rest of the dwelling, and Ethelreda calmed down enough to put the child down for a nap.

And then asked the other, obvious question.

"And where's my room?"

Shula hesitated for a moment.

"Well, this isn't quite the cottage in the magic woods," she said, managing to sound both apologetic and defensive at the same time. "I can't just wave a wand and create a room just because I need one. There was the extra bedroom, but I tarted that up for Dizzy – there's my office, but I do use that as an office on a day-to-day basis and there's no space in there for a permanent second tenant. There's the couch in the living room but it isn't really that comfortable as a bed – you wouldn't like it to sleep on for six months."

"So, what then? A sleeping bag on the kitchen floor?"

"There *is* a bed," Shula said. "It's a large one. King size. Lots of room. And it isn't as though I haven't shared that before."

Ethelreda roused. "I don't want to…"

"Oh, don't be silly," Shula snapped. "It may not be ideal but there's plenty of space for both of us. I'll clear some room in a closet for all your tat although I really don't know how it's all going to fit in there – your stuff takes three times as much room as mine does. And I do hope you brought… sensible shoes," she added, as an afterthought, unable to stop a sardonic payback comment in memory of her own unsuitable attire at Ethelreda's cottage.

The shoes were a matter for another time, though, as their first night in Shula's condo drew close. They settled Dizzy down, together, and then sat awkwardly together on Shula's sofa, nursing goblets of red wine and not meeting each other's eyes.

"I don't know if this is going to work," Ethelreda said eventually, grasping the nettle of the subject they were avoiding. "I haven't actually shared a room, let alone a bed, with anyone since… since I was a little girl."

There appeared to be more to that story than just the surface meaning because even as she uttered the words Ethelreda seemed to slam down something inside of herself, something she had almost said out loud but which she clearly did not wish to discuss further.

Shula chose to ignore that, for now.

"If you want, go in early. I have work to do. I'll just crawl in later and I'll try not to disturb you."

"Fine," Ethelreda said at last, after a long pause, and got up, leaving her half-full wine goblet on the table beside her. There was suddenly something awkward and self-conscious about her, and even her fiery hair seemed to lose a bit of its luster.

"You don't have to be *afraid* of anything," Shula said, not even sure why she thought that Ethelreda would be frightened, or by what.

But something flashed in Ethelreda's eye at those words, and she tossed her head, just a little, some of her defiance returning.

"I'm *not*," she retorted. "Good night, then."

"Good night," Shula said to Ethelreda's retreating back. And then rolled her eyes slightly as she drained her wine, sighing. "What was I thinking?" she muttered to herself. The whole baby thing seemed to be way too much trouble, and none of this had been in Shula's plans when she first put the idea of acquiring that first-born child into motion.

She did have work to catch up on, that much hadn't been a lie of convenience to Ethelreda, but there did come a moment when she finally decided that she was now inventing chores so that she wouldn't have to go to bed yet and closed her laptop with an air of resignation, blowing out the black candles infused with the power of her order which she used to enhance her performance at her job. She padded into the bathroom in bare feet, cleaned her teeth, gave herself a long apprising stare in the mirror and tallied up her usual imperfections, and stepped into the bedroom.

A dark shape that proved to be Gumby the skunk uncurled from the bedroom chair and looked up sleepily as Shula entered, and then made the decision that matters didn't require any further attention and tucked his head underneath his luxuriant tail once more and went back to sleep. On the bed, Ethelreda was curled up under the covers like a cat, barely visible, and judging by her deep even breathing solidly asleep. Her hair, unbound, had spilled over her pillow and onto Shula's side of the bed, its rich red curls dark by the dim light only barely provided by the luminous digits of the bedside clock – which registered that it was well after 1 AM. Shula stood by the bed with her head tilted to one side, contemplating the hair and wondering what on earth to do about it without waking its owner up out of deep sleep. She was conscious of several unexpected feelings – but it was one that she focused on most sharply, because she didn't quite know what to do with it. That feeling was an urge to pick up that hair and play with it, twisting it around her fingers, the sense of sliding strands almost physical in her tingling fingertips even though she had not touched anything yet. In the end, fully aware that she was potentially committing an act with far greater consequences than she might be aware of at the time, she succumbed to a purely irrational impulse and, taking a pair of cuticle scissors which had been left in the drawer of her bedside cabinet purely by oversight since before she had been forced to relocate to Ethelreda's country estate, carefully lifted and snipped off a long red curl from where it lay displayed on her pillow and carefully curled it around her fingers. She padded back out into the corridor, the lock of hair hidden against the palm of her hand, and placed the stolen thing inside a small lapis lazuli-inlaid box she took from a display shelf in the entrance hall, burrowing the box with the new treasure in it way into the back of her linen cupboard. It settled against another box hidden there, the concealment of the bath towels falling over both, tucking them out of sight. Shula stood staring at the neat stack of towels for a moment, a perfectly ordinary thing which gave no hint about what it protected underneath its folds, and then padded back to the bedroom, gathered up the spilled red hair as best she might and piled it between the two pillows, and spent the next hour wakeful and staring at the changing digits on her bedside clock as she tried to put it out of her mind.

When she woke it was to find herself alone in the bed, with interesting smells coming from the kitchen. Gumby had migrated to the bed sometime during the night and now slept majestically curled up at Shula's feet; Shula swung her legs out of bed trying not to startle or disturb the beast and, grabbing the vividly printed silk robe that had been flung across the bedroom chair, emerged from the bedroom, yawning and rubbing her eyes, to see that her usually quite pristine and rarely used kitchen had been commandeered by a red-haired fury cooking up a storm.

"You're out of everything," Ethelreda said cheerfully, her back still turned to Shula but somehow aware of her presence there. "I just used up anything remotely edible in this apartment, and even *that* was mostly stuff I brought with me when we came up. Just what do you eat, when you're living here?"

"Pizza, shop-bought salads, and Chinese takeaway," Shula said. "I don't have time to cook, woman. I have groceries delivered, when I need them, but I don't do that much..."

'You don't, at that, and what you had here was decidedly not fresh – do you actually get fresh food out here at all?"

"I'll take you to the market," Shula said, resigned.

"That's a start. In the meantime, there's a mushroom omelette, and we'd better use up the bread while it's fresh. I've already fed Dizzy."

"You're exhausting this early in the morning," Shula muttered, aggrieved, and then grimaced as she rubbed at her mouth with her fingers and came away with a long red hair. "Wow. Look, your hair is amazing, I grant you that, but could we have some sort of a compromise about that? A mouthful of *that* before breakfast is hardly an ideal situation."

"Sorry. I'll braid it tonight. I'm just not used to..."

"Fine," Shula interrupted, not wanting too much emphasis on the hair which she had just remembered she had lopped off a lock of without asking – and the moment to have asked seemed to have comprehensively passed.

The promised sortie to the market didn't go well, at first.

Shula considered making a snarky commentary about Ethelreda's attire. While her shoes were definitely not the kind of fashion statement that Shula's own footwear might have been, they were the least of Ethelreda's problems. The shoes may or may not have been 'wrong', in context, but almost everything else was, for Ethelreda. Her style had always been somewhat eclectic. She was given to wearing shapeless layers of things, handkerchief-hemmed skirts over underskirts which brushed her ankles, gathered peasant blouses or over-tunics in mismatched colors, her hair wild and free over all of that like a cloak. It looked fine in the woods, where she was an elemental spirit in her own domain. In the confines of Shula's condo she looked like a caged wild thing, a bird savagely fluttering her wings against the bars of a cage; and out in the city street she painfully obviously did not belong.

The market was a destination – but the first time Shula even managed to make Ethelreda conquer her uneasiness over leaving the comparative safety of the condo was something of an unmitigated disaster – and the two of them didn't make it very far. The outing lasted for less than ten minutes before Ethelreda started to look like she might bolt for the nearest hole she could pull in after her. Shula had thought it might be better not to bring Dizzy out with them (she had worried about leaving the child alone, but it was only going to be for an hour and Gumby had promised to make sure the human kitten didn't come to harm) but the child's absence only seemed to add fuel to the fire of Ethelreda's anxiety. So Shula gave up on the idea of simply throwing the metropolis and Ethelreda at one another and figured she'd better do this in incremental pieces. The day after the first catastrophic foray into the city Shula packed up the baby as well as the skittish country witch and headed through the crowded streets with the clear aim of one of the city parks. It was far from being Ethelreda's beloved woods, but there were trees there, and grass, and it seemed to work a little better as Ethelreda visibly allowed some of the tension to leave her shoulders as she stepped onto unpaved ground.

"Can't I just stay here...?" Ethelreda said, half joking and half pleading, when the time came for them to leave the sanctuary of the park.

Sounds like a wonderful idea, Gumby opined, rooting around in the bushes.

"There's laws against people just dossing down on a park bench," Shula said to Ethelreda, ignoring her feisty familiar. "It won't go anywhere. Promise. And really, my place isn't *that* bad..."

They made other stabs at it, but the city and Ethelreda didn't much like one another. Every city noise that Shula just took for granted – the distant roar of traffic, the occasional faint ululation of a siren, people's voices, occasional bursts of music or the battle scream of a feral alley cat – seemed to work on Ethelreda's nerves; she was constantly flinching at every new assault. Out on her rare forays onto the streets, her nose had wrinkled continuously over fresh insults at every turn – car emissions, the faint whiff of garbage or the occasional suspicion of urine, the inescapable ever-present smell of *crowd*. Shula had tried to herd her unwilling house guest – with a degree of malice aforethought, to be sure – into the subway at one time, but Ethelreda had not come out of the experiment all that well. The barred owl that was Ethelreda's own familiar, which had come with her to the city and had taken up a favoured perch out on the penthouse balcony, seemed to adjust far better to the new living quarters than Ethelreda herself did – but the bird balked at going underground at all, and Ethelreda didn't respond well to that. After the second attempt, when she'd had to help Ethelreda up the steps and back out onto the streets while the red-headed woman was all but hyperventilating and fighting back tears, Shula gave up. Ethelreda could handle cabs – and so it was either that, or walking. The city threw Ethelreda into a constant state of simmering anxiety, and it was only Dizzy seemed to be able to bring her out of it – the baby's delighted gurgle at some new stimulus could bring a smile to Ethelreda's own face almost instantly, to the point that Shula wondered with no small sense of exasperation if she should just tape that gurgle and play it back at Ethelreda every time the city threw her a curve that she couldn't handle.

But it was food that ultimately made Ethelreda call a truce with the city.

Ethelreda was nothing if not a foodie – she was a magnificent cook, herself, but it was mostly traditional stuff that she had always made, had learned how to make at her own mother's knee. The city opened up a whole a new world to her. When they finally made it to Ethelreda's first ethnic restaurant, a Thai place which was conveniently just on the corner of the road where Shula's condo was, Shula could literally see Ethelreda's nostrils widen as they walked in through the door, and her head come up like that of a bloodhound which had finally found an interesting scent.

"What *is* that spice?" Ethelreda asked breathlessly.

"There's probably half a dozen," Shula said, pleased that she had got a reaction that wasn't a recoil.

"Two?" a young Thai woman inquired pleasantly as they hovered by the entrance waiting to be seated, gathering up a couple of menus. And then, glancing down at Shula's feet, gave a tiny polite frown. "I'm sorry, but we can't allow..."

"It's a service animal," Shula said resignedly, following that disapproving glance to where Gumby the familiar, a creature which had attached itself to her with unbreakable bonds and whom she couldn't shake for long, who apparently had a choice about when he could be seen by other people but who chose to exercise that choice in a manner which brought maximum inconvenience to Shula, sat next to her foot with an air of completely entitled self-confidence.

"But it's a..."

"It's a service dog," Shula said grimly. "He's a mix of... of... Lhasa Apso, Papillon, and... and Border Collie."

The Thai hostess tried one more time. "Shouldn't a service animal be clearly..."

"Miss, my friend needs him. He's trained to prevent... anxiety attacks."

"Sure, blame me," Ethelreda said, grinning, just loud enough for Shula to hear.

"You want to eat? Zip it," Shula growled, giving Gumby, who gave every impression of not caring at all, the blackest of scowls. The skunk got a couple of startled and even panicked glances as he stalked elegantly into the restaurant at Shula's side, but then deigned to climb under the table and out of sight and most people promptly forgot about him. So did Ethelreda, as she got her hands on the menu and scanned it with a rising sense of excitement and anticipation.

"You ain't seen nothing yet," Shula muttered, ridiculously pleased at the success of the restaurant at making Ethelreda forget her instinctive recoil from the city while she was immersed in the new scents and tastes of the place.

It remained her comfort stop, as her first sanctuary from the encroaching urban menace she was so ill-equipped to deal with, but Shula had sensed a winner and had taken it further from there. They went to restaurants featuring Mexican, other South American, Japanese, Chinese, Bulgarian, Mongolian, Ethiopian, Moroccan, and various venues that practised different incarnations of fusion cuisine – and Ethelreda, quite literally, ate it up. She figured out how to search out ethnic recipes from the Internet and made stacks of printouts of them, ostensibly to take back home to her woods to try out, although Shula had trenchant opinions about just where out in her isolated woods she would be able to find access to some of the more exotic bits and pieces that would be required. But it was this that finally broke Ethelreda's resistance to plunging into the innards of the city, and

Shula couldn't find enough ethnic stores and marketplaces fast enough for Ethelreda to explore.

"And what's this?" Ethelreda would exclaim, homing in on some exotic fruit that Shula didn't even have a name for. "What do you do with it?"

"What do you use this one in? Or that one?" she's ask, sniffing over bulk bins of turmeric or cardamom.

There was only one time when they'd had to flee a market because of an avoidable disaster, and that wasn't even Ethelreda's fault. It was a sudden and inimitable whiff of *skunk* that made both women rear back in consternation while people around them began to gag and flee. Gumby, of course, had chosen *not* to make himself visible at that particular point, and Shula couldn't even find him to yell at him until the apologetic-looking skunk re-materialised next to Shula's ankle after they had made their escape.

"What the hell just happened in there?" Shula demanded.

Sorry. A rat got fresh. It won't happen again.

"It better not," Shula muttered. "You do this in the condo and I'll let Ethelreda *cook* you."

The food markets had proved to be a lifeline for Ethelreda. She'd bear down at a demonstration booth where someone would cheerfully be handing out samples of anything that was unfamiliar to her, and would sometimes unwittingly swallow large gulps of something spicy enough to have demanded sips rather than mouthfuls, leaving her standing there gasping for air and turning almost the colour of her hair; she would buy up quantities of things that Shula would have sworn were incompatible enough to blow up a kitchen if they were ever used in the same recipe; she came out of second-hand bookstores at the backs of the food markets with armfuls of cookbooks with recipes from Mali and Ethiopia, South-east Asia, Japan, and various locales in South America or the Pacific Islands.

Ethelreda was still skittish about city life, but food had opened a door for her, let her become a part of something new and wholly unfamiliar. Shula still occasionally had trouble getting past the city phobias long enough to plan a 'family' outing somewhere – but did have to admit that, on the nights they stayed in and Ethelreda cooked, she had never eaten so well.

❧

Shula was a thoroughly modern witch who actually dabbled at being employed – on a freelance basis, to be sure, and she made sure that she was paid well for it – and while the six month absences from the city as the twice-promised Dizzy's childhood unspooled were not insurmountable it was perhaps only a matter of time before the two obligations did collide.

Shula would have never thought that she would think that way, given her initial feelings about diaper changing and the very young baby's endless cycle of physical needs, but she quickly came to remember those times as being relatively easy – at least she could put down the child and know that she could find her there again when she went looking. The baby became a curious crawler, and then a toddler, and then a distracting if endearing babbler who could be counted on to shatter Shula's concentration on her work at the worst moments or require Ethelreda to drop everything and run to remove exploring little hands from things too hot or too sharp to investigate. Ethelreda's owl didn't show much of an interest in the baby but Gumby became something of a beloved and long-suffering baby sitter.

Both women had become increasingly aware of Dizzy's eventual destiny and obligations, and each in her own way had begun to shape the child into what might be needed for their own particular vision. Dizzy was still very young and malleable but that wasn't going to be the case forever. There were choices which would have to be made, and they loomed ever larger as Dizzy grew older.

In the city half-year which just preceded Dizzy's sixth birthday Shula battled valiantly to put to bed a particularly enormous project, but although she kept punching at it with increasing frustration until the last possible moment she finally had to admit defeat and tell Ethelreda she needed an extension in the city – just long enough to meet her contractual obligations. She had adapted as much as she could but there were certain things she simply couldn't accomplish outside the city, and her joint-custody duties as laid down by Baba Yaga fiat simply had to be postponed for a little while.

But Ethelreda was nothing if not nonplussed when informed, the day before their planned move back to the cottage, that Shula would not be accompanying her and Dizzy the next morning.

"What do you mean, you can't come? It's my time," Ethelreda said, mid-motion in her packing, as Shula announced that she wouldn't be travelling back to the house in the forest with them on the next day.

"There's a job," Shula said. Patiently enough. "It won't be long, but it needs finishing up and I cannot do that in your isolated little kingdom. That house of yours would implode if you ever got the Internet going there. I'm sorry, Ethelreda, you're going to have to muddle through on your own with Dizzy for the next couple of weeks. It shouldn't take any longer than that."

"Couple of *weeks?*" Ethelreda echoed, dismayed. More dismayed, in fact, than she had thought she had any right being. "Dizzy will..."

"Dizzy will be *fine*," Shula said. "It's been years since she's needed her diapers changed twenty seven times a day."

"She never..."

"Oh, E," said Shula. "You'll never get sarcasm, will you? Take Gumby back with you, too. I'll just throw together a suitcase and come down as soon as I can."

Gumby turned a jaundiced bright eye on Shula.

Where you go I go, the skunk reminded her.

"I'm not going to have time," Shula said. "Go on, go home. I'll be there as soon as I can."

Home is where you are.

Ethelreda let it go, for the moment, but came into Shula's office later that evening, and hovered in the doorway until Shula looked up from her computer in no small exasperation.

"What is it?" she asked.

"We need to start thinking about Dizzy's education," Ethelreda said.

"What, you're starting that conversation *now?* And anyway... you haven't been teaching her stuff already?" Shula said, pushing her wheeled office chair away from the cluttered desk to look up at

Ethelreda in her accustomed position of leaning against the doorjamb.

"Of course I have. And don't you think I haven't noticed that you have too. And she knows, too – she's going to be six in a couple of weeks and she isn't a baby any more. But that's just it – *you*'ve been teaching her things, and *I* have been teaching her other things, and some of those things cancel out and some grow into something neither of us thought we were teaching her at all and in the meantime we have to start covering stuff that neither of us has been dealing with."

"What? You mean reading writing and arithmetic?"

"She can read already," Ethelreda said with asperity. "She's been able to for years."

"I know. I taught her to."

"No, *I* taught her... never mind. What I mean is, should she be in – I don't know – school or something? Just what is it that we are teaching her to *be*, exactly?"

"We've actually never talked about any of our original plans, have we?" Shula said, digging her fingers into her hair. "Back when we first bargained for her..."

"So what did you intend to do with her?"

"Some day, she was going to replace me," Shula said quietly. "My particular order... is maintained by – I don't know – mandatory replacement. We are an organism, with every one of us playing a part. When it is my turn to go... I am supposed to have a trained replacement to take my place. That's what I want. That's what I needed from her. That's the sort of stuff that I have begun to teach her."

"And same here," Ethelreda said. "I am not of an order – I am more of a solitary – but that cottage.... It needs an heir..."

"So how did you get it?"

Ethelreda shrugged. "My first memories are of that place," she said. "If I was anything or anyone else, anyone other, before then, I have no way of knowing. Why, what did you think I wanted with Dizzy?"

"According to some or the tales the predecessors in the gingerbread house weren't averse to *eating* the children," Shula said.

She regretted it immediately because she saw the hurt that flashed in Ethelreda's eyes. She even began to apologize, but Ethelreda made a small sharp gesture that withered her words away into silence and turned to leave.

"We'll be gone in the morning," she said. "You can follow. When you are able. That's the contract, until she's eighteen. We're all bound by it."

Shula prepared to follow Ethelreda and Dizzy out to the woods five days later, having worked herself almost round the clock in order to put her project away, inexplicably bad-tempered and out of sorts over the less than a full week that she was alone. It was hard to fathom the fact that she wanted to leave the city where she belonged so completely in order to re-bury herself in the "gingerbread cottage" world that she had professed to despise so, but it was impossible to ignore the feeling that was almost anticipation with which she made the final rounds of her condo, preparing to abandon it for another six months of her life according to the terms of the ill-thought-through agreement that had landed them all in this mess. When she caught a glimpse of Gumby the skunk out of the corner of her eye in the first moment she thought she had conjured the image out of a sense of actually having *missed* the beast, as unlikely as that might have sounded to her only a very short while before. But she blinked, and looked again, and although it immediately became obvious that what she was seeing was just the equivalent of a holographic projection – edges wavering and undefined – rather than the real thing, the presence was real enough.

You are needed.

That, and no more. The apparition faded away, like a skunky Cheshire Cat, leaving behind only the afterimage of a luxuriant black-and-white tail.

Shula gathered up her keys, swept up the packed bag waiting beside her front door, and swiftly left the condo, barely taking the time to lock the door behind her.

A sense of urgency and a need for speed literally earned her a traffic stop from a zealous traffic cop who issued a citation – but Shula knew she could make that go away with the appropriate action and paid very little attention to it, continuing to drive at speed after impatiently waiting for him to finish up with the paperwork. The gravel road which turned off into the woods in the direction of the cottage, something that she herself had caused to occur in this untouched forest only after she had need of one for vehicular access to the property, seemed to have lengthened in the six months that Shula had been away; there were twists and curves she could have sworn had never been there before and it took an age before Ethelreda's cottage hove into view. Shula all but fell out of the car, leaving the keys in the ignition, and raced to the house – the door was unlocked, as it always was, and the place was empty. But she glanced out of the kitchen window and caught a glimpse Gumby hovering at the forest's edge – and, without a thought, followed.

She saw Dizzy before she saw Ethelreda – the girl was crouched beside a gnarled old tree, gently teasing a handful of mushrooms from the ground and into a basket she carried. But that was all she had time to see before the sparse underbrush seemed to gather itself against her. A vine snaked up to wrap itself around her ankle and then twist up her leg; a low-hanging branch stirred as if in a heavy wind and swung back towards her, with the apparent idea of knocking her head from her shoulders; a ragged handful of something that looked like poison ivy gathered itself together and reached for her.

Shula barely had time to take a breath and begin to utter a word of defensive power before the foliage all decided to abandon the attack on its own and fell away from her. She shook off the vine with a gesture that was part annoyance and part disgust, and while so engaged heard a step behind her; she whirled, ready to do battle, and relaxed only as she recognized the loose red hair falling about her companion's shoulders.

"Sorry," Ethelreda said. "I didn't know it was you."

"Who were you expecting?!" Shula said, brushing the rest of the vine off her leg and eyeing the poison ivy with a malicious glare.

Ethelreda hesitated. "I... there are things you don't know. About this place. About what it truly means – about how I belong to it, how it belongs to me..."

The two of them had never, perhaps out of nothing more than a misplaced sense of loyalty to their own brands of craft, discussed the fine details of their own natures, and their own particular means of practicing their vocations. They had wrapped their lives around the shared child – they had lived with one another, each sharing her home and (for years now) the same bed every night – but there were still secrets between them, and it was with an unexpected stab of hurt that Shula realized this as Ethelreda spoke. But she reacted with her usual defensive weapons, snark and sarcasm, hiding the soft spot that had been bared for just a moment.

"*Do* tell," Shula said sharply. "But can we do this without siccing the whole entire natural world against me? I have a hard enough time with this jungle as it is. I came as fast as I could. Gumby said I was needed..."

"*Gumby?*" Ethelreda echoed, looking startled. "But Gumby didn't... I mean..."

"Shu-ma! You're here!"

Dizzy, who had finally realized that Shula was there, had abandoned her mushroom-gathering activities and barreled into her with a hug. Shula slipped an arm around the girl's shoulders while mouthing *Later!* at Ethelreda over the top of Dizzy's tousled head.

'Later' came around after they'd all had dinner, played a board game with Dizzy, and then tucked her into bed, against her objections.

"But you only just *got* here," Dizzy sulked, being marched off towards her bedroom by Shula after she had tried one trick too many to extend her time up with the two of them. "E-ma lets me stay..."

"High time I came back then," Shula said firmly, her hands on Dizzy's shoulders refusing to yield to Dizzy's petulant squirming. "Bed. Tomorrow is a whole other day."

"Not fair," Dizzy said, fighting back a sudden huge yawn. "Gumby wouldn't let me go into the woods and get shrooms by myself, before, and now you don't want to..."

"Life isn't fair, baby girl. Go to sleep."

Dizzy grumbled some more as Shula was closing the door to her room on her way back out to the sitting room, but raised no real objections.

Sitting back in matching armchairs in front of a fire lit in Ethelreda's large homely hearth, nursing matching goblets of golden wine, the two women shared a long silence before Shula finally said, "Well...? Dizzy said Gumby wouldn't let her go into the woods alone – *Gumby* wouldn't – you have to admit that's hardly normal. What's been going on here?"

Ethelreda sighed deeply. "Look, when I told you why I needed Dizzy, why I claimed her, it's... not quite that simple." she said. "It's... this place... this house... it kind of claims you. It doesn't belong to you so much as you belong to it. You're – it's – I don't know. It's a kind of symbiosis."

"I know *that*," Shula said. "There's an attachment which I honestly thought was extreme, when I first met you. When you first came to the city – when Dizzy was just a baby – I thought you'd sicken from it. It was hard to find enough things to distract you, to make you forget even for a little while that you were *there* and not *here*. But what has that to do with my being needed? That was the case long before either Dizzy or I came on the scene."

"Your order functions on replacement, you said. Well, no less so this place. Dizzy was supposed to inherit it... and everything that goes with it. And it really does go deeper than you know. This entire forest – not just the house – even that road you made happen was an insult to the whole, and the wood barely tolerates it. It keeps changing it..."

"I know," Shula said again. "Now tell me something I *don't* know. What's going on?"

"There were two of us," Ethelreda said faintly.

"Sorry, I need more than that," Shula said after a moment. "Two what?"

"Me... and another," Ethelreda said. "The woman I called Mother – the one who is to me what I am to Dizzy, who came before me in this place – to this day I don't know why. Or which of us came first. Or which of us she thought was the wrong choice, and needed a plan be. The land bonds to the one who takes this place – but there were two of us, and only one of us could win. And I..."

"Win? Win what? Come on, E, this is me. Stop telling me fairy stories and just tell me the truth."

Ethelreda put her wine down and twisted her hands together in her lap. She would not look up to meet Shula's eyes.

"You've always thought that I was just... I don't know... fluff. Living out here, in this house, in these woods, standing knee-deep in earth magic – you've called me hedge witch before, and you weren't being kind when you said it..."

"You called me hedge fund witch right back and you weren't being kind either," Shula said. "But you're changing the subject."

"No, not really. You meant – pretty, sweet, selfish, wrapped up in my own world, the kind that has singing mice help to cook the dinner and clean the house. Admit it."

"A little," Shula said with a half-smile. "Okay, a little. So what's that got to..."

"You always thought it all just – came that way – that things just fell into my lap, that I was always, I don't know, entitled. You know – how you always had to fight for everything, and I had it all handed to me – "

"All *right*," Shula said sharply. "I acknowledge my faults. Now spill it. The stuff you aren't telling me."

"There were two of us," Ethelreda said at last, again, repeating her earlier words. And then, taking a deep breath, lifted her eyes to lock her gaze with Shula's. "I told you that all I remember was this place. That's true. But there was always... another here, too. The woman whom I called my mother, she had two of us here, in this wood. Call us Snow White and Rose Red, if you want – we were raised as sisters, although I have no doubt we came from vastly different places. I am..." Ethelreda made a gesture at herself, at her buxom body, her wild red hair. "I was the red sister, the wood-girl, always out there with animals and birds and trees and mushrooms and wild forest strawberries. She... she was white, all white, tall and thin and bony and pale pale pale and she had her own dreams and visions. And you see... there could be only one of us, here, after Mother died.. That's the way things work. Only one witch in this cottage, and these woods. And it was *I* who had the connection with the wood, by that stage, it was me that the woods chose."

"And what happened to this other one?"

"We... fought. She left. She had to leave. Because the wood was mine. But a *little* of the wood was hers. Will always be hers. She grew up here, same as I did, and that counts for something..."

"You drove her away?"

"I should have killed her," Ethelreda whispered, hanging her head so that her red hair spilled forward, hiding her face. "But I couldn't. There had been – we were raised as sisters, even if we were never truly meant to be – and I couldn't just kill her. I couldn't do it. But I exiled her – when I won – when the wood took my side – and in some ways it was worse – because we were both half-bonded anyway – and then she had to leave – but there was a loss of power, with the loss of being bound to the land, and I thought it would be okay – except that now..."

Shula frowned. "Wait. Let me see if I have this straight, There were two of you in this cottage and you fought a duel. You won, but didn't take it to a practical conclusion and now the one who lost is back and being a problem?"

Ethelreda glanced up, with a ghost of a smile. "Oh, you make it sound so *simple*."

"Well, isn't it?"

"No," Ethelreda said faintly. "You see... she has drawn new power. From somewhere. And now she wants... *this*...back."

"Correct me if I'm wrong but if you leave here permanently you're likely to just fade away, aren't you?" Shula said. "This other... she knows this?"

"Oh yes," Ethelreda said.

"But she'll take it anyway."

"This land... it's more valuable than you ever gave it credit," Ethelreda said.

"I don't care about *that*," Shula said briskly. "I care about what its loss would do. Why is she suddenly back...?"

"She tried to take Dizzy," Ethelreda said, her shoulders stiffening. "That's why the woods attacked you. I set up booby traps, for anyone who came near Dizzy. I was protecting..."

"Wait. Dizzy... is your continuing bond? Your heir? The one who is supposed to pick up your connection to this place, after you? So you've already started to pass it on to her – she's already started to form the attachment...?"

"But it's at a critical stage," Ethelreda said. "And if she's taken, the connection can be transferred. And then she'll have it too. My sister. And there can only be blood, after."

"She's been here? To this house? Recently?"

"Oh yes," Ethelreda said. "And she hovers, still. It's all I can do to keep her at bay, at an arm's length."

"Is she open to negotiations? I want to talk to her," Shula said, after a moment of silence in which she seemed to come to some hard-won conclusion. "Can you arrange that?"

Ethelreda gave her a strange look. "All I would have to do is drop the wards..."

"Do it," Shula said abruptly, setting aside her goblet. "Do it now."

"Dizzy..."

"Has both of us to protect her," Shula said, her expression grimly determined. "Bring this... other. Bring her."

Ethelreda hesitated, but only for an instant, for as long as it took to meet Shula's eyes and hold her gaze, exchange an understanding. Then she sighed, and bowed her head again, her hand falling away from her cup and making the tiniest of gestures.

It didn't take long. First Gumby manifested in the room, fur all on end, trying to make the small shape as large and threatening as possible – and then, in a shimmer of light, another form did. A woman wearing ice-white from crown to the pointed toes of her shoes, her long pale hair floating around her as though she were standing in a draft of cool air that nobody else could feel. She smiled, seeing Ethelreda and Shula sitting together, and her teeth were white also, almost sparkling.

"We haven't been introduced," the white witch said, her voice breathy and high-pitched like a young girl's.

"We don't need to be," Shula said. "You already know my name because you know Ethelreda's story, because you know of the child and how this came to be. But we both know of the power of a name freely offered and that isn't happening. You won't get mine from me. But I do have a proposal for you."

"*You* do?" the white witch said. "Interesting. Go on."

Shula carefully put down her half-full goblet at her feet and came to her feet. Her hands had been empty as she moved but even as she completed the rise she was holding something, dangling from her fingertips.

"I'll trade you," she said. "This is the key to my abode in the city. It is yours, and everything in it save for the things that do not belong to me but to my order which you will need to release to them, and one personal item of my choice which I can remove from the premises before you take possession. The place is imbued with my own brand of magic, and keyed to me, but I am willing to release that to you... in exchange for a promise fully and freely given that you will never come near this place again, and never plot harm on anyone who is connected to it. The woman, or the child, or anyone who comes after. You will relinquish all the hold that you have or have ever had on it. In exchange for what I offer, you will vow upon your own true name which only you know that you will do this. And I will make sure Baba Yaga knows of the bargain, and will enforce it if she is called upon to do so, and exact reparations, should you break the vow."

Ethelreda reached out to lay a hand on Shula's arm, but Shula shook her off, not taking her own eyes off the white witch.

"And what use would a suite of rooms in a city be to me?" the white witch said. "With no root to the land, with no power to..."

"Land isn't the only power," Shula said. "I am of an order that belongs more to air than to land but you would be foolish to pit the earth against a wind intent on blowing it away. I will leave a gift of power in this dwelling in exchange for that which you forfeit here."

The white witch considered, her head held at a slight angle, watching the set of Shula's shoulders in the dancing shadows of the firelight. And then her smile broadened, just a little.

"The bargain is made," she said.

"Seven days," Shula said. "I will remove the things my order owns, and I will set foot inside the dwelling only one more time, to retrieve that one personal thing that I will carry out of there. I will leave the keys in the hallway, and the door unlocked to you, and the word of power will be on the threshold for you to claim when you take possession."

"Seven days," the white witch said. "If I find a single thing out of order you will pay the price for it."

"You will not," Shula said. And then, without moving, said a single word to Ethelreda. "Wards."

Ethelreda moved her hand again, whispering a few soft words, and the white witch winked out, leaving the faintest of sparkles behind her as an afterimage before that too dissipated into the shadows.

"What have you done?" Ethelreda said quietly.

"I can always buy another condo," Shula said. "You cannot buy... another one of these."

"It isn't just a condo."

"No," Shula said, reluctantly enough. "She got a fair trade. She got what she valued, though. She wanted power. Not necessarily your power." She finally turned to look at Ethelreda, and in that look were both pity and a cool calculation. "I think you should have killed her, back when you had the chance," she said. "She would have killed you, you know. If she had won. Even I can see that."

"I know," Ethelreda said.

"I would have."

"You like to think so," Ethelreda said, considering the idea but dismissing it.

Shula allowed herself a small smile. "We'll never know, will we?"

"But why? Why do you do this thing? For Dizzy? It was a bad day for you when you made that bargain, you just lost everything that you..."

"Not for Dizzy, you fool," Shula said gently reaching out to let a light, gentle touch flutter down on Ethelreda's shoulder, and then leaning forward to plant a full and lingering kiss on Ethelreda's mouth. "For *you*."

❧

Shula left the cottage again before dawn, and drove back to the city, to the home which she had spent so many years lovingly building into her fortress. The deal had been made but there was still the one thing, the personal thing, that she could take from the place with her. And there was a little bit of work to be done, for that.

She had sent a text on her cellphone as soon as she got into signal range, and one of her sisters from the order was already waiting as she pulled into her spot in the condo parking area.

"Explain?" the woman said, wasting no words.

"A bargain has been made," Shula said.

"Another?"

"Yes. This place... it's a price. I'll lay a full account before the Mother Council and I will take what censure there may be due – but this was freely given away, and I will freely pay any price for that action. For now, I need you to take back and hold for me the Order's property. It needs to cross the threshold by tonight. After that, I will be in touch."

"This is something to do with your contract with the hedge witch, isn't it?"

"I owe," Shula said, economical with her own words because her own words thrown back at her by a member of her order carried the sting that Ethelreda has already felt. Except now it was aimed at herself, as somehow diminished because she had made the choice to be the companion of the hedge witch in question, and it burned more than she had thought it would. And she knew that if she wasn't careful she would defend that contract, the bargain, the relationship, to the point that might damage her standing with her own chosen order.

But Shula's sister-witch didn't hear that shortness or response, or didn't care to respect it. "Over and above what you owe to us?"

"Over and above," Shula said, biting down on her impulse to say something unwise in return. "Come."

There weren't many things to gather, but they were things of power. The black candles used in Shula's work – those were imbued by the Order, and they had to be taken into custody before some other could drain them for other purposes. The four insignificant objects from the four corners of the condo – the small statuette of an African drummer carved from ebony wood, the white king from the chess set laid out on the chess table in the corner of the living room, the amber teardrop hanging from a tarnished chain looped around a hook in the wall, and lastly, the red lacquered box which looked like it might open but was sealed shut, the hidden treasure she retrieved from underneath the stack of towels in the linen cupboard – the wards of the dwelling, laid out and imbued with the power of Shula's order, guarding her abode against intrusion, keyed to Shula herself and specific to this house, to these rooms, useless anywhere else. It was entirely possible that there might have been a way to subvert them, though, and they had to leave the place with Shula, be returned to be shorn of their significance by the people who had imbued them with the power of protection, or destroyed while new wards were made to fit a whole new place of abode.

Shula had lived in this particular dwelling for almost twenty years. She had laid down a lot of power in its walls, strong protection against all manner of attack, a sanctuary against every conceivable possible malicious intent – she was impregnable here, could not be touched, could not be harmed, could not fail at anything she set her hand to from within these walls. She could start again, to be sure – with a different home, different wards, different protections laid down. But all of this – all of what she had already achieved – she had laid down because it was no longer important that she herself – she, alone – was protected. Something new was long overdue to be begun. A place which protected Shula... and the one she loved.

The one personal thing she took from the place, in accordance with the bargain she had made, fit into the pocket of her jacket. The sister-witch had left with all the artefacts she needed to remove from the premises and Shula lingered only long enough to unhook the keys to the front door and the storage unit in the basement and leave them in plain view on a side table in the hall. And the last thing she did, taking care to step outside and stand clear of the threshold before softly and firmly closing the door behind her, was to write three words, in extravagant and almost impossible to read cursive – one on either side of the door and one on the lintel overhead. If one did not know they were there one could easily miss them, especially if one was some-body eager to take possession... someone who wasn't looking up, or to the side, someone who was looking down, looking for the word of power which had been promised.

She wrote that final word on her doorstep, a word of permission and release, allowing the first person to step across it to claim the dwelling it protected. And then she walked away, smiling, without looking back.

❧

"What did you bring out of the place?" Ethelreda asked, when Shula returned to the cottage in the woods.

"Later," Shula said. "I'll show you later."

"It won't be enough," Ethelreda said. "She'll... she'll come back eventually. She'll probably come for us."

"Two things," Shula said. "One, Baba Yaga, like I said. It was a bargain made and sealed. And two... I did leave a little surprise behind."

"You weren't supposed to entrap her," Ethelreda said, rousing. "If you did and Baba Yaga found out that would render the whole bargain..."

"A blessing," Shula said, grinning wolfishly. "A simple blessing. That is all."

"What did you do?"

"There are words," Shula said. "You don't have to know."

"Yes, I do. You said you did it for me."

"*Everything I Need*," Shula said.

"What? What do you need? Here? What are you going to do – "

"You can always teach me to cook," Shula said. "Or to knit. Or even how to weed a garden properly. Or how to make poison ivy dance to your music. But I haven't given up everything – before I left the city I put down a payment for another place. A nice place. It's getting properly warded before I move in there – I have six months to get it all taken care of, and I can always take a sabbatical from the job, if it all takes longer than that. But that wasn't what I meant, not really."

Ethelreda stared at her, brows furrowed. She looked so quizzical and so cross that Shula laughed out loud.

"It's what I wrote," she said, still chuckling. "On the door. *Everything I Need*. It became a binding which she accepted as soon as she stepped over the word of power she was expecting to find on the threshold. She doesn't even know it yet but that place... will become everything she needs, everything she wants. There will come a time that she won't ever see a good reason to leave it again. I locked her inside, without a key. She'll be her own warden, eventually. I don't think you need to worry about her again. And as for me..."

Ethelreda was smiling faintly. "As for you...?"

"Well, when I accepted this particular bargain it was Baba Yaga being obnoxious about things. Which was to be expected. That's what she's supposed to be. But in the years since... that has sort of become true for me, but outside of that other dwelling. Everything I need. It's right here, really."

"I know what you took from the condo," Ethelreda said. "You do know I already have a copy of it, don't you? That it was the seal on the bargain? You said so yourself..."

"You mean the photo? Dizzy, on day one? You and me? I already have a copy of that. I always do. On my phone. But as far as that goes... not the same as yours," Shula said.

"What on earth do you mean?"

"Bring yours. I'll show you."

Ethelreda slipped out of the room and returned with a single photograph in her hand. Shula waited, with her phone in her hand, and gestured to Ethelreda to bring her own copy closer. The two women leaned over the images, side by side, shoulders touching.

"They are the same," Ethelreda murmured. "...Aren't they?"

Shula pointed, without a word.

It was subtle but it was there. The photograph was indeed the same – baby Dizzy propped up against a pillow, with Ethelreda and Shula on either side of her, holding one hand each. But on Ethelreda's photograph she was turned ever so slightly towards the child and the other woman, her expression rather softer than the grim acceptance etched into Shula's features. In Shula's photograph, it was Shula who wore the softer expression, who was slightly turned towards the other two in the picture, and Ethelreda wore the expression of sullen submittal to something imposed upon her. In both pictures the baby stared straight ahead at the camera, an expression that was very nearly a smile upon her chubby as yet unformed features, as though she knew a secret that none of the others were privy to.

"Twice promised," Shula said. "Not *her*. Well, yes, her. But not just her. Us. *All* of us. Look at the pictures. They were supposed to be copies, identical in every way. But in yours, you knew, and in mine, I did. And I needed to bring it back here, to bring them together, at the proper hour, when the time was right. When choices had been made. Because... look, now."

The pictures had blurred, changed, both the electronic image and the one in Ethelreda's hand. Now both women were looking towards one another, lips curving into the ghost of a smile as they looked into each other's eyes. The spell had ripened, the spell each had cast on the other as they laid their hand to this joint enterprise.

"I fell in love," Shula said, smiling at her own image, and at Ethelreda's.

"With her," Ethelreda said, but her voice was dreamy, a smoky faraway quality to it. "With the baby. With the baby you thought you'd just won."

"Yes, of course. But that... became only a part of it."

"You didn't know I existed, before that moment. I didn't know you did. We knew nothing of each other, had nothing in common, no common path, would never have met, had it not been..."

"For the spell. Twice promised. Twice promised, E. Once to her – both you, and me. We took on the child because of our own needs and wants. But then – more than that – because we took her hands and through her touched each other... no, I didn't know you existed, not before that night we took our child home. But I knew then. And I have never not known about it, not for a moment, since. And now this stupid stupid stupid stereotypical gingerbread house...this weird wood, and Gumby ... it's all ... home."

"Well," Ethelreda said after a moment. She hesitated for an instant, but not for too long, and snaked an arm around Shula's narrow waist. "Welcome home, then, at last."

Shula let her own arm fold around Ethelreda, and gave a little squeeze. She thought for a moment about bringing out the lapis lazuli box, showing Ethelreda the only thing she had brought out of her abandoned fortress with her – the lock of red hair she had taken from Ethelreda's head on the first night they had shared a bed together. But then she thought again, and smiled to herself. There would be time, now. There would be time, for everything. Even this.

"I brought a portfolio to work on while I'm here," she said, smiling at Gumby, curled up comfortably in a corner of the room away from the direct heat of the fireplace, and then back up at Ethelreda. At her familiar, and her chosen family. "I'll go unpack properly first, though. Any of those wild mushrooms left? Dizzy will be hungry soon. And when all's said and done, I'm always starving after a good day's work. And we have a happily ever after to begin working on."

aris

Skyring

❧❀❧

The glimmer of artificial light which caught Aris's eye in the gathering twilight proved to be a disappointment. He had been hoping for a larger settlement, a place where he would be more likely to find a replacement for the snapped wire on his harp; a village as small as the one emerging in front of him was rapidly showing itself to be would have no hope of boasting a craftsman capable of doing work that delicate. Still, he would have to find a way to sing for his supper. The motley cloak on his back proclaimed that as his trade.

There did not appear to be an inn or an alehouse in the cluster of houses to which he came, at least not one that proclaimed its identity. Sighing, Aris knocked on the door of the nearest house which had light showing.

It was opened a crack, to present Aris with a being whose face was so seamed with age that it was hard to tell whether he was looking at a man or a woman.

"Good evening," he said, diplomatically omitting any form of gender-based address at all, but making up for it with a gleeman's bow every bit as dramatic as he knew how to make it. "I am a traveller, seeking shelter for the night. My means are few, but I would be happy to share a gleeman's tale or two for a bit of supper and a place by your hearth."

The aged eyes peered at him suspiciously from the doorway.

"Arrrr..." The sound was indeterminate, part-way between a growl and an exclamation of delight. The voice was neither male nor female in timbre, merely aged and cracked to the point of sounding inhuman – the voice of a tree, perhaps, or a granite cliff. Aris was on the point of giving up when the door was opened a crack wider, giving him a glimpse of the whole figure – a largely shapeless form swathed in a mismatched assortment of clothes. Its front may have just looked like it possessed a bosom, being beswaddled into oblivion as it was, but Aris took a chance.

"My good lady..." he began, with another bow.

"Arrrr," it said, motioning him inside.

It – she? – hadn't objected to being addressed as a woman, so Aris kept to that. "I thank you, my lady," he said with fulsome gleeman courtesy.

"Arrrrr..." she said again, and this time there was a genuine pleasure in the sound. Being addressed as a lady was obviously uncommon enough to flatter the crone immensely.

Within, the house proved to be no more than one large room with a beaten-earth floor, and an attempt at privacy being made by curtaining off areas with coarse, home-woven cloth; a half-finished piece of similar material, in fact, still clung to a standing loom leaning against a wall. A large hearth which doubled as a cooking range took up almost an entire wall of the room, and in front of this, on an assortment of homemade furniture, sat the rest of the household, looking up expectantly as Aris stepped inside and instinctively paused by the door, surveying his surroundings with some dismay.

His training kicked in almost immediately, though, and he swept off his hat with another courtly bow. "I am Aris the gleeman," he said, "at your service."

"Lena of Skoura, at yours."

The voice, low and smoky, belonged to a young woman who rose from her seat by the hearth and turned to face him as he entered. Aris had to consciously close his mouth before he could reply to her, and he did not think to do this for a few long moments – she was startlingly unexpected in a place like this, with hair like spun gold and eyes that were the colour of a harvest-born sky. She was of a height with Aris himself, perhaps even a hair taller, and no amount of shapeless clothes could disguise the full bloom of the body they swathed. It was a professional habit for Aris to inspect the hands of the people he met on his travels, since his own were so important for his trade, and Lena's looked like she could play his harp without conscious effort, strong and shapely with long fingers and clean, neatly trimmed nails.

"My lady," he managed at last, and Lena laughed lightly.

"Sir," she said, "your courtesy is greatly appreciated but it has no place here. We are simple folk in this house. But you are a welcome guest, indeed. It is seldom we have company. Will you share our supper?" She indicated the seat she herself had but lately quitted.

Aris demurred at taking her place, but was quickly persuaded; she turned to ladle a thick broth from a simmering cauldron hung over the fire in the hearth, while another young girl, barely more than thirteen or so, took it upon herself to introduce him to the rest of the family.

Lena, it seemed, was the oldest granddaughter of the crone who had opened the door to Aris. Lena's mother, Maira, and a sister named Claine were like enough to each other to be twins; between them they appeared to have bred a clan of daughters – Lena, then Mys, the girl who was making the introductions, and then, decreasing in age, another six girls the youngest of whom sat in Claine's lap silently watching Aris with eyes as blue as Lena's and her thumb very firmly in her mouth.

"Your supper, sir," Lena said, at the conclusion of the round of introductions, presenting Aris with a roughly hewed-off piece of homemade bread, a steaming bowl of broth, and a wooden spoon.

"I thank you," he said. This seemed to be a signal – it appeared that he had interrupted their own supper, for as soon as he started applying himself conscientiously to his meal other bowls appeared magically in the women's hands and for a while there was no more talking. It was Lena who rose again to collect the empty dishes, depositing them into a bucket where stray pieces of food floated on the surface of peat-coloured water. Aris swallowed, and looked away.

"Where are your menfolk?" he enquired, courteously enough, as he lifted out his harp to fulfill his half of the bargain, trying to think desperately of a song or a tale where could avoid the use of the broken harp string.

"Away," Lena said, and the tone of voice was so flat that Aris was startled into glancing up at her face. Her eyes had darkened to storm-cloud gray; this was obviously a subject to be avoided.

Aris pretended that he had not asked the question, and that it had not been answered; the women seemed content to let him do so.

"I will tell you," he began, instinctively shying away from the more 'current news' and harder-edged material in his repertoire, "the story of how the poppies came to bloom in the wheatfields." But with the first chord he tried on his harp he realised that he could not pull off the story of the poppies. There were too many minor chords, and the missing string would destroy him before he was halfway through. He hesitated, casting about for a replacement. "No," he said slowly, " on second thought...."

He looked up again, met Lena's eyes, and started strumming wholly unfamiliar chords on the harp. The tale that came to his tongue that night in the house of women was nothing he had heard anywhere before – a tale of earth and sky, when the world was young. He wove the spell with an instinct that was true; there was a part of him, outside the magic circle, that realised that he himself was under a sort of spell, for this was the first time ever that he had told a tale of his own and not simply retold a known and familiar legend or delivered a piece of news from the previous village where he had performed. Something in him tingled at the thought. *I am a gleeman*, he thought proudly, joyously. *I am a gleeman, and I am telling my own tales... oh, by all the Gods of my fathers!*

They must have been sitting in silence for some time before Aris, swept up by the glory of the night, became aware that he had actually stopped talking. The tale he had told hung before him like a jewel, perfect and faceted, throwing back unexpected gleams at him as though it was catching reflections off the fire on the hearth. It was Lena who spoke first, and her voice threaded through his tale as though it was a part of it.

"You have earned far more than your humble supper tonight," she said.

"You are generous," Aris said.

"No," she said, looking at him with a strange smile playing around the corners of her mouth. "No, I am not. Thank you."

The family murmured largely unintelligible thanks (the old matriarch offered another "Arrrrr!", this time definitely approving) and proceeded to drift off in small groups towards the curtained off areas of the room, the younger girls holding hands as they walked off, turning to smile at him shyly. It was only now that Aris woke up to the possibility of being in a very indelicate situation. He knew the subject of their menfolk had been met with something less than enthusiasm when he had first brought it up, but he felt honour bound to point out to Lena, who had busied herself with preparing him a pallet by the hearth, that his sleeping in this house, a strange man alone with a house-full of women, would not necessarily be an acceptable solution.

"I would not mind," he said, "sharing a warm stable. I am but lately a master; my journeyman years are not long past, and I have seen my share of stables in that time..."

"The house is big enough for all of us," Lena answered firmly.

Aris had his doubts; already he realised that he had carried on holding onto his harp for far more practical reasons than simply a reluctance to put away his first real solo creative effort – it served as an excellent shield for certain things that it were better Lena was not aware of. Aris knew that the knowledge that the ripe body, so ill-concealed by her strange, ragged attire, was upon a pallet a few steps away from his own, would make for at best an uncomfortable if not an absolutely unendurable night. But he did not know how to tell Lena this with delicacy, and so he doomed himself to suffer the consequences, because she finished making up his pallet, dropped him a small curtsey, and retreated behind the nearest homespun curtain.

In the pallid light of the dying fire, the house assumed a brooding silence, almost incompatible with Aris's sure knowledge of the number of occupants sleeping under its roof tonight. He had merely placed his harp beside his pallet, not wrapped it in its coverings, and the delicate metal harp strings seemed to pick up the remaining ember glow and shimmer with it as though with a low humming sound. Lulled by the light and the sound, real or imagined, Aris did what he had thought he would never be able to do that night – he fell asleep.

And dreamed.

Either dreamed, or else he was not asleep at all and this poor house in the isolated village hid more secrets than Aris would have suspected there to be room for behind the homespun curtains in the bare room.

For suddenly the room was enormous, so huge that its walls were lost in darkness, and the roof above him had dissolved into a sparkle of stars in the night sky. He was still on the pallet that Lena had made up for him, covered by his cloak of gleeman motley, but the pallet appeared to be floating on air, and he was caught by a wave of vertigo at the mere thought of peering over the edge of the pallet and checking out this idea. His harp, however, still stood beside him, reflecting the last dying light of a hearthfire no longer there.

A light brush of long fingers across the back of his hand made him sit up quickly, and his breath stopped as he looked upon the vision that had touched him.

It was Lena, but not the homespun-and-rustic Lena with whom he had shared her vegetable broth that night. Her poor rags were gone and in their place she wore a draped gown of shimmering white which concealed nothing of the shape the other garments had only hinted at. Her magnificent hair was floating about her head in a nimbus of gold, and her eyes were again the colour of a sunlit summer sky.

"I have a gift for you, Storyteller," she said, and the voice was the same, so achingly the same that Aris gasped at the pain of it – the pain of knowing that this was the voice he would more than likely wind up searching for in endless women over endless years knowing that the true one which he sought remained forever beyond his reach.

"Who are you?" he managed to ask, and his trained gleeman's voice failed him, the words coming out in no more than a cracked whisper.

She smiled, and the sight of the smile broke his heart. "I am Lena," she said. "Give me your hand."

Aris would have given her the world and everything in it. His hand seemed a small, inconsequential thing to offer instead, but she had asked for that and so he laid his right hand across the cool palm that waited to receive it. He found it hard to capture the feeling of his hand being held by another; it felt, rather, as though it was floating on a cushion of air. But the sensation of a ring being slipped onto his middle finger was very solid – the cool metal almost weighed his hand down with its presence, and as if to bear this out Lena withdrew her own hand from underneath Aris's and the glee-man's hand dropped as though a support had been removed. Lifting it up to inspect the ring that had been placed there, he found a simple gold band with a large blue stone set in it – the same colour as Lena's eyes.

"It is the Skyring," she told him. Her voice suddenly seemed to come from a very long way away, and he could not seem to bring himself to look up and realise that she was no longer beside him. "Look into it, and know its power."

And Aris looked, and the stone looked back at him. He thought fear and the stone changed, becoming purple thundercloud, and reflected back all the nameless terrors of his childhood, the dread of facing his teachers when they sat in judgment on his journeyman status, the apprehension of his first public appearance, the horror of pain and suffering which yet had to be faced because so many of his stories were true and revolved around those things. He thought awe and it changed into a night sky full of stars, and he remembered the first time he had heard a true master play a harp, the first time he had heard a pure trained voice lift a melody up into the heavens. He thought sadness, and the stone responded with the amethyst skies of deep summer twilight, and the memory of his mother's death, and the loss of first love. He thought joy, and the ring blazed scarlet with the flame of passion, with the memory of dawn breaking through clouds heralding a brand new day.

Aris looked into the stone and knew that he could be anything he chose, do anything he chose, merely by wishing for it and seeing it happen in the blue stone.

"Why?" he whispered.

"I am Lena," the voice, more distant than ever, repeated. There was the sound of laughter, far away, and then Aris found himself staring open-eyed into the cold hearth ashes of the house where he had told his tale last night, his harp, dull now in the grey light of early morning, still standing guard beside his pallet.

"Arrrr?"

The old crone's ubiquitous sound had a questioning tone. Aris sat up, wrapping his cloak around him, and the crone nodded at him as she shuffled past and busied herself with lighting the fire. There was no sign of the other women.

"A dream," Aris said, half under his breath. "It was a dream."

And then his hand moved to gather the cloak closer around him, and a ring with a blue stone was on his finger. He gasped, staring; the crone half-turned back to him.

"Where is Lena?" Aris asked her. Her only reply was a blank look. Aris leapt from his pallet, casting all convention aside, and strode to the concealed spaces beyond the homespun curtains.

The room, except for himself and the old woman, was quite empty.

"The other women...?" Aris asked a little desperately. "Where are the others?"

The old crone shook her head with her back still to him. "Arrrrr..."

She had the fire going, and now she shuffled towards him bearing a platter with more of the bread that he had had with the broth the night before, and a small pottery jar which might have contained lard. "Arrr?"

"No," said Aris. "No, thank you, good lady. I think I had better be on my way..."

He was thoroughly spooked; he had been almost convinced that the ring put on his hand by such unconventional means would never come off again but in fact it slipped on and off his finger easily as he twisted it with the fingers of his other hand. He knew of its power; he also knew – somehow – that it was tuned to him alone, and that to anyone else the ring would be a pretty trinket. And the weight of the ring on his hand terrified him.

He left the old crone puzzled and alone in the house, taking to the road as soon as he wrapped his harp to his satisfaction and collected his gear. Walking along the empty country road, alone in the sunshine, Aris recalled with a gleeman's precise and focused memory the sensation he had had when he had shaped his tale in that strange house that night – and knew with all the force of a prophecy that he would never be able to do that again so long as he wore the Skyring on his finger. He would never feel the pure joy again, because he had been handed power, and he would never be sure whether what he crafted was his own, or just something stolen from a magical realm where others could not go.

I will never be a true gleeman while wearing the Skyring, he thought bitterly. *What have you done to me? Do you know how hard it is to cast away power when it has been given into your hand?*

He could be a prince. He could own countries. He could be a wizard that the world would fear. But as long as he did it with the Skyring…. he could no longer be himself, Aris the Gleeman, telling others' tales and his own, knowing that he lived by his wit and no more magic than any human soul could create.

Maybe – if he had been younger, if he had been older – maybe the temptation would have been too hard to resist. But Aris had just had the first taste of his own power, untainted by any magic trick, and he was bitterly reluctant to let that go. Maybe, in a few years, when the world started going colder… maybe then…

The road forked before him as he mused, and he paused to consider his direction. In the actual fork an ancient gnarled tree had rooted itself, looking like it had stood there for hundreds of years and would likely strand for just as long. It was hollow, half-dead, and still it obstinately showed young green on its ancient, grizzled, belichened boughs. Aris found himself smiling as he looked at the tree, tapping his lower lip with his finger. He looked around, almost furtively – the crossroads was deserted. With a quick, apologetic motion he twisted the Skyring off his finger – it caught the sun and sent a last vivid blue gleam of light into his eyes before he swept it out from under the sky and into a deep fold of the ancient tree. He felt it nestle securely in a hollow; almost, almost, his hand closed around it again to take it out, but when he brought the hand out again it was empty. And if there was regret in his mind, he acknowledged it – but his soul felt free, and something in him leapt and took wing into the sunlight.

"Yes," he whispered to himself, "wait for me here. Maybe, one day, I will be back."

He took a fork of the road at random, humming a tune that had claimed possession of his mind. A new tune – his own. He needed to get to a town and get the harp string replaced. He needed to play this tune, to memorise it, to claim it. He needed to prove something to himself.

Many things.

He thought joy, and anticipation, and an edge of pleasurable tension at what was still to come. Back in its dark hiding place, the Skyring glowed blue with it.

Shadowsword

Strangers were rare in this place, perhaps because the locals appeared to believe there could be no sane reason why a traveller would actually *choose* to pass this way. When Aris pushed open the door of the local tavern one cool autumn evening, it was as though the gust of wind and rain he allowed to enter with him had extinguished all conversation and laughter like a candle flame. Under the wary scrutiny of every pair of eyes in the room, Aris stood shaking the damp from his hair, and wondering whether he might yet be forced to seek shelter elsewhere that night. The atmosphere in the inn was hardly welcoming, if not overtly unfriendly. But then a man wearing a long linen apron which might once have been white wiped his hands on it and took a few steps towards the unexpected guest.

"Can I be of service, young sir?"

"A bed for the night, if it be possible... and a bite to eat, perhaps?"

The innkeeper smiled - it was a creaky smile at best, out of practice, but it was a smile. Aris couldn't accuse him of not trying.

"Aye," he said. "Mayhap we could manage that." It sounded as if he had just tried to make a joke. Aris smiled wanly. "The roast's nowt but bones by now — but there's hot broth out in the kitchen. Would that do you for your supper? We're simple folk here."

"Broth will be just fine," Aris said, setting his wet pack and another small package wrapped in oiled leather his precious harp, down by the door.

The innkeeper turned and retired into the kitchen, wasting no further words. Aris slid behind one of the empty tables. The rest of the inn's patrons were still staring at him, some with tankards frozen half between table and lip as if they had seen a wraith and been paralysed by the sight. Aris nodded at them equably, and that seemed to release them - motions were completed, sips taken, and a low murmur of conversation began again. The broth arrived, and Aris sent the innkeeper out again to bring him a tankard of ale of his own, applying himself in the meantime to his supper. But the ale, when it arrived, was not brought by the innkeeper but by one of the men who had been sitting by the hearth - he bore two, one for Aris, one his own.

"May I join you, stranger?"

Aris cocked an eyebrow at him. "If it pleases you," he said.

"Your ale."

"So I see. My thanks."

Aris continued eating. The other sat down, his tankard before him on the table. Aris could feel the intensity of his gaze; it was an almost physical thing, fingers brushing his raised hackles.

Aris cleared his throat, wiping his mouth with the back of his hand. "I am not accustomed," he said mildly, "to supping under such scrutiny, sir. Is there something in which I can be of service to you?"

"You must forgive me," the other said abruptly, looking away, somewhat abashed at the rebuke. "I don't mean to be rude. It's just that people from the wider world do not come to us, and when one does... we...."

"Wonder what he is doing here," Aris finished for him.

The other man suddenly stuck out a calloused hand the size of a small spade. "Erchik," he said. "I am the smith. I suppose I am more used to strangers than most, for even those who do not stop in the village oft-times stop off at the smithy. You have no horse that needs shoeing, stranger?"

"None, Erchik the Smith," said Aris, pushing away the empty bowl. "The name is Aris, Aris the Songmaster. You many have heard...?" The blank look on Erchik's face was answer enough. Aris shrugged. "No matter. A small fame. I travel the roads, sir, singing for my keep where songs are desired, collecting tales for posterity, telling in the next village the legends of the town I just left behind, and the chronicles of both in the hamlet I find waiting down the road. I am something of a vagabond, you see - all I own is in yonder pack, and I only carry a change of clothes and enough coins for a single night's lodging should I find no patron to offer me a bed for the night. The harp beside it is the only possession that I treasure. Horse or beast have I none - that way I am always responsible just for myself."

"So it's tales you collect, is it?"

The question was asked with such a wealth of understanding that Aris narrowed his eyes. "You have one for me?"

"Oh, no," Erchik said complacently. "Not I. The Hero might, perchance."

"The hero?"

"The Hero," Erchik corrected him, re-introducing the capital that Aris had left out of the title when he had said it. "The old man that lives alone at the end of the village, in the small cottage with the wild garden. He hasn't spoken much to a living soul, mind you, but he might well speak to a collector of tales."

"Why is he a hero?... The Hero?..."

"As to that," Erchik said, "it's himself you should be asking. He's been living there in that cottage, alone, for more years now than I care to remember, and nobody in this village remembers any other name for him but that - The Hero. He seems to have no family, and few enough friends, though the good innkeeper's wife occasionally takes him a meal from the tavern. He's never seen about in the daytime - when he goes out at all, which is rare indeed, he chooses twilight and hides in the shadows, and even then folks are never sure that they have seen him pass by. The Hero? I grant you, it sounds like a strange name for a man like that. Perhaps he knows why he owns it, for I surely don't." He leaned closer in a conspiratorial manner. "That's why you're here, isn't it? You've heard of our Hero, and you're here to collect his tale. Come to think of it, maybe I *have* heard of you before somewhere. Perhaps it was one of my customers who stopped to shoe a horse that told me."

Aris had been about to disavow any such intentions, but the sop of being known and spoken of on the roads stopped his mouth and he merely smiled. But his curiosity was thoroughly piqued, and if he had thought himself exhausted enough to go up to the room the innkeeper showed him after his supper and do nothing more strenuous than simply throw himself upon the bed and sleep, he soon discovered that the vision planted in his mind would not let his body rest. Eventually, after tossing sleeplessly for the better part of an hour, he gave in. He rose resignedly, reached for the damp cloak he had draped across the back of the chair to dry, and let himself out into the wet autumn night again.

The lights were still on in the cottage with the wild garden. But it was getting late, and Aris stood there in the rain, irresolute, not so sure now that he was here that this had been such a good idea after all. But even as he hesitated the door was opened with a creak. An old man stood there, hair and beard quite white but with an unbowed back, peering outside.

"Well, are you going to come in or do you plan to stand there the whole night?" the old man asked testily.

"How did you know I was here?"

"One knows," the old man said. "When one lives alone for so many years, one develops a sense for company." He stepped away from the door. "Well?"

Aris climbed the three shallow steps leading up to the small verandah outside the cottage's front door, paused for a long moment beside his impassive host as he looked into the old man's eyes, and then entered the house he was bidden into, doffing his cap.

"I am..." he began.

"I know who you are," the old man said, shutting the door and dropping the latch back into place. "Or at least I know your ilk." He fingered the motley of Aris's cloak, the unmistakable badge of his profession. The touch was oddly gentle, almost as though the old man was rediscovering something he had lost a long time ago. "The name isn't important to me. Names have ceased to be important... long ago."

"What is yours?" Aris asked.

"I forget," the old man said. "Nobody has called me by it for so long."

"Why do they call you The Hero?"

The old man laughed dryly. "Direct, aren't we. I like that. Well, I am no hero, boy. I can tell you that." There was a blazing fire on the open hearth, a single rocking chair beside it. The old man pointed at it. "Sit."

"But where will you...?"

"Sit, sit," the old man repeated impatiently. "I spend my life sitting, you spend your life walking from place to place. It won't do you any harm to sit by a friendly fire awhile, nor me to pace my own floor." His white eyebrows were bushy and knitted into a solid line above his eyes; when he cocked one towards a niche by the fireplace it seemed as though his entire face rose towards his hair. "There's a cup in there, and some liquor," he said. "I have no use for the stuff, myself - but you young 'uns, you seem to like it, and that's been sitting there for some time, should be nice and mellow. You try it and tell me." He rubbed his mouth. "I haven't really touched that stuff since I quit the roads. I suppose I was afraid."

"Afraid of what?"

"Of a lot of things - but mainly that if I started, I couldn't stop. I tried to forget without its help. It wasn't always easy."

But Aris had caught another phrase, and put it together with the old man's long-fingered hands, his way with words, the manner in which he had handled the cloak of motley. He gazed at the old man over the edge of his cup.

"You were one of us, weren't you?" he said.

The old man's eyes flashed up at him, startlingly dark in the white-ness that framed his face. He looked as though he was about to deny the charge, and then sighed deeply.

"One of the best," he said, and the words did not have the air of a boast.

"You're Alay," Aris said, surging to his feet out of the chair where he had been installed. "You're Alay of Angwin... you've been lost for forty years! The Guild thought you had vanished in the Ophar Moun-tains in that terrible winter when so many died - or that you'd died in the Salarcan War... Why, Alay, for all the Gods' sakes? Why did you disappear? You were mourned, mourned more than you could know, across the breadth of the land..."

"Ha!" said the old man crisply. "While I was alive they couldn't find a kind word. When they thought me dead it was finally safe to say all the fine things they had been holding back for so long, is that it? I don't need that kind of mourning."

"Where have you been all these years? Here?"

"A lot of them," said Alay. "After the mountains, I needed a quiet place... where nobody knew me."

"What mountains?"

"The legend, boy. The legend. I broke a cardinal rule of the gleemen. I believed a legend I told, and went hunting it myself."

"And was so ashamed when you failed," said Aris, suddenly under-standing, "that you found the darkest hole you could to crawl into."

"Are you so sure I failed?" Alay said challengingly.

"Of course," Aris said. "Else you would have been back at the Guildhall making a song of your success. What was it, Alay? Which legend?"

"Once," Alay began, his voice lapsing into bardic sing-song, "once in a hundred years, it is said, a golden moon rises above the triple peaks of Asphorel. There is a secret valley in the mountains; the road to it lies hidden for all the hundred years, but when the golden moon shines, it is open for those who know where to seek it. If a man should find the road to the valley of Asphorel on the night of the golden moon, he should seek the place where the shadows of the triple peaks become one, and sleep the night beside the fire he builds on that spot. And when he awakes, he should rise and hunt the creature whose tracks he discovers in the cold ashes of the morning. Where he finds and kills that creature, there should he dig in the ground a hole three times his own height. If he does all this then will he be rewarded, for he will lift from the bowels of the earth where it has been kept hidden for so long Ondur Caras - Skysword, the sword of Gods and heroes."

"The Skysword," Aris breathed. "You went looking for the Skysword?"

"I was in the foothills of the Asphorel," Alay said in his normal voice, "when a golden moon rose one night, and lighted a path I had not known was there."

"Is it true?" Aris asked, his eyes ablaze. "Did you find the valley?"

"I found the place where the shadows of Asphorel's peaks were made one in the light of the golden moon. I built a fire there, and slept beside it."

"And in the morning...?"

Alay turned away and bent his head, staring into the fire. "In the morning," he said, "there were no tracks in the ashes... except my own."

"What did you do?" Aris asked softly after a beat of silence.

"I took my dagger," said Alay, "and I buried it to the hilt in the ground where the heart would have been in the long shadow that stretched from my feet."

"And then?"

"And then I dug into the ground."

There was something in the old man's face - no, his eyes - that was strange. Aris narrowed his eyes, trying to focus, to pin it down - and then he realised that Alay's eyes were dark with a darkness not their own. That there was no reflection of the leaping flames in them as there would have been in his own if he'd been standing over the fire, leaning on the mantelpiece, as Alay was now doing.

Everything in this cottage, lit only by the flickering fire on the hearth and a single small lamp, had a long, trembling shadow stretched out behind it... except Alay.

Aris raised a white face to Alay.

"What have you done...?"

"I won the sword," Alay said huskily. "In a way."

He turned away and rummaged in an iron-bound wooden chest which stood beside the fireplace, emerging a few moments later with a long, disreputable-looking package wrapped in a tangle of old rags beneath which Aris could glimpse the gleam of silk and the unmistakable shape of a sword.

"I won the sword," Alay said, "but I cannot touch it."

"You are holding it," Aris said uncomprehendingly.

Alay shook his head. "No. Watch."

He unwrapped the package, and Aris saw... nothing.

"Alay," he said gently, "there is nothing there."

For answer, the old man simply reached out and took Aris's hand, placing it gently down on what seemed to be empty silk - and Aris jerked it back as though burned when he felt it rest on empty air... shaped like the pommel of a sword.

"It was shadow that I killed to gain it," Alay said, "and shadow it has been to me ever since. I can see it, but not touch it without this silk between my hand and the blade - it was only by wrapping it in my cloak that I was able to take it from its resting place." Only now, thus warned, did Aris recognise the outer wrapping of the sword of shadow - it was the remnants of a gleeman's cloak, twin to his own. He shuddered.

"You, on the other hand," Alay continued softly, "can't see it... but to you it is as solid as a real sword. I killed my soul and bartered away a life I loved because of this thing - and now I am its prisoner. My shadow lies pinned through the heart in a hidden valley under Asphorel. Men would burn me for a warlock if they saw me walk the world without a shadow. So I stay in this house and cling to the shadows of twilight, and they think I am a Hero." His mouth quirked in an ironic smile. "What a tale it would make."

"Tell it!" said Aris, rising again from the chair into which he had subsided. "Come with me, come to the Halls, come, tell it! It is yours, no other tongue..."

"I am dead!" the old man said harshly. Then his eyes and voice both softened as the younger man recoiled from him. "I am dead. But you... you are young. You have a future out there. I give you leave - spin the tale that you will. Make your own name. A name that will make the name of Alay pale..."

"But you..."

"I," said the old man, "will do what is necessary. Do you wish to take the sword?"

"No!" cried Aris, snatching his hands away.

Alay smiled. "Probably wise. Very well. I will deal with the matter. And you... you can do what it is not given to many to achieve. You can start a new legend."

"What?" Aris said numbly.

"Look for the Skysword, those who dare," the old man said, his voice back into the sing-song of the gleeman's chant. "Search for a shape of shadow and air. Know that the Skysword is to be found... where its last Keeper shadowless lies in the ground."

Without knowing how he had got there, Aris found himself standing in the doorway of the cottage, his still-damp cloak over his shoulders. The weather had worsened; behind him, the world quailed beneath the scream of the wind and the lash of torrential rain. But inside the cottage a silence reigned, the silence into which legends are born. A shadow in the shape of a cross burned black and sharp against the far wall, and a man with no shadow at all held thin air suspended above him for a moment, wrapped in ragged silk so that his hands could touch it − before turning the invisible sword in his hands and falling upon it, plunging the blade that was air and darkness into his breast. The shadow of the sword and the body of the man merged, twisted, tangled, rolled into one; the fire guttered, and suddenly died. And in the stormy night Aris turned and fled, running from the cottage in superstitious dread, waiting for the Gods to strike him from behind for laying impious eyes on too holy a mystery.

He left a silver piece on the pillow of the room he had not slept in when he returned to the village inn, shouldered his pack and harp, and crept out into the night again like a thief. On the way, beside the path he took out of the village, the lights burned in Erchik's smithy; Aris bowed his head and passed by. He was a gleeman with a tale to tell – and he knew that tales were best told otherwhere than the place where they had begun.

And there would be another village down the road, just like this one, like a hundred others. But the one he was leaving...

The one he left behind was already changing – from a forgotten hamlet on the side of the road to nowhere to a crossroads where all roads met. It did not know it yet.

Hourglass

I could get RICH in Ghulkit!
Prove it...

Aris cursed the cosy inn whose potent ale had made him utter that boast and then have his bluff called. Wyn and Allyc, the two fellow gleemen who had provoked his words, were at this moment no doubt ensconced beside another warm fire in some congenial hostelry, nursing mulled wine and laughing quietly over Aris's stubborn insistence to honour the rash boast he had made.

Spend a winter in Ghulkit, come back with wealth, and he could return and spend many a satisfying evening telling avid listeners across the length and breadth of all the Kingdoms how one gleeman had dared to defy almost impossible odds. He would get rich in Ghulkit, and then get rich all over again telling stories of Ghulkit in the tame lands afterwards. No other gleeman could compete....

Aris allowed himself a grim smile as he struggled through the snow-drifts on the lonely back road. Spend a winter in Ghulkit. He should have known there was a good reason why people did not do this. He had already found out − the hard way − that if he was not totally focused on the road he was travelling he could find himself mired in innocent-looking snow banks which were hip-deep or worse. At least once he nearly lost his harp in the drifts; and even without that, he could almost physically feel the effects of the killing cold on the fragile instrument. Whenever he gained some sort of sanctuary and obtained a spot to ply his trade, he would have to thaw out the harp for half an hour or more before he could usefully employ the instrument to assist him in the simplest of songs.

This day was worse than many a day before it, because often the cold would be ameliorated by a thin and watery kind of sunlight which would even manage, weak and etiolated as it was, to render the muffled, frost-sparkling landscape beautiful in Aris's sight. That, at least, had been a sort of gift – he had composed several songs about the beauty of the snow country – but after a while even that had not been enough to make him forget how *cold* he was. And this morning – this morning it had started snowing. By the time he had hit the road it was not just snowing, it was snowing heavily; he should have stayed another day where he was, at the village where he had been given adequate if not lavish hospitality. But he had thought it a flurry. The locals could have told him it was not, had he thought to ask – but he had not asked. The blizzard had grown steadily worse; in the white light Aris lost all track of time and could not have possibly said if the sun was meant to be overhead or setting. He only knew that he had been walking for hours, that he was on the verge of losing all feeling in his feet, that he could see no further in front of him than the length of his outstretched hand, and that he was in real trouble.

Spend a winter in Ghulkit.

If he was not careful, he was in real danger of spending eternity here.

He could have missed the house by the roadside altogether, so camouflaged was it in the snowdrifts; and in his snow-blanked mind Aris had been focused for so long on just putting one foot in front of another that he would have had considerable trouble recognising even familiar things, let alone something that barely differentiated itself from his frigid environment. But he retained enough wit to pause briefly when he smelled what he thought was smoke; even so, he almost did not see what lay right before him and it was quite probable that he could have shrugged the smoke smell away as a hallucination of his fevered brain and struggled on. But even as he halted, a black hole suddenly yawned in the nearest "snowdrift". It took Aris precious moments to realise that someone had just opened a door.

"Whuh..." he muttered, in a cold-cracked voice, through lips that seemed to have stiffened into icicles.

"You walk to your death, stranger," said another, lighter voice. It sounded very young. "This is not a day for travelling. I have a fire inside. Come."

"Whuhuh... thhhan...thank you," Aris managed to force through chattering teeth.

He allowed himself to be guided through the doorway. When it closed behind him, he found himself in close darkness, and fought a rising panic – but then, a moment later, what appeared to be a heavy curtain was lifted at the far end of the hall and beyond it Aris could see the inviting red glow of a fire. An involuntary sigh escaped him at the sight, and his host chuckled softly at this.

"Come inside," he said. "Let's get you out of those wet clothes."

By the time he was fully in command of his senses, Aris was a little startled to find himself wearing a fur-edged woollen robe, sitting beside a hearth whose sheer size made it look as though it belonged in a king's hall and not some lost and snowbound cottage in the wilds of Ghulkit, and clutching a pewter mug full of some hot drink. It was the mug that made him snap back to himself because the scalding heat from its contents had made him jerk away the palms of his hands which had been wrapped around it. He very nearly spilled the whole mugful into his lap, only saved by a steadying hand on his own.

"Easy," murmured his host. "That is better *inside* you..."

Aris remembered his manners.

"I think," he said, "you saved my life."

And at that he looked up and finally saw the face of his companion.

Standing beside him was a very young man, almost a boy. His untidy shoulder-length fair hair and two engaging dimples he produced as he smiled, together with the small hands and the narrow child-sized hips, made Aris initially guess his host's age as fifteen, maybe sixteen at most. But then he met the eyes of blue fire that sat in that young, unlined face, and felt his stomach knot. The eyes were ancient beyond measure, all-knowing, all-seeing, *old.* This was someone of no age at all, or perhaps all the ages of the world; beneath the intensity of those eyes Aris dropped his own, utterly confounded, feeling as though all the sins that he carried in his soul – the pride, the arrogance, the ambition, the selfishness – were open to their scrutiny.

"Who are you?" he asked after a beat of silence.

The other laughed softly.

"You may call me Bek. Now drink that. Slowly."

He raised an eloquent eyebrow when Aris hesitated, and Aris, feeling obscurely shamed, lifted the mug to his lips and drank. The scalding liquid burned its way down his throat, to the extent that tears came to his eyes as he swallowed. He coughed.

"Sorry," said Bek. "It needs to be hot. You were on the verge of snowsleep."

"Snowsleep?" repeated Aris blankly. He suddenly roused. "My harp..! My harp!"

"Rest easy," said Bek, one hand on Aris's shoulder. "It is here. I took the liberty of unwrapping it and wiping it down. It is a fine instrument. You are a gleeman?"

"Yes," Aris said, subsiding, his eyes on the harp he now saw glinting on the far side of the enormous hearth.

"Well, then," said Bek. "Perhaps you could honour me with a tale later. Perhaps even the one of how a solitary gleeman came to be trudging the Ghulkit roads in mid-winter."

"Foolishness," muttered Aris under his breath.

Bek laughed out loud. "Ah, a longer tale than that, I think," he said. "But there is no hurry. First we get you warm. It is certain that you will be going nowhere for a while. It is only getting worse outside."

Aris sipped his drink and stole an apprising glance around the room as he did so. It did not appear to have windows; this nagged at him obscurely, as though it should have occasioned at least one important question to surface in his mind. He could not pin it down, however, and he let go, knowing that the stray thought would return all the faster if not pursued. The room was larger than it first appeared, with the far corners lost in dark shadows. Aside from the firelight, it was lit by candles – groups of them, placed on any flat surface with enough space to bear them. There was a desk in a nook beside the fireplace, overflowing with parchment, ink bottles, quill pens, and a quantity of leather-bound books. It also bore a stuffed owl and an hourglass which looked about to spill the last of its sand into the lower chamber. Further out, there was an armchair which presently served as sleeping quarters for three identical black-and-white cats who were tangled in a knot of paws and whiskers on the cushioned seat. More books lay in piles on the floor beyond that. Whoever the owner of this cottage was he was no humble tiller of land – these books were riches, even had their bindings not gleamed with subtle inlays of silver and gold.

Feeling Bek's somewhat sardonic gaze upon him, Aris finally turned back to his host.

"I would," said Bek, his voice hiding a suspicion of a smile, "be happy to answer questions. Within reason."

Aris gestured. "There is a king's ransom in books here," he said, and it was not a question. Quite.

Bek inclined his head. "Some of them," he said, "probably were. I am a collector. Of books, amongst other things. For example..." He rose, and fetched a wooden case from a shelf, opening it up on a hinged edge to reveal rows of meticulously displayed butterflies. "This one," he said conversationally, pointing to a midnight blue specimen with silver flecks on his wings, "I had to travel far to find. Very far. You might say it was worth more than any two of those books."

Aris had gulped down the last of the fiery liquid in the pewter mug, and it dangled from his hand as he examined the butterflies with interest. Bek took the cup from him.

"Good. Another, I think."

"What is it?" Aris, who was feeling quite ridiculously invigorated, asked.

"Secret recipe," Bek said. "Amongst other things, I am a healer."

Aris cast his eyes around the windowless room again, and felt the question he had been chasing earlier coalesce clearly in his mind.

"There are no windows," he said.

Bek, who had been pouring more steaming liquid into Aris's mug from a kettle that had been hanging in the hearth, nodded without turning. "This is so."

"Then how do you know that it is getting worse outside? And how did you know that I was there?"

"One does not," Bek said, "necessarily need to see with one's physical sight in order to observe one's world." He walked the few steps back to Aris with the steaming mug in his hand. "And there is no need to look quite so alarmed. It is a gift, much like your own with the harp."

"Magic," said Aris, and could not keep his distaste out of his voice. Aris and enchantment had a relationship akin to that of a cat hater and any kind of cat – magic pursued Aris, flattered him, cajoled him, tried to climb up to his lap to be petted, while he spent all his energies trying to shoo it away and keep it at arm's length. Using his experiences he had composed a number of songs and tales and the irony was that he was becoming known for his tales of magic even while fleeing it with all his might.

All Aris had ever wanted to be was a singer of songs, a teller of tales. He knew he was good enough to achieve this with no magical intervention. He was just having an inordinately hard time proving it to himself.

"If you wish," Bek said equably, "then yes, magic. None that will harm you. You yourself just said I saved your life. This is no less than the truth. I could show you what it is like outside now, and it is considerably worse, if you can imagine that, than when I called you in here. But I suspect you would think that I was just showing off... and you would probably be right." He held out the mug. "Drink it. I promise you there is nothing harmful in it at all. If you have to know, it isn't even *magic*." The word was emphasised, lightly, with something akin to amusement. "It is herbal knowledge, no more."

Aris accepted the drink after a brief hesitation. Bek inclined his head in an acknowledgement of this acceptance, put away his butterfly collection, and on the way back bent over to inspect Aris's harp.

"I think it has taken no harm," he said. "I would be very grateful if you would play for me later. If there is something here that I miss, it would have to be music."

"I owe you my life," said Aris. "A song or a tale is small enough price for this."

"We all place our own value upon things," said Bek cryptically. "I may not even choose to count it as payment. I may consider your offering something to place me in *your* debt."

Aris looked at him for a long moment, and then put down the mug he still cradled in his hands. "If you would pass me the harp," he said courteously.

Bek did so, with infinite care and gentleness, and Aris spent a few moments adjusting the strings and tuning the instrument to his satisfaction. This done, he glanced up, cradling the harp against his body.

"Is there something specific that you would hear?"

"Whatever you choose."

Aris bent his head over the harp, strumming a few experimental chords, letting the beloved instrument guide him, as it had done so many times before – it almost had a gift itself, this battered harp of his, of passing the *right* song, the *right* tale, into his head. It did not fail him – the melody that came flowing from under his fingers was a tale of vivid spring, of bluebells in ancient forests, of young love blighted and lost through blundering and malice. As always Aris lost himself in the telling, pouring his body and his mind into his art, making his voice an instrument of his soul. When he was done, he "woke" back to his surroundings as the last chord of the harp still hung brilliant and sparkling in the air, and saw the glint of tears on Bek's cheeks.

"That," Bek said, "could easily have been a tale of my own youth. How could you know?"

"I, too, do not require windows to see," said Aris.

"I told you it was the same kind of gift," Bek said. "I thank you. That was well chosen, and well done. We can discuss your fee, gleeman, when we rise. I do not often entertain visitors, but I have readied a pallet here by the fire for you. I hope you will find it comfortable."

"Thank you. I am sure I shall. But as to the fee..."

Bek raised a hand for silence. "All in its time," he said, "although here we do have the luxury of choosing our moment... For now, I wish you a good rest and a pleasant night. You may dream, in this room. Pay it no mind." He chuckled. "It is just a little bit of... *magic.*" Again, the word was emphasised with an unspoken smile. "I think I do not have to warn you to touch nothing here that you do not begin to understand... ah... perhaps it is safer to touch nothing at all, then, if magic is your bane."

He saw Aris flinch, and his face assumed a contrite expression.

"I do apologise," he said, " I have absolutely no intention of plaguing your rest with fear or anxiety. Rest easy – what is here, is mine, and will not harm you."

Aris bowed. "It would be ungracious to find fault with sanctuary," he said. "I owe you."

"No," Bek said. "It is I who am in your debt."

He bowed lightly, vanishing behind another curtain, twin to the one through which they had entered the room from outside and blowing out one bank of candles on his way out.. Aris doused the rest, put away the harp, and settled onto the comfortable sleeping pallet, piled high with furs, which had been provided for him. But sleep was elusive, especially after one of the armchair cats decided to leave its companions in favour of the furs of the pallet and curl up, purring imperiously, against the pallet's occupant. The room was palpably benign, to one as sensitive to atmosphere as a trained gleeman was, but there was something about it that made Aris's hair stand on end even so, especially in the deep silence of the night shadows. Not even the comforting, anchoring presence of the cat helped. Something was brushing along the edges of his mind, lightly, and would not let him rest. His fingers ached for his harp – inconveniently, for he could hardly take up the instrument and start improvising on it while his host was asleep in the next chamber. So he lay back with wide-open eyes, wakeful and worried, his thoughts in curious chaos, until his body rebelled and presented him with a violent cramp in his leg. He kicked, dislodging the disgruntled cat, and rose to his feet.

Mindful of the injunction not to touch anything he nevertheless embarked on a quick wander around the room, peering with a measure of real curiosity at some of the more accessible books – but the fire had burned low and in the half-light he could make out little except the glint of their precious bindings. The owl on the desk proved to be companioned by a pair of tiny stuffed mice which sat somewhat smugly right under the bird's lethal claws secure in the knowledge that the talons would never be reach them, even though the owl had been caught in a position of stretching one foot for possible prey. Beside it the hourglass... the hourglass had not moved.

Aris took a closer look. Yes, there was a still a very small pile of fine sand in the upper chamber, but now that he was close enough to see he became aware of the fact that it was not seeping into the chamber below, in the manner of hourglasses. In fact, it was frozen, in stasis, as much as the owl forever reaching for prey which would never be caught.

Touch nothing here that you do not begin to understand...

It was too late. It was a gesture as instinctive as time. Aris watched his hand reach for the hourglass, and turn it over.

He shivered in a sudden blast of cold. An owl hooted somewhere close by. The friendly house had melted away around him, and he stood beside a huge snowdrift with the hourglass in his hand and his harp, his travelling pack, his gleeman's cloak and a fur-piled pallet with one first startled and then very irate cat at his feet. Upon closer inspection he appeared to be standing barefoot in the snow, with his boots a step away at the edge of the pallet. Aris hopped onto the furs of the pallet, displacing the hissing cat, and quickly drew the boots onto feet already blue with cold – then, before doing anything else, working swiftly to wrap the exposed harp into its multi-layered pack. Only once this was done did he pause and stare at the hourglass, which he had dropped into the snow when making the dive for his footwear.

The sky was clear, hung with stars and a huge close golden moon, but it was bitterly cold and his breath hung in white clouds before his face.

A deep sigh behind him made him spin in the direction from whence it had come, and he found himself looking at a wizened old man, bent with age, his sparse hair white and straggly across the collar of his robe. He leaned heavily on a carved staff, both gnarled and twisted hands, bare of gloves, upon its head. There was nothing in this ancient being to suggest the almost childlike youth of Aris's erstwhile host, Bek. But then the old man looked up and the eyes were the same glowing embers of blue fire.

"The Eternal Hour was a high fee to choose, gleeman," the creature that was Bek said in a low voice cracked with the passage of time.

"The Eternal Hour?" repeated Aris blankly.

"What you hold," Bek said, "made me and my home timeless. You could have spent a century inside my room and emerged young and beautiful the next morning."

Aris picked up the hourglass gingerly and held it out. "But I don't..."

Bek shook his head. "Too late. It is in *your* hand now. I mean – take a look around you... nothing made it that was not part of your immediate environment when you touched the glass. Your own belongings, and then the pallet you slept on, the mug you drank from, the chair you sat on..." This was correct; only now did Aris notice these items, incongruous in the snow. "And one careless cat," chuckled Bek, with real amusement. "Well, they're yours now, cat and all. And the hourglass. You control your life now, to use however you choose. You may take whomever you wish into the stasis with you, and they may then leave unmolested... unless they touch the glass, and you may not warn them directly not to do so. Just be warned – it is a treasure with a price..."

Aris shivered, and not with cold. "What?"

"Keep it too long and you forget what time is," said Bek. "I received it when I was very, very young... and kept it for too many centuries...." He coughed. "They do catch up with you..."

"But I don't want it," Aris said obstinately, a hint of panic in his voice.

"Then," said Bek, "you had better give it away within this hour – before the sand runs out to the last few grains, and then stops, starting your Eternal Hour."

"But if someone else..."

"If someone else turns the hourglass over before the end of the hour, it is theirs," said Bek. "But just as you may not warn them not to touch it when it belongs to you, so you may not hide its nature while it is still free. It may be taken in ignorance or innocence, but never passed on willingly under the same geas. If you *give* it away, you give away everything – including the knowledge of its power." Bek chuckled. "And you may find it hard to find people who love eternal life enough to take it over by choice...."

He began to flicker and to fade against the gleaming moonlit snow. Aris threw out an imploring hand. "No! Wait!..."

"Be careful with your gift..." Bek's voice came drifting back, and then he was gone, completely gone, leaving Aris alone in an empty wilderness with an hourglass that held his destiny. He sank down onto the furs that had been his pallet, dropping the hourglass beside him in the snow, and buried his head in his hands.

The cat came high-stepping daintily back to the furs from the snow where it had initially fled. It approached the human, butting Aris's knee with its head, purring loudly, but this elicited no measurable response. The cat came round the back of Aris and settled against the side of his leg where he sat on the furs, starting to clean itself.

Spend the winter in Ghulkit.

Aris allowed himself a bitter chuckle at the memory of a stray thought that had accompanied him on the road before he had found Bek's house – a thought that took on the force of premonition, seen with hindsight. *If he wasn't careful he could find himself spending eternity here.*

The cat leaned more insistently against him, letting out a small whimper. Aris lifted his head and turned to look at it, resting his chin on hands folded on his knees.

"Poor beast," he murmured, "you hardly asked for this..."

He reached for the cat, awkwardly, at an angle; the cat shied, backing away. Its hind leg slipped off the edge of the fur, onto snow... and into the side of the hourglass.

Which tumbled slowly, and then righted itself.

On the opposite end.

Sand began flowing back into the chamber it had just left.

Aris sat frozen in mid motion, staring, unable to believe his eyes. He had not fulfilled the geas of explaining the nature of the hourglass to the cat, but the cat was an animal – would such an explanation have made any difference? And could he really take a serendipitous accident as a gift from the gods and walk away, free?

The cat had gone over to investigate the hourglass as Aris carefully rose from the pallet furs, slung his harp-pack securely diagonally across his shoulder and chest, and reached for his pack. Slowly, quietly, like a thief stealing away, he backed off from the cat that would never die. He gained the edge of the road he had been travelling before he had found Bek's house, and hesitated, very briefly, as he cast a glance first in the direction in which he had been heading, then back along the way he had already come.

I could get RICH in Ghulkit!

Would they laugh at him if he returned destitute, frozen, in rags?

Would they miss him if he never came back at all?

But he was a gleeman. It was their appointed task to seek, to find, to experience. If some chose to hide from that task in comfort and safety – well – they would sing the same old songs to tired audiences till the end of time....

The end of time.

Aris shivered, irresolute for a moment under the golden moon. He glanced back briefly and then turned, staring. The pewter mug and the chair in which he had sat in Bek's house were still there – but the pallet, its furs and the cat were gone. And so was the hourglass.

A voice inside his mind screamed at Aris to flee this enchanted place, to seek familiar places and more hospitable lands. But there was a shimmer of moonlight on the horizon, and the snow gleamed with promise underneath the stars. He was Aris, gleeman, storyteller, and there were more stories out there to be found.

There was no choice at all.

The moon pooled and shimmered in the footsteps of the trail he left behind him, following the snow-mantled road into the future.

almost fairy tales

Go Through

❧

I t's a street. There are houses. They are old, built of brick, mortared, painted; the windows are framed in carved wood. There may be gargoyles on the edges of the roof – I don't know. I don't look up. I never look up.

At my feet, the cobbles – uneven, gray, worn. Sometimes wet with a persistent annoying drizzle, or with rain that has already come and gone leaving just puddles in its wake. Sometimes dry, dusty, absorbing sunlight, radiating heat back. I have to keep looking down as I walk because the street looks as though it might once have been a wave of water – a wave rising and falling, a memory of motion now caught and frozen for eternity under the old cobbles. If I don't look where I am going I will turn an ankle, twist a foot, stub a toe. There will be pain.

Pain. There is always pain. I think I carry it with me. I brought it here. I wear it. I leave it in the tracks I leave behind on the cobblestones.

. . .

Right until I fetch up once again at a door that should never have been in front of me.

That's the way I live my life. I stumble and stagger in the direction that I am perfectly certain I am supposed to be moving in – and then I find myself yet again in front of the unexpected door, the door I should never have met, never have touched, the door I should never ever ever even consider walking through – because I know where it goes, because I have no idea where it goes, because it is not a door that was meant for me, but here I am and there it is and I open it and step through...

She doesn't know, when she wakes, where she is. Not quite. The bed – the room – they look vaguely familiar but she can't be sure whether it's because she's seen this particular room or slept in this particular bed before or because she's seen a thousand rooms just like this one.

Beside her on the other pillow, he sleeps. He snores. There is the shadow of a beard on his face. She tries to hunt through her mind for his name, but fails. It's a man. That's all she knows.

She gets up, slowly, carefully, disturbing as little of the bed as she can. She lays one long-fingered hand on the dusty curtain, brings her face up close and inhales the musty scent of fabric which hasn't been washed for years, puts her eye to the crack where the two wings of the curtains have been pulled together, peers outside. Nothing is quite familiar. Nothing is completely strange. She almost thinks she recognises the place. She is not sure enough to swear to it. If she walked down this street and turned a corner she is almost-but-not-quite-completely certain that she would see an open square, with a tree whose outlines she has known for years, with certain shops lining the square, with a worn path through the grass where people persist in taking shortcuts. But perhaps none of this is real. Perhaps she has just dreamed it all, there in that bed which is still warm with the memory of her presence – perhaps she has put together that square in her mind from dozens of mental snapshots of places she has known but it has never existed, in the shape or form that she now visualises it, outside the confines of her imagination.

She glances back to the bed. He is still asleep. She suddenly knows that she could not bear it if he woke, if he looked up and frowned as if he couldn't remember her face at all, or worse, if he woke up and smiled and called her by name or called her his darling. She can't face any of it. She's alone, here, now, in a cold room with the grey light of early morning gathering outside and the first shadowy shapes of scurrying people hugging the houses, scuttling along the sidewalks with their heads down and their shoulders hunched, their hands gloved and their collars raised. That tree in that square which may or may not exist no longer has its leaves, she knows this for a certainty – it's autumn, late autumn, sliding into winter, the light tells her so.

She dresses in silence. There is a run in her pantihose, draped across the back of the chair. No help for that. She slides her feet into the stockings, smoothes them over her legs. Pulls on a nondescript dark skirt, a sweater. There is a battered handbag lying by the door; she pads towards it in stocking feet, carrying a pair of sensible shoes in her left hand, picks up the handbag with the fingertips of her right hand – there is no other woman here, the bag must belong to her, after all. Somewhere, soon – not here, not now – perhaps over a cup of coffee in a cheap diner nearby – she's going to open the bag and rummage inside it, for identity, for something to tell her who she is, what she is doing here.

She hesitates at the door, shoes in one hand, bag in the other. It is not a door she remembers seeing before. But she remembers the fact that she has often hesitated before strange doors. That doors never quite lead where she expected them to. That she quite probably never meant to be in this unknown room in this unknown house on this unknown street with this unknown man in the bed – she was never meant to be here at all.

She doesn't know if she can leave – if she is able to leave. If, when she walks through the door, it will mean leaving life behind. But she knows nothing about what's on the other side of this door, just as she knows nothing at all about the things which she can see on this side of it, hesitating before it. She knows nothing at all. Nothing. So – stay or go – it matters very little.

She reaches out, with the edge of hand holding the shoes. She pushes down the handle. The door opens, just a crack, silently. She doesn't look back as she slips through, into shadow. Behind her, the room sinks back into shadow, too.

It's a road. A dirt road. I've been on it forever, or perhaps I've only stepped on it moments ago. I don't know. I don't remember. Time is elastic, after all, bulging and distending, sometimes worn very thin, thin enough to lift up to your eye and look through and be able to glimpse other things on the far side as though you were looking through a fine chiffon scarf. But this... this is a road. It's dusty. There's nothing on either side of it but fields, empty ones. No cows. No horses. Not even hay bales. Just windblown fields, in between stands of trees. There are wire fences between the fields and the road – I'm not sure if they're to keep me off the fields or to keep the things that don't exist in those fields from stepping onto the road and gobbling me up. There's a crossroads. It's just a place where four roads meet, in the shape of a geometric cross, a gigantic plus sign drawn on the landscape. There's a signpost, right there in the middle – it has signs, pointing in the four directions – but the signs have either worn down into illegibility or else they're in a different language altogether. I don't understand them.

. . .

Beside the signpost, there's a door. Just a door. A doorframe, with a closed door within. There's even a key in the lock – but it's just a door, and I can walk right around it, and it's a door from either side, leading absolutely nowhere at all. I am certain, utterly certain, that those travellers for whom the signpost is intelligible will never see this door at all – but for me, for those like me, there's always a door. A strange door which leads nowhere. A door that is an alternative to directions that are unknowable, and unknown – a part of the signpost, just as mysterious as all the rest.

Every door opens into something. There are just too many doors that I should never even have seen, let alone passed through. Too many doors that lead from darkness into shadow, or into light too blinding to see. Doors that make me stumble. Doors that never allow me to pass them by, once I've seen them. Once seen, never unseen. Always there.

A door ignored will return – again and again and again – until I reach for that key, for that handle, and crack it open. A door that should never have been in my path; a door without which my path would not exist.

❧

She gets out of the car, slowly, her movements hinting at fatigue. She isn't sure how long she's been driving. She isn't sure where she started from, not any more. There is a large black and battered duffle bag in the back seat – as far as she knows, it's her only luggage. She has, in the moment she thinks of the bag, no idea as to what it contains – what items she had thought essential enough to carry, to bring with her, instead of leaving them behind... wherever it was that she had come from. Her toothbrush? Her childhood teddy bear? Her Bible? Her shotgun...?

. . .

Around her, darkness is beginning to rise, to seep into the sky from the black shadows underneath the trees ringing the parking lot – empty, except for her. There's a house looming just in front of her, a house with a sign illuminated by a single dim light, a sign that proclaims it to be an inn. It's a haven. A refuge. A place to rest for the night.

There's a light behind the drawn curtains of windows facing out to the parking lot. Somebody's home. But there's a door. And the door is closed.

She hesitates, before she knocks. The house feels like a stage set – a two-dimensional thing, no more, behind which lies the chaos of backstage – fake potted plants, and a cracked coffee cup, and a ratty moth-eaten sofa with the doilies from last year's production of *Arsenic and Old Lace* still draped on it, and a typewriter with no ribbon in it, and a bunch of dusty silk roses, and a stuffed dog, and half-painted wooden cutouts of trees and of people and of a fireplace with a painted fire which gives no warmth at all. If she passes through this door she might simply be stepping into all that fakery, living a life in which nothing is real at all. Or she might be stepping *from* that fake life into something warm and real and waiting – a world where that fireplace is real, and so is the fire, and she can curl up in the corner of the sofa with a real dog curled up at her feet and real coffee in the cup. All just waiting for her. Maybe the bag in the back of the car is empty – just a stage prop; maybe the car doesn't run at all. Maybe all of it at her back – the gathering twilight, the vehicle whose keys even now dangle from her fingers (ah, but are they real keys or fake...?) the mysterious piece of luggage supposedly belonging to her – all of that – perhaps all of it would simply vanish if she stepped through this door, as though none if it had ever been.

What a strange dream she's been having. Of lying, and running, and hiding, and looking for sanctuary.

. . .

She should never have come here. Never have been on this empty and isolated road so late in the day. Never have known this inn existed. Never hesitated in front of its door.

She should never have seen this door in her life.

If she passes through, she will be a different person. She knows this. It frightens her.

It makes her happy.

She reaches for the door handle – if it opens to her touch, she decides, arbitrarily, on the spot, then she will walk through. If not, if it's locked and she has to ring or knock to ask for admittance, she will not stop here. She will drive on. Into the night.

Into the doorless night.

The door gives under her hand. Swings inwards. There's a light, somewhere, within.

Just as well. She knows, without knowing, that she would have come up against this door again, if she didn't choose it this time around. That's the way things are.

. . .

She steps through. She has already forgotten about the bag on the back seat of the car. Nothing it contains has anything to do with her, not any more. The future is behind a curtain; the past is a long-lost foreign country, almost forgotten.

ॐ

It's a gate made of wrought iron.

It's a coal hatch.

It's an airlock.

It's a gaping hole in the ground, only darkness within and beyond.

There are many doors.

They lead from memory into oblivion, from darkness to light, from warmth into icy cold, from dream into wakeful reality, from life into death and then back again.

I've seen many. Too many. So have you. We'll see more. They're portals, they're gates; they are inevitable, and they are everywhere, and there are some which you should never have seen or passed through at all... but you go where the waters of life wash you up, flotsam and jetsam, lapping at the steps leading from the sea up to the threshold of a door you don't recognise and yet always knew would be there. Doors are choices. They are wishes. They are sacrifices (oh yes, they are - look down at the old blood stains at your feet, traces of those who came here before you...)

. . .

They are passages.

I wear a key on a string around my neck. It fits any lock. You carry one too. We all do. We are latchkey kids, the grown-ups are away, we're home alone and must do the best we can. A door can lead home, or into frightening alien places you cannot ever hope to understand.

They are doors. Even the ones you should never have seen, never touched, never listened with your ear against the grain of the wood for the faint sounds of what might be stirring beyond – even those, even the ones you don't know, don't recognise, don't understand – especially those – they're yours. They're meant for you.

It's a street. It's a road. It's a sidewalk. It's an alley. It's a path between the stars.

Stop, and look. There's a door.

You'll never recognise it. You might.

Go through.

❦

Vision

FAR FUTURE/MYTH

This way, please. This way.

This is the heart of the last remaining ruins of a Temple of Istynn, the Goddess of Truth and Prophecy.

Watch your step, it's a little crumbly over there at the edges.

Madam, could you please make sure your youngsters don't venture beyond the ropes? They are there for a reason, and we don't want any damage to the site... er, that is, of course, we don't want the children to come to any harm. Thank you.

Sir, a word, if I may – this is unfortunately not a dual-language presentation –I lack a Translation Cube at this time – will your K'Dynn friend be able to follow? Ah, the reason I ask... I have seen what happens when some of her people give way to strong emotion, and the preponderance of orange on her facial fur suggests that she is... well, as long as you think it will be all right....

Is that everybody? Gather around, please, so you can all hear me clearly.

We are standing on what remains of the Altar Plinth in what was once the heart of this Temple. You will observe the shape of this raised dais, where it hasn't crumbled at the edges – please, do be careful there, sir – was once a perfect circle, and in fact we are all standing here at the center of that circle, in precisely the place where the Eye would have opened in the roof of the Temple – and that would have been hundreds of feet above us. Please note the buttresses to the sides of this area, which once supported the structure and the weight of that roof.

This particular construction was traditional for Temples of Istynn – we believe that the original instructions for the architecture of these Temples were brought all the way from the First World when the Migrations started although of course we can no longer be certain of this provenance after the First World was destroyed a thousand years ago.

For those of you who may not be familiar with the cult of Istynn, she has been described as the daughter of Moc, the Elder God, and variously a number of the Goddesses of that Pantheon or human women. You will find that the lineage any particular Temple believed to be true of Istynn would be incorporated into the design of the Temple decorations – for instance, you can still clearly discern, over there on the right, that zig-zag shape that portrays the lightning bolt, the symbol of Moc, and next to it the cup, which is known to be the emblem of Jivan, one of the senior Goddesses.

Sir, please do not stray outside the demarcated areas. Some of these old ruins still have areas whose properties have not been fully explored. Thank you.

Is there a question back there? Well, yes, you are right – as the Goddess of Prophecy Istynn would have had an oracle at a Temple of this nature, and in fact we are standing at the precise spot where the oracle – or at the very least the Temple acolyte who was chosen to be its voice – would stand in order to answer the questions posed by an supplicant.

Yes, under the Eye of the Goddess – who was, as you correctly state, always depicted as blind or at the very least lacking in organs of *physical* sight. The myth of Istynn had it that her physical blindness was what opened her inner eye and she was therefore able to see every-thing, even the things that were hidden.

She could see into shadows, and through time; she could tell you things from your past, and yes, she could foretell the future. The oracle was not under anyone's control, however, and it was made clear to those who came here that they might – and in fact they almost always did – get far more than they bargained for. Someone who came in to ask about their harvest or their child's marriage might also learn that their spouse was having an affair or that they only had less than a year left to live, for instance. It would always be the truth, to be sure, because it was impossible for the Oracle to lie while speaking for the Goddess. One came here for answers at one's own risk.

And yes, people came anyway. Always. Constantly. This was one of the last cults to wither, after the Gods of Istynn's Pantheon began to fall out of favor. The Temple whose ruins we stand in right now was only abandoned after the necessary operational knowledge of keeping the Eye opening, which would have been directly above us right now if the roof structure was still intact, in good repair was lost. The conse-quence of that was that the direct connection between the Goddess and the oracle was also severed. The attraction, both that of a despera-tion to know some truth and the bracing against learning things unlooked for in the bargain, vanished, and Istynn shriveled into nothing more than a little sightless idol. You can still see crude carv-ings of the idol in the remnants of the cultural detritus left behind by the civilization which came in the aftermath of the cult of the pantheon of Mos. You can find replicas of those on sale in the gift shop on the way out of the ruins, on the far side of the catacombs.

The carvings are said to still possess a certain kind of power. Modern-day devotees of Istynn, and there are still some even though there has been no operational Temple for hundreds of years, will tell you that if you ask a question and make sure that the person you ask it of is holding an image of Istynn, you can get nothing but stark unvar-nished truth in reply – as you would still, technically speaking, be standing under the Eye of Istynn, the Eye that sees all. You will have to decide for yourselves.

Sir...? Oh, that – yes, that is one of the early depictions of Istynn. It has not proved possible to determine how or why the carving was vandalized – yes, the Goddess was always known as blind but in that particular instance, it does seem as though someone went to some trouble to actually gouge out the eyes of the carving. It has been dated as quite old, maybe as old as the Temple itself – maybe one of the original defacements that was done after the Temple was abandoned. We have no reliable record. It seems to have been a common thing in Istynn's Temples, however, and you will find similar things in many other locations.

There is a school of thought that posits that it may have been a part of the original depiction, but other authorities doubt very much that a goddess would have been depicted in this way on purpose. Istynn may have been blind but she was a Divinity and it was unlikely that it would have been the sort of brutal blinding as depicted here that would have rendered her so.

Moving on, ladies and gentlemen. Please, take a moment to linger if you would like to take a closer look at something – but please do refrain from touching anything. The Temple is quite old, and very fragile, and we would like to preserve what is left for others to be able to enjoy. Do remember that you will be able to purchase souvenirs later, in the gift shop...

FUTURE/LEGEND

Once upon a time, there was a girl.

When she was born, the fairies who gathered at her cradle were silent, and one by one they drew back into the shadows without giving the child their gifts. When only one remained, the Dark One, the one who did not fear the shadows, the child's parents cried out,

"What is it? What is the matter with this child, that all of you draw back from her?"

"She sees. She understands. She sees too much. She will be much loved, and she will be feared."

"But she is a babe – she is nothing yet, and this can be turned from her!"

The Dark One turned her head and gazed on them. "Do you not want your child to be special?"

"Of course," the child's mother said. "Does not every mother wish this?"

"Then know, she already is – and any gift that any of us would have to bestow would merely take away from that," the Dark One said. "But I will give her one, anyway, if you truly want me to."

The parents bowed their heads. "If that is your pleasure," they said.

The Dark One stretched out a hand over the child.

"You will live your life in pain, and end it in darkness. But you will bring light unto others. Light, and understanding, and always, always, the truth. You will be known as the truth speaker, and eventually the oracle of your people."

"Thank you," the child's father said timidly.

"But the price...!" whispered the child's mother.

They had asked, and it had been given, and it was done. The Dark One withdrew into the shadows from which she had come, and the fairies were gone.

The child grew, and became first a bright-eyed toddler and then a happy little girl whose fair hair was dressed by her mother with vivid red ribbons and who skipped and sang her way through her days.

Until the morning that the Dark One's words began to come true.

On that day she came home from the woods where she had been playing, and she was very quiet. Her mother asked her what was wrong, and she stumbled over the words as she tried to explain – how she had seen a rabbit in a clearing in the forest, and had seen the fox waiting in the shadows, and had then suddenly seen the rabbit as the fox had seen it, had seen the fox as the rabbit saw it in the last moments of its life, had felt the light of the rabbit's vision dim and die as the fox's teeth closed about its throat.

"But that is the hunt," her mother said. "And creatures of the woods have always lived the lives of the hunter and the hunted. And even we, out here, do the same."

"How?" the child asked, lifting her big, beautiful eyes which were brimming with tears.

"Well," the mother said, "you have seen me kill the chickens for our supper..."

"I did not think of it that way," the girl said, looking away.

The mother thought that maybe that would be the end of it but the next time she prepared one of the chickens for the family's dinner, the child pushed away her plate and said that she was not hungry. And she never ate anything again that had once looked out upon the world through its own eyes.

It was a year later that her mother found her sitting by the side of the road, comforting a weeping woman traveler.

"No matter how bad it seems now," the girl said, her hand laid on the hand of the weeping woman as they sat side by side on a grass bank, "there is light that is waiting for you – and someday your daughter will be there to take care of you when you are old."

"But I have no daughter," the woman sobbed. "And I am lost, lost, lost and alone..."

The mother took her daughter home, after offering some food and comfort to the footsore traveler, and then forgot about the incident until the woman returned, almost a year to the day after the encounter by the roadside, and sought out the cottage where the child who had comforted her made her home. She carried with her a small bundle wrapped in swaddling clothes, and on her face was wonder.

"I had to come," she said, when she found the girl who had spoken to her a year before. "I had to come, and bring this one to show you – for how did you know that before last year was out I would be blessed with a daughter of my own, the light of my life, that child you spoke of who would take care of me in my old age.... How did you know?"

"It was the truth," the girl said simply.

And after that, they started to come. One by one, and then four or five or ten or a dozen, waiting patiently in the yard until she would speak to them. And then a hundred. And then more.

There were some who heard things they did not like, and hated her for saying them, and then went away and spoke ill of her – but the bad things came true for them anyway, and the girl's reputation only grew. But she herself grew thinner and quieter, her pretty face getting gaunt and hollow-cheeked, her eyes haunted.

"Tell me how to make it stop," her mother said, "because it is hurting you, and it needs to stop. How do I make them go away?"

"They will not go away," the girl said. "Not ever. Not while I can see through every one of their eyes, into the shadows of their lives, into their future, into their past. They will never go away. Not so long... as I can see."

And she grew even quieter after that, as if she had given herself an answer to a question she had not known that she had asked, had not even known could be asked. But it seemed to be an answer that she was afraid of, and recoiled from – right until the moment when she disappeared from her home one night, and somehow crept past all the people who were huddled out in the yard and by the roadside waiting for the dawn so that she would wake and speak to them again like the prophetess that she was, and vanished into the woods.

Her mother missed her when she rose to greet the new day, and the crowds outside roused at her cry. They fanned out to look for the girl, and there was no lack of searchers that day – but they had no luck in finding her, not until the sun was low in the sky and the horizon was blood red with the sunset in the west. That was when they came across her, huddled in the back of a shallow forest cavern away from the light, and what remained of her beautiful eyes as blood-red as the sunset as the tears of blood ran down her cheeks from where they had once been, from where she had plucked them with her own hand. So that she could no longer see. So that she could buy her freedom from the weight of truth, from the press of expectations from everyone out there who wanted to know the things that were hidden from them but not from her, never from her.

"We found her! We found the Oracle!" the searchers clamored, as they brought the wreckage of the girl back to her mother's house. "She is hurt, but she is alive, and we found her, we found her! And after she is better..."

The mother saw the ruined eye sockets and wept, and washed the blood from the girl's face,, and asked, "Are you in very much pain...?"

And the girl whispered, "Yes – but it is not what you think..."

"What is it? What did you do? Why did you do this? Are you sorry...?"

"I did it so that I would no longer see anything," the girl whispered. "But oh... Mother... Now... now I can see *everything*..."

And her mother remembered the Dark One's blessing at the child's birth – *You will live your life in pain, and end it in darkness. But you will bring light unto others. Light, and understanding, and always, always, always the truth. You will be known as the truth speaker, and eventually the oracle of your people.*

Such are the gifts of Dark Ones, offered over cradles of innocent children in the dawn of their lives.

NEAR FUTURE/HISTORY

"It's all screwed up," Liam Muller complained, tapping at his keyboard and squinting at the shifting screens on his monitor. "There are dozens of different versions of it in the media, and then thousands of testimonials of those who swear they met her and she was a saint or that they met her and she was the devil or that they met her and she was a goddess, or an angel, or just a scared little girl. And that's just online. There's stuff in that folder back there which pre-dates the Net, and it's all mired in all kinds of exaggeration and improbability "

"Go back to the primary sources," Stelli Carr said, peering at her own computer.

"Stelli, this was a hundred years ago, all the people who actually knew her are *dead*," Liam said sourly. "I can't question them; all I have is what they wrote."

Stelli sat back, removing her spectacles and rubbing the bridge of her nose "Well, what do you expect *me* to do about that?"

"Listen," Liam said, leaning closer into his monitor. "Here, just take the three articles that I'm looking at right now. One says she blinded herself, and that she was institutionalized after that or perhaps because of that and that her fame as the oracle really began *after* this. Another says that it was actually one of the people who asked her a question and who didn't like the answers he got who attacked and blinded her, and *then* she was institutionalized, etcetera. And the third one says that she was never institutionalized at all but that her sister took care of her for the rest of her life." He paused, rubbing at his own face. It was past midnight, and he was more tired than he would admit. "And then there's a fourth one which speaks of her as an only child."

"And...?"

"As in, she *had* no sister to take care of her."

"Cite everything," Stelli said. "Just write that there are conflicting accounts of her life and cite every single damn thing you find. You can let whoever reads this find their way through the maze. You're giving them the maze, not the map."

"We are supposed to be journalists. We're supposed to tell the *truth*," Liam said, exhausted but obstinate. "And even if... well... it would just be the crowning irony of all if we didn't tell the truth now, here, about a woman so many believe was an oracle."

"You've done a hundred of these profiles before and you've done them in half the time and with a quarter of the kvetching. Just get on with it!"

"I can't," Liam said helplessly. "This one's different."

"No, it isn't!" Stelli said, exasperated. "She's just another..."

"No," Liam said, with conviction. "No, she's not. This one is just special. Something really unique happened here."

"*Really* unique. Tell me you didn't just qualify that word."

"No... yes...but you know what I mean. Yes, we've done a hundred of these profiles. But this particular one is going to outlast both you and me, Stelli. People will be telling *this* story a thousand years from now."

"You know this *how?*" Stelli demanded. "Look, it's late. Why don't we just knock off for the day?"

"No," Liam said, after a short hesitation. "I have to get it done. I have to find what the truth was."

Stelli sighed, and pushed her chair back, yawning. "Fine. I'll see you in the morning, then."

Liam's attention was already back on the computer screen. "Sure."

Stelli shrugged and left the room, rubbing both hands wearily on the nape of her neck.

Liam spared his partner a glance as she vanished through the door, and the glance had a good deal of regret in it – in some ways he knew that Stelli was right, that they were both tired, and that he was putting far more work and effort, far more meaning, into this particular profile than it probably deserved. And yet... and yet. There was something. There was something waiting for him, if only he dug deep enough, if he was careful enough.

The truth was there. *Her* truth, the one whom they had called the Oracle in her own lifetime. The girl who could only tell the truth. The blind girl who could see everything...

The blind girl who could see everything,

He shivered, with an almost superstitious awe and understanding starting to wash over him. It was as though all the confusing accounts of one little girl's life, one young woman's pain, suddenly coalesced for him for a moment into a vivid pattern of understanding – as though he had asked the question of the Oracle herself... and she had stepped out of the past and given him an answer, *his* answer, the truth he had been groping after all along.

In some ways, nothing that was said of her was true. In some ways, all of it was.

In that sense Stelli was right, and making judgments on what was 'true' became almost irrelevant in the face of the greater truth, the greatest truth of them all.

"It isn't sight," Liam said, leaning forward, his hands curling over his keyboard, suddenly inspired. "It's *vision*. And she had the vision. She didn't need anything other than that to be able to see..."

The night closed in, around the glow of a computer monitor lighting up a face that had assumed the expression of an apostle, against the sound of soft but rapid clicking of the keys on a computer keyboard, as the chrysalis of a life once lived trembled and cracked along its seams and something else, something different, something greater, waited to be born.

PRESENT/TRUTH

I think it all started when I was six, and we moved into the house in the tree-lined suburban street which was supposed to be the fairy tale castle – or so my little sister, then four, and I were told. I remember standing on the sidewalk looking up the garden path to where the house sat, innocent and sleepy amongst the trees, with my mother holding my hand on one side and my sister's on the other.

"Look," she said to the two of us, "Look, the house is smiling at you. Can you see it? See those windows up there? One of them will be your room. Aren't the windows just like a couple of twinkling eyes, smiling down at you?"

Once she said it, once I saw it, I could never unsee it again. The house had eyes from that moment, forever more. Mother had wanted to make the house seem welcoming to us, as if it were something living, a friend, something comfortable and sympathetic which we would see as our ally and our sanctuary and thus love immediately.

Instead, the house *looked* at me. And saw me. And I stood there on the pavement, rooted to the spot, for that moment at least so completely terrified that I could not move at all – and when I did, finally, it was when Mother dragged me forward, step by unwilling step. The house stared me down with its unblinking eyes of sparkling glass panes, and when I crossed its threshold it reached inside of me, owned me, knew me, and I knew it. And those "eyes" that looked out onto the street, they became mine, too; there were times I could simply close my own lids and the street would unfold before me – sometimes in the bustle of the rush hour when all the neighbors were coming or going, herding children or dogs, husbands and wives racing to work, gardeners mowing lawns, a constant and turbulent motion; sometimes in the middle of a moonlit night, empty and still, with cars parked somnolently in driveways and just the occasional dog barking at nothing in particular as a lonely counterpoint somewhere in the distance.

And that, I believe, was the beginning of it all. Because once I saw, I could not unsee – once I saw *anything*, I could not unsee – and the world was full of eyes. I kept on seeing them. I kept on watching, and I kept on being conscious of being watched.

"She's changed," I overheard my mother tell my grandmother once, maybe a year after we had come there. I was seven, and it was late, and I was supposed to have been tucked away in my bed and asleep but I had been thirsty and I'd come down the stairs for a drink of water... and instead walked into these voices, talking just out of my sight, talking, I knew, about me. "She used to be so happy, you know. She was my laughing one. Now – she's so quiet. She doesn't talk to me anymore and when she does it's about things I don't understand, and they're beginning to scare me. Even in her sleep, you know. Once I was walking past her room and I heard her saying in this funny little singsong voice, 'I can seeeee youuuu! I can seeee youuuu!' And I looked in and she was fast asleep. Honestly, it freaked me out."

"She's probably going through something," Grandma said soothingly. "She's of an age..."

"She's seven," my mother said. "They go through *ages* at the Terrible Twos, or when they're teenagers. Not now. Now they're supposed to be happy little children. Do you suppose she's just unhappy that we moved here? She loved our old house..."

"She was a baby," Grandma said. "She can't remember that much about it."

Maybe I did, maybe I didn't. That wasn't the point.

The point was that *this* house had eyes, and that it had made me see through them. And then it just got worse, and worse, and worse. Because there were eyes... everywhere.

They took us down to the central city one day, and there were *windows all around me*, and every one of them was a gaze aimed squarely at me – and then I could see through all of *them*, I could see people scurrying in the streets and waiting at traffic crossings, and tapping impatient feet and talking on telephones – and I could see the birds that zipped in and out through the canyons of glass and steel – and I could see the rats burrowing through the dumpsters in the service alleys. All of it. And I got quieter and quieter, more and more still, until I could barely move at all and could hardly speak, and the outing was cut short and we went home again.

I saw a woman taking a photograph of her children in the park. And the camera in her hand was an unblinking eye.

The stuffed animals on my bed stared at me.

I began to cry when I saw a dog or a cat; our own cat, Mimsy, began to hiss and arch its back when I came into the room, and we could not look each other in the face.

And worst of all... mirrors. With my own haunted eyes looking back at me, and my vision swimming as it doubled, tripled, multiplied, me looking at my mirror self and my mirror self looking at me and me looking back and she looking back until my brain swam from the echoing images and I would sometimes enter strange hypnotic fugue states, standing in front of a mirror frozen in place until someone came to shake me loose and away. Eventually the mirrors in the bathroom I used were taken down, and so were the ones in my room – but there were others in the house that would catch me sometimes.

Out of the house, every plate-glass display window was a danger. I walked with my eyes downcast when I left the house, wary of meeting my own eyes through a careless glance cast at a pair of pretty shoes in a shop window.

I was filling up with vision and I was struggling to cope with it, stumbling under the weight of it, being driven into either catatonic sleep or white wakefulness for twenty hours or more at a time as I tried to find a way out of it. I would merely look outside – through a window – from within a house – and I would happen to lay eyes on a bird on a tree branch, and the things it could see would flood into my own mind. At night, sometimes, lying awake, I would stare at the slightly lighter shape that was the window in the darkness of my room and I could swear I could see eyes out there, staring right back at me through the windows, sometimes plaintive and weeping and sometimes demonic, red, malevolent, seeking me out to do me harm because I was seeing it all and it was crushing me, crushing me...

Mother was right. I had gone quiet. Who could I possibly have talked to about this? Whom could I have told about it and not been considered to be mad? I could not tell my parents or my grandmother because they would have never left me alone again, I would have never had another day of being on my own again, I knew they would do their best to help and to try and 'cure' me but what that would mean would be endless tests and medical procedures and probably therapists and psychiatrists and drugs and perhaps they'd even end up locking me away somewhere, so that they wouldn't have to worry about me, so that I could be safe, so that I would be away from them and they would not have to worry about me or think about it. And I could not talk to my sister, who had not heard what I had heard, who had not seen what I had seen, who was a normal and happy little girl and whom I loved and could not destroy by dragging her into the nightmare with me.

So I endured, and withdrew, and soon they took me out of school and my mother and grandmother tried to give me lessons in the basics at home – but I became a recluse inside my own house, inside my own room, sometimes huddling in the darkness of the depths of the closet because there were no eyes there and I could find some peace. My sister had posters on her walls, with people on them – I could not, my room was bare, almost monastic, with nothing in it except what I absolutely required and even that pared down to the barest and simplest minimum – a bed, a chair, a plain table for a desk.

And even then sometimes the eyes played on the blank walls and stared at me as I lay in bed at night, looking, always looking, seeing everything – I saw everything and knew everything, and they all looked right back at me. I don't know if they were even aware of it but all those gazes could have seen me for what I was if they had had any idea that I was there. But they did not. And instead I began to scribble down things on pieces of paper, on that plain desk in my room, answers to questions I had never been asked. I was naming names I had no right to know, and giving them answers to problems they had no idea that anyone other than themselves knew anything about. I would write the answers down, and then I would shred the paper on which they had been written, ripping it convulsively into confetti, trying to hide what I had done, feeling guilty, feeling resentful, feeling helpless under the onslaught of it all.

It was my little sister who broke it eventually, despite my silence – she found one of my notes and took it to my parents and they started keeping an eye on me and more of the notes found their way to them and then one day something I said *came true*, right on the news, and that scared them all.

It was a name – no more than a name – a name they had found on one of the notes that my sister had taken to my parents. It had been a bad one, it was a pair of eyes that had haunted me, and I had not been able to escape him, in the end. I had never met him, never spoken to him, he never saw the note that I wrote with his name on it – but I had scrawled on that note that he was going to die, and violently – and when the name turned up on the evening news I could see them recognize it, and blanch, and I saw them recoil from me. They tried to hide it, but I saw it, and I had, after all, a gift for seeing, and for truth. I knew that it had been real. And it had been that which cracked open our cocoon because it was *that* story that scared them – scared them enough to let what had still been a family secret out, and the world in. The people through whose eyes I saw suddenly knew that I could see... and they came, they all came, until the quiet street became choked with people seeking to come to me and ask me things which they all just *knew* I would know – ones and twos, and then handfuls, and then dozens, and then hundreds, and then more.

We had to move again, eventually. But people who wanted to find me did not stop looking, and they found me again, in the new place. And they kept coming.

Eventually it was thought best that I should be separated from the family, so that they could have some semblance of a normal life, and from the world, because people would pay and cheat and kill to get to me, to get to the Oracle. And so my family found a place where I could live behind high walls, almost like a prison even though I had done nothing wrong, and they left me there. And they went away, my mother and my father and my little sister.

Trying to find a life with a little peace.

I could not blame them, really.

But that night they left me alone, that was the night I cried, and cried, and cried, until the tears were dry and the blood came, until I reached for the eyes that were showing me all the truth in the world, giving me all the insight and all the answers, all except what to do about it all.

With clawed hands, with pushing thumbs, with hooked nails, I started tearing at those eyes that could not help seeing things, until I could see no more. I understood the pain, I accepted the agony, I did it with full awareness, I knew when the wetness on my cheeks changed from tears to blood.

Darkness had once been a sanctuary. There was a time when I could bury myself in the back of my closet, stuff my face into a fold of my coat, shut the sights of the world away, and I could find a few moments of peace.

But that had been before. When the seeing was still young. When it had not yet fully taken root in me, perhaps.

I was willing to accept the pain and the blood. I had freely offered up my physical sight, paying the price I thought I needed to pay. I wanted... *needed*... to abdicate from this high place of being a witness to the world's suffering, and I was almost happy to embrace perpetual darkness if I could have that quiet place to which I could go, and be free.

But I had not realized until it was too late... until it was far, far too late...that I had merely liberated myself from the shackles of the sight that was of the physical realm, of flesh and of blood.

Instead of the quiet black emptiness I had reached for – instead of giving up the sight that had caused me so much anguish – instead of the rest and solitude that I had craved – instead of seeing *nothing*... I could not help seeing *everything*.

I could not help... suddenly, vividly, with no chance of escape and no place to hide... seeing it all.

Iron and Brass, Blood and Bone

BODY

There are moments I look back over the events that have brought me to this point, and I can look at them quite dispassionately, from a distance, analytically, as though they happened to somebody else entirely and not to me.

I remember clearly the sort of person I was. I was mild, and polite and dedicated; I was near-sighted, with round wire-framed spectacles, and I always tried to hide my lanky height by walking a little hunched over, with my shoulders sloped inwards and my hands wrapped anxiously around each other before me. I worked long hours in the back room of the lawyer's office, dealing with contracts and inheritances and judgments, keeping the accounts. The lawyer, my employer, had a lavish office out front, all decked out in leather and dark wood; he would receive clients there and take on cases, and then he would turn the details over to me to write up. I was the only other employee there, other than the woman who came in mornings to clean the offices and make the first pot of tea (anything of that kind, later in the

278

day, that was my responsibility too). I was paid barely enough to make the rent and to keep from starving, but I was mild and polite and dedicated, I didn't deserve more, I never asked.

The lawyer didn't know about my monster, the creature I came home to and dedicated long hours of painstaking work to. The lawyer never knew that I was capable of independent thought or original invention, that I could ever conceive of, let alone build, the mechanical man which I put together over weeks and months during long nights lit by lamp and by candle, poring over every wire, every connection, every tiny detail.

The reason? Because I wanted to. Because I could. Because I believed – with all the passion that I was capable of mustering – that I would be the one who would find the mystery of what makes a thing alive – that I would be the one who would provide that divine spark that animated my mechanical man, and make him live. I had never thought beyond that monent, not really – I was just dedicated to the idea of that one instant when I would see my creature look at me, and see me, and recognise me as the nearest thing it could have conceived of as his God.

He was a thing of beauty, my mechanical man. I never really gave him a proper name, but I thought of him as Ludo – why that, more than anything else, I do not know. But his body was iron, and his legs were iron, and his arms were iron, but his hands and his feet and his head were golden brass. I gave him two glass eyes. I even contemplated providing him with a head of hair, with a wig I could have purchased a few shops down the street from where I worked and which I passed every day, but I finally dismissed that idea – he was perfect enough as he was, Ludo, with his shining brass pate and his blank eyes.

He was almost done, almost, when I ran out of materials late one night – twelve more rivets I needed. Just twelve. And he would be complete. But I was all out, and it was late, and at any rate I would not get paid for another week – and in that time he would have to sit there unfinished, Ludo, just a pile of scrap metal until I could complete him and start the real work, that of giving him life and motion.

It was well past midnight that I rose, frustrated, and put on my hat and coat, and stalked out into the foggy gas-lighted streets, walking aimlessly, blundering along the cobbled alleys without a destination in mind, too hyped and upset to sleep.

I must have taken a turn somewhere into an unfamiliar part of town because I found myself hesitating before a shop – lighted, and, it looked like, open, even at this hour. There was something coming out of a vent on the side of the house that the shop occupied the front of – smoke, or steam, something white that mingled with the fog – it smelled vaguely of hot metal, and something else, something chemical, sulphuric perhaps, certainly acrid enough to make me catch my breath and cough. But more than that, the windows of the shop made me stop and stare.

It was a machine works.

They had, perhaps, the rivets I needed – the last twelve.

They were closed – they had to be closed – it was well past midnight – but it was like a miracle laid out before me. I needed something and God had provided, here it was, the very thing, right in front of me, right now.

I pushed open the door, and a bell jangled somewhere in the back. Very soon a balding man with a pencil moustache and a pair of thin, elegant eyebrows pushed aside a curtain hanging over an alcove and stepped into the shop.

"Good evening," he said.

"Rivets," I said, after a beat of silence.

"Indeed." He pulled open a drawer behind the shop counter and pulled out a box, putting it softly on top of the counter and pushing it towards me with one long, white, bony finger. "Will these do, sir?"

I looked. Inside the box, there were twelve rivets.

Exactly the kind I needed. Exactly the number I needed.

"How much?" I managed, through a mouth that had gone suddenly, inexplicably dry. I was afraid – I did not know why I was afraid – I was exhilarated, and suddenly flooded with ecstasy, with a heady excitement.

"Thirty silver pennies," he said.

I gave him a sharp look; he gazed back at me out of a pair of limpid pale blue eyes, one of those eyebrows arching over like a delicate dark caterpillar.

"Too much," I said at last, after a long pause. Which had told him far more than I, perhaps, had intended.

But hre responded instantly, without hesitation.

"I'll take a down payment," he said, "or in kind..."

"In kind? Rivets?"

"Let us just say that I am perfectly willing to let you take these with you through that door, right now. And I will defer the payment."

"How do you know that I won't just take them and never return?" I muttered.

He smiled, and some part of me shivered in terror at that smile.

"Oh, I will be paid," he said.

I thought of Ludo, sitting propped up in the corner of my bedroom, slumped over, his brass hands between his iron knees, his head lolling without support for lack of these very rivets.

I thought hard.

"I'll take them" I heard myself say.

And I took them. And walked away. I don't remember looking back, but somehow I knew that the lights had gone out the moment I had stepped outside that small strange shop – that it had never really existed, except for the small box of rivets in my pocket. The world was empty and sleeping – all except for me, and for my Ludo, who would wake once I hurried home with the last small thing I needed to finish him...

SOUL

He remembers that night – but he remembers it as if it was a story that was once told to him. He remembers it as though he watched it happen, floating above the streets like a crow, watching the hunched man with the box of twelve rivets in his pocket hurry home through the dank fog in the early hours of that morning.

I remember the rest of it, when he returned home, and took the rivets out of that pocket, and began to work.

I remember, because that was the beginning of me.

It is not given to many to remember the moment of their own birth, but I do.

It was slow; it came by painful degrees; it came rivet by rivet, a little bit at a time, and I could feel it slipping into me, dripping into me, oozing down the wires and pooling in the glass eyes out of which I could suddenly see. With every rivet, a bit of him, into me. With every rivet, a little piece of his soul. Until, at last, it was all done, and all twelve of those accursed things in place and tightened, and I was all soul, and he was none at all – and the sky was lightening in the east already. He would need to be at work soon, very soon.

He should have been too tired. He should have fallen onto the bed in an exhausted heap, fully dressed, and slept the sleep of the dead. But he was not. He stood gazing at me where I sat at his workbench, giving me a dispassionate and apprising look as though I was a piece of merchandise that he was contemplating buying and weighing the money bag in his hand as he appeared to find me, on some level, wanting. But he had no real time for anything more, not right then. The work was done here. The final rivets were in place. I was finished – I, Ludo, was finished. At least the form of me was. The rest would have to wait on his other obligations and responsibilities.

He left me there in the cold pale morning light. Alone.

He didn't know that I could think and feel. Not then. Not yet. But already he would not have cared.

The hours crawled by – and at first I sat as he had left me, without moving, because that was what he appeared to expect me to do. But he had no reason to think of me as anything other than a doll, a mechanical thing without life – and I was no longer that. Not with all of his soul animating my iron and brass body. When I moved, the first time, it was in every bit as mechanical and graceless a manner as he might have expected – but even though he had made my brass feet a little too small I found a way to stand, and then to balance myself upright, and then to take a step. It had not occurred to him to dress me – I was just a metal man – but something had passed into me with the soul he had transferred there with those rivets he had found in the night, and I felt the need. His clothes fit me badly, too tight in some places, too loose in others, too short in sleeve and leg, leaving long naked vistas of iron wrist and iron ankle – but I was dressed, tgh it did not fit me well, which he would probably want to take back when he returned. But it felt proper, to be dressed in an acceptable manner, even though I had no watch fob to tuck into the waistcoat pocket as would have been correct. But I didn't need to tell the time, after all.

I was empty, except for feeling and instinct. I looked out of the window and the streets were strange to me, unfamiliar – I carried his soul, not his memories. The tiny set of rooms he rented – bedroom, small parlor he had turned into the workshop where he had built me, a nook of a kitchen which contained very little by way of sustenance – I explored it all as though it was new to me, which it was. I had been born here, but there was nothing here that I, myself, knew – I took in the details, the faded wallpaper, the brazier in the bricked-in fireplace, the narrow single bed in the bedroom which had not been slept in that night and was still neatly made, the scattered tools on a small bench in the corner... the empty rivet box.

I understood it first, the bargain that he had made. I was the receptacle of a soul that was sold, already no longer the property of my creator. Those last twelve rivets – the ones that he had so desperately needed for me to live – had cost him his own salvation.

He knew nothing of it yet. But he would. He would. And I was afraid of what he would do when he found out.

Oddly, I was never afraid of what he could do to me. Perhaps I already understood more than I knew – and I knew far more than he did...

BODY

Work was strangely different that morning, the morning after I had finished Ludo and left him sitting there in the shop. I arrived early as I always did, despite the sleepless night, there long before the lawyer got to the office, making sure everything was in order for his first client. Then I went back to my room and started on my own work, which was never done – the moment I made any headway, a new pile would be deposited on my desk for me to deal with. Usually that was just... the way things were. But that day, it was different.

I worked mechanically, at first. I had been doing this job for twelve years, would be thirteen years come that February, I could do it with my eyes closed. I didn't have to think, so I didn't think, and the paperwork was dealt with methodically, tidily, efficiently, as always.

But then... then I heard the cleaning lady leave, and then the lawyer left for a court date.

And I got up... and left my desk... and went into the lawyer's office. I had never done this before. This office was not for the likes of me; I had only been in there to deliver some important paper, or to receive a swift last-minute instruction if required – always with the lawyer present, often sitting there behind his desk with his horsehair wig still on, smelling of cologne and old leather and dry justice. But now... I was in there alone, and it was as though I was seeing it for the first time. The high arched windows, the plush curtains, the shelves lined with thick dusty books, the large desk inlaid with red leather which was almost hidden beneath an untidy pile of papers and files. I actually went over, pushed some of the files out of the way, brushed my fingers against the leather. It felt good.

Outside, the streets were grey under cloudy skies. People looked cold, hunched against the wind, hands tucked into the sleeves of their coats and their collars up around their ears. Carriages drawn by black horses, with liveried coachmen up on the high seat, passed busily by underneath my gaze; I could hear the faint sounds of hooves on cobbles through the closed windows.

It looked as though it might snow.

There was no colour outside, other than black and white and gray. Nothing at all. The world had turned monochrome.

The red leather on the desk. That was the only colour in the world.

I stood at the window, staring at the desk. I could not take my eyes off that red leather. Red leather. Red leather. It had... some strange subliminal meaning. Red. Leather. Red.

There was red, later, too. When I found myself looking down at the lawyer's body, at my feet. Red pooling around him, from the gash in his neck... dripping from the knife I held between the thumb and forefinger of my right hand.

I held it as though I did not know how it had got there, finding myself gazing upon it – at first, at least – with a measure of astonishment. I wondered why I had killed him, and could not remember.

It did not matter. Not one little bit. I wiped the knife on the curtains, tucked it away into the lawyer's own leather satchel, and walked out of there without looking back. It was as though I was walking out of an illustration, a two-dimensional thing, an etching from some book, not my reality for the last dozen years. The lawyer's office was already forgotten, gone, behind me, over. I knew I would not go back there again. The satchel, besides the knife, contained what money there had been in the lawyer's safe – I knew the combination, of course. They would find him, and the empty safe, and they would find me gone, and they would begin to hunt for me – but I could not find it in me to care.

I came home... to Ludo, standing in the middle of the parlour.

I didn't think I had given it a voice, or even intended to attempt to do so – but somehow, it had one. A flat, metallic one, befitting the flat metallic mouth out of which it came – but a voice, nonetheless.

"What," Ludo asked inflexionlessly, "have you done."

I shrugged. "Everybody dies," I said, "eventually."

"You have killed."

"Yes," I agreed. Without any guilt, or shame. It was a simple fact, it was the truth. And inside of me, there was a vast and glassy emptiness, nothing at all for any emotion to cling to or survive.

My insides... were *his* insides, the empty tin man I had made.

And yet...

SOUL

And yet, he contained me. And I contained him. He was the man, the human, the blood and the flesh and the bone and the sinew, with the muscles in his face which he could move to make himself smile or frown, with eyes that could weep, with a voice that could scream. I was the brass and the iron, doomed never to express an emotion – I could not move the metal skin on my face, or clench my hands into fists, or howl with rage or with pain.

He could do all these things – and would never do any of them again.

I could never do any of these things, but carried every painful urge to try, and was doomed to fail forever more, for as long as I existed.

He looked at me and if it was still possible for him to feel any emotion at all, he hated me. I looked at him and I adored him, and I pitied him, and I loved him. He was my creator, my God; he was me. I was him.

"I could destroy you," he said at last, after a long silence.

"No," I said. "You cannot."

And he knew it for truth.

"What if I die?" he asked.

"You cannot," I said. "Not while I live."

"And you will live... forever?"

"I do not know. But some day this body that you have given me will fail. Some day, the bill for those rivets will come due."

We were tied together now, he and I.

He could not die — because there was no longer a place for him in either Heaven or Hell — because I carried his soul, and I would not be admitted into either of those places. I, who had never lived. I, who would carry all his guilt and all his pain, from here on, into eternity.

"What do you plan to do," I asked, my voice flat, without the inflexion of inquiry, but he understood it as a question.

"Well, I no longer have a job," he said. "I guess, if I need money to live, I will have to get it some other way."

"You will kill again."

He smiled, a little, but his eyes were cold, cold, cold — colder than my glass ones.

"I will kill," he said equably. "And why not? Who among us deserves to live so much that another must give way? I have needs — and I will meet them however I am able. And the beauty of it is..."

He stared at me, and I knew that he knew, and that I was lost.

The beauty of it... for him... was that he would feel nothing, when he killed. Nothing at all. I would feel it, all of it, everything, every ounce of anguish and fear and pain and moral recoil. His hand would wield the knife and the soul which he no longer carried would pay the price for it.

"I will be your conscience," I said.

His smile was a thing of terror. "I have none," he said.

And so it began. The shadows gathered around him, and swallowed him. He remained ageless, stuck forever more at the hour in which he had poured his soul into me. Within a few years they had stopped looking at him when they sought the man he had once been — because logic and common sense told those who hunted him that the killer they were looking for must have aged as the years passed and now looked different. They no longer hunted the younger man whose features he continued to wear, whom he remained.

He lived well enough – he dabbled in things occasionally, sometimes picking up a transient occupation when it amused him to do so. For a while he even worked as a lawyer, out of the offices where he had once clerked – and he had learned enough law that none suspected a thing, until he grew tired of it all and simply walked away. He became a merchant, a doctor – even, for a little while when it became necessary to remove to the country when the heat got too close to him after a killing spree, in a grim mockery of all that was holy, a soul-less priest in a rural parish where the poor came to him for succour and advice. He found that he excelled at sermons and speeches. He became a politician, several times, in several different incarnations, and he was good at it. But sooner or later he would kill again because he could, and the stain of it slipped off him like water off oiled brass, and came to me.

I have no memory of the details of his crimes. He carries the memories, not me. I sleep, in a way that I sleep, and on the mornings after the nights that he has killed I wake to a day of agony and recrimination – because the guilt comes home, to me. He kills, he spills blood, and he walks away from it all – he can tell you the names and the places, all of it, he remembers it all in detail, but he does not care about it. That is my burden. My anguish. The tin man with the glass goggle eyes who follows him when he moves lodgings – sometimes he tries to give me the slip but I always know where he is, how could I not, and if he moves and leaves me behind I simply wrap myself in a cloak and trudge after him, slowly, on my too-small brass feet on the dark roads that lie between places, and I always find him. He never drives me away – when I turn up and take my place in his new home he simply carries right on doing whatever he was doing, as though it was the most ordinary thing in the world that I should be there. I had always been there. I always would be.

BODY

I sometimes wonder what would happen if my brass-and-iron shadow followed me into a shop that wasn't there, that shop I never found again to pay my dues for the twelve rivets I had got there on a foggy midnight in the city, so long ago now. What would happen if he came into that room and I was there, and that devil also, the one who had sold me those rivets – I was still not sure about the ultimate price, but I did not really care, not any more – and if he stood there, my metal man, Ludo, with my soul behind those goggle eyes that I had given him. What would the devil take? Him? Me?

He has done nothing – nothing, except carry the guilt.

It is my hands that drip and reek.

And I don't care. And he does.

I wonder what would happen. Would he offer himself? To the Devil? To God?

Does he belong to either of them?

Do I?...

SOUL

I wondered if it had an end. If some day something would happen to me, and the soul was free. Would that be the day he paid that final bill, would I – his soul – watch his physical body crumble into the dust that it should have been long ago, and then be taken, after all? The devil can wait. He has an eternity.

So do we, him and I, as things stand. Unless things change for one of us. Unless one of us makes things change.

I questioned my own beliefs – which were partly his, and partly forged out of my own metal. Was I – Ludo – the metal man – insane to even ponder the idea of salvation? It could not possibly affect me. I could not go to Heaven or Hell, after all.

But "I" was that soul I carried within me. And it was black with sin.

He would probably never again set foot inside a church, ask for forgiveness – because he no longer knew how to ask, because he no longer needed it. And I, who knew, who did, well...

...Forgive me, Father, for I have sinned...

I said those words. I meant them. If I had had the tears, I would have wept over them. If I had had a real heart it would have broken in two. But although I now carry all the emotion that it was ever given to my human creator, I lack the basic means to express any at all. There were no tears. There was no inflexion to my voice when I spoke, hidden behind the curtains in my half of the old wooden confessional – nothing that would indicate true penitence. I said those words flatly, because I had no choice to do otherwise. But I, who felt every agony and every anguish now, could not show it – and he, who suffered none of it at all any more, would never again do so himself. Broken, both of us. Damaged. Wounded.

Sold.

Alive, but dead.

Dead, but existing.

The priest in the other half of the confessional heard the voice that asked for forgiveness. The flat and metallic voice. The voice that was so wrong. He had leapt from his seat, flung back the red plush curtain, saw me sitting there – machine, iron and brass and glass. He saw none of what was inside of me because I had no means to share it other than in plain words and those words he would never believe from me. He shouted, and screamed, and clung to his crucifix, and damned me (as though I could be damned) to everlasting Hell for heresy and for daring to profane the holy sacrament which was, as he said repeatedly, "...only for true men who hold a soul that God Himself gave them!"

And then, with surprising strength and determination, he was done with words, done with anathemas; he had said what needed to be said. It was time to do, now – he reached in with both hands, hauled me out of the confessional, pushed me staggering down the aisle, all the way out to the front door, all the way out, down the steps that led out from the main portico, into a pile onto the path below.

I felt struts snap, something shatter.

I did not care. It did not hurt. That which was inside of me did, and that I could not heal, ever again.

Ever again.

Only for men who possessed God's gift of a soul...

Little did he know but that it was that very soul which I took into the church and tried to cleanse. But the priest that drove me away did not know, could not know, could not possibly have understood. All had to give in response to my presence was fear, and fury, and holy righteousness.

And yet...what he felt... what he did... it was the right thing to do.

He broke me that night. For all that I was made out of iron and brass I was a fragile enough construct; when he threw me down those stairs, he smashed things – essential things – and I knew that Ludo was done. The monster was done, the metal body was twisted and snapped, there were wires and connectors that were split, there were bolts that were sheared. I would not get up again, I would not follow the man whose soul I carried within me again.

They would find me here, where the priest had thrown me down.

The priest would tell them what had happened, what he had done, where to look. They will call me an abomination or a saint, but they will destroy me, they will destroy this body of iron and brass that had been a secret for so long.

I was right when I had believed that we would have immortality, he and I, the body and the soul and the metal man who carried it – so long as we existed, together. But perhaps salvation lay in the simple fact that it could not endure forever.

Immortality seems to have lasted a little shorter than its usual promised span. This I knew – I knew, as I lay there, dying.

They would free this tortured soul – and perhaps, if it... if I... could cling to holy ground, to these hallowed stones, when they send the earthly remains of me to the scrap heap... perhaps it will be well. Iron and brass, expiating the soul of flesh and blood and sinew and bone.

I wonder if I will see him again. If I will ever again look into my own eyes.

There were two headlines in the newspapers that week.

One was the strange case of the metal monster who had tried to confess his sins to a parish priest.

The other was the body of a very, very old man which was found in a back street of the city. His hair was down to a few white wisps on his head, his face deeply furrowed, and his expression seemed to indicate that he had perhaps died of a stroke – because one half of his face was smiling, and the other had the corner of the mouth turned down. There were even traces of tears on the cheek of that other, anguished, side. As though... as though half of him had wept.

There was nothing to connect the two things.

Nothing, except that the metal man was oddly... unfinished.

And the old man in the street had a box of twelve twisted rivets in the pocket of his coat.

Finley's Joy

Nobody thought it would last. They were oil and water, empirical science and magical intuition, yin and yang, complete opposites; when aeronautical engineer Josh Pearson and ethereal Wiccan folk singer Isabella Mallory met, fell in love, and married, even their best friends were prophesying that the partnership would soon run its course after the first heady days of infatuation were over and most gave the marriage maybe a year or two. Maybe three or four. Seven at the most. Well, maybe ten.

Except that the number kept changing and growing, and if anything Josh and Isabella were more in love with each other every day.

They wanted children – they wanted something that was part him, and part her, and a culmination of the best of both of them. But the years slipped by and Isabella's waist remained as slender as a girl's, and the hopes began to slip away.

And then, as though they were touched by magic, in the thirteenth year of their marriage Isabella's belly grew round. And then, as the months slipped by, she became huge – carried her pregnancy high up, tight, her maternity smocks (which she made herself, only out of material that would bring health and peace to the child) draped over the bulge of what was not so much a baby bump as a baby balloon, hanging over in almost helpless gathered folds.

The little girl who was born to them was named Finley. And it was immediately clear that Finley was no ordinary child.

She glowed. There seemed to be a light behind her eyes, which faded from their baby blue into a pale blue-gray, and when she bent her luminous gaze on somebody that person would be instantly smitten, ready to lavish all the love in the world on the mite. Her hair was allowed to grow long and silky, and either lay over her shoulders like a cloak of liquid pale sunshine or got braided into a pair of pigtails finished off with white ribbons that made the child look even more sweet and exquisite than anyone had thought possible.

But she was silent. Long after most babies began to babble and coo, Finley would only turn those extraordinary eyes on someone and smile – and managed to communicate her needs perfectly by doing no more than that. It was as though Fate had played a cruel joke on Isabella, the singer, whose own voice was so beautiful – by giving her a child who would never speak, let alone sing.

Isabella did not give up hope. She did the singing – she sang all the lovely lullabies she knew, when Finley was only a tiny baby, and then other songs, sharing everything that she knew and loved, as Finley grew. And it was to Isabella that Finley gave her gift – the first sound that bubbled from her lips – her laughter.

Finley laughed, and it was almost more than Isabella could take. It was so beautiful, so perfect, so completely filled with joy, that Isabella felt tears spring to her eyes. The laughter had come as a response to a particular song, and Isabella, who had been alone with Finley when the miracle had happened, grabbed a cellphone and began to record, first herself singing, and then, somehow, catching Finley's laughter as it came again, spilling out, itself a song, voice given to joy..

Isabella played the video snippet to Josh when he came home from work – and then tried again with the song, but Finley would not give the gift of her laughter again, not for her father to hear.

He was disappointed, and made it his business to find a way to make his daughter laugh with him, too. He clowned for her, pulling faces, but that elicited no more than an indulgent smile. It was beautiful, like everything about Finley, but it was not that liquid bubbling laughter. It was more of an indulgent 'Silly Daddy!' moment – no less treasured by Josh for all that but still, not what he had been looking for. He did not give up, trying different things, and it was something quite unexpected that made Finley offer him her joy.

Isabella had gone out briefly, leaving Josh with Finley, and Josh had begun reading to her – reading something dry and dusty, an engineering tome, explaining to her how stars worked, and then he looked up and caught her eye and put the book down.

"No, but all that is true but irrelevant," he said to his daughter. "Isn't it? You know what stars are. You understand perfectly how out there in the real world they're these huge balls of burning gases – but you also know, don't you, that you and I and everything living was made from starstuff, don't you? They're alive, Finley, they're as alive as..."

And Finley laughed. With Finley's joy.

Josh grabbed his own phone, and babbled some more about the stars, and Finley rewarded him, her laughter, her love, captured on the video. He showed Isabella, proudly, when she came home, and they danced together in their living room, with Finley smiling her blessing on them.

After that, they competed – and Isabella succeeded one more time, to elicit the laughter and the joy and to capture it on tape, and then Josh did so once more, talking to his daughter about the mysteries of other worlds where the seas were made of molten metals and it rained diamonds. Twice more, Finley laughed, shared Finley's joy.

And then, one day, just before she turned four, Finley simply... disappeared.

They were both at home when it happened. They could both swear that their daughter was right there one moment... and was not, the next. She had vanished, like a ghost, like she had never been. Only the four videos of her luminous laughter remained, as proof that she had existed at all.

The recordings themselves were curious. For one, they could not be copied – they existed, as and of themselves, four discrete moments, but they could not be shared in email, or reproduced in any way – they did not transfer. They existed in their own particular space, simply four unique moments in time, four captured instances of Finley's joy. They lived on the phones on which they had been captured, and only there.

"This has to have a purpose," Josh said, finally, after a year had passed – a year in which the parents of the missing child had been investigated thoroughly by police, private detectives, and even the FBI. Nothing was found; Isabella and Josh were finally and grudgingly acquitted of any wrongdoing but the child's disappearance had not been solved. Finley was a ghost who lived in their house, a memory who could be called up by playing the videos of her laughter; her spirit was still there, but her small body had inexplicably dissolved into bright air.

"Meaning? The meaning was that we had her," Isabella said.

"What do you hear in that laughter?" Josh asked.

"I hear Finley," Isabella said.

"Yes, but more than that. What do you hear?"

"I don't know what you mean…"

"I hear so much," Josh said, and for someone like him this was hard, this was almost impossible. Nothing about this was empirical or provable – this was instinct, more the kind of instinct that was usually Isabella's province. "I hear… everything. I hear, above all, Finley's joy. I hear a greeting from the human race to the listening stars and the message is joy. The message is joy…"

And this took hold in Josh's mind, and became almost an obsession. He listened to the sounds of Finley's laughter. He tried to interpret it, to understand it, to translate it, but it defeated him – there was no hard data there. Just, as he had himself said, the joy.

He did not know what to do with these feelings. He became brittle with it, thin, transparent.

It was Isabella – taking on his role as he had leaped into hers – who gave him a release.

He was in the throes of creating probes to be sent out into space, four of them, identical, sent out in different directions, their only purpose to listen, and learn, and transmit home what they found. The team working on the probes had already put together an elaborate 'greeting' from the human race, like the original Voyager probes, to be sent out with the new probe family – but it was Isabella who put both the phones into Josh's hands, hers and his own, and folded his fingers over them.

"Send Finley," she said quietly. "Send Finley's laughter. Send Finley's joy. Send that out there. Let that be the greeting of humankind to the stars."

He could not do it officially. It would never have been sanctioned. But in the end, he did it anyway – and it was the first and last time Finley's laughter permitted itself to be copied and transmitted. Josh put one of the four recordings into each of the probes, and when the probes were safely launched he triggered the secret codes he had buried in the software and released Finley's laughter into the void.

He never knew what happened, after that – he and Isabella had released Finley, and she was free; the two of them moved on. A couple more years went by, and Isabella quickened again – they had another child, this one quite ordinary in every way, who walked and talked and passed every milestone precisely on cue. They never forgot Finley but they had a family, and the world, their world, was complete.

Out there, the probes hurled out into the void raced out into the vast spaces between the stars.

The first probe went far, far away, and was finally captured and examined by the M'rzelin, a warlike race whose only purpose was conflict and conquest. They did not know peace, nor understand it – to them it was merely surrender, and weakness. But while they were solving the mystery of this alien probe, determined to find out where it came from so that they could aim their war machine in that direction and go out and conquer the intelligences who had sent them this thing... they triggered the sound of Finley's first laughter, the one that she had offered Isabella for her song.

And Finley's Joy swept over them, and they were disarmed.

The meaning of peace was made clear to them, and for the first time in their history they embraced it. Their worlds were changed by it, and transformed, and they prospered. They revered the sound of that laughter as the voice sent by a God.

The second probe tumbled in a different direction, and eventually crossed the path of a race called the Bolassi, in a time of great crisis. There was a plague that had swept their world, and they were dying by the thousands, with no release, and no cure in sight. They had become resigned to dying, to being erased, to vanishing from the fabric of time completely.... when the second probe fell into their sky.

They heard Finley's second laugh, the one she offered to her father for his starstuff story, and the Bolassi were healed, the sound of Finley's Joy conquering the unconquerable disease, giving the Bolassi back their health, their dreams, their future. They never knew where the sound of that celestial laughter had come from, but they knew what it had done, and it was enshrined in their history for all time, becoming legend.

The third probe found a world of fools who could not agree on anything at all and wasted their entire existences on squabbling with one another, sometimes for very little reason, only so that they could be proved 'right'. This race was degenerating into something squalid and terrible, something small, something petty, something that was destined to reduce itself to oblivion arguing about nothing at all.

They heard Finley's third laugh, another she had offered to a mother's song, and they woke up as though from a bad dream. They looked at their lives, and their world, and themselves, and they suddenly knew that they could be so much more than they were. They heard Finley's Joy, and they grew wise. To the smouldering ends of their civilization, they treasured the sound of Finley's laughter as a balm, as a release, as something that changed them all and made them *better*.

And so Finley's Joy echoed out among the stars, and everything it touched it transformed.

. . .

What Finley's fourth laugh might have done, we will never know. It came too late.

The last living sentient being on a dark world without hope saw a bright star burn across his sky as the probe immolated itself in the shredded veils of the world's atmosphere. If the last being on this world heard the last sound of Finley's joy, her fourth and last laugh, it was already too late for it to bring anything that perhaps a hopeless regret, a final glimmer of understanding of what might have been. If it had accomplished even that much, Finley, whose spirit flew in that laughter, might have found something to be content with. But the probe died a hard and fiery death, the fourth laugh was stilled into silence, and no gift was brought to that corner of space by Finley's joy.

Perhaps some day another star child will laugh – and the laugh will bring peace, and healing, and wisdom.

Until then... the echo of Finley's joy is still out there. In revered memory. In serenity. In glory. The stars heard her laugh and the stars laughed with her, and the universe gave its gifts in return.

If you listen – if you listen very hard, in the quiet moments of twilights, and starlit nights, and bright summer mornings – if you close your eyes and listen you might hear it still, the bright lilting laughter, the pure bright gift of Finley's Joy.

Author's Notes

The First Book: The Three Fairy Tales

I wrote these three stories an almost fairy-tale span of years ago – a thousand years ago – back in the last millennium. It was so long ago that I no longer even really remember how they landed me my first agent, and how that agent came to write me a letter (this was before the days of email) telling me that I had sold a book. For the longest time after I got that letter I kept on thinking, I sold three stories, and they will appear in a book somewhere. But the agent kept insisting – no, YOU. YOUR book. ONLY you. It took a while for that message to penetrate. But the thing I remember quite clearly was the incandescent joy that lit up inside of me when I finally understood.

I had sold a book. And my name would be on a book cover.

It was an added grace that the book was a collection of fairy tales.

These three tales were, to a greater or lesser degree, inspired by Oscar Wilde and his take on the fairy tale – and then there are the subcategories of inspiration – "The Perfect Rose" was a nod to Scheherezade, Niklas and his fiddle owe their existence to the lyrics of an old song that haunted me enough to produce a story, and "The Dolphin's Daughter" was perhaps the truest child of Oscar of the three, with direct roots to things like "The Nightingale and the Rose".

The book was published by an educational publisher and was used – during its nine printings – in schools; I'm pretty certain there's a generation of English schoolchildren who hate me (because they had to answer those terrible questions of "what did the author mean by..." for actual marks...). But these stories – this book – this beginning – this was a gift. I have never stopped lighting a small candle of gratitude at its altar, ever since.

Ever After: A Story of Four Princesses

The first one of these stories, the "Ashes" one, was written in a white hot if bleary fury at 5 AM, curled up with cold feet tucked underneath me in my husband's office across the hall from our bedroom, barely able to see what was happening on the screen where the words I was typing were coming out – but it didn't matter because I wrote that story not with my fingers on the keyboard but with my heart and mind straight onto the screen. I went back to bed after I put down a shaky early-morning first draft of a story that came to me and took me by the throat and demanded it be told, and I slept again. And when I woke, eventually, it was with the other stories almost fully formed in my subconscious, swimming like something glimmering through dark waters.

The inspiration for all of this WAS dark. It was the early days of the Trump era and the world was even more awash in refugees than usual – and I was in the throes of producing my charity anthology, "Children of a Different Sky", a collection of stories about, and created to help, refugees. The idea of "what would your Disney princess look like if she were a refugee?" came a-haunting like an unquiet spirit and wouldn't be laid to rest until these stories were written.

You'll know them, these four. You'll recognize them. You may call them by name – Cinderella, the Little Mermaid, Aurora, Snow White. What you will see in their eyes when they answer is nothing like you've ever seen there before. These are not the pretty privileged princesses of your own sheltered childhood. There is nothing Disney here. This is what happens when you strip fairy tales to the bone, and you discover a reality more painful than any "real" world might lay claim to...

Tales Re-Told

I wrote "Rum Pelt Stilt's Skin" for a fairy tale anthology released by Book View Café a few years back, "Beyond Grimm". I had no idea when I began it that it would turn... so dark. Some reviews called it "borderline horror" – well, I don't know about THAT, but it is still not the Rumpeltstiltskin you knew. Miss Letitia's "Butterfly Collection" was written, I remember well, while I was sick unto death with something flu-like, and it was a fever dream. I remember typing it mechanically, as though I was taking dictation, while my eyes kept watering with these hot welling tears, and I do recall that I had an actual temperature at the time. Being a lousy patient I simply took what came and ran with it. What better time to write a weird fairy tale than when you are being racked with illness which is altering your mind...? "Glowstickgirl"... was the product of our times, a retelling of the Little Match Girl in the harrowing context of what was going on in the United States when children were ripped from their parents and stacked like cordwood into camps, places where nobody knew them or loved them. This was a story that told itself. "Hunting the Wolf" was an experiment in fairy tale told as "noir"... and a flirtation with punnery. It was literally written in the dying hours of 2020. You may find references to the "plague" year in there, and you will certainly recognize the role that masks get to play...

New Tales

This one's a bit of a mixed bag. "Color" and "Safe House" were both written for themed anthologies ("Human Tales" and "Mystic Cat", respectively). "For A Coin of Silver" was literally born of the headlines where a weird little story along those lines had been reported – one where a particular sum of money was literally being passed around a neighborhood from one person to another in exchange for goods and services and it was a tale sitting up and begging for a fairy tale-like retelling. "Spiderhair", oddly, came from a conversation on Facebook about what to do with long hair when in bed at night. If you're me, you go and write a story about it...

Witches

"Wedding of the Weed Witch" was something unlooked for and I honestly didn't even know what it was going to be until I was in the middle of writing it. Although it is, on the face of it, fairly traditional in terms of the fairy tale tropes, the story has some very Oscar Wilde-like turns of language in it and I think it has an ethereal quality which gives it a purity that I remain very pleased with. My favourite bit is the blooming of the flowers in their pots.

As for "Twice Promised", the longest offering in this compendium, it arose from a very throwaway conversation that popped up on social media once upon a time:

jcatgrl:

copperbadge:

persinetteinthetower:

moriartythetease:

So what happens if two people who have promised their firstborn to separate witches have a child together? Do they both just pop up in the nursery and have a custody battle?

I need a book about a little girl whose parents had promised their firstborn to different witches and the only way that both ends of the deal were fulfilled was for them to have joint custody of the child.

I love it!

And then the witches, forced to share a cottage while raising their joint stolen child, fall in love...

#more witch-centric lesbian fairytale rom-coms#....a sentence I never thought I'd type

Source: moriartythetease

79,190 notes   ···   ⇄   ♥

And I said, that's almost irresistible.
And people said, so why are you resisting?
Admittedly, reservations existed – particularly since it seemed from

the conversation as it unfolded that there were a number of people whose interest had been tickled by this particular idea – and therefore there might have been any number of attempts at it. But it was pointed out to me, and rightly so, that no two people would be telling the same story anyway, and whatever I did would be (by definition) a unique contribution to the new subgenre of #morewitchcentriclesbianfairytaleromcom – and anyway by this stage the damage had been done. The story which that particular hashtag began unspooling in my brain was already underway.

It was supposed to be a short story. But in the usual manner of my stories, it ran away with itself until it was well past the "short" in that context. Before I knew it I had a novelette on my hands. And here's something else: this particular section of the story, the novelette now in hand, is in all probability the basis for something that might yet become a full novel someday. Slightly changed, a little deepened, with the world worked out a little more fully. But that's for the future. For right now – this is the story which a random social media conversation and a challenge arising from it brought into being.

Aris

Aris the Gleeman and his Tales might be considered straight fantasy as opposed to fairy tale... if it wasn't that they were so firmly grounded in folk and fairy tale. The story of the sword, written first (and considerably before the other two) , arises out of a folk tale I carried with me from my own cultural literary baggage – except that I embroidered and embellished upon it. Having created the character of Aris, however, it became hard to let him go – so I wrote two more stories about him, something that might have been his origin story ("Skyring") and a tale from a more mature time ("Hourglass"). I think these stories have quintessential fairy tale qualities – and once again, as I do, I feel as though there may be more tales to tell in this world. For now, however, there are only three – these three. If anyone wants more Aris, do let me know...

Almost Fairy Tales

Sometimes a fairy tale is a feeling, a sense of wonder, a shiver as you look sideways and glimpse something unusual, even impossible. It's a whisper in your ear, telling you a secret name, or offering you passage into the undiscovered country...which, yet, comes to feel oddly familiar as you step inside, as though you had lived there all of your life. Oscar Wilde did this beautifully in his fairy tales (something like "The Fisherman and His Soul" comes to mind), and I have written several stories that take on this mantle – although they may not be classic "fairy tales" in any strict sense. "Go Through" is the kind of story that makes you look around or back over your shoulder, to see just what you might have missed by walking right by it all unawares; "Vision" explores how a distancing in time might turn a strange turn of contemporary truth first into history, then into legend, then into myth... from which it's a short step into the fairy tale. Or, going back to Wilde's soul questions, there's the steampunk take on that, in "Iron and Brass, Blood and Bone". "Finley's Joy"... is a science fiction fairy tale, which I don't think come round very often.

Fairy tales come in all guises. You'd be surprised sometimes to see one smiling at you from deep in the shadows of a drawn-forward hood of a concealing cloak.

But here's the thing, and it applies to all of the stories above.

Everything that you have read in this book...

...in its own way...

...is true.

That is the power of the fairy tale.

Acknowledgments

The Brothers Grimm, Charles Perrault, Hans Christian Andersen, Oscar Wilde, the legions of unnamed story tellers who have shared the worlds of the fairy tale – my debt to these storytellers and their imaginations and their touch of magic that has shaped my world since I was very very young – my debt is immeasurable. Without them, without their stories, I would have been, quite literally, a different human being. Without them, this book could never have existed.

The storytellers who came later and left their imprint on the malleable clay of the fairy tale – Jane Yolen (known as the American Hans Christian Andersen), Theodora Goss, Catherynne Valente, Terri Windling, Robin McKinley, Neil Gaiman – my debt to them is just as immense. They showed me the way into the lands of dream and power, and I have walked in their footsteps, with gratitude and with humility. Without them, too, this book could never have existed because I would never have known how to write it.

To the people who helped bring the volume alive – to Book View Café which published it, to James Artimus Owen for the cover art, to the people who crowdfunded it in Kickstarter (your names are listed below) – my thanks. For EVERYTHING.

Kickstarter supporters:

Janicket, Marva Grossman, Jack L.Z. Frost, Landon King, Jennifer Fournier, Jed and Finley Speer, Rana Elizabeth, E.J. Kelly, Elizabeth Livingston, Rosanne Girton, Noelle McMillin, Barry Buchanan, Elyse M Grasso, Cathy Sullivan, Christine Ethier, Intwo, Tiffany Hall, Liz M, Robert Tienken, Lily Ibelo, Caitlin Bramwell, Margaret B. , Cathy Green, Brooks Moses, Joshua Spencer, Jenn & Drew Bernat, Riccardo Sartori, John WS Marvin, Victor Meng, George Reissig, Charlie Kinsella, Rosina Lippi, Jean-Philippe Guérard, Caroline Griffin, Erin Cashier, Courtney Walter, Anthony R, Cardno, Douglas Wyman, Max Kaehn, Liz Copeland, Siavahda, Ian Harvey, CE Murphy, Susan P Carlson, Kristi N Austin, Deirdre Schwein, Joshua Palmatier, Steven Goodall , Vida Cruz, Jules Dickinson, Mare Matthews, Brendan Sheehan, Camille Lofters, Keirsten Gustafson, Ellen Kushner, Kari Blackmoore, Don Lloyd, Janis Gaines, Karen Broecker, Claire O'Dell, ADMHatter, Mary Kay Kare, Matthew Mole and Elizabeth Thompson, Charles Boyd (Brandon's father)

And others, who asked not to be thanked publicly but whose support is still greatly appreciated and hereby acknowledged.

Alma Alexander
2021

About the Author

Alma Alexander's life so far has prepared her very well for her chosen career. She was born in a country which no longer exists on the maps, has lived and worked in seven countries on four continents (and in cyberspace!), has climbed mountains, dived in coral reefs, flown small planes, swum with dolphins, touched two-thousand-year-old tiles in a gate out of Babylon. She is a novelist, anthologist, and short story writer who currently shares her live between the Pacific Northwest of the USA (where she lives with the obligatory two writer's cats) and the wonderful fantasy worlds of her own imagination.

You can find out more about Alma and her books on
    her website (www.AlmaAlexander.org)
    Amazon author page (https://amzn.to/2N6xE9u)
    Twitter (https://twitter.com/AlmaAlexander)
    Facebook (https://www.facebook.com/AuthorAlmaAlexander/)
    Patreon (https://www.patreon.com/AlmaAlexander)

About Book View Café

Book View Café is a professional authors' cooperative offering high-quality DRM-free ebooks in multiple formats to readers around the world. With authors in a variety of genres including mystery, romance, fantasy, and science fiction, Book View Café has something for everyone. 90% of the profits from the sales of BVC ebooks goes directly to the authors.

Book View Café authors (past and present) include Nebula, Hugo, Endeavour, and Philip K. Dick Award winners – Nebula, Hugo, World Fantasy, Rita Award and regional State Book Award nominees – as well as New York Times bestsellers and notable book authors.

http://bookviewcafe.com